FIVE BAD DEEDS

FIVE BAD DEEDS

A Novel

Caz Frear

HARPER

NEW YORK • LONDON • TORONTO • SYDNEY

HARPER

Also published in Great Britain in 2024 by Simon & Schuster UK Ltd.

HarperCollins books may be purchased for educational, business, or sales promotional use. For information, please email the Special Markets Department at SPsales@harpercollins.com.

FIRST U.S. EDITION

Emoji Artwork © Cosmic_Design/Shutterstock

Library of Congress Cataloging-in-Publication Data has been applied for.

ISBN 978-0-06-309111-5 (pbk.)
ISBN 978-0-06-309110-8 (library edition)

23 24 25 26 27 LBC 6 5 4 3 2

To Edie & Albert, with love and excitement for all the stories you'll tell and the worlds you'll create.

FIVE BAD DEEDS

Three months after

The Meadowhouse went on sale this week. Twelve viewings already, I'm told. Although there's probably more by now; I haven't called home since Tuesday. No phone credit, you see. No deodorant either. Thank God it's canteen day tomorrow. If I use my spends wisely, skipping all my old life essentials that in here we call luxuries, I'll be able to purchase a few more minutes of agonising chit-chat with the people who still speak to me. Mainly Max and Kian, my four-year-old twins.

Four years old.

They were three when I last held them; I missed their birthday by two weeks. When the dreaded day came, I crooned "Happy Birthday" down the phone to them, inhaling the musty scent of hair grease on the receiver and ignoring the Code Red mayhem kicking off just behind.

Code Red: a bloodied brawl. Otherwise known as the matinee entertainment.

We made the decision early on—*we* being Adam, and almost certainly his parents—not to subject the boys to prison visits. Too traumatic, *we* decided. Too alien. Too counter to the plans we'd made for their curated little lives. I agreed, or conceded, on the promise that we'd discuss it again once I'd "settled in properly"—Adam prefers to talk like it's my first term at boarding school—but I've been "settled in" now for months and he still refuses to sanction it. The women here say he's punishing me, *because that's what men do, Ellen.* But I try to believe he isn't one of those men. That he could never be that cruel.

And I know I'm one of the lucky ones. A lot of the women here don't have anyone to keep the home fires burning. No family or real friends to take care of their kids, pay the rent, store their possessions, and, in my cellmate's case, feed their budgerigar. In losing their freedom, they lose everything.

Although not all deserve pity.

There's a woman three cells down—Joy, could be Joyce; I'm too scared to ask for clarification—who tells anyone who'll listen that she lost her kids over a Dyson hairdryer. It isn't the full story, of course. It never is in this hellhole. She always neglects to mention the twenty prior "hairdryers" and the four previous jail sentences, or the fact she threatened to stab the security guy in the throat when he asked to search her bag.

Still, it makes a good sob story, and they're stock-in-trade in HMP Holbeach.

Not that I have one to tell.

Our story is pure spite.

I suppose it *is* harsh, though. Fifteen months for a hairdryer.

I mean, no one likes a thief.

But at least no one died.

1

Ellen

Before

"Apparently, you're fourteen per cent more likely to die on your birthday than any on other day of the year. Crazy, huh?"

And with that truly uplifting statement, my sister, Kristy, blows out her candles. Today is her thirty-ninth birthday, although on close inspection, the candles only number thirty-five.

Orla, my eldest, is typically unimpressed. "Seriously, this candle ritual needs nuking. It's, like, *totally* unhygienic. You might as well just spit all over the cake." She picks a potato wedge off my plate—the massive crispy one I was saving—and breathes all over it. "See, would you want to eat that now? No, didn't think so."

Welcome to my life, which, so the story goes, is a happy one. And later, I'll post a photo on Facebook to further back that story up. It'll be all smiles and crumpled wrapping paper. Clinking glasses and soft filters. No mention of death, or germs, or the draughty table by the back door that they allocated us in the Cricketers pub, or the fact that neither the birthday girl nor the minimal number of guests particularly wanted to come.

"Hey, remember what Dad used to say?" says Kristy, now marginally more engaged after two vodka Red Bulls. "'You're a great man the day you're born, the day you're buried, and on your birthday. Every day in between, you're just a gobshite like everyone else.'"

Ah yes. The wisdom of Patrick J. Hennessey. Epic drinker. Average philosopher. I never did get around to challenging our not-so-dear departed dad about this and so many other of his lager-soaked theories, but I assume the same held for women. Not that Dad had much time for women. Not unless they were minding kids or handing out beer money.

He'd have been proud of me today, I think. Picking up the tab in the pub, three cranky kids in tow on account of it being Orla's half-term holiday and there being no one to mind Max and Kian. No one I trust, anyway. Anyone brave enough to run that particularly dicey gauntlet—my friends Nush and Gwen, Adam's parents, and Kristy (at a push)—is either here or, in my in-laws' case, cruising around the Galapagos Islands on board the five-star *Symphony of the Sea*.

I wish I was on a cruise. Actually, I'd settle for a bus trip. Just some time to myself. To read and think and rest.

The thought's been coming and going all morning, sharp as a menstrual cramp.

In truth, my hangover isn't helping. Neither is Orla.

"Y'know, even by Muriel's standards, that cake is an atrocity, Mum." She eyes the vaguely rectangular slab like it's a lump of rotten meat.

Gwen, usually kind to her core, agrees. "Yeah . . . I mean, I'm no Mary Berry, Els, but *grey* cake? It looks like a tombstone."

"Yeah, a tombstone inscribed 'Kirstie,'" says Kristy.

"I did ask for silver," I protest, quickly glossing over the misspelling.

Nush sighs. "And yet I bet you said nothing, even though you were paying her."

"Even though you can't stand her," adds Kristy.

"She didn't say nothing, she said, 'Wow, it looks amazing, Muriel. You're a natural, so talented.'" Orla mimics me, her voice as sickly sweet as the hair-of-the-dog cava that Nush just foisted on me. "Seriously, Mum, you're *such* a bloody hypocrite."

Hypocrite, or just polite? I'm not certain there's a difference. And anyway, firstly, the little ones will gladly wolf it—cake is one of the few things Max eats without morphing into the Antichrist, while Bella, Gwen's daughter, and Kian eat *everything*. I once caught them licking a slug. But secondly, and more importantly, everyone knows it pays to flatter grumpy neighbours when you're about to embark on a renovation, and ultimately I'm happy to lie about cake if it spares us a noise complaint.

I put my cava down untouched and stare across the table at Orla. "So what should I have said, smart-arse? 'Jeez, Muriel, I'd rather staple my tongue to a moving train than take one bite of that shambles?' It's called manners. You used to have them, remember?"

Orla gives me the glare of a serial killer, all five-foot-nine of her bristling with adolescent disdain. Two can give good glare, though, and after a few seconds she tires of the stand-off and stalks off towards the bathroom, her spindly heels narrating her exit across the treacherous cobbled floor.

Mother Me wants to shout, "Be careful you don't twist your ankle," but mothering Orla these days is pure kamikaze, and in any case, my daughter isn't the type to take a tumble. Orla has a solidity, a swagger. A watertight contract with the world that states she's sixteen, she's invincible, and she doesn't have time for busted ankles.

She's also taller than me already. Orla gets her red hair from Adam's side and her height and bra size from mine. Everyone jokes that we're in for a rocky few years.

The last few months haven't exactly been peachy.

Moments later, with Nush answering emails and Kristy chasing the boys and Bella around the table, Gwen taps her fuchsia-pink lips, code for "Fancy a sly smoke?"

"Christ, no, not here," I say, as though she just suggested we strip naked. "Sylvia's cronies are over there. It'd definitely get back."

"And Mummy-in-law would *not* approve," confirms Nush, still tapping away—demanding some poor schmuck do something better or faster, no doubt.

"Approve? She'd get our marriage annulled," I say, and Nush laughs, ever bemused by my Sylvia-based anxiety. But then perfect, polished, proficient-at-bloody-everything Nush isn't married to Adam, much to Sylvia's barely concealed disappointment. "She'd have the power, trust me. There's priests in that family. Well, there's a deacon, whatever that is."

"Chrissake, Els, man up," mutters Kristy.

Gwen stands, bouncing on her ballet pumps. "Ah, *come on.* We'll hide behind the bins. It'll be like being fourteen again."

I laugh but shake my head. Gwen clicks her tongue, mumbles, "Spoilsport," then breezes out the door to smoke alone like the easy-peasy friend she is.

"Doesn't she feel the cold?" Nush says—a blatant dig at Gwen's pineapple-print romper. "It's the end of October, for heaven's sake. Tights season."

"If I had her legs, I wouldn't feel the cold either." I sigh. "Sadly, I got Mum's sturdy pins. They looked OK when I was younger—you know, strong, athletic—but now they've gone kind of farmer's wife. Good for rescuing sheep out of ditches, not so good for shimmying around in rompers." I roll up a jean leg, produce a robust calf as proof.

"How about shimmying around Pelham High?" Nush puts her phone down with a smile. I sit up straight, practically panting in anticipation. "Oh look, now don't count your chickens, darling. It's not in the bag yet, *officially.* But 'sources'—well, Joanna Plimpton—say you're the clear front-runner."

Kristy stands still. "For that job?"

"Hell, yeah." I puff my chest out a little. "Bow down and

behold Pelham High's new head of English." Nush shoots me a warning look. "Yeah, yeah, not in the bag yet. I hear you." I can't help a smile, though. "I must have *nailed* the panel interview for J-Plimp to say that, though. Which isn't bad given that twenty minutes before, I was cleaning Kian's vomit off the hall carpet."

Nush nudges my cava towards me. "Well, I think that *definitely* deserves a drink, don't you?"

"I shouldn't really. I hit the wine a bit hard last night, and I've got the car outside."

"Oh relax, one won't hurt. It's practically fizzy water." She hands me my glass and clinks it against her own. "To *potential* good news."

"Forget 'good news.' It's salvation . . . deliverance." I take a long sip, then another. "Seriously, I'm like a sitting duck since Muriel's husband died. She's got no one else to moan at during the day now except me."

"You know, she isn't *all* bad," says Nush, absently stroking her own hair the way you'd stroke a pedigree cat. "She's crabby, no one disputes that, but she does a lot for charity. Knits blankets for the homeless. Deep down she's a good person."

And what's the point of that? I feel like saying. Surely your goodness should be right there in the shop window? What good is being good if all others see is bad?

And obviously Muriel isn't all bad. Few people are. Few people are all good either. When it comes right down to it, we're just a mishmash of roles, and we can't be good at all of them. You're generally a top-notch friend but an impatient sister. An A-star colleague but a B-minus wife. I mean, only an hour ago, we had to listen to Nush insist *again* that while her ex, Tom, was undoubtedly a faithless cockroach of a husband, he was "such a wonderful father to Jasmine in so many ways" (as though the construction of one rocking horse in 2007 made him the Lord of All Dads).

"Still no word from Adam?" asks Kristy as she sits down with the pained wince that's been pretty much a reflex for over a decade. I'd feel sorry for her if her question had been a genuine one and not a glaringly obvious shit-stir. I let my face do the talking, then issue a menacing "No!" towards Max, who's currently karate-chopping the table for reasons only a three-year-old brain can fathom.

"Now be fair," says Nush. "He only landed at midday; he's probably gone home to bed for a few hours. They didn't fly him business, did they? Complete joke, given he was in New York on, *hello*, business."

My sympathy is finite. I haven't been to New York or New Anywhere since the arrival of the twins.

"Yeah, well, any time Adam wants to swap, he only has to say the word. I'll happily watch porn and order room service for four nights straight. He can stay here and sift toddler turd out of the bath."

"Oh, here we go, another War of the Walshes," Kristy groans, even though it's usually her who stokes them. "Round One: who has it worse, Ellen or Adam? Round Two: second verse, same as the first. Over and over until one of them dies."

"You could always get your own place," Nush says to Kristy, setting me up for another evening spent convincing my sister that *of course* she's welcome to stay with us, *of course* we're not fed up with her, *of course* I don't moan that she never double-locks the door or replaces any of the wine. "Because, honestly, living in a shed at thirty-nine—"

"It's a garden cabin," I snap, not for the first time. "It's got a veranda, for God's sake. The shower's better than mine."

Nush knows this. She was there when they installed it. She was all for it, in fact, back when it was a potential office-cum-gym and not a halfway house for errant sisters.

"Maybe I should move in with *you*," Kristy replies to Nush, a nasty glint in her eye. "I mean, husband gone, kid gone. You've got plenty of room these days."

Kristy always had a mouth like a rusty machete.

It's been five months since my younger sister showed up on our doorstep from Ibiza, carrying a depressingly light suitcase and the hauntings of a black eye. I asked about the eye, of course; she chose to lie about it, spinning some yarn about a dropped toothbrush and the unyielding composition of a porcelain sink. Later, she told Kian she got it fighting a bear over a pot of honey. Adam got a wink and "the perils of rough sex."

It'd been four years since we'd been in the same room together. Four years of FaceTiming, of communication from the collarbone up. Not that we were estranged as such. Kristy and I had always had an on–off thing, casually falling in and out of sibling love at various points in our history. And certainly since the twins, a combination of life, geography, and the fact that we're profoundly different people with profoundly different priorities had meant that getting together was always something we talked about doing rather than actually ever did. We spoke regularly, though, the distance giving our calls an almost confessional feel, allowing us to spill secrets safe in the knowledge that our lives never entwined. Kristy knew I was pregnant with the twins three days before Adam did. I was the only person she told about a termination late last year. A decision apparently made because "You make motherhood sound worse than hara-kiri."

Do I? Sometimes.

Is it? No.

Kristy takes things too literally. She doesn't get that cooing over your kids then crying over the sheer tedium of looking after them is all part of the standard playbook. The motherhood Magna Carta. I mean, does it matter that I said I'd rather have cystitis for a year than attend the twins' nativity play for half an hour? I was there, wasn't I? Clapping and smiling and cheering on my two little shepherds in their 3 a.m.-assembled costumes. Hell, I even managed to feign interest during the fifteen mind-numbing minutes when mine weren't on stage.

And OK, maybe I often claim that I'd love my old life back, but *clearly* I'm joking. A scrap of my old life would do. Just ten blessed minutes of no one needing me to find something, or cook something, or explain for the twenty-fifth time that while it might look cool on Kristy, they're definitely not getting their septum pierced.

It was different when it was just Orla, when we had routines inscribed in family law: Library Tuesday, Disney Friday, Pancake Sunday. Twin boys brought anarchy to the house. For the first couple of years, we lived under a landslide, waiting for the next bumped head or dropped biscuit to spark domestic Armageddon. Suddenly there was never any silence anymore, any structure. Just a never-ending soundtrack of bangs, thuds and yelps. Like sharing your house with two malfunctioning robots.

It got easier, of course. I got better at it, at *them*. But in surprise news to no one, Adam and I got lost along the way, and we've still not found a path back. We're still feeling around our marriage like guests in an unfamiliar kitchen; some instinctive, ingrained sense of how the standard bits operate—the kettle, the toaster, the tin opener, the sink—but no clue whatsoever how to fire up the Belgian waffle maker.

I never dreamed Orla and I would get so lost, though. Everyone says it's normal, par for the teenage course. Blame hormones, they say. Blame TikTok. Blame the Kardashians. Blame it on anything you want, Ellen, because it sure ain't on you.

Only Orla and I know this isn't exactly the whole truth.

I'm crouched down disciplining Max, or rather threatening him with an iPad-less future if he doesn't stop kicking things, when Nush's voice summons me.

"Ellen, quickly, you need to see this."

I stand ready to *oh-my-God* at whatever's caught her eye, expecting something like a neighbour's bad dye job or some sap trying his luck with Gwen. However, Nush's face tells a different story. Following her line of sight, my eyes land on something far more urgent.

Orla at the bar.

Rather, Orla leaning over the bar. Legs at full stretch, back arched, neck craned forward. Her coppery head is dipped as she smiles at something in the barman's hand.

"Hard to tell with the whole man-bun-and-beard thing, but he must be what, thirty?" Nush says, wobbling on tiptoes, her heels raised out of her elegant nude heels. "They're doing something with their phones. Swapping numbers, maybe?"

I vault forward, seeing red. Kristy shoots out an arm, blocking my path. "Look, maybe Cool Aunt should handle this. If you go over, you'll only embarrass her."

"That's the plan."

Yesterday, over the vegan pot pie I spent nearly two hours making for her, Orla announced that my email address embarrassed her. It's bad enough I use email, apparently, but Hotmail—"peak cringe."

I bat away Kristy's arm and steam straight towards the bar. Kristy follows but hangs back, still weighing up which horse to mount: Cool Aunt or Supportive Sister. The barman clocks me first, causing Orla to turn and her smile to fade instantly. Sensing trouble, she skitters away, quickly attaching herself to the first person she thinks might offer protection—in this case, Bella, as I'm less likely to bawl at her if she's carrying a small child.

I've no interest in bawling at *her*.

"She's sixteen," I bark, catching the attention of Greg, the Cricketers' long-time manager. My anger feels elastic. Like it could stretch me ten feet tall.

The barman says nothing, green eyes twinkling, biceps flexing as he pours a pale, cloudy ale with the lazy precision of a pro.

In the reflection of the bar mirror, Orla is chatting breezily with Gwen while making pig faces at Bella, but I can tell that she's livid. I know her. My baby. I can sense my daughter's mood just by the way she cleans her teeth.

"Did you hear me? I said she's sixteen." My knuckles are pearl white as I grip the dark, grainy oak. I have to hold on to something or I might claw him like a rabid cat.

"Yeah, I heard you. So she's old enough, then." There's a second where he seems genuinely confused by my death stare before the penny doesn't so much drop as hit him square on the nose. "Oh God, no. No! I meant to model. She's old enough to model. Not to . . . y'know . . . Jesus!"

Model? *Seriously.*

"Everything OK, Ellen?" asks Greg, hovering a bit closer.

I point at the barman. "*He* swapped numbers with my daughter, and I want him to delete hers, that's all. That's me done." I shrug. "Then what you choose to do about your staff hitting on schoolgirls is entirely up to you . . ."

Greg doesn't get a word in.

"Hitting on her? No. No way. You've got this all wrong. She's got this *all* wrong, Greg." He casts a panicked look at his boss. "I was showing her my cousin's Instagram—she's a model." He looks back at me. "And, see, she looks a bit like your daughter, and she's always saying redheads are 'in,' so I said she—your kid—should follow her, that's all. See what it's all about. She *could* be a model, you know. She's got the height."

"She's also got exams next month."

Kristy's hand on my shoulder says *leave it now, Els*, and with the twins brawling in the background, I'm forced to rain-check every threat, every insult I'd love to hurl at this insect for using such a cheap, clichéd line on my bright, brilliant daughter.

"And anyway . . ." I point back at Kristy, unable to resist a parting shot, "her aunt here was a top model. So we're all sorted on that front, *thanks*."

His eyes scan Kristy. The barely-there scar bridging her faintly crooked nose. The way her body arcs slightly, *like a bloody cheese Pringle*. I spin around, wishing I'd never said anything, praying that Kristy didn't clock the bemused look on his face.

"Come on," I say, shooing her, then I shout over to Orla. "And can *you* go and get your brothers, please. We're leaving in five."

Orla turns, her face as sour as citrus. "Er, I'm not your babysitter. Not unless you're paying me nine pounds an hour, hey, Gwen?"

Poor Gwen, caught in the crossfire, throws me a sympathetic look. "Els, if you're in a rush, I can walk the boys back. It's no problem."

"Thanks, hon, but it's fine." My resolve hardens. "Orla, I said go and get your brothers."

She slowly steps towards me. Her lemonade breath is hot against my ear as she whispers, "And I said I'm not doing it. Go get your precious boys yourself."

You said we're leaving in five, so I'll be out in five.

Like a chauffeur waiting on a high-profile client, I sit and wait for Orla as five minutes pass, then a few minutes more. I try and keep my temper in check by speaking as little as possible, just the occasional "Lads! Please!" as the twins demolish packets of Pom-Bears over the dump we call the back seat.

Kristy, however, doesn't do silence.

"So what was last night about?" she asks, rummaging in my bag for her own packet of Pom-Bears. "Not like you to hit the wine on a week night. And the less said about that pouty selfie . . ."

"Oh Christ, you saw that?" I rest my forehead on the steering wheel, my nose squashed against the Audi badge. "I thought I'd got away with it. I deleted it off Facebook after, like, five minutes."

"Oh, I saw it," Kristy laughs through a mouthful of crisps.

"You won't have done yourself any favours in the Orla embarrassment stakes."

"I wouldn't worry. She's sixteen. She wouldn't be seen dead on Facebook." I twist my head to face my sister. "And to answer your question, I was bored. Adam away *again*, everyone busy, no one to play with. I knocked on the cabin door, but you were . . ." I glance back at the twins, lowering my voice, "off shagging Shane, I suppose?"

"Shay. There's no *ane*. And you suppose right."

"Are we ever going to meet him then, this international man of mystery?"

"So yeah, anyway, thanks for my birthday lunch." Blithely sidestepping unwanted questions are a particular skill of Kristy's, if not her superpower. "I mean, Lady Nush and Gwen are your friends, not mine, and I *really* wish you'd stop trying to turn us into an awesome little foursome. But it was a nice thought, I guess. And my biker boots are . . ." She mimes a chef's kiss.

"I thought you liked Gwen?"

"Correction: I don't *dis*like Gwen. There's nothing to dislike. She's got the personality of a milky drink." Which is unfair and untrue. Gwen's problem is she's gorgeous, barely thirty, and she tends to see the best in people. Three strikes and she's out as far as my sister's concerned. "So it'll be bye-bye week-night wine, then—once you start this new job, I mean. You never could hack hangovers. Seriously, you look like dogshit."

"God, don't say that. It's bad enough one of Sylvia's cronies caught me dry-shampooing in the toilets. That'll be around the village by teatime, you wait."

Kristy rolls her eyes. "Els, you need to loosen up. You've passed your probation by now, I reckon."

"What's that supposed to mean?"

"It means you're not on the outside looking in anymore. You can stop trying. You're one of them now."

One of *them*. A Nush. A Sylvia. A Thames Lawley pillar of impeccability. No trace of the kid from the rough council estate who shared bunk beds with Kristy for the best part of fifteen years.

"Nah, I'm not. Not yet. If—*when*—I get the Pelham job, I might be. I'll have 'standing' then, lucky me." A horrific thought occurs. "God, do you think Sylvia might ask me to join one of her committees?"

"You won't have the time. Beats me why you want to go back to full-time teaching, to be honest. I thought flexibility was the pot of gold these days."

"Well, there's this thing called ambition, Kris." I didn't mean that to sound so harsh, but by the looks of it, she isn't bothered. "And there's also this thing called money. It might be the root of all evil, but it comes in mighty handy when you've got a huge renovation to pay for."

"When Adam's folks have, you mean."

"It's a loan," I bite back.

"It's a shackle." She lets out a huge yawn—Shane without the *ane* must be keeping her up way past her bedtime. "Just think, a lifetime of being grateful to Sylvia . . ."

Admiring her carrot crop. Pretending to like that fucking cat. *Dear God, is it worth it?*

I drive the thought from my head. "Anyway, it's not just the money, it's the challenge. Private tutoring's fine, but all I'm doing is cheerleading bright rich kids through exams they'll pass easily. Would you punch me in the face if I said I want to make a difference?"

"Repeatedly." She taps a knuckle on the window. "And besides, the only difference you'll make is giving a few teenage boys someone new to wank over."

"Good luck to them. It's teenage girls I can't cope with." I shoot daggers at the dashboard clock. "Jesus, five minutes, I said. She literally has *no* respect for me."

Kristy snorts. "I don't remember us having much respect for Mum at Orla's age."

I snort louder at the comparison. "Mum was in court for handling stolen goods on my sixteenth birthday. Anyway, it's more than that, Kris. It's . . . She . . ." I shake my head. "Oh, just forget it."

I shut myself down because I have to. Because if I start, I might never stop.

And do I *really* know my sister?

I know she's wearing an expensive bra of mine. I recognise the lime-green spots peeking through the gauze of her white top. *She* knows I've been looking for it everywhere—tearing through drawers, scrabbling through washing baskets, blaming Orla.

Four years apart is a very long time.

"Well, *of course* it's more than that," she says, and even for Kristy, it sounds salty. "Always is with you. Always was. Can't be just a regular problem. Has to be special, has to be different."

I wait for her to smile. She doesn't. She's deadly serious.

"Whoa, what's eating you all of a sudden?"

But now she's looking past me. I sense a presence moving towards the driver's-side window.

"About bloody time," I say, relieved by the interruption.

I fire up the ignition, then turn to look at Orla, quickly weighing up whether to read her the riot act, give her the silent treatment, or throw her off completely by being calm and unnervingly nice.

But it isn't Orla standing there. It's a police officer.

I let down the window, offering a wide, flummoxed smile. "Hey, Jason. You OK? Are you looking for—"

He doesn't let me finish. He doesn't return the smile either.

"Could you step out of the car, please, Ellen."

2

Ellen

I laugh. I actually laugh. Not my brightest idea, and frankly not how I ever imagined myself behaving in front of a police officer. When I was fifteen, I once asked a security guard if he "fancied me or something" after he eyed me suspiciously while I sniffed perfumes in Debenhams, but until now, that's the closest I've come to disrespecting anyone in uniform.

Confused, I step out of the car.

Unlike his sister, Gwen, PC Jason Bale has an exceptionally bland face, the kind that's forgettable yet familiar. Muddy brown hair matching muddy brown eyes. A straight, harmless nose and lips of no definable shape. You could plan a meal, a holiday, a full-scale military operation while looking at him, and there'd be nothing to distract you. No point of interest to draw you in.

"Name, please?" he says, rubbing the place I suppose you'd call a jawline.

I stare at him, bewildered, waiting for the world to come right again.

"Name," he repeats.

"Ellen Anne Walsh."

I instantly regret the *Anne*, kicking myself for sounding like a been-around-the-block criminal.

"And can you confirm your full address?"

I can, and I can confirm yours too, Jason Bale of 12 Wavertree

Crescent. I can confirm that your front door is painted a dark denim blue. That the porch light needs replacing. That the windows are brand new. I can also confirm that you're thirty-six, Sagittarius, and while I'd never come out and say it, that I've always found you pretty rude.

And that you're holding a small black device in your right hand.

Shit.

"Um, address is the Meadowhouse," I stutter. "Number four, Caldicott Lane, Thames Lawley."

I don't add that he knows this. That he can see my house directly across the village green. That his sister spends half her time there, and he's been invited himself often enough (invitations he always ignores, never bothering to offer a polite excuse).

"Have you had a drink today?" he asks.

"No . . . Oh, actually, hold on, I had a mouthful of cava. No, two mouthfuls," I add, determined to play a straight bat. "Maybe a third of a glass."

"And last night?"

This is a nightmare. An absolute nightmare. And it's not being remotely helped by the fact that the twins rate policemen even higher than dinosaurs, and they're now hollering *Nee-naw! Nee-naw!* at an excruciatingly loud pitch. Kristy is trying to shush them, which she should know only encourages them, and to cap it all, it's starting to rain for the first time today. Sparse but fat droplets pooling in the potholes at our feet.

Sadly, the rain doesn't stop the rubberneckers from pouring out of the Cricketers. There must be twelve, maybe fifteen of them huddled together in a knot of suppressed glee.

Yes, *glee.*

I'm not so sensitive as to think it's personal. People like scandal, end of. People here *love* it. They live for it. They have a vampire-like need for something other than the occasional funeral and pothole petition to break up the usual run of play.

"Look, is this some sort of spot-check thing?" I say, knowing I sound desperate.

"We don't do spot checks," he replies in the tone of a man bored to his back teeth with life. "I have reason to believe you may be over the legal limit and intending to drive."

"What reason?" I give a brittle laugh. "Look, I know my parking isn't going to win any awards, but I was in a rush. Kian, you see—"

"We had a call," he cuts in, raising a hand to pre-empt my obvious question. "A concerned citizen. That's all I can say."

"I beg your pardon?"

I barely recognise my own voice. I sound prim and comically officious. Next I'll be demanding to see the manager or making thinly veiled threats about how I play golf with his boss.

My brain stutters as I try to compute what he just said, to translate his words into stark facts.

Someone reported me?

"So, last night?"

I stare at him, speechless. So sucker-punched I can't recall the context of the question. I rub at my arms like I'm trying to start a fire, but the cold, or maybe the shock, feels stitched to my skin.

Jason sighs, trying a third time. "Last night, Ellen—did you have a drink last night?"

"Well, yeah, I had a few wines."

"How many?"

"Quite a few." He waits for specifics. "A bottle, I guess?"

"And when did you have your last drink?" he asks. "Today's mouthful aside."

God only knows. Even sober, I'm not a great clock-watcher. Nursery drop-off, pick-up, and my regular weekly tutoring gigs are the only times that seem to implant properly in my brain. Everything around that feels abstract. Simply the space in between where all the other shit gets done.

"Um, well it was definitely late. Maybe one a.m.? Slightly

later?" I give a pathetic, hopeful smile. "I'd eaten a big dinner, though—fish pie. And I had a glass of water before bed."

He checks his watch, does the calculations. "You know it can take at least twelve hours for 'quite a few' drinks to leave your system, so you're sitting right on the cusp. I assume you're happy to take a breath test?"

He presses the device. The screen lights up in anticipation of my answer.

"Oh, well, *sure*. I'd be honoured. My first breathalyser. Woo-hoo!"

I'm not proud of my sarcasm. The *woo-hoo* was unnecessary.

But this feels wrong.

I feel wronged.

"You can refuse," Jason says, lifting the device towards me, the rubber tube at mouth level. "But you'd be charged with failing to produce a specimen."

And so I dip down, draw a breath, then give the rubberneckers the money shot.

I blow.

3

Orla

WHATSAPP GROUP: WHO RUN THE WORLD?

Members: Esme, Orla

ESME: OMFG, La-la!!

ORLA: Well look who's back

Was starting to think u weren't speaking to me

ESME: Always speaking to u babe.

ORLA: Er, except the five days u haven't been

ESME: Busy busy. Serious tho—u ok???

ORLA: Any reason I wouldn't be?

ESME: Oh u kno . . . climate change, world peace.

ALKY MUMS!!

ORLA: Who told u? Abi Devlin? I thought I saw her nosy

bitch nan in the pub.

ESME: Aaaaaand???

ORLA: Aaaaaaand whaaaaaat???

ESME: La-la!!! Spill the tea!!! It's either ur mum's drink

problem or geography homework. Need drama!!!

ORLA: No drama. She blew under.

It's all gucci, my sometime friend.

ESME: Fucksake, I kno she blew under. Tell me more!

Something Abi-D doesn't kno.

ORLA: Why'd u care? I don't.

ESME: Cos it's ur mum!! Like if it was my mum it'd be

whatever cos everyone knows she's a hot mess. But UR
MUM!!! She's apple pie.

She's like the CEO of Squeaky Clean, Inc.

ORLA: U have NO idea how off the mark u are.

Like if the mark is Thames Lawley, ur in New Zealand.

ESME: Whaaaa? I mean, she probably sucks ur dad's cock
occasionally but she's pretty basic.

ORLA: Thanks for the image

ESME: I mean, ur dad's kinda cute

ORLA: I think I preferred it when u ignoring me

ESME: Hey I like an old guy can't deny it. I'm done with
guys our age.

ORLA: Same. Dickwads, the lot of them.

Barman in the Cricketers hit on me earlier . . .

ESME: OMG that spunk rat with the man-bun!!! No way!!!

ORLA: Way.

Said I could be a model.

ESME: La-la he is FINE!! Hotter than the sun in a frying pan!!
Could ditch the beard but 10 out of 10 would
recommend.

Did ur mum see?

ORLA: Yep

ESME: OMFG!!! How r u not dead?

ORLA: Why would she kill me? Not my fault he
thinks I'm hot ☺

And anyway, I've been dead to her since the twins so . . .

ESME: OK now that's a little extra 😴

ORLA: But true.

The boys, the renovation and keeping secrets. That's all
she cares about.

ESME: Secrets?

Being cryptic doesn't make u interesting, u kno? It
makes u annoying. Spill or zip it.

ORLA: Forget it. So u going to Scotti Lund's party
tmrw night?

ESME: Yup.

ORLA: Thought ur done with guys our age??

ESME: I'm done sucking their cocks. Happy to drink their
vodka. U going?

ORLA: Nope.

ESME: That dickasaurus Roan Howells isn't going if that's
what's stopping u??

ORLA: Nah. Babysitting

ESME: At Creepy Jason's?

ORLA: At Gwen's

ESME: Same thing. Same house

ORLA: U kno he's the one who breathalysed my mum?

ESME: Awks

ORLA: Not really. Was funny

ESME: Ur SO harsh on ur mum. Poor Mrs. W 😭
Serious, have mine for a week. U be begging for urs
back. She drove off with her bag on the car roof this
morning. Dopey AF.

ORLA: Harmless AF.

ESME: And what's Mrs. W? Serial killer? Trained assassin?
Actually she looks a bit like Villanelle. With curly
hair obvs.

ORLA: She's not as innocent as people think.
My mum is dark AF.

4

Ellen

If yesterday was surreal, this morning borders on revolutionary.

Adam and I have sex. On a Thursday.

We don't *talk* about getting around to "some sex," and we don't just *think* about it either—lying there eyeing each other like pieces of unused exercise equipment, knowing for sure we'd feel better afterwards if we only popped our metaphorical running shoes on.

We actually *do* it.

Proper sex, too. Not the cursory maintenance mount fuelled by wine, guilt, or an almost regal sense of duty. No, this morning is the dynamite kind. The kind that makes you wonder why you don't do "some sex" more often.

Not too often, though. Let's say a diligent twice a week.

"You're not usually this horny after a work trip," I say, hunting for my knickers in the twisted bedsheets. "Were there no adult channels on the TV? You should complain to HR."

"It's the police thing," Adam says, performing a theatrically languid stretch—one more suited to a perpetually stoned rock star than the finance director of a mid-sized management consultancy whose train leaves in thirty minutes. "The whole bad-girl thing, you know? It's sexual catnip."

I aim my knickers at his head. "Er, sorry to pop your balloon, sunshine, but my good-girl credentials are firmly intact. I blew under, remember?"

"Just."

I grab my dressing gown and follow Adam into our gruesome en suite (currently avocado and peach; the mould is easily its best feature). Sitting on the side of the bath, I take a moment to properly survey him naked for the first time in eons.

Not bad at all, I conclude, all things considered. Age. Stress. Kids. A predilection for craft beer and pepperoni pizza with extra cheese.

We met in Warwick Student Union in 2001. I thought he was flashy, buying champagne when I'd asked for Guinness. He thought I was called Helen, which I didn't correct until halfway through our first date. We were inseparable after that, except for the holidays, of course, when Adam would head back to Thames Lawley before going skiing in Mont-de-Lans or Val Thorens (depending on the season) and I'd troop home to Leicester to stack supermarket shelves and pull pints.

"Home" was a vastly different experience, as we soon discovered during our nervous first forays into each other's non-university lives. Adam's was a six-bedroom pile that housed a nice neat five of them. The Walshes had "grounds." They had an orchard. They had the holiest of grails: Sky TV. Home for me was six irritable people crammed into a three-bedroom council flat on the Highfield estate. There were no orchards, rarely even apples (or any fruit, although Mum fiercely disputes this). And it wasn't an entirely uncommon occurrence to find that Dad had sold the TV.

Still, there was always music, fights, and drama. Every day the final act of an overwrought Italian opera. Back then, Adam, with his tendency to romanticise hardship, couldn't have loved it more.

I couldn't wait to get away.

"Hey, I wonder if I'll hear from Pelham today?" I say as Adam sponges his crotch vigorously under the measly trickle of the shower head. "Do you think I should call them, get the state of play?"

"Hmm . . ." He pulls a face. "Not sure. Might come across a bit . . ."

"Presumptuous?"

"Desperate."

"I *am* desperate."

He stops sponging. "That doesn't sound good."

I think about shrugging it off, restoring post-coital equilibrium. But he's here now. A captive audience. Albeit one with a flaccid penis in his hand.

"It's just . . . I want my career back. You know, appraisals, promotions, back-stabbing, meetings. Yeah—*meetings*."

"Okaaaay."

"Now *that* doesn't sound good."

"No, no, it's fine. Obviously. Good for you." A tad patronising, but I let it pass. "And I'll support you one hundred per cent, you know that. It's just not nice hearing your wife say she feels desperate, that's all. I thought you were a happy camper."

"I am." A *moderately* happy one. "But forget head of English, Ads—I was on track for the top job at St Mike's before your swimmers sneaked through." I give his balls a mock scowl, although technically it was my fault. It was me who'd declared, "Ah, don't worry about it" when we were anniversarying in Paris and I realised I'd forgotten birth control—Adam had offered to go to the pharmacy, rolling his tongue around *pilule de lendemain*. But I'd taken the morning-after pill before and it'd made me dry-heave relentlessly, and I'd been looking forward to Paris for months, and . . . well, as they say, you live and learn. "I mean, *obviously* I wouldn't change the boys for the world, but you know I always had that goal of being head by forty. And now I'm forty-one and what goals do I have? Find Kian's Crocs. Take Muriel's dead husband's clothes to the charity shop."

Adam smiles. "Set up that true-crime podcast, concerned citizen.com?"

We mulled it over for hours last night. Me still stunned and stress-eating Doritos. Adam bewildered. Kristy heartily entertained. The best we came up with was the barman I'd basically called a pervert, or the guy who lives across from the Cricketers who once accused me—*falsely*—of cheating at the pub quiz.

The worst we came up with was Kristy suggesting Orla, then Adam suggesting Kristy. "Just a joke," apparently, but one that ignited a firework of *fuck you*s.

"Actually, speaking of Muriel, maybe it was her?" Adam says. "A delayed act of vengeance for Max trampling her begonias."

"No plural, Ads. It was *one* begonia." Which I replaced with fifteen more and an absurdly grave apology. "Anyway, I'm not even sure there *was* a 'concerned citizen.' It might have just been Jason trying to embarrass me."

"Oh, here we go." Adam rolls his eyes to the cracked, stained ceiling.

"No, no, hear me out." I raise a finger. "Means: he's a police officer." Another finger. "Motive: I'm sure he doesn't like me; it's like he resents me being friends with Gwen." I hold up a third finger—what I believe to be my smouldering gun, if not quite smoking. "And then guess who was in the next aisle in Costcutter when I was moaning to Susi Sands about my hangover yesterday morning? Jason bloody Bale. So there's opportunity right there—he knew I'd been drinking the night before."

"OK, Poirot, but so did anyone who saw your Facebook selfie. All two hundred and whatever of your so-called friends." Adam doesn't do social media, although he enjoys a shoulder-lurk at mine. "And anyway, this thing with Jason. From what I can see, he's not wild about anyone. Remember when I asked him to join our quiz team? Complete tumbleweed. Even Nush couldn't persuade him." Wow. *Even* St Nush. Imagine. "How was she yesterday, by the way?"

"OK." That word, usually so meaningless, feels apt in this circumstance. She was nothing more, nothing less. "OK" seems to be her permanent state. "Still banging on about Tom, obviously."

"Banging on? Jeez, Els, you're all heart."

Yes, but you don't have to listen to it. You get to "uh-huh" and "oh dear" at my post-Nush rundowns without ever having to engage.

The faint sound of Lego being tipped signals that it's time for me to get moving. I slip off my dressing gown and step into the shower, unceremoniously shooing Adam out. "I know I sound mean," I say, fiddling with the temperature dial out of habit rather than any expectation of success. "But it's been a year since Tom left . . ."

"And you'd get over me in a year?"

"No, but I'd have got under someone else by now. For the ego boost, if nothing else. Probably some young stud. Thick as mince and twice as pretty." Adam towels his hair, pretending not to react, but I can see the twitch of his grin through the gathering steam. I grin back. "Oh yeah, didn't you know—early forties is *peak* cougar. I read it on Mumsnet. Young enough to still have 'it'—whatever 'it' is—but old enough to have an air of 'seasoned mystique.'"

Ah, the mystique of aching joints, two-day hangovers, and sporadic chin hairs.

Adam pokes his head around the shower door. "Well, you've definitely still got 'it' from where I'm standing, Mrs. Walsh." *Sweet.* I draw a heart in the condensation. "But you know Nush, she's not like that."

I wipe the heart away. His reverential tone grates on me.

"Oh yeah, *of course*, I forgot. St Nushelle of the Holy Virtue. She's on a higher plane to the rest of us."

Adam goes back into the bedroom, too late for work to take the bait. I raise my face to the dribble, savouring the last few minutes of solitude before the day and all its duels begin—kids, students, other drivers, "concerned citizens." When he comes back moments later, he's dressed and gelled and infusing the steam with the same woody scent he's been wearing since the late nineties. He says see-ya-later-hope-you-hear-from-Pelham-can-you-call-the-electrician-and-fuck-da-police.

I ask if the electrician is a young stud who might fancy a tepid shower with a peak cougar.

Adam says he's called Bert, he's sixty-three, and when he's not rewiring houses, he plays dominoes with his dad.

Fancying ourselves as future high-flyers, we'd moved to London after uni, the plan being for Adam to earn gazillions crunching numbers on the corporate hamster wheel, leaving me free to inspire young minds (aka change the world) for a far more modest salary. While the gazillions never materialised, an OK-ish standard of living did—for London, anyway—and it took nearly fifteen years, including one wedding, three flats, two redundancies, and one Orla, before we turned against the capital and said *enough, we've had our fill.* Orla's secondary schooling had sealed it. Financially, private was a stretch (and back then I was made of sterner stuff when it came to rejecting handouts from Adam's parents), but with local comprehensive schools ranging from "average" to "apocalyptic," we had to do something, we reasoned. And as the old saying goes, if the best state schools won't come to Mohammed, Mohammed must go to the best non-fee-paying schools.

So we did, to Foxton Grammar—the pride of Thames Lawley. Former pupils included a Labour MP, a three-time Olympic medallist, and a lesser-known finance director, my very own Adam Walsh.

Leaving London wasn't easy. You don't realise how much you miss thought-provoking graffiti and twenty-four-hour taco stands until they're a dull and distant memory, and for the first year, "fifty minutes" became our mantra, the fast train to London our saving grace. In just fifty minutes, we'd reassure ourselves—the time it took to, say, cook a lasagne or skim a newspaper—we could be right back in the thick of the capital. Day trips. Nights out. Picking up London where we'd left off.

Until the twins arrived and we stopped bothering.

And Thames Lawley wasn't so bad. Gradually I came to love it. The sense of community. The safety. Even the small-mindedness, on a good day, seemed harmless and oddly sweet. I didn't love our first house, though. Our pleasant-but-drab semi-detached house on the main road out of the village. The type of property we'd have killed to own in London but that here seemed run-of-the-mill. Even after several years, it still felt like a stopgap to me. Just somewhere to eat, sleep, and keep tidy until the perfect-but-affordable house miraculously showed up.

The Meadowhouse was that miracle.

While others crush on celebrities and sports stars, and to get quite Thames Lawley-specific, Nathaniel the coach from Soccer-tots, I've always crushed on houses. And boy, do I crush hard. It started in 1988, when I sent Santa a three-page missive on why I deserved a Barbie Dreamhouse, and when it sadly didn't materialise, I sent the same letter to the PM. In the nineties, it was the *Home Alone* house. In the early noughties, Carrie Bradshaw's brownstone. And they were only my chief crushes. There were so, so many more. But there was never any particular style, or size, or specific feature that hooked me. The only thing they had in common was how they made me feel.

Charged. Aspirational. Like life might have something decent to offer me. That I might be worth more than boarded-up windows and persistent coughs caused by damp.

Having notions, my mum called it. I called it having hope.

I'd been crushing on the Meadowhouse for twenty years (not exclusively—it had competition). I'd even taken a sneaky photo of it once during a visit to Adam's during Easter break.

"For my vision board," I'd told him.

"That's probably illegal," he'd said, laughing.

"What, photographing houses or having vision boards?"

"The former, although both should be."

And then, *wham*, around fifteen months ago, there was it was, winking at me on a property website.

Mine, I decided, before I'd even booked a spot at the open house.

It wasn't the biggest house in Thames Lawley, nor the most expensive by a country mile. That crown had been well and truly seized by a McMansion on the outskirts, a real eyesore of a home that seemed to hang back from the rest of the village with the slightly embarrassed air of someone who knows they've overdressed. The Meadowhouse was the most beautiful, though. *Enchanting*, to use the estate-agent speak. A traditional Cotswold stone farmhouse, with golden bricks draped in clematis and peach climbing roses. Cherry blossom forming a guard of honour over a winding gravelled path. Several years ago, the exterior had featured in a Hollywood Christmas movie. It was without doubt, as the agent declared, "the quintessential English house."

Inside, it was the quintessential money pit, last updated in the mid nineties. A warren of small, suffocating rooms, each one more oak-panelled than the last. Only the kitchen provided any space that you could swing the proverbial cat in. But even that was uninviting, unless congregating next to tobacco-stained cabinets was particularly your thing.

It wasn't a complete surprise, of course. There was obviously a reason why it'd been on the market for a while and why it was *just* within our budget (due to a recent price reduction). And to be fair, the agent had been clear from the outset that it was "ready for a revamp." But revamp we could live with. Revamp we could afford. What we found, however, was a house screaming to be remodelled. To have its entire layout reconfigured into something light, bright, and fashionably open-plan. This meant walls removed, ceilings raised, stairs reshaped, rooms extended.

Finances depleted.

Enter my fairy mother-in-law, Sylvia, albeit two months later. I'd almost given up on the dream when suddenly she offered to help us out.

"You'll pay it back when you can," she'd said with impeccable, chilling grace.

No more ducking out of Sunday lunch for me, then. No more pretending I'd missed her call.

Adam, to use his own phrase, was "Meadowhouse agnostic." Deep down, I think he knew Sylvia was buying our gratitude, and while I'd fallen hard, he'd have been happy to walk away. Even now he refers to the renovation as Operation Ellen. He says it with a smile, but I know it's his way of distancing himself, of saying: *On your shoulders be it—don't ever lay this on me.*

Kristy was vaguely sceptical, although she is about most things. My mum, still using my dad's death as an excuse to be relentlessly loathsome to everyone, offered, "Since when did you have the first clue about renovating houses? Who d'you think you are? Bob the fucking Builder."

In the end, Nush was the only person to take a firm stance on the subject, warning us not about the double whammy of planning permission and building regulations, but about something surprisingly more woo-woo.

"That place has bad energy. First the Merricks' dreadful attack all those years ago. They were never the same after that, so I hear, and neither was the house—they stopped caring, stopped looking after it. And then you've got the Sharps' divorce. Rock solid for twenty years before moving in—less than three years later, they're communicating through solicitors. I'm telling you, it's cursed. Nothing good ever came from living in that house."

Bad energy, bad luck, and bad marriages be damned.

One year in and we're still here to tell the tale.

5

Ellen

The Gwen in my kitchen is a Gwen I don't recognise. Bella is her predictably buoyant self, felt-tip-marker-jousting with the boys and eating me out of breadsticks as usual, but Gwen, usually so at home here, seems like a stranger today. At a guess, I'd say she hasn't slept, or at least not soundly. Her eyes are tinged pink and her scarlet pixie-crop looks like it hasn't seen a brush in days.

"I should have come over last night," she's saying, standing rigid in the kitchen doorway, "but I was just *so* embarrassed. Seriously, I could kill him, Els. God knows what you must think of him. And me."

My first thought is *bless her*. My second is *I don't have time for this*. It's gone eleven and the breakfast table still resembles the aftermath of a medieval banquet, and despite several attempts, the twins still aren't dressed.

"You? Don't be daft, G. Why would I think badly of you?" I yank her into a bear hug, staring over her shoulder at the pot racks I can't wait to get rid of. Had the Sharps never heard of drawers? "And I don't think badly of Jason either," I lie. "He was just doing his job. I get it."

Her voice is muffled in my curls. "No, he was *way* too heavy-handed. That's what he's like. A sergeant-major type, you know?" She pulls back slightly, but I'm still close enough to smell her toothpaste. "He blames our childhood, all the crap, the instability. But I had the same. I had *worse*—he forgets that. And I'm not such a bloody stickler for rules."

"He's police, hon. Be weird if he wasn't." I give her a small squeeze. Conversation over, as far as I'm concerned. "Honestly, it's history. I could have done without the audience, sure, but no real harm caused." I laugh. "*And* I got to keep the rubber tube. Best souvenir ever. There isn't a toy in this house that Kian hasn't breathalysed. Looks like Catboy's going down."

I loosen my grip and move away, but she's still not settled. A few unshed tears blur her wide hazel eyes.

"Hey, don't cry," I say softly, disguising an inner scream of, *for God's sake!*

"Ignore me, I'm just being stupid." She blinks hard, stemming the flow. "My period's due tomorrow, which probably isn't helping. I cried over that Katy Perry song earlier—you know, 'Firework.'"

"Oh, don't talk to me about the tears. I cried over a squirrel last month. It kept dropping its acorn. It *killed* me." I push her towards the window seat, or Gwen's throne, as we've taken to calling it, due to her being the only person in Christendom who thinks the pheasant-embroidered monstrosity is "kind of cute." "But seriously, you and me—we're good, OK? All good."

Gwen and Jason live in the bland, boxy newly-built houses on the opposite side of the village green. They arrived a month or two before us, newbies to Thames Lawley as well. As Gwen later explained, after a tough few years raising Bella alone in the centre of busy Reading, she wanted a change of scenery and pace, a better quality of life for them both. And as Jason was effectively homeless after the break-up of his marriage in London, it made sense for them to move in together and split the not insignificant rent.

I met Gwen a few weeks after we arrived at the Meadowhouse. She was passing with Bella while I was standing in the front garden, feeling overwhelmed by the jungle of flowers now under my dubious care.

"Doesn't seem fair," she announced, her smile wide and toasty warm. I stared, not quite following. "I mean that I get to look at your lovely house every day, whereas you have to look at mine."

Well, yes, but across a lush village green known for its daffodils in spring and its epic cricket matches in summer. Not to mention puppy school on a Sunday morning, which I get to watch from my front wall.

The view from my childhood bedroom was a derelict pub.

I liked Gwen instantly. Her breezy nature, her lack of ceremony. I also liked the fact that Bella was the same age as the twins and raising hell over a scooter helmet. I could do with a friend with a badly behaved kid, I thought. Someone to remind me I'm not the only one getting it wrong.

"Oh, I don't know about lovely," I replied, aiming for modest but possibly sounding ungrateful. "You should see the inside— it's grim. Actually, do you want to see the inside?"

And that was that. A coffee turned into a large glass of wine. The glass into a bottle. The bottle a regular thing.

Only ever Gwen, though.

"Jason's not really a people person," she always insists, which would be fine if he was a lighthouse keeper on a remote island, not a public-facing police officer. "And he isn't in a great space right now, what with the separation, the move, the new job. It's complicated."

Or it's just him, I want to say, although I can hardly judge, what with my own complicated sibling having taken root in the back garden. But at least Kristy's entertaining. Jason's the perennial Grinch. The type who'd refuse to wear his Christmas cracker hat for fear of looking frivolous.

"OK, well I'm glad I came over now," Gwen says, sounding genuinely more chipper. "Orla's babysitting tonight, though. I hope she doesn't feel awkward if Jason's back before me."

"Awkward? Orla? That's a good one." I grab a bowl off the table, scrape mushy Cheerios into the pedal bin. "Orla doesn't do *feeling* awkward. Now, *being* awkward—she wrote the book on that."

"Is she in?" Gwen tips her face towards the ceiling, Orla's lair being just above our heads.

"Nope. She got up, guzzled a glass of orange juice, went out. Not one word."

Her face is all concern. "Look, shall I have a chat with her? We often shoot the breeze before I go out or when I get back, so I can do it subtly. I worked in PR, remember? Still do, if you count being a failed freelancer. Point is, I'm good at sly messaging. 'Mother knows best,' that sort of thing. Worth a try?"

"Probably not." I open the dishwasher. "You can have a chat with your brother, though. See if you can wheedle out of him the name of the bastard who reported me."

She scowls. "I'd whack it out of him, Els, if I thought it'd work. But it won't. And to be fair, he might not even know. Sorry."

"Forget it," I say, fearing another onslaught of apologies. "Let's talk about something else. Something fun." *Something quick.*

Gwen grins. "So, what is it now? T minus two months till lift-off?" She means the renovation. Apparently, with my white minimalist "fetish," I'm turning the Meadowhouse into NASA HQ. "I'm going to miss this kitchen," she says, looking around as if for the last time, her bottom lip stuck out playfully. "Can't believe you're ripping the pantry out, for a start. An *actual* pantry. It's like *The Wind in the Willows*, or what's that show? *Downton Abbey.*" I smile, roll my eyes. "Yeah, I know. I'm a closet granny. I love a bit of rustic charm."

"Rustic, yeah. Geriatric, no." I slam the dishwasher shut.

"And Christ, I said something *fun*, G. I've been talking about this renovation for approximately three hundred years."

Although that reminds me, I need to call Bert, the electrician. The light in the kitchen has taken to tripping every few days.

I grab my phone, scroll for his number. "So why's Orla babysitting? Hot date?"

The sound of the postman outside halts her answer. I make a dart for the door before Max beats me to it and I have to spend the next ten minutes wrangling bills from his clenched paw.

As I walk back in, Gwen says, "No hot date. Not even a lukewarm one. Just a drink with a friend." She hesitates. "You're welcome to come."

The pause suggests she was only being polite. I'm not offended. I do the same thing. In fact, I'd say over half of the offers I make, the favours I grant, come with the internal wearied plea, *Please don't take me up on this. I only said it to be nice.*

"Thanks, hon, but I can't," I say, letting her off the hook. "Adam's playing badminton tonight. Yeah, *badminton*."

My disdain has nothing to do with the sport and everything to do with Adam never being home.

While Gwen embarks on a badminton anecdote, I sift through the mail, surprised to see there's actual news—bad and good—to be found among the junk. Due to an accounting error, I unfortunately underpaid last year's taxes. However, on account of a healthy cervix, my recent pap smear was clear. The final letter in the pile is addressed to me in a hand I don't recognise, postmarked High Wycombe. My heart sinks at the prospect of another bloody wedding invite. We've had five already this year: attended two, dodged three.

It isn't an invitation, though. It's a lined piece of paper. Neat handwriting in black ink.

SOONER OR LATER EVERYONE SITS DOWN TO A BANQUET OF CONSEQUENCES

Do you know who said that, Ellen?

I bet you do.

Because you know everything. You have everything.
You want everything.

But I know things too.

<u>*I know you.*</u> *And I know that people have to learn*
there are consequences.

I'm going to teach you that lesson.

Right under your fucking nose.

I read it twice, then a third time, my body calcified by shock
while the words pinball around my skull.

Consequences. Have. Want. Know.

They *know* me? Who does? *How?*

Casually? Have we hunted for lost shin pads at Soccertots on
a Sunday morning? Have I taught dangling modifiers to their
polite, bored-stiff kids?

But the capitals, the underline. That implies something deeper.
Something damaging.

I swallow. No.

No.

It *can't* be about him.

I've been careful. That was the deal. That was the pact I solemnly made with myself.

*Be careful and you can do this, Ellen. Be careful and no one
gets hurt.*

So no, this *has* to be about something petty. A small-town
storm in a teacup.

Think, Ellen.

Have I offended someone recently? Been caught gossiping,
or judging, or ridiculing someone with a cheap quip? Sober Me
wouldn't do that. Sober Me is always the first to slap down any
hint of mean-girl bullshit, but white wine is a bad influence and

Drunk Me likes to bitch. I'm never cruel, but slightly waspish and, on the odd occasion, indiscreet.

Except when it comes to my own secrets, of course.

"Els? Ellen? *Hello?*" I look up, startled by the cheery bounce in Gwen's voice. "I said what about tennis? Whistlebrook Park has clay courts. We can pretend we're playing in the French Open. That's right, isn't it? That's the only one played on clay?"

I stare, not sure how to reply or what the hell she's even on about. I feel bone tired all of a sudden; the adrenaline of wild panic has been replaced with the exhaustion of pure dread.

"Mate, are you OK? You look a bit strung out." Gwen frowns at the note in my hand. "Bad news?"

I take a breath, giving myself seconds to decide whether to pour forth or pull the shutters down.

I choose the latter.

"No, no, everything's fine," I say, smiling and shrugging and probably completely overdoing it. "It's just a quote to have the gutters cleaned. Daylight robbery. I might tackle them myself." I shove the note in my jeans pocket, feeling bad that I'm about to exploit Gwen's misplaced guilt over Jason. "G, I know it's short notice, but you couldn't do me the biggest favour, could you?"

Of course she says *Of course I can.*

"Could you mind the boys for a bit? I've got a few errands to run, and you know what it's like—it'll be ten times easier if I don't have The Destructors with me."

And I'll feel ten times safer once I know this isn't about Zane.

6

Ellen

When I first noticed noses wrinkling at the mention of Lower Lawley, Thames Lawley's distinctly poorer and far less photogenic cousin, I assumed that what it probably lacked in organic apothecaries and experimental gastropubs, it made up for in decent houses you could buy for under half a mil.

I was off the mark with my inverted snobbery. It turned out that less than a ten-minute drive away from the world of grammar schools and garden cabins lay an entirely different microclimate. One not entirely unfamiliar to me.

However, while I grew up on the Highfield, where crime was a constant but so was community, Zane Jackson just about *survives* on the ground floor of the Lomax Tower, a place where if you're not buying drugs or guns, you might want to check you've got the right address. The Lomax reeks of ground-in apathy. The lift is invariably broken or uninhabitable. And sometimes when I'm sitting outside in my car, trying to talk myself into—or out of—plunging my hand into the hornets' nest again, I wonder if he lived on the top floor instead, and I'd had to brave the lift or take the stairs that first time, would that one physical obstacle have made me stop and see sense?

But this will be the last time.

I swear it every time I come here and every time I leave. I even mean it sometimes. Usually when he's been difficult, or occasionally when he's been delightful. Which covers most of the time, frankly. Zane doesn't really have a neutral state.

And there will be a last time some day. One way or another.

Zane is seventeen, but Lomax-seventeen. Shrewd and life-savvy, like all the posturing man-boys I grew up with on our estate. Bright but erratic, and the kind of handsome that creates as many problems as opportunities, he was permanently excluded from sixth form earlier this year after either a "mix-up" or a "set-up" involving the carrying of a weapon. Which version he deploys depends on how he wants to play you that day.

The first time I tutored him, he was rude and pointedly topless. A six-foot streak of attitude in low-slung sweatpants and bare feet. Now when I come, he wears aftershave and slim-fitting polo shirts. In terms of his work, he's conscientious, although given half a chance, he'd rather discuss me.

You seen Black Panther, *Ellen?*

Been to Koh Phangan? Apparently the Full Moon parties are pretty epic.

Ever tripped on Benadryl?

Had glandular fever?

Do you like Hemingway?

Do you like me?

One afternoon, when he was in a particularly melancholic mood—*Death of a Salesman* can do that to a person—he asked me, in a tone I couldn't quite decipher, "What's your mum like, Ellen? D'ya get on?"

Zane's mum is long gone and not missed, if you believe the word of a hurt teenager. She's also "probably giving some bloke a blowie in a pub toilet somewhere," if you believe Paulo Jackson, Zane's bitter dad.

And so I answered Zane truthfully that day. I didn't dilute Mum's character, like I do with most people. I didn't laugh about her, or make excuses, or dress her up as a harmless kook.

Instead, I told him about the court appearances and the episode at my graduation. I said that while she could be funny and occasionally wise, she was inherently selfish and prone to spite. It felt liberating to say it out loud to someone. To not feel judged, or embarrassed, or somehow diminished by her failings.

And Zane was a good listener. He didn't need to probe. He understood.

"Wanna know something about *my* mum?" he said later, with a stare I should have turned away from. "She'd hate your fucking guts, Ellen. Gorgeous and clever—seriously, you'd make her combust."

I should have left that day and never gone back.

Paulo Jackson answers the door, confused to see me standing there. The feeling's entirely mutual, given that he's usually sleeping off last night's excesses on his red leather La-Z-Boy, and, unless I'm very much mistaken, this is the first time I've seen him standing up.

"Fuck me, is it Friday?" he says, knuckling his shaved head. His eyes are predictably bloodshot, but he sounds lucid, almost perky. "What happened to Thursday? Have I missed a day? Wouldn't be the first time."

"It's Thursday, don't panic," I tell him, although God knows what he'd be panicking over. Paulo doesn't exactly follow a schedule. I doubt he has many appointments to keep. "I was just passing, that's all."

I follow him into the flat, down the dark, narrow hallway that's needed a new bulb the whole time I've been coming here. He seems steady. Christ, he seems sober. But while I'm pleasantly surprised, it isn't exactly ideal. A passed-out Paulo means peace. And privacy.

Zane appears in his bedroom doorway: blue eyes, white boxers, dark curls sticking out at wild angles. He has a crease down his left cheek and a smile that could stop wars.

"Just passing?" he says, one hand circling taut abdominals. "Scoring some smack for a dinner party, were you? Well, I hope you didn't use Danno, 'cos he cuts his gear with his dog's de-worming tablets." He frowns at me with mock concern. "Maybe play it safe, yeah, Ellen? Stick to the cheese and biscuits."

I don't rise to it.

"Have you just woken up?" I ask. He rubs both eyes, answering my question. "Zane, we talked about this. Sleeping till noon is a bad habit to get into. You need routine."

"You might as well talk to the wall," Paulo shouts from the small kitchen, his rasp cutting through the sound of the extractor fan and sizzling bacon. "I keep telling him he's gonna end up like me if he doesn't stop acting the prick."

Zane and I share a smile, although the thought of Paulo being right, the *likelihood* of Paulo being right, is as depressing to me as the fading of a rainbow. "Zane could have aimed for the stars" were the parting words of his former head teacher, and the reason I first got involved was to make sure those stars stayed within reach.

Now my reasons are so muddled, they're incomprehensible. Not so much reasons as impulses, and none of them any good.

I mean, *why* have I even come here today? It's not like I'm going to be brave enough to ask him outright.

What do you think you know, Zane?

Did you send me a letter?

Does anyone know about you and me?

He makes an "after you" gesture, then follows me into the living room, where I lay claim to the La-Z-Boy and stick the TV straight on mute. I think about telling him to get dressed. I *should* tell him to get dressed. Instead, I pluck a T-shirt off the radiator—Paulo's, almost certainly—and throw it at him with authority. Pulling it over his head, he says, "Don't ever tell *anyone* you saw me in an Iron Maiden T-shirt," and I take a minute to imagine a world where I'd tell anybody anything about him.

He hurls himself backwards onto the sofa, taking up the entire length of it. "So come on then, spit it out. 'Cos obviously you weren't 'just passing.' What's so urgent it couldn't wait?" He gives me a preening grin. "I mean, I know I'm pretty hot, but it's not like I'm going anywhere."

I open my mouth, but nothing comes out. The words bottleneck in my throat, clumped together like dried glue. Twenty different versions of the same volcanic question.

Was it you?

Zane's antennae shoot up. "What's the matter?" he says, sitting bolt upright, his swagger drained in an instant. "Seriously, what's happened, Ellen? Are you OK? Have I done something wrong?"

Has he?

Right here, right now, cocooned in the warmth of this poky little flat, it's hard to believe that he has. It certainly doesn't *feel* like he'd ever hurt me.

"I might be taking a full-time job," I say. It's the first thing I can think of that won't lead to confrontation. "It's not confirmed yet, but I wanted to give you the heads-up."

"Oh, right, OK." He chews a thumbnail, clearly finding this something of an anticlimax. "Fair enough, I s'pose. Yeah, good for you. Why not?" He tips his head towards the kitchen. "Hey, at least you got to see him being useful just the once before you piss off. Always told you he ain't too bad until his fourth or fifth can."

"He isn't bad full-stop, Zane. He tries in his own way. He loves you. He's cooking bacon."

"He's cremating bacon." He smiles, then his expression quickly slides back to confusion. "Seriously, though, a new job? You made a special visit to tell me that? That's some next-level personal service, Ellen. Definite five stars on Tripadvisor, that."

"Just wanted to get it out of the way. Tomorrow's for work. We've got a lot to get through."

"Nah, we ain't, not really." He sits back, his long legs splayed across the worn brown carpet. "I finished *The Changeling*, but I ain't got a lot to say about it, to be honest. Themes, subplots, all that shit you get excited about—it's just a load of posh people in heat, you ask me. Alonzo wants Beatrice, Beatrice wants Alsemero. De Flores is a nutjob, and Diaphanta wants Alsemero too." He pauses. "Oh yeah, and some jealous old dude has a hot wife that *everyone* wants." I start to speak, but he hasn't finished. "And, like, it's *so* obvious Beatrice is thirsty for De Flores. All that pretending she hates him?" He stares at me intensely, his top lip twitching, more a sneer than a smile. "No way does she hate him, Ellen. She hates *herself* for wanting to fuck him."

I stiffen. Is he trying to shock me, or impress me, or flirt with me, or *threaten* me? My Zane radar, usually so spot-on, has been totally flung off kilter by the poison contained within that note.

Paulo comes in with a stockpile of bacon, saving me from having to attempt a response.

"Eh, I might not be useful very often, son, but I ain't sodding deaf." He lays the plate on the coffee table next to what I suspect is the remnants of last night's coke sesh, then drops cross-legged to the floor, far nimbler than I expect. "So you're leaving us then, Ellen?"

I should seize this, this out. This chance to say: *It's certainly looking that way, sadly.*

"No. Not if you don't want me to." Relief sweeps Zane's face; blink and you'd miss it. "But obviously Friday afternoons aren't going to work. We can set up an evening thing, maybe?"

I've no idea how I'll make that happen. What I'll say to Adam. What story he might swallow. Adam has no idea I come here, and if I manage this right, he never will.

Zane shrugs. "Give it a go, I s'pose." His tone says *whatever*, although we both know it's bravado. "Gonna warn you now, though—my head's proper fried by, like, five o'clock. I'm talking ADHD central."

"Boy ain't lying. He was always like that, never did grow out of witching hour." Paulo grabs four slices of bacon and dumps them on the nearest makeshift plate, an unopened gas bill. "He *is* lying about reading that *Changeling* thing, though. He watched it on YouTube. S'quicker, to be fair to the lad."

Zane throws me a weak grin. "Well . . . same thing, innit? Same story. You should give it a go. It was good, had Hugh Grant in it."

"And that short fat fella," adds Paulo. "The guy from *Roger Rabbit*."

It takes a minute, but I get there. "Bob Hoskins, you mean?"

He clicks his greasy fingers. "Bob Hoskins, that's 'im. Here, is he dead or alive? I lose track of who's dead and who ain't."

"Dead," I confirm. "Ages ago."

Paulo grins at Zane. "Should have known she'd know, eh? Got a brain the size of a planet, that one."

"Only Mercury, though," Zane says. Paulo's face is blank. "It's the smallest planet, Dad. It was a joke. A shit one."

Paulo rolls his eyes. "Thought the moon was the smallest?"

"The moon's not a planet," I say.

"It functions a bit like one," Zane adds. "But it's a satellite really."

"Check you out, Stephen Hawking."

Paulo's tone might be mocking, but he's peacock-proud of his son, despite the school expulsion. On the Lomax, getting thrown out of school isn't extraordinary—in truth, it's barely noteworthy—but knowing about planets, and Hemingway, and everything else Zane turns his whip-smart mind to when he can be bothered most definitely is.

I stretch forward and scavenge for the least charred piece of bacon. Paulo, as ever, is disproportionately charmed.

"See, that's what I love about you, Ellen. You ain't got no airs and graces. You don't think you're the Queen of fucking Sheba just 'cos you got a degree and nice teeth. Not like that other one they sent. That stuck-up cow who won't even take a cup of tea."

"That other one" being Zane's *actual* tutor. The one who tasked him with reading *The Changeling*. The one appointed officially—*finally*—by his local education authority.

The one Zane knows not to tell about me.

7

Adam

Adam had hoped that the goodwill spawned by their sublime impromptu shag this morning might be carried into the evening, maybe even spark a rare repeat.

But it's the hope that kills, he muses as he throws his bag down on the table. He could tell there was something wrong as soon as he saw her rage-slicing that spinach quiche.

"Are you *actually* kidding me?" she's saying now, and he wishes she'd put the knife down. Not because she's a homicidal maniac, but because when she's angry, she's all thumbs. "Someone sends me a threatening note and I'm stressed out of my skull about it, and the best you can do is 'It's got to be a prank.'"

And yes, thinks Adam, right this second, it *is* the best I can do. I've been in meetings all day and I walked in the door less than two minutes ago. I need to decompress. Kiss the kids. Eat some crisps or a bowl of cereal. What I don't need is the day's headlines delivered at falsetto pitch and lightning speed.

But OK—*OK*—maybe his response was a bit flippant. As usual, it's her timing—problems, arrangements, convoluted anecdotes about people he's only ever met in passing, all fired at him like Nerf pellets before he's even taken a leak.

Rogue builders.

Ringworm at nursery.

Cancellation of a dinner with Jed and Kay—to which Adam thinks *hallelujah*, followed by *remind me, who are Jed and Kay?*

And now this. Some sort of nasty note, apparently. Well, he did warn her there'd be a ruckus once more people got wind of the renovation. There was nearly a punch-up in the Cricketers once over builders' vans clogging up Caldicott Lane.

Sooner or later everyone sits down to a banquet of consequences. Jesus.

He tries to act normal as his breath is knocked clean out of him, and for one panicked second, he thinks that the words are aimed at *him*. But then he scans them again. It's OK. It clearly says *Ellen*. He knows it's profoundly shit of him to feel such a powerful sense of relief.

"So?" She puts the knife down and folds her arms, her body as rigid as concrete. "Any advance on 'prank' now you've read it, or is that your final answer?"

Adam pictures her this morning; so loose, so fluid as she writhed—yes, *writhed*—underneath him. If he tried to hug her now, he's not sure she wouldn't break.

Although he should hug her, shouldn't he?

"Christ, Els, I don't know," he says, opting *not* to hug her. He knows enough about body language to know it's a gesture he might regret. "Whoever was behind the breathalyser, I suppose—which kind of puts Jason Bale out of the frame." Ellen tilts her head in that way that suggests she wholly disagrees with him but she's going to let him tie himself in knots first. "Oh, come on, why would Jason Bale be sending you hate mail?"

"Er, why would anyone, Adam? I think that's the whole point."

He doesn't mean to be unhelpful, but he can't make head or tail of this. Ellen might drive him nuts from time to time, but she's a straight shooter, a good egg. He can't think of one single person who would want to psych her out like this.

Unless . . .

No. No, she wouldn't, would she?

Christ, if she has, it's a bit over the top.

It was one kiss, for God's sake. One kiss and, OK, many,

many hours of candid conversation. *Real* conversation. Hopes and dreams. Past regrets. The best macaroni cheese they'd ever tasted. The weirdest Wikipedia rabbit holes they'd happened to stumble down.

A far cry from home, where rubbish collections and mislaid keys form the main topics of discussion, occasionally punctuated by a row over who's the more tired.

And yet despite how good—*so* good—it was, despite how young and refreshed and full of possibility their *thing* had made him feel, he'd nipped it in the bud, hadn't he? Kept his dick in his pants and the thoughts in his head. Far safer, he'd decided, to secretly masturbate in the shower. To fantasise about her un-Ellen-ness within the confines of marital sex.

He doesn't feel guilty about that, either. No way. He's a realist. After twenty years together, he'd be surprised if Ellen's mind doesn't roam too. He's heard her laughing with Gwen about the merits of a certain DHL delivery driver. He's read the comments in the Soccertots WhatsApp group about that "obscenely buff" coach who can't be long out of his teens.

But they're just crushes, silly fantasies. They pass the time and no harm done. And he'd crushed his crush kindly, he thought. They'd *both* agreed it was a phenomenally bad idea.

Hadn't they?

He flops down at the breakfast table, pulling out the chair beside him—an invitation to Ellen to sit down. "Look, this is bonkers, Els. Beyond bonkers. I mean, who on earth would have an issue with *you*?"

"You know, Adam, sometimes you make me sound really bloody boring."

When you're anything but, he wants to scream, or at least former Ellen wasn't. The girl who danced like a demon to the Prodigy in Warwick Student Union. The girl who wiped away a Guinness moustache to reveal the most perfect Cupid's bow of a mouth. And *of course* he knows people change, but my God, he misses former Ellen. Firebrand Ellen, who'd argue long into the night about inequality and the correct pronunciation of David Bowie. The Ellen who could mine the fun out of anything and never took setbacks personally. New Ellen—or let's be honest, post-twins Ellen—constantly flaps over nonsense, then complains he never listens to her, when he'd gladly listen to her all day if she'd talk about something other than school-gate politics or the latest thing Max won't eat.

He says none of this, though. Instead he looks at the note again and says, "So, do you know who the quote's by?"

"What?"

"Well . . . this person seems to think you will. I just wondered if you do."

Her face says he's an imbecile. Maybe he is. Maybe he'd like to be one. Life must be less stressful if you're stupid, Adam's always thought.

"It's Robert Louis Stevenson. And no, I didn't know. I had to google it. Now, is there anything more constructive you want to bring to the party? You know, something that might actually help?"

The pressure.

"Well, have you spoken to Nush—"

She cuts in before he can finish. "Nush? No. Why?"

It's not just her tone that implies he's said the wrong thing *again*, but the fact that she's sat down at the table but not at the seat he pulled out for her.

Former Ellen never went in for all these passive-aggressive moves.

"I was *going* to say have you talked to Nush, or Kristy, or Gwen? Have you shown anyone else, basically?"

She shakes her head. "Gwen was here when it arrived, but I was too stunned to say anything."

A look crosses her face, but it doesn't have time to settle before Orla sweeps in, brandishing a letter of her own. Adam stares at Ellen, whose face immediately drains of colour. If Orla's been sent something too, then this is definitely way beyond a prank.

She thrusts a printout under Adam's nose. "Dad, there's a Frankfurt trip next February. It's only seven hundred pounds." Ellen audibly exhales, but Orla's too busy lobbying Adam to notice. "It's focusing on business German—how to pitch my ideas and opinions with *way* more precision." Heaven help Frankfurt, thinks Adam. "I need a parental signature and a two-hundred-pound deposit by Monday."

Ellen stands up, drawing almost eye-level with Orla. "You don't, because you're not going."

"Oh, let me guess, we can't afford it." Orla kneads her chin theatrically. "Remind me, Mum—how much is that new fridge the size of France costing?"

"Heaps, but that concerns you how?" Ellen doesn't blink, although Adam knows she's conflicted about the price tag. On the one hand, his wife loves *things*: expensive things, showy things, things she could only dream of owning when she was growing up. On the other hand, and to his slight annoyance, she can sometimes lean a little Chairman Mao. "You're not going, Orla, because firstly, 'only seven hundred pounds.' Do you have any idea what you sound like?" An entitled brat, thinks Adam, but show me one kid round here who isn't. "And secondly, you don't need to go. You speak German better than some people speak English. You're already predicted a top grade."

Adam wouldn't put it past his daughter to fail now out of spite.

"Dad?" Orla looks at him expectantly, as though Ellen's judgement isn't binding or in any way important.

"What if she pays half?" he says, certain that Orla would sooner cut her own throat than fund her own school trip. "She's got her babysitting money, her monthly allowance."

"Oh, just forget it if it's *such* a big deal." Orla registers Ellen's satisfied smirk, then matches it with her own. "By the way, Mum, where were you earlier?"

"When?"

"This afternoon. Well, lunchtime."

"Out."

It's a simple exchange, but as is increasingly the case with these two, Adam suspects he's missing the subtext. He leaves them to it and scrolls his phone, half reading headlines, half eavesdropping.

"It's just I called in to Gwen 'cos she owed me a fiver, and the boys were there, trashing the place, *obviously*." She pauses. "Apparently you had 'a few errands' to run." Exaggerated air quotes. Adam has no idea what they're about. "Why didn't you bring the boys with you?"

"Why didn't you wait to get the fiver?" Ellen says. "You're babysitting tonight."

"And why didn't *you* wait to run your errands tomorrow? I thought that was the whole point of the boys doing a full nursery day on Friday. So that you have time to 'do errands.'"

Adam looks up. "Hey, enough with the air quotes. This is an air-quote-free house, remember?"

Ellen stares hard at Orla. "You'll find out when you grow up a bit that life doesn't always run to plan."

Orla gives her a harder stare back, then flies out of the kitchen, issuing one final statement from halfway up the stairs. "And by the way, I'm lucky to still have a babysitting job after yesterday. It doesn't do me any favours, you know, being the spawn of a drunk driver."

A few more protest stomps, then the door above them bangs closed.

Maybe *he* should go to Frankfurt, Adam thinks. He could do with learning how to express his opinions with—how did Orla put it?—"*way* more precision." Maybe then he'd have more sex, less renovations, and fewer chats about ringworm.

And that's when he sees them.

Felt-tip marks on the breakfast table. They trigger a vigorous, broiling fury in no way proportionate to the crime.

Fucking kids. Fucking Frankfurt. Fucking felt-tip marks on fucking everything. The new breakfast table, the one commissioned by Operation Ellen, is costing £2,000, and what's the betting it ends up being used as a glorified fucking colouring book.

Well, if he sees *one* mark on it, just one tiny smudge, he'll . . .

He'll *what*?

He'll leave it to Ellen, as usual. Even though he swore it wouldn't happen, he knows he's turning into his dad. Good old anything-for-a-quiet-life-just-keep-me-out-of-it Roger Walsh.

Could he be depressed, he wonders, or having a midlife crisis? He's never really understood if they're actually one and the same thing. But the latter suggests Lamborghinis and shrill, pneumatic girlfriends. The former seems more his tempo.

On the flight back from New York, he wrote his own epitaph on a BA napkin.

HERE LIES THE BODY OF ADAM RHYS WALSH.

DEVOTED (ISH) HUSBAND, FATHER,
BROTHER, & SON.

COMPETENT FINANCE DIRECTOR.
SIX-FIGURE SALARY.

FUNDER OF BREAKFAST TABLES.
SUFFERER OF HEARTBURN.

LAPSED SKIER. LAPSED ROWER.
LAPSED EVERYTHING, REALLY.

ALWAYS PICKED UP LITTER.

CONSIDERED CHEATING ON HIS
WIFE BEFORE BOTTLING IT.

MAY HE REST IN PEACE. AMEN.

He briefly considered showing it to Ellen (penultimate line and all) in the hope it might spark radical change. One of those seismic, clear-the-air conversations that, as painful as they are, often mark the start of something good, or at least something better.

Breathalyser-gate put an end to that. He tore his epitaph into shreds then flushed it down the toilet. Probably a wise move, in light of all this.

"Are you still going to badminton?"

Ellen's voice pulls him back, although as he wasn't paying attention, he can't quite decipher if it's a loaded question.

Should he *not* go to badminton? Is that what she's implying?

He glares at the felt-tip marks again and, in an admittedly bizarre mental leap, decides he *deserves* to go to badminton.

"Sure am. Cal's booked a court." He pauses, adding grudgingly, "Why? Is that a problem?"

"No, no, it's fine. Kristy's *obviously* around." A faint thud of techno is pulsing around the garden cabin. Loud enough to irritate, but quiet enough to make them feel like fossils if they ask her to turn it down. "I'll explain what's happened and get her to mind the boys for a bit. They're already bathed and in their PJs, so she won't have much to do."

Is that a dig at him? He does *try* to leave work on time.

"Why, where are you going?" he asks, hoping he hasn't been told twice already.

"I need to see Nush. Tonight." He frowns, puzzled by the urgency. "It was what you said before," she explains, "about whether I'd spoken to her. I don't know why I didn't think of it sooner, to be honest."

"Think of what?"

"That *this*"—she snatches up the note—"could be the work of everyone's favourite arsehole."

He's fairly sure that's what she used to call Orla's first cello teacher. And her brother, Cahill. *And* the guy who lived above them in Streatham, who played the bongos after midnight and would never sign for their parcels.

But he knows who she means now, and he has to admit it's not a bad theory.

"Tom," she says, as if Adam needed the confirmation. "I always had a feeling he'd come back to bite me."

First Bad Deed

The Messenger

Ellen

"Wow, Ellen. Great to see someone's gone down the sexy bunny route. Most of our guests are more Thumper than Playboy. What a splendid addition you are."

Strictly speaking, I met Tom before I met Nush. That's the version he tells, anyway. The Tom Delaney director's cut.

It was barely a month after we'd moved to Thames Lawley. I'd arrived alone to the Delaneys' annual costume "Eggs-travaganza"—Adam had been held up for reasons I've long deleted from memory—and with these opening words, delivered at the door with a grin that somehow managed to be both sheepish *and* wolfish, Tom had instantly made me feel awkward, not to mention dirt cheap.

"Hate" was too strong a word, but it's fair to say that from that moment on, *everything* about Tom Delaney riled me. The fact he used hand lotion. His overuse of the word "splendid." His tendency to walk around with his hands clasped behind his back, like a minor royal visiting a packing plant.

Not that a living soul would have guessed my true feelings. If anything, I overcompensated. No favour too big, no hurdle too tall. It was only later, when I understood more about Tom's psychology, that I realised it was precisely my unwavering niceness that actually made *him* dislike *me*. Tom saw me as a doormat, a yes-person, and if there's one thing Tom Delaney doesn't like, it's a smooth, easy ride. I met his father once at a cheese and wine thing—another annual Delaney event—and let's just say it explained plenty.

Nush and Adam went way back to Foxton Grammar, although until we moved to Thames Lawley, she'd been just a name in a Christmas card, not someone I'd ever met. They'd kept in touch sporadically—a quick drink whenever she was in London—but I admit I was taken aback at first by their easy-breezy intimacy. He'd make fun of her but know just when to leave it. She'd call him "Walshy" and knew exactly how he liked his beef.

Nush and I weren't natural buddies; we became so because of Adam. On the colour wheel of life, she was rich mulberry while I was neon pink. Nush rolled her own sushi. She played piano. She wore cashmere. She'd built two successful businesses from her kitchen island (aromatherapy and plumbing materials, so you couldn't even snipe *cliché*), and the truth was, I felt intimidated by her and a touch Z-list by her side. It wasn't her fault—she couldn't have been any more welcoming—but her air of benevolent superiority made it hard for me to fall hard.

And then there was the pub quiz.

The question had been: "In southern France, who or what is a *calisson*?"

While Tom and I had made stumped faces, Adam and Nush chorused, "Oh my God!" with sheer delight.

"A sweet!" declared Nush.

"A bit like marzipan," explained Adam.

"But with melon," added Nush. "God, we must have eaten hundreds that fortnight."

We.

By this time, I knew that Adam and Nush had had "a thing" when they were teenagers, but I'd imagined photo booths and mix tapes, I WUFF U teddies and crap sex. I *didn't* know that Adam had spent two weeks at Nush's family's French villa. Or that they'd gone missing for twenty-four hours, first hitching to

Cannes, then on to Antibes, so that Nush could visit the Picasso museum, where she'd cried in front of *La Joie de Vivre*.

I'd cried too that summer. My brother, Cahill, had burgled two flats on our estate and Dad had been so affronted he'd put him in hospital with a fractured jaw.

So did it sting, this sweet, cinematic, sunlit pilgrimage they'd embarked on? Well, yes, in a childish way. It sure beat me and Adam bickering the entire three miles to Palma Cathedral only to find the place closed for the week and covered in tarpaulin.

But I got over it, of course I did. It was more than twenty years ago, and I'm not a complete and utter moron. Soon I forgot all about it, and over the years, Nush, by her own admission, transitioned from being Adam's friend to my friend. "Inseparable" would be a stretch, but we regularly shopped together, moaned together, socialised and exercised together—if by exercise you count me trudging to a few sessions of Nush's latest devotion (Powerhoop? Floatfit?) before bailing due to "cartilage issues" and a complete lack of any interest.

We also confided in each other often, although only ever about lightweight issues. The type of stuff you'd tell a taxi driver after one too many G&Ts.

Until last year, when things got unexpectedly heavyweight.

It was one of those nights when you wish you hadn't bothered. The train into Oxford had been delayed, turning a twenty-minute hop into a sixty-minute swear fest, and Max had smashed Orla's iPad in protest at me leaving the house.

I was heading back to the station, hurrying down past Oxford Castle, when I saw them. They were coming out of the Malmaison hotel, hand in hand, laughing intimately. To this day, I can still picture the thwarted look on Tom's face.

"Ellen, goodness, what are you doing here?" he asked, all fake bonhomie.

"Susi Sands's fortieth," I replied, matching his chirpy tone.

"Nush was invited too, but she thought she'd spend tonight with Jasmine—you know, what with her going back to uni tomorrow." I looked at the woman—the *girl*—then back at Tom. "So? Aren't you going to introduce us?"

She looks exactly like Nush, that was all I could think. Tall and willowy, with coal-black hair spiralling way past her shoulders. Sri Lankan descent, maybe. Definitely South Asian. She even had Nush's manner: the ballerina poise, the blithe self-possession. The cool, expectant smile of someone used to charming people at will. I'd always assumed the whole point of infidelity was the thrill of something different, but clearly the same was perfectly fine with Tom as long it was fifteen years younger. Actually, nearer twenty.

"Um, Jessie . . ." he stuttered, flicking his index finger between us, "this is Ellen. She's a . . . a friend." I pulled a manically friendly face. I must have looked demonic. In my defence, I was more than a little shell-shocked and under the influence of three mai tais. "Ellen, Jessie is a colleague. My star associate, actually. We've just had drinks in Malmaison. They do a surprisingly good Merlot."

"Hi, Jessie." I arranged my face into a smile. "We had a dog called Jesse when I was little. A randy little cocker spaniel. Seriously, he'd hump anything."

Yes, it was catty, but also it was true. And in any case, Tom's wedding band was clearly visible, so while Jessie certainly wasn't the main villain here, she wasn't exactly an ingénue.

What followed was two minutes of excruciating conversation. Another plug for Malmaison's surprisingly *splendid* wine list. A load of work stuff, presumably designed to imply that they had just been talking shop. Then, finally, a suggestion that Orla apply for the company's "highly prestigious" internship programme. Presumably a not-so-subtle hint that she'd be a shoo-in if I kept quiet.

I called Kristy from the train platform, full of indignation and regret—at Tom for being a shitbag, but more at myself for playing along.

"I can't *believe* I stood there chatting, but it was just so bloody awkward. I should have called him out there and then, shouldn't I? Why am I such a coward?"

I expected Kristy to agree; she's never been one to shy away from confrontation. However, her advice was quite the opposite and completely unequivocal.

"Stay out of it, sis. This is real life. You're not the ballsy best mate in a 1990s rom-com. Don't worry, Tom-fuckery will trip himself up eventually. His type always do. The best thing you can do is go home and forget about it. 'Cos the messenger usually gets shot, remember that. Save yourself the aggravation."

So when I got home and into bed, I curled into lovely, faithful Adam. And with my head still spinning, I lied and said that I had nothing to report from my evening, except a typically delayed train and Susi Sands's husband's recurrent gout. There was no point in telling him, I reasoned. Not yet. Not until I'd decided what to do. I had to let things percolate. I had to let Tom stew.

It was barely twelve hours before he served his first volley.

We need to talk about Oxford.

Then half an hour later, three more texts in quick succession:

It's not what you think.

Ellen, can you answer pls.

OK, cards on the table. It was a one-off, I swear.

The email came later.

From: tom4567x29@gmail.com
To: elsbelswalsh@hotmail.com

Ellen,

Can we talk? Maybe grab supper? I need to
explain and I need to know if you're going to tell

Nush, although I would beg you not to. Nush
hasn't said anything to anyone, but she isn't
in a great place right now. Serenity Scents is
struggling, and to make matters worse, Shani is
off her medication again and all that entails.

Please, Ellen. This isn't about protecting me.
I just don't think Nush could take it right now.

I know I am flawed, but I also know you are
a good person. Please think carefully before
causing unnecessary pain to a dear friend.

Tx

What could I do?

While Nush had never gone into much detail, I'd gleaned
enough over the years to know that her mum, Shani, sometimes
experienced chaotically high highs and cavernously dark lows.
So now a fragile mum, a rocky business, and potentially a marriage breakdown. Did I want to be the person who saddled her
with that lousy mix?

I fired back one message, figuring that Tom deserved no more
than five seconds of my time and two simple words.

End it.

Avoidance could only last so long, and having lied my way
through illness, busyness, and a sudden burst of back-to-back
tutoring commitments, eventually I was out of excuses and had
to accept an invite. Ten days later, I found myself stationed back
at Nush's kitchen island, being rebuked for using a fork to eat
her homemade vegetarian dim sum while Tom bored us senseless
on the best way to appeal a parking fine.

Everything felt so normal, I almost relaxed. Not in the sense
of enjoying myself, but zoning out, keeping quiet, "uh-huh"-ing
when expected. I was actually a million miles away, working out

my feelings towards their new voice-activated smart taps, when the name "Jessie" wrenched me back.

"Anyway, it was sweet of you, darling," Nush was saying while inspecting a dot of chilli oil on Tom's shirtsleeve, "but I'm not sure parking ticket advice comes under mentor responsibilities. I know you feel responsible, but HR ended her contract, not you."

I dropped my frowned-upon fork, fearful I might gouge Tom with it.

"Ah, but it was me who advised she wasn't quite up to scratch." He threw me a glance then, one that reminded me of Kian—all puffed up and proud that he'd tidied his toys like I'd asked. "Of course, I had hoped they'd consider her for something less . . . challenging. She definitely has talent. She's just not fixed-income material."

End it.

I felt sick, murderous. Worse, I felt complicit. While Jessie was hardly my favourite person, she didn't deserve to lose her job over *him*. The idea that Tom would use his power in this way, and that he thought I'd be happy about it, repulsed me to my marrow.

"So how come you're still mentoring her then, mate?" Adam's complete lack of guile made me want to stroke him, then slap him.

"Yeah, how come, *mate*?" I echoed, my jaw clenched.

Tom shrugged, picking at something lodged in a back molar. "Oh, it's just an informal arrangement, an occasional session." He glanced at me again with the faint glimmer of a smirk, and I knew then. *I knew.* "I really enjoy the mentoring side, but actually it makes far more sense to have a mentee outside your organisation. It's less . . . well, messy, I suppose. There's no politics to navigate. You can explore things a lot more deeply."

"How's your mum, Nush?" I asked abruptly. Tom grinned *touché* across the island. "Is she well? You haven't mentioned her in ages."

Nush frowned, confused by the hairpin turn in the conversation. "Oh, well, yes, she's fine. She's great, actually. There's been nothing much to mention, thank God." I believed her instantly; you can't fake that inner glow that shines through when a loved one you've been worried about is thriving. "Obviously I've learned not to get my hopes up, but it must be almost a year since the last episode."

Tom didn't flinch. Instead he leaned over and said, "Anyone mind if I have the last cream cheese wonton?"

Later, when Nush was upstairs grabbing a thriller she thought I'd enjoy, and Adam was outside getting annoyed at our lost Uber, Tom said to me, and not in a particularly quiet voice, "OK, Ellen, it was a bit low, I'll give you that. But let's not pretend you not telling Nush had anything to do with poor Shani."

I was mystified by what he meant, and even though part of me, *all* of me, didn't want to give him the satisfaction of my curiosity, before I could stop myself I said, "And what is that supposed to mean, you prick?"

He smiled at the vulgarity, as if it were further proof of his argument. "I'm talking about the fact that you're loving all this. Having one over on St Nushelle. Knowing something she doesn't." He took a step closer. "Oh yes, because I see you, Ellen. That deep-rooted inferiority. You've always felt a bit *nothing* next to her, haven't you? But now you feel pity. And that's intoxicating, isn't it?"

Much later, in bed, once the shock had worn off, I faced Tom's accusation head-on.

Was there any truth in it? Was there even the slightest piece of me that enjoyed viewing Nush as a victim?

Nush the entrepreneur, who'd never use a fork instead of chopsticks. Nush who'd hitched along the French Riviera to sob over Picasso with my now-husband.

No, I concluded, as first light peeked through the bedroom curtains. There wasn't, not one iota. I might be childishly amused if she had a small trip in public, or if Jasmine started dating an unemployed thrash-metal freak. But this? I wouldn't wish this kind of hurt on anyone. Not only was her husband cheating, but he viewed it as one big game.

She had to be told.

First, I sounded Adam out.

"I need to tell you something," I said, seizing the opportunity the next morning as he brushed his teeth.

"Shounds shominous," he replied through a mouthful of foam.

"That night a couple of weeks ago, Susi Sands's fortieth . . ." I paused, taking a breath while Adam eyed me in the bathroom mirror. "Thing is, when I was walking back to the station, I saw Tom with a woman."

He kept brushing. "Who, Nush?"

I gave his reflection the look it deserved. "No, Ads, because if I'd seen him with Nush, I'd have said 'I saw Tom and Nush.' Another woman, you plank. A colleague. The one he got rid of. The one he's still 'mentoring.'"

I knew Adam hated air quotes, but some occasions called for them.

He stopped brushing. "Okaaay."

"And they were holding hands. They were together—as in *together*."

After a quick spit and rinse, Adam spun around, armed with his reasonable face. "How do you know they were *together*? I mean, *I* don't walk along holding hands with other women, but you know what Tom's like."

"He admitted it. He was wetting himself that I was going to tell Nush, so he sent me these cock-and-bull messages about it being a one-off and Shani not being well, so maybe don't say anything, blah blah . . ." I paused, expecting shock, or at least disgust. Adam's face was unreadable.

"So you haven't told her, then?"

I laughed, despite everything. "Well, obviously not! I don't think he'd have been wolfing down her cream cheese wontons if I had, do you?" I lifted my chin. "I'm going to tell her, though. I have to."

"No." Adam shook his head vehemently. "No, leave it, Els. It'll blow over."

Blow over? As though cheating on your wife was just a passing fad, like carp fishing or learning the trumpet.

"Will it? 'Cos it doesn't sound like it's going to any time soon. All that guff last night—'an occasional session,' exploring things 'more deeply.'" I rattled with rage. "Seriously, Ads, he needs to be neutered, then served with divorce papers."

Adam stared at the floor mournfully, drumming his fingers on the basin. I assumed he was weighing up whether he should offer to play a supporting role when I spoke to Nush, or whether, as with most unpleasant conversations, he could leave the lion's share to me.

He looked up.

"Leave it, Ellen."

It was as close to an instruction as he'd ever given me.

My reply was every bit as resolute. "No, Adam. I won't."

He straightened up, widening his stance, and I almost laughed at his attempt at a power play. "Look, this may or may not surprise you, but this isn't the first time, or even the fifth time, that Tom has done this. And Nush has always turned a blind eye before, and it's likely she will again. Which means all you'll do is create a load of awkwardness."

"Oh my God, how have you never told me this?" I didn't know what I was more stunned by: Adam's discretion, Tom's bastardry, or Nush being such a doormat. "And, I mean, you and Nush—you haven't been close for ages, not really. Why would she confide in you and not me?"

"She hasn't confided in me in years, not since London, not

since we've been living here, socialising with them both." He sighed. "We just don't talk about it. It's like those conversations never happened."

It made sense now. Tom's manner last night. His smug, fearless goading. When it came right down to it, he wasn't overly concerned if I told Nush or not. While it might be temporarily inconvenient, he knew she'd forgive him. The fun was in unsettling me.

A fresh swell of rage rose up. "Problem is, Ads, he's not just a bad husband, he's a bad person, and I can't ignore that. He used Nush's mum's mental health to dig himself out of a hole. He got that girl, Jessie, fired. It stinks."

"You're angry, I get it." Adam moved towards me, putting his hands on my shoulders. "But don't confuse punishing Tom with helping Nush."

"That's *not* what I'm doing," I said, barely convincing myself. "If it was me, I'd want to know."

He sighed again and dropped his hands. "Yes, *you* would, but you're not Nush. You're only seeing this through Ellen-cam. You need to take a step back."

I took a breath and dialled myself down; fighting Adam would help no one. "Look, if she accepts it, she accepts it. Fine. I won't say another word. But I can't pretend I didn't see it."

"Maybe we should speak to Shani, see what she thinks."

I dialled right up again. "For God's sake, Nush isn't thirteen! This isn't about whether she can get her ears pierced. Her mum doesn't get to decide what's best."

"Oh, and you do?"

"Yes," I said, and in that moment, I was never more certain of anything. "Because I'll be telling her the truth. And the truth is always best."

I can't say that Adam didn't warn me.

*

"Oh, Thomas, you silly fool."

I stared at Nush, thinking about the last time I'd called Adam
something similar. He'd been halfway through filling up a diesel
hire car with petrol. He hadn't been sweating up the bedsheets
with a lookalike half my age.

Although that's not to say Nush didn't go through a full suite
of emotions. We had surprise, agitation, something resembling,
I'd say, regret. But what shocked me most was how fundamen-
tally unchanged she seemed by the revelation. As though Tom's
infidelity was just a tiresome chore she knew she'd have to
address once in a while.

"Are you OK?" I asked probably twenty times that morning.
Each time, she'd play it down.

"Well, I think it's fair to say I've had better news, Ellen."
Or:

"I'm not going to stick my head in the oven, if that's what
you're worried about."

After a while, after our second coffee, I tried a different tack:
actions in place of feelings.

"So what are you going to do, then?"

"*Do?*" To Nush, one of life's doers, the concept suddenly
seemed bemusing. "Why should *I* have to do anything? He'll say
sorry, he'll promise his way out of the doghouse, no doubt, and
then we"—she waggled a finger, indicating her and me—"will
forget we ever had this conversation." My face gave away my
wholesale disapproval. "Listen, we all have different marriages,
Ellen. My marriage isn't your marriage."

Adam *had* warned me, and yet it still seemed so absurd,
so 1950s housewife. And it wasn't even as though I viewed
forgiveness of infidelity as an automatic middle finger to the
sisterhood. But *repeated* infidelity? I couldn't reconcile that with
the Nush I knew.

"Nush, this girl was, like, twenty-four, twenty-five," I said, not wanting to hurt her, but rather to rally her into *some* sort of revolt. "Doesn't it make you feel—"

"What?" she snapped. "What is it you want me to feel, Ellen?" I gave her wide, surprised eyes and she quickly backtracked, reaching for my hand across the kitchen island. "Oh look, I'm sorry. I'm *sorry*. And thank you for telling me, darling—honestly, I mean that. There's plenty of people around here who'd be telling everyone *but* me." As she withdrew her hand, she slid me a look of pity. *Me?* "But if I'm supposed be shocked that a forty-five-year-old man is attracted to a twenty-five-year-old woman, then I think it's you who's a bit naïve."

All I could do was laugh. "Oh, is that right?"

She gave a small sniff, tracing the rim of her coffee mug. "Well, don't tell me you haven't noticed Adam holding his stomach in every time your pretty little friend pops over in her denim cut-offs."

My pretty little friend.

She meant Gwen, and she knew she meant Gwen. Despite her air of indifference, Nush was too sharp and well-mannered not to remember someone's name. It could have been playground jealousy—you never fully grow out of feeling territorial over friendships—but more likely it was the way men looked at Gwen. Like she was a glass of iced water on a hot summer's day.

"I dare say he does," I replied evenly. "But holding your stomach in and getting your cock out are *way* different ends of the spectrum." Her lip curled in disdain, the way Tom's had that night he called me *nothing*. And it hurt, it triggered something, so I hit back. "Seriously, Nush, how would you feel if someone treated Jasmine the way Tom treats you? Don't you think you should be setting a better example?"

As soon I said it, I wished I hadn't. It wasn't that I didn't think it, or that it wasn't a perfectly fair opinion, but when you tip into moral judgement, it's quite hard to take it back.

Surprisingly, Nush bypassed the criticism. "Look, Ellen, Tom occasionally has sex with other women. I know that. It's an itch he feels the need to scratch, and it's got nothing to do with how he treats me. He treats me wonderfully." She paused the "stand by your man" routine, tilting her head. "How're things with Adam, by the way? Still leaving all the childcare to you and signing up for every sport going?"

The question was rhetorical. She was making a point, plain and simple. A point that made absolute sense to her, even though I couldn't believe she equated the two crimes.

Still, I hadn't planned on saying what I said next. In my defence, her snarky references to Adam had *really* started to grate.

"You know, Tom suggested Orla apply for that summer internship thing next year." Nush frowned, not following. "Well, what's to say he won't be in the market for a new 'mentee' in the future. He obviously likes them young."

"Ellen! How could you . . . Orla's practically a child!" She jumped up, grabbed a cloth and ferociously wiped down the island—a surface already so clean you could perform surgery on it. "I really think you should leave now."

But something had got through. She couldn't meet my eyes.

This was no time to relieve the pressure.

"Oh, I'm not saying it won't be a few years before she's fending him off. I assume he isn't *that* much of a deviant." I assumed nothing of the sort, although if he so much as looked at her, I'd ram his head into the ground until it resembled a smashed birthday cake. "What about Jasmine's friends, though?" Nush froze. "This girl was maybe five, six years older than your own daughter, Nush. Who's to say her friends won't be fair game before long?" I paused. "Imagine that. Go on, imagine it. The humiliation."

She put the cloth in the sink, then stared out into the garden. While I couldn't see her face, the sag of her shoulders said it all.

I went back in one final time. "At least teach him a lesson."

"And how do I do that?" she said, murmuring the question into the ether.

I joined her at the sink, shoulder to shoulder, woman to woman. "Kick him out, at least for a while. Don't just settle for an apology and bullshit promises. You're Nush Delaney, for God's sake. You're a titan. You're Boadicea." That raised a weak smile, at least. "Seriously, if you don't take a stand, where's it going to end? You need to give him a fright, a reminder that even if he gets horny, there are still rules in place. There's only so much you'll tolerate." She nodded, more resigned than resolute. "But he has to know you mean it, Nush. You have to *show* him you mean it. No more words. You need to kick him out."

So.

Did I go too far? Was I too pushy? Was bringing Orla and Jasmine into it a gratuitous low blow?

I've thought about it since, and no, I don't think so. It might have been sparked by my frustration at Nush's passivity and her digs about Adam, but there was merit in what I said. I still think it's a matter of time.

And my shock therapy did the trick. Whatever scale Nush had been previously working with, where mid-twenties colleagues were regrettable but ultimately forgivable, the mere suggestion of Tom leering at her daughter's friends was where her *no more* kicked in.

She didn't turn a blind eye. It didn't blow over. Within days she'd thrown Tom out—swift, brutal, and, to everyone's huge surprise, final.

The past year hasn't been easy. For someone who's achieved so much professionally, Nush defined herself primarily as "Tom's wife" to an astounding extent. But she'll get there, I know she will. She's bright and attractive, and when she isn't playing up to her Queen Bee persona, she's also funny and generous. She deserves someone kind.

So maybe I was a little bullish, but I did the right thing.

Only Tom Delaney, currently living in Jessie's one-bedroom flat while he awaits the financial fallout of divorce proceedings, thinks otherwise.

8

Nush

"Fame at last, darling. Your name isn't quite up in lights, but you're next to the cryptic crossword in *The Echo*, so not a bad billing."

There's silence down the line, at least from Ellen. As usual, there's the background din of carnage that Nush has come to associate with Chateau Walsh: TVs blaring, Orla whining, the twins running feral around the house.

Nush awards herself a smile in the hallway mirror, knowing that Ellen's total silence can only mean one thing: distress.

"Oh God, no, darling. I don't mean that business yesterday," she says, reluctantly putting Ellen out of her misery. Although does she really think she's so important that *The Echo* would class her breathalyser test as quite the exclusive scoop? "No, last week, I mean, at the Retro Food Fair, when you guessed the number of jelly beans. There's a photo on page nine. It's a lovely one. I'll keep it for you."

Ellen had acted astonished when she'd won. *What, me? I never win anything!* But later, over a glass of prosecco, she confessed to Nush that there's a knack to it. A rough calculation you can apply. Something to do with diameters and radius and glass thickness, and who cares, really?

Lucky Adam, was all Nush could think. The nights in Chateau Walsh must really fly by.

Still, to come that close, within eight tiny sweets. It *was* impressive. Even Nush can admit that. But then life, love, everything—even jelly beans—comes easy to Ellen bloody Walsh. She's the classic "good at maths and English" girl.

The girl who always gets what she wants.

Right now, she wants to come over to relay the latest Ellen saga, and she's using that cloying, grateful tone, like she's angling for a flight upgrade rather than a chat and a cup of tea. It sometimes makes Nush laugh, but mainly it just mystifies her, how someone so self-absorbed as Ellen can have so little self-esteem.

As she witters down the phone, Nush fixates on the photo in the paper, tracing her index finger hypnotically around the shape of Ellen's head. It's a flattering photo, actually. Ellen's jaw doesn't look quite as square, and her collarbone appears quite sculpted. It helps that Ivan from *The Echo* is a retired fashion photographer who knows a thing or two about angles. He's a master of masking flaws. An arch manipulator of what people see.

Ellen will pretend to hate it, of course. The publicity. The photo. The whole twee, provincial fuss over community newspapers and jelly beans.

"So, am I cracking open the Pinot?" Nush asks as soon as there's a break in Ellen's self-pity. "As long as you're not driving over, of course. You might not get so lucky a second time."

She suppresses a grin, although heaven knows why she's suppressing it. There's no one here to judge her anymore. Not since she lost her daughter to Pembroke College, Cambridge, and her husband to a flat in Amersham, thirty miles away.

Ellen, disappointingly, barely registers the dig. She replies, "No, no Pinot," but says she's going to walk over anyway. She needs to stretch her legs, clear her head. The past twenty-four hours have apparently been "more stressful than Dunkirk."

Hmm.

So, there's problems at the Meadowhouse, but frankly, when aren't there? If you ask Nush, Ellen's problem is that she has no real problems. Nothing of any substance, anyway. She doesn't know how it feels to lose everything. Ellen's world comes crashing down if she can't locate her keys.

No, what Ellen has is drama, and drama is a self-created construct.

Renovation dramas. Twin dramas. Orla dramas. Adam dramas.

Is it any wonder, Nush often thinks, when they have to put up with so much *you*?

And then there's the "stand-alone" dramas, as Nush has come to think of them. Last week it was A Worrying Mole; the week before that, Possibly Offending Sylvia. The week before *that*, it was Ants in the Living Room—a great swarm of them, in fact, attracted by a rogue ginger biscuit that had been left festering under the sofa. It was all Nush could do not to point out that if Ellen actually vacuumed under the furniture once in a while, instead of just around it, it wouldn't have happened.

But as in vacuuming, so in life.

Ellen's only ever concerned with the parts people see.

9

Ellen

It's unspoken etiquette, and it could be one-sided, but even after several years of friendship, I still don't turn up to Nush's uninvited. And unlike Gwen, who once popped over to ours to borrow a charger and ended up cooking a Thai green curry, I certainly don't commandeer Nush's kitchen. I've never even made myself a hot drink.

Fortunately, Nush is an exceptional host.

"Sweet tea for the shock," she says, handing me a mug and a slab of something sticky across the kitchen island. "And home-made Sri Lankan coconut cake for the sheer bloody hell of it."

Nush is on good form tonight, always galvanised by a crisis. And on the subject of her soon-to-be ex, she's absolutely resolute.

"Darling, I know he has a flair for the dramatic, but poison-pen letters would *so* not be his thing." She bites her bottom lip, her eyes narrowed and perplexed. "But then, really, whose thing would they be? Who on earth would have something against *you*?"

"Adam said the same." I laugh weakly. "I didn't realise I was so bland and inoffensive."

A flash of the Lomax. Of Zane. The guiltiest of secrets.

The place and the person that expose the worst of me.

Nush hops onto the stool opposite. "Well, listen, I assure you it isn't Tom. I don't think I ever remember him writing a letter, never mind going to the trouble of posting one. He never even used to write to Santa—discouraged Jasmine from doing it too. Can you believe that?"

I can, no problem. For a man with such a baggy relationship with the truth, Tom always held tight to the belief that adults shouldn't perpetuate "childish falsehoods." The Tooth Fairy was his ultimate bugbear.

God, I hate him.

I also know that I'm projecting, that I *desperately* want this to be him. Because at least a hostile strike from Tom is a strike that I can talk about. I could even talk to the police if it came to it. If nasty letters became nasty deeds.

But without knowing who I'm dealing with, involving the police could be self-destructive.

"And anyway," Nush continues, "quite apart from the fact that he's never been much of a wordsmith, he's been in Zurich since last week, five hundred miles from High Wycombe."

I look at her. "I thought you two were pretty much incommunicado these days?"

"Oh, I have eyes and ears."

I wish she'd let him go. And I hope she isn't using poor Jasmine as her snitch.

"Well, even if he's in Zurich, he must have a lackey who'd post a letter for him." I try a corner of the cake, making the requisite cooing noises while I formulate my next thought. "What about the breathalyser?"

Nush points her fork. "Now *that* I wouldn't put past him. But how would he have known where you were?"

"You didn't put anything on Facebook? A photo, a status update?"

Her body curls into a defensive knot. "You think I'm so tragic that I wouldn't have unfriended him on Facebook?"

I cringe. The last thing I want to do is pick at Nush's wounds when they're still at the red and scratchy stage.

"Well, look, regardless of the *how*, I still think Tom's a strong

contender. He obviously blames me for you throwing him out."
A nip of doubt pulls me up. "Although why now? I mean, 'revenge is best served cold' sounded great in *The Godfather*, but
this is real life."

"Yes, well . . ." Nush pauses. "Life is about to get very real for
my darling ex, it seems." She looks down at her tea, going quiet
again for a few seconds. I'm about to explode from curiosity
when her head whips up. "The cocker spaniel is pregnant."

"Whoa." I put my fork down. This is turning out to be quite
the day all round. "God, so it's . . . serious?"

"So it would appear. A pup is for life, as they say."

"But . . . I thought he was just staying there for convenience?
Keeping his dick wet and his pants washed until he knows how
the land lies financially?"

Nush raises an eyebrow. "So you think Jessie's the pant-
washing type, then?"

"I've no idea. I wasn't being literal."

"Oh, come on, you must have got some sense of her." We've
been doing this routine for a year: Nush probing me for detail
I don't have, pumping me for insight into someone I spoke
to for less than five minutes. "Although cocker spaniels are
known to be quite a doting breed, aren't they? I'd say she does
his laundry."

I humour her with a grin, even though I'm slightly mortified
about "the cocker spaniel." While the term served its purpose
during the first few weeks of the post-Tom apocalypse, I kind
of hoped we'd move on from it, or at least tarnish Tom with a
similarly snide tag.

"So when did you find out?" I ask.

"Oh, days ago. Not through him, of course. Jasmine."

The lily-livered wuss couldn't even tell her himself.

"Days ago! Christ, why didn't you say anything?"

She rakes a hand through her hair. "You're always so busy. I
didn't want to burden you."

"Well, you should have. This is big, Nush." I blow out a long breath. "So how do you feel about it—you *and* Jasmine?"

"Jasmine's OK. Mainly concerned about me, darling that she is. But I'd be lying if I didn't say it hurts, Ellen. It hurts right here." She raps her long, slim fingers hard against her breastbone. "I always wanted us to have another child. Obviously, it didn't happen."

I always wondered, although there's no way I'd ever have asked her. Nush is the kind of person you wait to receive info from, and in any case, how many kids a woman has—one, two, ten, none—has always struck me to be entirely her own business. I assumed she was happy with her lot, though. She's always referred to Jasmine as "such a treasured child" (as though I'd come across mine in a rubbish bin and thought I'd find use for them), and the three of them seemed so contained, so content, at least on the surface. I suppose she was a bit distant when I announced my jaw-dropper pregnancy a few years ago, but I put that down to a touch of melancholy over the fact our friendship would inevitably change.

"Well, it'll be hell for him, if that's any consolation," I say. "Seriously, he hasn't wiped a shitty bum in nearly two decades." Nush's expression suggests he didn't wipe too many back then, either. "And then there's the broken sleep, the endless sterilising. *And* he'll have to put up with all the older-dad jokes. Who's going to lose their teeth first? Who takes more naps?" A trace of a wry smile. "And then wait until they hit the twins' age and life becomes one long supermarket meltdown."

"Enjoy them, darling. Before you know it, they'll be off to university and your house will feel like a mausoleum." She throws me a sheepish look, an acknowledgement that *just hang in there for another fifteen years* probably isn't overly comforting. "So how many meltdowns this week, then?"

"Oh, just the three." She winces. "The last one was so bad I called Max 'Satan' in front of Mrs. O'Leary at pickup. I don't think she appreciated the joke, but hey ho." I hack at the cake again; sugar and fat is *always* comforting. "Honestly, between them and Orla . . . You know, Kristy thinks she could have been the one who reported me for driving over the limit."

"Orla!" Nush finds the idea reassuringly outlandish. "She wouldn't do that, surely? She's just going through a phase. They all do." Easy to say when Jasmine's phases involved photographing viaducts and launching a campaign to save the pangolins. "Really, Ellen, Kristy shouldn't have said that. But then Kristy shouldn't say a lot of things."

"Hey, what do you make of Jason Bale?" I say, swiftly changing course. It doesn't feel right to Kristy-bash. Not when she's at home taking care of my babies.

"Jason Bale? In what sense?"

"Oh, it's probably nothing. I just get odd vibes from him. It's hard to explain." Particularly hard after the day I've had. My brain feels like it's running on gloopy rice pudding. "He's a bit off with me, that's all."

"Can't say I've noticed." Nush leans forward, arms folded—classic gossip's pose. "But I'll tell you something—it *is* strange that he's wound up here administering breathalyser tests."

"He split up with his wife," I say. "Wanted a fresh start . . ."

"He split up with his *life*, according to Stu Bartlett." I haven't a clue who Stu Bartlett is, but Nush is nosy and well connected, and I am suddenly all ears. "He used to be a senior officer in the Met . . ."

"Who? Stu Bartlett?"

"Noooo." Her tone suggests the very notion is laughable. "Stu works on the front desk at the station. His wife, Pia, runs Bootcamp on the Green. She's Danish, he's . . . I don't know, from somewhere up north." She gives me a frustrated look, as if I really should know all this. "Jason, I mean. *Jason* was with the Met. Murder, counter-terrorism. Inspector-level, I think. A real high flyer."

"He was demoted?" I say. It could explain the gruffness.

"Well, no. That's the strangest part. According to Stu, Jason effectively demoted himself. Turned his back on his big career, and next thing he's applying for a lowly constable role in our humble little parish." She sits up straight, pleased as punch with herself. "If you ask me, darling, there's some very 'odd vibes' about that."

10

Kristy

Does Kristy mind if she's back a bit later, she's *a legend*, and *so sorry!!!* That was the gist of Ellen's rambling, grovelling text. And of course, Kristy said *fine*, because them's the rules of her free tenancy. Every inconvenience must be met with *stop stressing, Ellen. I understand.*

And she does. She really does. She understands that Ellen thinks her time is more precious than everyone else's. She has three children, see, *three*, and endless noble responsibilities: widowed neighbours to check on, *Othello* to teach, tradesmen to mobilise. Quite simply, Ellen has more on her plate than possibly any living human, and because she has more, you should expect *less*. So if she's running late, don't get snappy. If she's snappy, please don't judge. And you can't complain, not really. Not when you're living in her house and she's put you on the car insurance, and she's saying it honestly isn't a problem because *these things even themselves out.*

Don't they fucking just. Ellen doesn't know the half of it.

The twins are in bed at last, although God knows if they're asleep yet. Kristy's job was just to settle them and, frankly, that was work enough. Now in the peace and quiet, she's standing in front of Ellen's heaving wardrobe, marvelling at what kind of pretentious dipshit pays £90 for a plain white tee.

Beyond baffled, she drags the offending item off its velvet

padded hanger, inspecting the front for even a faint logo, but of course there's nothing there. See, Ellen Walsh doesn't do designer logos. She thinks they're naff, "a bit lottery winner." Her Svengali, Nush, would probably call them *the mark of nouveau riche*. Thing is, Kristy remembers Ellen *Hennessey*, the Undisputed Logo Queen of Leicester. Ellen Hennessey was more than happy to wear her self-worth across her chest.

When she was seventeen, Kristy bought Ellen a Gucci T-shirt with the cash from her first photo shoot, then they drank posh wine at The Case in Leicester. Ellen kept saying, "Imagine if the Highfield lot could see us now . . ."

It's strange, given that she's been Ellen Walsh for almost as long as she was Ellen Hennessey, but Kristy still can't help thinking of them as two completely different beasts. She once shared a flat with a therapist, who asked her which Ellen she'd prefer to get stuck in a lift with, and when Kristy instantly replied, "Hennessey," she asked if that meant she resented Adam. Did she blame her brother-in-law's well-to-do-ness for her sister's apparent change?

What she resented was the *apparent*, and anyone would think Adam was aristocracy. But for the record, Kristy has never blamed Adam. Not for Ellen's baseless grandeur.

And certainly not for what she did.

She stuffs the T-shirt back in the wardrobe then rifles through the pockets of a red pea coat. Annoyingly, there's no cash, just a desiccated wet wipe and the heads of two Lego men. Coats are often a gold mine. She must've found at least £50 in Ellen's bank of coats alone. Just last week, she discovered a twenty in an All Saints puffer marked for charity. What kind of ditsy, privileged dipshit loses track of twenty quid?

The first time she stole money from Ellen, she was only looking for decent painkillers. Something to combat the latest wave of decimating back pain that makes over-the-counter drugs as

much use as sweets. Through the agony she'd remembered a chat
she'd overheard weeks earlier—Ellen on the phone extolling the
merits of low-dose Elavil to a cystitis-stricken friend.

High-dose, low-dose, anything was better than no-dose to a
desperate Kristy. And so she went hunting for medication and
the money was just there—£12.75 to be exact, discarded in a
drawer underneath a tangle of old phone chargers and bottles
of kids' medicine.

I'm long forgotten, the money whispered. *Go for it, honey.
Help yourself.*

So she did.

And tonight, she was honestly only searching for Kian's imag-
inatively named Brown Bear when she spotted the silver charm
bracelet gathering dust under Ellen's bed.

"Happy birthday to me," she whispered.

All yours, it whispered back. *She hasn't even realised I'm
missing. You'd get thirty quid for me on eBay. Maybe forty after
a decent clean.*

That's probably ambitious, Kristy thinks now. She'll get
twenty if she's lucky. Jewellery is never the easiest to shift, not
unless it's boxed and new, or you can prove its actual prove-
nance. Branded clothes, still tagged, and luxury beauty products
still wrapped in cellophane, that's where the good money is,
and luckily Ellen has boatloads. A whole fleet of wardrobes
and drawers stuffed with clothes she's never worn, creams she's
never opened, perfumes she didn't ask for. Mainly guilt gifts
Adam bought while killing time in duty-free. Every time Ellen
whines about Adam's work trips, Kristy wants to shout, *Shut
your mouth! He's my main supplier!* Just this week he brought
back a Dior serum that Kristy knows she'll get £50 for. And it's
not like Ellen will notice. Kristy's checked. She already has three.

So is it really theft if the owner doesn't even miss it?

She knows she should look for a job, and she does occasionally, to show initiative. But *taking* a job is more complicated.

Taking a job would mean admitting she's sticking around, and she can't see that happening. Not now. Not since she met Shay. He's already talking about them moving away, making a fresh start. He's got this obsession with North Cornwall. She can't picture him on a surfboard, and she can barely shuffle ten yards some days, never mind execute a perfect cutback. But still, it feels nice when he talks about it. This future where she isn't always relying on other people's help.

See, people say they want to help, but it's a short ride to them feeling exploited. Years of sofa-surfing and ruined friendships have taught her that bitter truth. Because people don't *really* want to help. What they want is to feel good about themselves.

And Kristy believes it's high time that some of those people started feeling bad.

11

Ellen

Someone is watching me. My nerves are shot. My pulse is flying.

Or more likely, *someone* is feeling jumpy, and they should probably go easier on the caffeine.

It's late and it's chilly and I should have called a taxi, and the stifling suburban silence is only fuelling my unease. As I dash down the shuttered high street, I try to recall the basics of a self-defence class I took a few years ago. Do you kick them in the nuts or key them in the eye? A chop to the throat rings a bell, but in all honesty, I hadn't paid that much attention. The class was nothing more than an excuse for a night out. *A chance to kick ass instead of wipe ass*, as another new mum put it.

The dark void of the village green looms ominously on the horizon, and I can't help thinking, a little crabbily, that if the boot was on the other foot, I'd have insisted on giving Nush a lift. Although maybe she'd had a drink before I got there, and that's why she didn't offer. Who could blame her, really, what with Tom planting his seed in her twenty-five-year-old doppelgänger? I'd sink a whole vineyard if it was Adam about to embark on a new family.

I'm at the edge of the green now; one steely breath, then decision time. Do I do the sensible thing and walk the long way round, or do I dart across the middle and have my key in the door in less than five? Despite my jitters about the letter, the short cut is, as ever, sorely tempting. The cold is in my bones now, and it's not like I haven't done it before.

But I should at least *try* not to be a hypocrite, I tell myself, knowing I'd ground Orla for life if she even thought about doing it.

Despite what my daughter thinks of me, all I've ever wanted is for her to be safe.

12

Jason

From the darkness of his car, Jason watches Ellen teetering on the edge of the village green, no doubt deliberating whether to cut across or use that famous brain of hers and walk around.

It stuns him that people make these kind of calculations. Grown adults. Supposedly educated people. Idiots with children, responsibilities, long lives to look forward to, weighing speed versus safety like it's a choice between coffee and tea.

Don't they watch the news? Don't they realise that all it takes is one bad decision?

If that's how much Ellen values her life, well . . .

But then *Thames Lawley is SO safe!* That's the mantra they all repeat to themselves. It's the lullaby that fast-tracks them to sleep. Their justification for their stale lives.

Feel safe! Be safe! Stay safe!

The slogan's everywhere. It's on the town sign. It's in the newsletter. Ellen's drummed it into his sister without a single fucking clue. He can literally her voice every time Gwen starts quoting crime stats at him (yeah, *him*, a police officer), or when she's cooing, "Everyone's got your back here, Jase. They're all so caring. Everyone's cool."

That so? Well, tell that to the Merricks, who owned Ellen's house a good few years ago. Evidently, no one had their back the night they were beaten black and blue. Tell it to the old guy who got mugged while walking his dog in Proctor's Park yesterday, or the kid from that ugly McMansion they all bitch about—the brat with his own gaming room, the angry stepdad, and the broken ribs.

Jason knows there's no such thing as safety, just naïvety and blind privilege.

It's only a matter of time before Ellen learns it too.

Sometimes he can't believe she doesn't remember him. Other times he wonders if anyone really sees him. Even when they were kids, he was the stage dressing; it was Gwen who got the attention. It's partly why he joined the police, he thinks. Why he worked so hard, so long, so late—God, *so* late—on some of the more high-profile cases. It was all to form an identity that made him more than good ol' Jase.

And now look at him. Hiding in his car—the car he can no longer afford the repayments on. Hiding from Ellen, from Gwen, from the second-hand futon he bought for fifty quid off eBay and the six plastic wardrobe hangers that constitute his sad-fuck life.

She's taking the long way around. Good.

Wasn't that hard, now was it, Einstein?

He's in no rush to go home, as usual. He might as well sit here and watch her, although he'll probably lose her as she moves between the dense sycamores on the west side. But when she reaches the main road, the street lights will pick her up again, and he'll be able to track her right up to the moment she puts her key in her front door. Swallowed up again by the cocoon of her "safe" life.

He's not sure how long he can do this.

Burnout, he lied the day he quit the job that meant everything to him. He blamed all the murderers, the terrorists, the company he'd been forced to keep.

But living in this limbo in Thames Lawley has taught him the true meaning of burnout.

Watching her is exhausting. It's a full-time career.

*

He could do without Gwen tonight. He could do without Gwen full-stop.

"Where the hell have you been?" she asks, as though he's got some fucking nerve having his own life to deal with. "I told Orla you'd be back by eight thirty. I had to pay her extra. I thought you were working ten till eight?"

Jason fishes in his pocket, retrieving a five-pound note and a few coins. Gwen can't be paying her more than that, surely? Not for speed-reading *The Bumblebear* and Snapchatting her mates for three hours. When *he* was sixteen, he worked on building sites, digging trenches and shovelling topsoil for a wage the Walsh girl would laugh out loud at. He didn't have a choice, though. Gwen was only ten, and someone had to put clothes on their backs and food on the table. All their worthless parents had ever contributed was the sperm and the egg.

He throws the money on the sofa. "There you go, Mary Poppins's overtime." He moves towards the stairs. "I'm knackered. I'm going to bed."

Gwen moves, blocking his path; a brick wall with sparkly hairclips. "I asked you a question, Jase. Where've you been?"

He could move her. *Shove* her. He's got at least seventy pounds on her. Instead, he fires back his own accusation. "You went over there this morning. I saw you."

"Oh, for God's sake," she stage-whispers, then louder, *much* louder, "Seriously, Jase, what is *wrong* with you? I want this to stop, OK. I want *you* to stop." He holds her stare, waiting for the answer to his implied question. "Of course I went over! I had to apologise."

"Why?" He claws at his top button. One year on, and wearing the uniform still feels like a slow form of asphyxia. "I questioned some thug off the Lomax about that mugging in the park earlier. Turns out he had an alibi. Are you going to apologise to him, too?"

"No, because offending him doesn't mean losing my babysitter."

"Oh, and what a loss that would be." He's truly had it for today. He pushes past Gwen and up the stairs, pausing two steps up to add, "You know, when I got back the other week, she was in your room, trying on stuff. Clothes and make-up everywhere. I'd check everything's still there if I were you."

"But you're not, are you? You're nothing like me."

The house falls convent-quiet. No sounds from outside, either. No sirens, no shouts, no traffic, no life. Nothing whatsoever to remind him that there's something other than them. Than *this*. Gwen's frustration and his . . . what?

Resentment? *Obsession?*

"Look, I didn't *have* to apologise," she says suddenly. "I wanted to. Ellen's my friend."

She's doing her petulant face now and fiddling with her right ear lobe. A stupid childhood tic that was irritating enough when she was a kid but drives him crazy now.

"Your *friend*." He oozes scorn. "I suppose that's why you were gossiping about her last night?"

"I was *what*?"

She could win an Oscar, she really could.

"On the phone, Gwen. That's the problem with these new-builds—thin walls, no privacy."

She thinks for a minute, or pretends to think, anyway. "*That*. That wasn't gossiping. Susi Sands called to see if I'd put Bella's name down for Twirler Tots, and then she asked what happened at the Cricketers and I had to say something. Better she heard the facts from me rather than the spiced-up version, don't you think?"

"And do you give all your friends names like 'the Home-wrecker'?"

She throws her hands up. "For God's sake! I call Ellen that to her face. You remember what a joke is, right? I just don't get why she wants to turn a lovely cosy house into something out of *Space Odyssey*. I mean, it needs a lick of paint, sure, but she's pretty much sending the tanks in."

"And that's none of your business."

"Oh, that's rich coming from you." She stares at him unblinking, then drops dramatically onto the sofa. You'd swear she'd just done a gruelling ten-hour shift, not three hours perched on a bar stool, sipping wine with God knows who. "But you know, you're right, as it goes. It *is* none of my business. Just like it's none of Ellen's business who I met for a drink tonight, but I bet she's over there now, discussing it—sorry, 'gossiping' about it—with Adam or Kristy. And you know what, Jase? That's fine. That's what people do. They talk about each other. It's *normal*."

Normal. He wondered when that word would get an airing. When Gwen isn't prizing it above everything, she's using it as a stick to beat him with.

She lets out a small conciliatory sigh. "Look, can we just leave this. There's a casserole in the fridge if you're hungry. Make sure you reheat it properly, though. Chicken can be lethal. Use the thermometer." Jason almost laughs at the predictability of it all: first her fury, then exasperation, and finally the peace offering. "There's baked beans in it," she adds with a crumb of a smile. "Just the way you like it."

He fucking hates baked beans. Hasn't liked them in two decades. Gwen is stuck in some rosy reconstructed past where comfort food made them happy. Where sugar and carbs offered a respite from the constant shit that life threw.

But he doesn't have any fight left. Not tonight. He's too tired. He can't even be bothered to point out that she smokes and drives too fast, and he's never once seen her apply sunscreen, but yeah, he'll reheat the chicken properly. Wouldn't want to mess with 'lethal' meat.

"Thanks," he says. "I'll take some to work tomorrow, have

it for lunch." He points up the stairs. "But now I really need to sleep. It's been a long day."

He won't sleep, not for hours, but in the meantime, there's social media.

Might as well spend some time judging other people's lives rather than lying there blaming everyone—well, just one person really—for the absolute shipwreck of his own.

13

Ellen

As I close the front door, bolting both inside locks with a neurotic flourish, the sound of laughter from the living room immediately catches me off guard. I'm aware that recoiling from laughter must make me the world's most miserable human, but I assumed Adam would still be out having a post-badminton snifter, and that Kristy would fly the coop as soon as my toenail was in the door. I was hoping for a Baileys in the bath, not more conversation.

I walk into the living room.

"What are you pair up to?" I ask by way of a tart hello.

The room is dark. Kristy is sitting on the floor with her back against the leather sofa. Adam is perched on the arm, bony elbows on swollen knees. *Was there any point buying him a knee brace?* Their heads are almost touching as they stare, smiling, towards the glow of Kristy's ancient laptop. There's a rainbow sticker by the mousepad: *IBIZA PRIDE 2014.*

"Ads is helping me fill out this application," Kristy says, finally looking at me. Her eyes twinkle with something toxic. "Hey, what song do you think best describes my work ethic, Els-Bels?"

I draw a blank, but it doesn't matter; it's not a question, it's a challenge. An invitation to be snide so that she gets to reciprocate the spite.

"Application? That's great," I say, refusing to bite. "What's the job?"

"Gourmet popcorn."

Right. Making it? Packaging it? Marketing it? *Eating* it? It could be any one of a hundred different verbs. There's no end to the jobs Kristy will turn her hand to for, ooh, a matter of weeks.

"A-Salt and Buttery," Adam says, giving me *shoot-me-now* eyebrows over Kristy's faux-hawk. "They're 'disruptive innovators,' apparently, whatever that means."

"It *means* they're a progressive start-up," Kristy snaps, leaping to the defence of the company, who if she does end up working there will soon be deemed "worse than North Korea" for simply suggesting she turn up on time. "They set up a few months ago. They're aiming for street-food fairs, festivals, that kind of thing."

Sounds like more of a prize than a job, basically a free ticket to Glastonbury. I keep my own counsel, though, muttering a vaguely encouraging *cool*, then say, "So, how was it? Were the boys OK?"

"Yeah, they had a whale of a time playing with scissors and sticking their fingers in the plug sockets."

Adam snickers. I give a testy sigh. "Look, I wasn't implying—"

"I know. It was a joke. Of course they were OK." She slams the laptop shut and, using Adam's thigh as a platform, pushes herself up to standing. "We played 'throwing the sock up the stairs' around, oh, four hundred and twenty-seven times, then they went to bed, no bother." She flexes left to right, stretching out her back for, *oh*, the four hundred and twenty-seventh time this week (sometimes, God forgive me, I think she slightly milks it). "Well, apart from the Brown Bear crisis, but I found him in the end in the towel cupboard."

"Is Orla back?" I ask, although I know intuitively that she is. The house feels different when my daughter's in it. It pulses with a distinctive energy, a slow, queasy sway. Like the roll of a boat on a rough body of water.

"Didn't you see the flag at full mast?" Adam says. "The queen is in residence."

"Forget Orla." Kristy's on to spine rotations now. "I want to hear what Lady Nush had to say."

And so I tell them about soon-to-be Papa Tom. When I'm finished, a now fully stretched Kristy offers a few *poor cow* platitudes. Adam shakes his head and asks, "Shit. How's she taking it?"

"Oh, you know, she's on-brand Nush: hurt but elegantly stoic. Think Princess Di on *Panorama*." Was that mean? Maybe. I shift to a more supportive tone. "She's actually doing OK, considering. Better than I'd have predicted."

"Happy pills, I bet." Trust Kristy to take the cynic's view. "What?" she protests in response to my eye roll. "Her mum has issues, doesn't she? That kind of thing runs in families."

"And what runs in ours, Kris? Lack of compassion? Or is that just you and Mum?" I unzip my coat, addressing Adam. "Makes you think, though, doesn't it? If Tom isn't exactly over the moon about this pregnancy, you know who he'll blame? Me. For telling Nush about Jessie. For upending his cosy little life. 'Cos that's how his mind works. He's never to blame for anything."

Adam's fists clench. "You really think it *could* be bloody Tom then, this letter?" His voice shakes and I can't help but smile at his mild-mannered machismo. Angry—sure. Protective—yes. But slightly panicked at the thought of being called on to punch someone.

"I think it's possible," I say. "Thing is, Nush doesn't. She's adamant it's not his style."

"Well, hold on to your hats, but I think I agree with Her Royal Smugness." I look at Kristy, half expecting a punchline. "No, seriously, Els, listen—whoever sent that note wants to see your reaction, that's a given. That's, like, Psychology 101. And unless Tom's bugged the house, or microchipped your arm or something, he's not going to get that kick living in Amersham, is he?" She gives a little shrug. "But then, of course, if not him, who?"

My phone pings in my pocket, giving me a jolt of pure anxiety. If whoever sent the letter knows my address, there's a chance they know my number too.

Please let it be Mum, I pray. She's the only one who ever messages this late. Sometimes to tell me we're "a shower of wankers" for not visiting. Other times to ask for money. Always when she's drunk.

It isn't Mum. It's Gwen.

Your Facebook. WTF??? Who's Ciara Harkin? What's her problem???

"Ciara Harkin?" I say, looking at Kristy, who hasn't the first clue what I'm talking about. "Weren't there Harkins on the Highfield?"

"You're thinking of *Haw*kins. Jimmy Hawkins. He hung around with Cahill."

Harkin. The name *does* sounds vaguely familiar, but I can't summon a face, or an event, or one single memory. I bring up Facebook, ignoring a "What?" from Kristy, who at the first sniff of drama has jumped back on her laptop, and an "Eh?" from Adam, followed by "Earth to Ellen" when I don't respond.

Five notifications. *Ciara Harkin has tagged you in a photo on Facebook.*

Ciara Harkin doesn't have a profile photo, just a standard greyed-out silhouette. We're "friends," though. Maybe the Irishness of the name made me assume she's a third cousin twice removed and accept her request.

I click on the first photo, captioned: *STATE of this and she's a MOTHER!!!*

The next carries the observation: *Sad really* 😞 *She obviously needs help. #ItsTheKidsIFeelSorryFor*

In every photo I look blotto, and yet, to my shame, I originally posted them. This Ciara Harkin has obviously screenshotted the originals then reposted them with her own commentary. So who the hell is she, and to quote Gwen, what *is* her problem? And why oh why did I ever post this stuff? What was I thinking or trying to prove?

A yard of ale at a charity event.

Holding two cocktails while, with the help of an ex-colleague, sipping a third.

Fast asleep on a beanbag, cradling a six-pack of Carlsberg like a newborn.

"Hey, look at you! Never saw you as a Jack-Daniel's-straight-from-the-bottle girl." Kristy's barely concealed amusement brings me up to speed with the fourth photo.

The fifth is the oldest: Courchevel 2010. Adam's sister Zara's hen weekend (or week-long atomic bender, rather). In it, I'm pushing thirty and a mum to a then four-year-old Orla, and it's the first time I've been away since the day she was born. I say this to explain the exuberance. To give context as to why I'm dancing on a bar, glugging from a magnum of Moët being held by a rich teenager, the overflow soaking my then collagen-rich cheeks, my skirt barely longer than the cigarette we've just shared.

It was taken by Zara on the rare occasion she wasn't mauling the nearest stag party. It captured a wild day. It capped off an *expensive* day. Champagne. VIP booths. More powder up the nose than on the slopes—although not for me. Downing fizz with Etonian sixth-formers was the extent of my debauchery.

Zara had the photo framed and gave it to me as a joke the following Christmas. "Something to scandalise Orla with," she suggested. "Something to laugh at when you're old and creaky."

I'm creaky now, and I'm not sure Orla even cares enough to be scandalised.

What I am sure of, though, and what has literally just occurred to me, is that like so many of the photos taken that week, my antics never made it on to the internet. It wasn't that it was *that* bad, more that social media wasn't the go-to it is now. Back then, things were occasionally kept private.

So the stark and alarming fact is that this particular photo couldn't have been screenshotted.

That photo is on a collage that Adam put together for my fortieth, a collage that hangs in the spare bedroom.

I'm ninety-nine per cent sure it's never left this house.

"You should go to the police."

We're in bed, scene of the revolutionary sex this morning. The idea of intimacy now seems so incredibly naïve that I feel almost embarrassed by the act, for giving myself so completely.

And yet I completely trust Adam. As much as I trust anyone.

I stare into the darkness, stress-tugging my eyebrow hairs. "No."

"You have to, Els. I'll come with you."

"I said no."

"For God's sake," Adam shout-whispers—there's no way he's risking waking one of the boys and spending the night having his scrotum pummelled by a squirming, restless toddler. "The breathalyser, the letter, now *this*. It's stone-cold harassment."

"Look, shall I try a different language? Which one do you want? No? *Nein*? *Non*? *Méiyǒu*? That last one's Mandarin. Aren't I clever?"

He gives an irritated sigh. "That's right, make a joke of it. Meanwhile this Ciara Harkin plots her next move."

I mouth a silent scream in the dark. Is he being deliberately dense?

"What part are you not getting, Ads? There *is* no Ciara Harkin. Someone set up a fake profile and sent me a friend request, knowing I'm the big fucking fool who almost always accepts them." I'd untagged myself from the photos immediately to limit the audience, but God, I'm an idiot. The hours I've spent lecturing Orla about being cautious online. "And it's very likely that that someone has had access to this house."

"What makes you say that?"

"Well, because unless your sister's behind it—and I *really* can't see it, can you?—the only way that Courchevel photo ended up online is if someone took a photo of it in the spare bedroom."

"Oh, and *that* isn't a police matter, no?" He sighs again. "Seriously, is this some kind of hangover from childhood, some honour code? *I don't talk to the filth.*" I smile, despite everything, at Adam's standard-thug impression. So far from who he is. "You do realise this is Thames Lawley? 'Feel safe! Be safe! Stay safe!' The police aren't the enemy."

I pull the cord switch above the bed; another feature from the dark ages. Adam squints at the abrupt light.

"And what exactly do you think the police will do?" I ask, sitting up. "I'll tell you, shall I? They'll a) do nothing—remember when Kristy was being stalked by that fruitloop years back? What was their response? Come back when they've actually *done* something."

"But this person *has* done something . . ."

I keep going. "Or b) they'll start prying into every corner of our lives, our friends' lives, our family's."

He props himself up on his elbows. "Let them pry. I haven't got anything to hide, have you?"

Why did I switch the light on? Telling lies in the dark is so much easier.

"Look . . ." I take a deep breath, dodging the question. "Now you're not going to like this, and I'm not saying it *is* her, not at all. But I honestly wouldn't put all this past Orla."

I'm not sure if I believe this, or if I'm simply trying to misdirect Adam. I think it's the latter, but then she *was* acting kind of weird earlier. Questioning where I'd been. All the air quotes around my "errands." She usually couldn't give two damns about my whereabouts, so why the sudden interest?

Adam's "No' is instant, followed by a flummoxed "Why?"

There's no way I'm answering that. I press on. "And yeah, the police probably wouldn't actually *do* anything if it was Orla. They'd see it as a family matter. But still . . . *the police.* Is that what you want? Remember, whoever this person is, they've been in this house, they've been upstairs. It's almost certainly someone we know well, Ads. We need to think carefully, that's all I'm saying. Like Kristy said, this person wants a reaction, so they'll show themselves eventually. We can deal with it then."

He looks shocked, as though it hadn't occurred to him that it could be someone very close to home. So what *has* he been thinking? A plasterer with a grudge? The woman who came to measure up for the blinds in the spare room whom I never called back?

After a minute, he says, "Look, maybe you could ask Jason for some advice off the record—isn't that the term they use?" Pre-empting my *no*, he adds, "Or ask Gwen to sound him out."

"He used to be an inspector, you know," I say, diverting the conversation. "Me and Nush googled him. He was on that big case in London—the sniper a few years back, remember?" Adam's wide eyes say *And?* I shrug. "Just a bit weird, don't you think? Dirty Harry becoming Dixon of Dock Green."

"What's weird is that you seem to think this is just going to go away if you ignore it."

"Maybe it will. Maybe whoever it is has had their fun."

"The letter, though . . . that seems to promise more than a breathalyser stunt and some Facebook embarrassment." Rallied by his own words, he gives a grim, determined shake of his head. "No, you have to log it with the police. If you don't want to make a big thing of it, fine. I'm sure they'll be more than happy to file it under 'not urgent.' But at least if you tell them, it's logged for when—*if*—something else happens."

He's so right. He's so rational. And yet there's zero chance of it happening.

Because if I go to the police, they'll ask if I know why someone might have a grudge against me.

And what's the point in going to them only to lie to them?

Because I'm certainly not telling them the truth.

14

Gwen

I always warn my clients that they can do twenty good deeds, but all people will remember is the one bad one.

The words of Gwen's old boss, Angie. Her first mentor in PR.

And it's true. Just look at poor Ellen. Always the first to offer a lift, water your plants, lend you her hedge trimmer. But Gwen knows without a doubt she'll now forever be known as "Ellen the Breathalysed." Doesn't matter that she blew under. That she was driving off moments later. The optics just weren't good. And in the modern world, optics are king.

Not that Gwen blames Jason, despite what she said to Ellen. He *was* just doing his job, and it isn't his job to protect Ellen's brand.

But *holy guacamole*, those Facebook photos. They were bad. Like, superbad. Individually, they were fine, but collectively Ellen looked like a total lush. Gwen knew she'd have to warn her. She'd be a lousy friend if she didn't. But she'd waited a few minutes. Around ten minutes. OK, maybe fifteen.

See, Gwen *tries* to like Ellen.

She *does* like Ellen.

Or does she just *want* to like Ellen?

She's pondered this a lot, and she can never quite work it out.

She knows she *should* like Ellen, that she's only ever been welcoming to her *and* to Jason (even though he flinches every time her name is mentioned—what the hell's that all about?).

She knows that Ellen's kind, if a bit martyr-ish. Easy company, if kind of hectic. And she can be fun, really fun, when she drops the whole *I don't have time to wipe my arse* routine. Case in point—they had a boozy "kitchen disco" a while back. Sounds lame, but it was hilarious. They both gave it the full Rihanna, and cracked two tiles dancing to "Rude Boy." They only stopped when Ellen thought she'd wet herself, and Gwen nearly wet herself laughing at that.

"Yeah, well, that's what happens when thirteen pounds of human flesh muscles its way out of your vagina in one sitting. Your twerking days are over."

Such a funny night. So much laughter. *So* much rosé.

And miracle to end all miracles, Ellen didn't once moan about that fucking house.

Actually, Gwen shouldn't be sour about the house. She loves the Meadowhouse. In fact, she'd *love* the Meadowhouse. No, it's the owner that winds her up. Her lack of awareness is *so* grating. Not a thought for Gwen's generation—the much-maligned millennials who've got actual *real* problems to fucking moan about, given that *one third* will never own their own place. Not even a piddly one-bedroom flat.

Gwen hasn't plucked that figure out of nowhere. She's done her research. She's a bit obsessed with it. She's also worked out that with the deposit the Walshes paid (seriously, Ellen overshares about *everything*), their mortgage payments on the Meadowhouse are only £200 more than her and Jason's rent.

And *still* Ellen comes out with things like "God, not the renovation, talk about something fun, G," as if creating your perfect home isn't a total privilege. Then, there was the day they met, when Gwen remarked how lovely the place was, Ellen said the inside was "grim," then gave her a tour of everything supposedly wrong and naff.

Doesn't she realise how lucky she is? How lucky they all are, Gen X and Baby Boomers. And God, don't get Gwen started on the Boomers. They think the only reason "youngsters" can't buy property is because they spend too much on avocado toast.

So really she shouldn't be mean about Ellen. They're all like that, and Ellen isn't the worst of them.

But she's the only one Gwen has to listen to, and a bit of self-awareness wouldn't go amiss.

15

Ellen

It's usually my twin-labour-ravaged bladder that provides my 2 a.m. wake-up call, or the subconscious scratchy feeling that I've forgotten to call someone back. Tonight, I can partly blame the weather, the mediocre wind that sounds like a Category 5 hurricane through the gaps in our rattling windows. But mostly I'm awake because of Courchevel and plain old-fashioned guilt.

The joke's always been that it should have been me in the wheelchair. How did I, it's often wondered, with my limited skiing experience and my famed clumsiness, manage to fly down a mountain without a single bump or scratch, while back home Kristy only ran down the stairs to fetch her phone charger and wound up with a broken spine?

The call came the night of the bar dancing, except I didn't receive it, having rather cleverly dropped my phone from a cable car a few days before. Only Adam knew to contact me on Zara's phone in an emergency (*Where are Orla's wellies? Naughty step for throwing a boiled egg??*), and he didn't hear about Kristy's accident until well into the next day. Mum claimed she didn't have his number, which in fairness was probably true. She occasionally forgets his name. She once addressed a birthday card to *Dear Alan*.

As soon as Adam called me, I packed my bags and fled to the airport, but a frustrating lack of flights meant it was almost another day before I arrived at Kristy's bedside, bearing

Lucozade and stifling sobs. If I was paranoid, I'd say that she was pissed off with my late appearance. But then she was pissed off with everyone at that time—family, friends, nurses, phone chargers—and it only took one atom of empathy to conclude she had every right to be.

It's always haunted me that while my sister was secured to a stretcher in the back of a London ambulance, I was shaking my tush in the French Alps with not a care except for my next drink. The guilt I carry is, I know, both pointless and irrational. Sometimes, for instance, I think that if I hadn't gone to Courchevel, Kristy's accident might never have happened. Why I think this is a mystery, given that she lived miles from us, and anyway, since when was I an expert on household safety? But then guilt is narcissistic. It erodes perspective. Makes everything *me me me*.

But as if I didn't feel bad enough, it was actually Kristy who'd loaned me the money for Courchevel. It wasn't peanuts, either. My share of the chalet alone cost more than our monthly bills, and things were tight for me and Adam back then: mortgaged to the hilt, the financial crash of the late noughties still affecting Adam's job and both our overdrafts. Kristy, on the other hand, was always flush, her modelling career at its peak.

Courchevel was the last time Kristy loaned money to me or to anyone. Even after months of physiotherapy, her wonky gait and loss of muscle tone, not to mention her inability to stand in one position for more than five minutes, meant that the modelling work dried up and she was ghosted by her agency. It might be different now, I often think. For Orla's generation, the notion of beauty is broader, more interesting. Sadly, back when Kristy had her accident, models were still mannequins with pulses, not real-life women who had real-life catastrophes.

Clearly I'm not going back to sleep tonight.

Bubbling with bleak thoughts, I take my phone and head downstairs, seeking distraction. I could do the boys' lunch boxes for tomorrow. Declutter the spice rack (what even is a caraway seed?). Or maybe I'll sort through that heap of clothes I've been meaning to take to the charity shop for weeks.

The overhead light in the kitchen promptly dumps on my good intentions, teasing me with a few hopeful sputters before throwing in the towel. I could park myself in the living room, I suppose, but the door is haunted-house creaky, and I swear Max has bat hearing. So with little else to do, I grab a glass of water then settle myself on the window seat.

First: Facebook.

Since I unfriended the account earlier, there's no more "Ciara Harkin," and in fact the only shock I'm met with is the green dot signalling that Nush is online. This is *most* unlike her. Nush has never been a night owl, always the smug proverbial lark, slaying chores and building businesses to the backdrop of a dawn chorus. I tap out a message—*Couldn't sleep?*—then delete it, not wanting to invite any late-night Tom chat. Instead I scroll mindlessly, trying to subdue my brain. Unsurprisingly, my feed is quiet right now. Just Zara—now living in Sydney—posting photos of the gorgeous gummy niece we haven't got to meet yet, and my younger brother, Mikey, claiming that a much-loved singer has a punchable face.

Instinctively, *compulsively*, I switch to Zane's Instagram. I don't have an account myself—and even if I did, I wouldn't follow him—but as his account is surprisingly set to "public," I can still view his eclectic page. It's a patchwork of supposedly funny memes, brooding selfies, and far too many Hemingway quotes. Today's is set against a white background with a single blue teardrop:

Life isn't hard to manage if you've got nothing to lose.

Before I can work myself into a lather trying to guess at what inspired this, the sound of the wind attacking the patio umbrella summons me reluctantly outside. Cursing Adam, then myself, for not packing away the garden furniture weeks ago, I thrust my size six feet into Adam's size ten Nikes, then clown-run across the lawn, the flashlight on my phone just about lighting my way. As the wind whips my hair, I lock horns with the umbrella, calling it every name under the sun while trying to wrestle it from its base.

The laugh comes from a short distance away—male, gravelly and terrifyingly unfamiliar.

I stop dead.

Is this it? Is this the moment I'm taught a lesson about consequences?

Fear spears me to the spot, my breath hijacked halfway between my lungs and my dry throat. I open my mouth to scream, but there's no way I can attract attention without the kids hearing the commotion, and the thought of them tearing down the stairs and barrelling into danger is enough to freeze my blood.

I need to deal with this myself.

Quickly. Quietly. Efficiently.

I look down at the rock garden by my feet, the small armoury at my disposal. I don't fancy my chances, but the will is there at least.

I will stone this fucker if I have to.

I drop the umbrella and snatch my phone off the table, giving the intruder one single chance to retreat.

For the love of God, please take it. I don't want the police here. I don't want their questions, their spotlight on me.

"I'm warning you, I'm calling the police," I say, masking my blinding terror with the stern, steady tone that lets the twins know I mean business.

I turn around to offer proof of the phone, then instantly regret it. He's more likely to flee if I haven't seen his face.

But he has no interest in fleeing. A shadow emerges from beneath the chestnut tree behind Kristy's cabin. It moves towards me slowly, cautiously, crunching leaves with each step. As it gets closer, I see hands half raised as if in surrender. A lit cigarette held in place of a white flag.

"Hey, let's back up a bit, OK?" the shadow says, that same gritty laugh again. "No need for the five-O. I'm a friend of Kristy's. Shay."

I point the torch in his direction.

I might not have recognised the voice, but I know the face.

"*You?*" I'm staring at the bearded barman from the Cricketers. "What in the name of . . .? How . . .? Why . . .?"

Shock has rendered me tongue-tied, only capable of short, ragged breaths and incomplete sentences.

He sighs, amused. "Shit, we really do keep getting off on the wrong foot, don't we? You were trying to get me sacked yesterday, now you're threatening me with police. Ever tried 'ello'?"

His green eyes glow almost radioactive in the torchlight, as does his thin white t-shirt, far more suited to a summer's day. Not that I can talk. All I'm wearing is a pair of trainers four sizes too big for me and a shrunk Gucci T-shirt that stops an inch above my knickers.

But this is *my* garden, and if I want to run around it dressed like a madwoman, that's my right. Him and his biceps have no business here.

"Fine. *Hello,*" I growl. "Now, what the hell are you doing creeping around my property?"

My property. Who am I, Clint Eastwood?

"Hey, I was stood under that tree, minding my own business. I don't remember creeping anywhere." He actually sounds offended. "And I told you, I'm Kristy's friend. Her 'international man of mystery.'" He takes a last drag of the cigarette, then extinguishes it between two fingers without so much as a flinch. "Well, you got that wrong for a start. I've only ever been to Holland. Three days in Antwerp on a school trip. That's as international as I get."

"Antwerp's in Belgium." I jab a finger towards the cabin. "And you being her 'friend' doesn't explain why you're stalking around my garden."

Another laugh. "Oh, I'm stalking now? I was creeping a minute ago. God, you can tell you're an English teacher." I go to say something, but he prattles on, seemingly oblivious to everything: my fury, the wind, and, I hope, my bullet-nipples. "Not that I'm saying that's a bad thing. Not your fault I was brain-dead at English, is it? Brain-dead at geography too, eh? Could have sworn it was Holland we went to." He stops for a moment, dips his head a fraction, eyes lasering mine. "Now, numbers, they're more my thing, Ellen. Numbers are truth, you know? Absolute."

What I *know* is this guy is really getting on my nerves.

"OK, nine-nine-nine, how's that for a number?" I fold my arms across my chest, partly to give off no-nonsense vibes, mainly to cover my nipples.

He nods. *Yeah, good one.* "Look, relax. I came over to see Kris, same as I always do after my Thursday shift . . ." Which is breaking news to me, so that's tomorrow's row sorted. "We fell asleep, the wind woke me up, and I fancied a smoke, that's all." He gives a shrug. "And OK, fine, I probably shouldn't have laughed at you swearing at that umbrella without announcing myself first, but what can I say? I'm a dickhead. That's well documented, trust me. I didn't mean to scare you, though. I'm sorry."

And yet the laugh in his voice suggests the exact opposite. It's not a nervous laugh, the kind you'd emit if you'd just scared the holy living shite out of your "friend's" bra-less sister. It's overfamiliar, suggestive of something, although God only knows what.

"You fancied a smoke in this weather?" I say, eyebrow cocked, ignoring his apology.

"Ah, you know how it is." He reaches into his back pocket, proffers a nearly full pack of cigarettes. "You want one, by the way?"

Forget they're Marlboro Reds; right now I want several. Lined up like little cannons in the gaps between my fingers.

"No, I don't smoke."

"Course you don't." His smile is far too knowing. "Nor me. Not unless I'm drunk, or I'm wearing blue, or the day's got a Y in it. You know what I'm talking about."

Again the familiarity. The awkward sense that I'm the butt of a private joke.

"Actually, I don't," I say starchily. "I bum the odd cigarette here and there, but I'm not a proper smoker."

"Oh, sure, *usually* you're not. But you've had a rough day, haven't you, Els-Bels? I mean, that was one pissed-off letter. No shame in needing a nicotine cuddle after a shock like that."

I might be shivering in next-to-nothing but my face burns oven-hot.

Is there anything Kristy hasn't told this chump? The letter, my smoking habits, *Els-Bels*, my job. What else? Does he know that my first crush was on Harv from *Cagney & Lacey*? Does he have any thoughts on whether I should go back on the pill?

Riled, I push the spotlight back on him.

"Why didn't Kristy say anything in the pub yesterday? About who you were when I . . . you know . . ." *Implied you were a sleazebag.*

Credit where credit's due, he doesn't let me squirm for more than a few seconds.

"You tell me. I don't know why she's all secret squirrel about it." Frowning suddenly, he says, "But listen, you didn't *seriously* think I was trying to hit on your daughter, did you? Don't get me wrong, she's a good-looking girl, but she's Kris's niece. She's a kid."

"Well then let me give you a tip. Going around telling kids you've got modelling contacts is *not* a good look. It's a bit 1970s. A bit 'pop your clothes on the chair, darling.'"

"Yeah, all right, all right." He lifts a burly arm and tugs at his man-bun—a stress tell for sure, so at least he has some shame. "S'just Kris mentioned her niece wanted to be a model . . ." She does? Last I heard, it was environmental lawyer. "And so

I thought if I put her in touch with my cousin, I'd be kind of ingratiating myself. Scoring a few future Brownie points for whenever Kris got around to introducing me. But I got it wrong. I fucked up. It's what I do."

The doleful eyes, the hanging head. I'm clearly supposed to think he deserves pity. What I do think is that *ingratiating* is a fancy word for someone supposedly brain-dead at English, and that I've had enough of freezing my arse off with Kristy's latest waste-of-space.

"Look, I'm going in," I say, swivelling back towards the house. "But just for the record, admitting you're a fuck-up isn't a great way to ingratiate yourself either." I point behind me. "Fixing that umbrella *might* be, though."

He offers a salute. I nod a grudging thanks.

I'm two paces from the back door when he calls after me.

"You know, we're all fuck-ups, Ellen. Some of us just accept it. Makes life a whole lot easier when you do, take it from me."

I turn to take one final look at him. Standing in the centre of the lawn, with his feet planted wide and his body anchored against the wind by his bulk, he looks more solid and unshakeable than the chestnut tree he emerged from under.

He looks immovable.

Like he's built to outlast us all.

16

Ellen

Next morning, unfairly, *unfathomably*, it's me who's the bad guy. Orla's still grouching about Frankfurt and something's clearly eating Adam (and it can't just be the felt-tip marks on the breakfast table that, as principal child-wrangler, are *obviously* my fault). Max hates me because today isn't his birthday, and it appears to be only Kian who can stand me, gazing at me like I hung the moon when I sanction his request for Coco Pops.

It's Kristy, though, leading the revolt from her spot in front of the fridge. Evidently I didn't get the best write-up from Shay.

"*You* said I was welcome here, Els. 'Make yourself at home,' you said. *Mi casa es su casa.*"

I scoop a fistful of Coco Pops out of the box for myself, my nutritional standards always shaky on less than three hours' sleep.

"Yeah, *su* casa, Kris. *Yours.* Not every Tom, Dick, or Harry who fancies slipping through the side gate for a booty call."

"He's my boyfriend."

A loose term where Kristy's concerned. The "boyfriend" she brought to Orla's First Holy Communion was some guy she'd met in the dance tent at Glastonbury barely a week before.

"Hey, what happened to Stefan?" asks Orla, probing the yolks of her poached eggs—made by me, her arch-oppressor—with her tip of her fingernail. "He was, like, loaded, wasn't he?"

"Turns out he needed to be," says Kristy. "A wife and four kids costs a whole heap of pennies."

Orla mumbles, "Shit, sorry."

Kristy gives a curdled laugh. "Not as sorry as he was."

God knows what that means, and God's welcome to the knowledge. As much as I can, I tend to turn a blind eye to my sister's darker traits. Her ability to hold a grudge longer than most people hold a mortgage. Her inability to be the bigger person. To let sleeping dogs lie.

"Anyway, this is different. Shay's different." Adam snorts into his coffee. I play nice, my mouth a neutral line. "We've both come off Tinder, you know?"

"Oh, well then . . ." Adam breaks into the wedding march.

"Yeah, very fucking funny," says Kristy. Kian shouts, "Not nice word," banging his spoon like a judge's gavel. I shoot him a *good boy* and Kristy a hot stare. "I mean, was the internet even invented the last time you were on the dating scene, Ads? How did you let a girl know you were interested back then? Draw your hankie across your left cheek?"

"So if it's so serious," I say, my mouth full of dry Coco Pops, "why the secrecy?"

"Just because something's serious doesn't make it public property."

I swallow. "Christ, you're not Harry and Meghan! 'Thames Lawley Barman Dates Sister of Local Woman.' I doubt there'd be a media firestorm." It's catty, but she's being ridiculous. "You let me stand there and pretty much call him a paedophile in the pub. Why?"

"Yeah, that *was* harsh, Mum," says Orla, standing up. "In front of his boss, too." She walks over to the bin and scrapes both eggs off her plate, every act a hostile gesture. *Or maybe she actually has gone vegan?* "And anyway, I'm sixteen, post-pubescent, so he wouldn't be a paedophile."

"He isn't from Thames Lawley, *actually*," says Kristy, lips pursed. "He's from London. Brixton. Not far from where you had that flat. And I don't know why I didn't say anything, Els. Maybe 'cos I told you to let me handle it, but no, you had to go steaming in as usual." She smirks. "Or maybe 'cos it was funny."

"Funny?"

Adam makes the face I've come to recognise as *Jesus, your family*. The Walsh sibling dynamic is all earnest debates and fun, gentle teasing, whereas my rabble, myself excluded, are never happier than when they're brutally winding each other up. I blame our parents. Survival of the meanest.

"Anyway, forget that. What did you think of him?" Kristy asks before I get the chance to explain that it wasn't particularly *funny* last night when for the briefest moment I thought I might never see my kids again.

"He's young," I say, keeping it factual.

"He's thirty."

"That's young in man years. Everyone knows women mature quicker than men."

Adam scoffs. "You're eating dry Coco Pops for breakfast."

What is eating *him*? Is he put out because he wasn't called upon to deal with Big Scary Garden Man? Still smarting over my claim that Orla could be behind the recent grief?

It doesn't take Orla long to pile on.

"Mum, you're *so* hung up on age," she says, opening the cereal cupboard. "Too old for me. Too young for Auntie K. What does it matter? Gwen's ex—Bella's dad—is, like, fifty. And loaded. He gives her a shit-ton of child support."

"Oh well, that's OK then," snaps Adam. "Shame he didn't go to the hospital when Bella had that scary rash thing. Or bother to send a birthday card."

"You're very well informed," I say, bemused. "I've never heard about any 'scary rash thing.'"

Adam shrugs as he walks to the sink. He swills his coffee mug under the tap, then turns to look at Kristy. "Look, to get back to the point Els and I are trying to make . . ." *Els and I?* Not that I don't appreciate the belated united front, but I'm a bit thrown by the timing. "It would just be nice if you told us if you were having guests over, that's all."

"Not *nice*," I correct. "Essential. There are three minors in this house and we know nothing about this guy."

"Fine. What do you want to know?" Kristy pushes herself off the fridge and scrapes a chair across the cracked kitchen tiles to the centre of the room, making herself the focus. "Five minutes—ask me anything." She shouts over to Max. "Hey, Maximoo, want to ask me a question about my friend Shay?"

"When is mine birthday?" he asks me. The only question that matters.

"A while yet, buddy." I stroke his head. "Remember what we said?" *Five thousand times.* "Auntie Kristy's birthday first, then Santa comes, *then* your birthday." He scowls.

"Actually, there's a question, Kris," says Adam. "What'd he get you for your birthday?"

She shrugs. "Nothing. I told him not to bother. I don't really need anything, and he's a bit skint right now."

I give Adam a look—*another skint one.* Kristy sees it.

"I know, Els—if only he had some rich in-laws to prop him up, eh?" she snarls.

"OK, so I've got a question," says Orla, opening a box of Cheerios. "Has anyone else ever falsely accused him of preying on a teenager *and* criminal trespass within the same forty-eight hours?"

On the wall next to the cereal cupboard, there's a photo in a heart frame: Orla with her arms outstretched, aiming a two-toothed grin at some guy dressed up as Freddy Krueger. That's how she was back then. So open, so cheerful. She loved everyone, even fictional child-killers with melted skin and blades for fingers. More than anything, though—God, how she loved me.

"Don't you have studying to do?" I say, my tone more *don't you have traffic to go play in?*

"At seven thirty?" Her eyes say *moron.* "I'm going over to Esme's at ten. Is that early enough for you?"

I have the kind of dislike for Esme Eavis that I usually reserve for fraudsters who scam the elderly. If she serves one positive purpose in my life, it's to remind me that Orla isn't that bad.

"As long as it *is* to study," I say.

"Oh, who cares? They're only mock exams."

"Orla, every exam from now on is prep for applying to Oxbridge. And don't give me that face—*you* set that goal, not me."

"Yeah, like, a year ago."

"And what's changed?" Adam asks.

Orla looks at me. Looks away twice as fast.

"It's just . . . it's not the be-all and end-all, is it? Loads of people don't go to uni at all and they *somehow* manage to exist." Kristy laughs at this. "I mean, you don't need a degree to be an entrepreneur, do you? Or, like, Jodie's aunt is a plumber and she earns stacks."

"Shay trained as an electrician." Kristy joins in. "Says there's good money in it." She bites her thumbnail, a cautious smirk slowly spreading. "He took a look at the kitchen light, actually. Reckons there's asbestos behind the fuse box, though, and he doesn't have the right licence to go meddling with it."

"He's been in the house?" My scalp prickles. "When was this?"

"Couple of weekends ago. You were down at the coast." She looks guilty for a second before reverting to defensive type. "Jeez, it's not like I threw a party, Els. I didn't empty your drinks cabinet into a punch bowl then shag him on your bed. We were in and out in twenty minutes. I was trying do you a favour. Or *he* was, to be fair. It was his idea."

Oh, it was, was it?

An idea of my own forms. An idea that runs directly counter to how I'm feeling at the moment: off balance, exposed, and distinctly unwelcoming.

It's an idea that makes sense, though. I can even shroud it under the guise of being friendly.

"Bring him to lunch tomorrow," I say to the palpable shock of all assembled.

If this guy wants to poke around my fuse box, maybe I should have a good poke around his.

The kitchen is cleared of kids, and Kristy, and as many catapulted Coco Pops as I can locate, when Adam makes his announcement while hunting for his house keys.

"It wasn't Orla, the Facebook thing," he says, peering in the breadbin; they really could be anywhere. "I checked the search history on her phone when she was in the toilet. All clear."

"You did *what*?"

In a matter of seconds, Adam yo-yos in my estimation—up, down, then up again, before settling there. At the end of the day, while I've always believed Orla should be allowed a certain level of privacy when it comes to boys, friendships, and slagging us off to high heaven—standard teenage stuff—when it's something like this, I'm sorry, but we pay the bill.

Although I'm glad it was Adam who did it. I could do without more guilt.

I laugh a little shakily. "God, remind me not to leave my phone unlocked near you."

"Why? Afraid of what I might find?" Crabby, not teasing.

"No," I lie. "Although I did google 'Does Crazy Crocs Soft Play have a fully licensed bar?' the other day."

I expect a laugh, at least a smile. All I get is more grumpiness and passive-aggressive key-hunting.

"By the way, did you have to invite that Shay guy to lunch?"

A noisy rummage in the fruit bowl. A third check in his coat pocket. "I thought Gwen and Bella were coming over."

I spy his keys in the bucket of Max's toy tractor by the back door.

He can find them himself. He's getting on my nerves.

"They are, and so's Nush. I didn't realise we had a cap on numbers?" This isn't like Adam. He's usually the king of "the more the merrier." "I want to get the measure of him, Ads. I mean, I'm not suggesting anything—I'd never even met the guy until the other day, so God knows what he'd have against me— but a nasty letter *and* a garden prowl on the same day. Don't you find that a bit fishy?"

He shrugs. "I suppose. Maybe. Maybe not."

"Well, thanks for that helpful insight."

He huffs. "And did you have to say evil Esme could come? You say no to Orla often enough. You could have said no to that."

I sigh. "If Orla senses we're anti-Esme, she'll fawn over her even more. Better to play nice. Don't worry, Esme'll dump her again soon."

"Is that the strategy with *him* too?"

"*Him?*" I land a playful punch. "Adam Walsh, are you jealous, is that it? Is it because he pretty much saw my nipples?"

He ignores all mention of my nipples. "Why's he working in a pub? That's what I find 'a bit fishy.' I mean, how many electricians do you know can't find work? Most are turning it away."

"Lots of people love bar work," I say, although, in fairness, it's a good point. I can't even get Bert the electrician to call me back, and they say the old guard have manners. "Trust me, there's days I'd rather be back pulling pints than dissecting Jacobean revenge tragedies."

But not today. Not when there's Zane.

I feel an ache of shame so deep, it's bottomless. I quickly move away, certain the guilt must be etched across my face.

"Here." I retrieve his keys from the tractor bucket, then glance at the clock, avoiding his eyes. "Now scoot. It's half-past seven. And leave the paranoia to me, OK?"

"Can I leave the pay-off to you, too? It cost us two thousand pounds to get rid of the last waster, remember?"

17

Orla

WHATSAPP GROUP: WHO RUN THE WORLD?
Members: Esme, Orla

ORLA: *ALERT* If my mum asks at lunch tmrw, I was
studying at urs earlier

ESME: What were we studying? Ur mum will want deets.

ORLA: She won't. She pretends to give a shit but
she doesn't.

Like she goes on about me needing quiet to study but
she's banging and crashing about right now, smashing
up wardrobes by the sounds of it.

But say atomic structure if she asks.

Oh yeah, and I was at urs Monday night too 😊

ESME: OK spill!!

Pls not Callum Rudd tho (Abi-D will cut your liver out)

ORLA: It's no one u know (and I'd cut my own liver
out before I went near Callum Rudd or any of
those dickwads)

ESME: AGAIN u mean.

A bit of buyer's remorse is fine but don't be rewriting
history now, La-la.

U and Declan O'Dell were hot stuff.

ORLA: Says Declan.

ESME: Whatever. But lemme get this straight—it's defo NOT

the fit barman from the Cricketers? He wasn't flirting?
Just sucking up to ur aunt?

ORLA: Maybe he was flirting.
Maybe he's a groomer. Using Auntie K to get
close to me.

ESME: He can groom me any time. He's soooooo wasted
on ur aunt.
She's pretty in a skanky sort of way but she's like way
older than him.

ORLA: Gwen's ex is fifty!

ESME: Different. Less weird when the guy's older

ORLA: Can u even spell misogyny?

ESME: I can spell harsh truth (bad feminist! shoot me!)
So what time's lunch tmrw?

ORLA: Dunno? 2ish? Whenever. It's no big deal. Just pizza.

ESME: Ask ur mum to get Papa Johns. Vesuvios are way
too stingy on the cheese

ORLA: She's making them from scratch

ESME: Who the actual fuck makes pizza???

ORLA: IKR? It's cos Nush is coming (Jasmine
Delaney's mum)
She goes weird around Nush #inferioritycomplex

ESME: #lesbianaffair

ORLA: Ha! Maybe. She's definitely up to something.

ESME: Ok u have my attention.
Hello???
Remember what I said about being cryptic, La-la

ORLA: Look, I don't even kno. She just goes AWOL
sometimes.
And like she put the little brats into nursery for a full day
Friday a few months back. Says it's so she can get shit
done, but I can't see what shit's getting done??
House still upside down.
She's still only got the same four or five clients.

ESME: Maybe she's having "me-time." Getting her nails
done. Having her vag waxed.

ORLA: Have u seen her nails? Don't think so.

ESME: Ouch.

U should give ur mum a break tho.

ORLA: Ur worse than Gwen!

ESME: Eh?

ORLA: Gave me a lecture when she got back last night.
"U only get one mum . . . mine didn't give a shit . . . ur
lucky urs worries about u . . ." blah blah.

SO obvious Mum put her up to it

ESME: Just holler any time you want to swap employers,
Miss £9 an Hour.

Skinflint Susi only pays me £6 to babysit her chubby
little fuck.

ORLA: That's tight. Is that why you're always nicking my
fags? JOKE 😜 😜

Anyway, at least u don't have Creepy Jason
spying on you.

ESME: WTAF!?

When? Last night?

ORLA: No. Coupla weeks ago. Didn't I tell u?? I was trying
on some stuff Gwen was going to throw out and I
caught him looking at me thru the bedroom door.

ESME: In ur knickers???

ORLA: Not when I saw him but dunno how long he
was there.

ESME: Dirty little perv.

U deserve £9 an hour for that. Call it the Creepy
Jason Tax.

ORLA: Could do with £900 at the mo. Mum refusing to
cough up for Frankfurt 😫

ESME: Serious? Why?

ORLA: More important things to spend her money on obvs

18

Ellen

The first time I bought Zane something, it was nothing to feel *too* weird about. Just a four-pinter of milk and a packet of chopped parsley he needed for a sardine stew.

I expressed surprise at the stew. He was straight-up offended.

"S'pose you think I live on frozen meals. Think veg is for rabbits, yeah?"

I didn't think that; two minutes in Zane's company and you knew not to make assumptions. But still, *sardine stew*? A meal straight out of a World War II ration book.

"Exactly. And what do you need in a war, Ellen? Strength, and your wits about you. Can't be eating nothing but processed shit if you gonna do more than just survive."

I almost joked that I'd quote that to Max, my relentlessly fussy eater. But I rarely mention the kids when I'm with Zane. It's not so much a rule as a safeguard, a way of keeping everything in its correct box. He did see a photo of Orla once, early on, while giving my new iPhone the once-over. After snatching it back, I asked him testily if he was ever taught not to touch other people's things without permission. He laughed and said, "Keep your hair on," followed by, "Pretty girl, not my thing."

After the milk and the chopped parsley, my generosity steadily grew more expensive. Soon it was bags of groceries. Salmon. Walnuts. Blueberries. Premium coffee. Brain food, I'd tell myself.

A holistic approach to modern learning. But then the brain food became treat food, and the treat food became money. A fiver here, a tenner there. Forty pounds once to get his phone reconnected. On that occasion he insisted he'd pay me back. Said he was owed a few quid for giving someone an alibi for a break-in.

He never did pay me back.

Today I haven't brought food, and I've barely got any cash on me. I do have a gift, though. A day-glo Ralph Lauren polo shirt that I bought Adam for his fortieth. Limited edition and stupid pricey, it was meant to be a nostalgic wink back to our brief days as ravers. Adam said, "Wow," then never wore it. I doubt he'll even notice it's gone.

"Fuck, wow," says Zane, echoing Adam—except his is the *wow* given to a new bike on Christmas morning. "Don't know what to say. What did I do to deserve this?"

We're in his bedroom, as we often are. It's the only place we can be when Paulo is comatose in the living room, and the kitchen doesn't have a table. It's a dark, stuffy room infused with boy, weed, and body spray. But at least in here we can spread out a bit, make a pretence of actually working. Zane slouched against the headboard arguing that every modern take on Hemingway is bullshit revisionism. Me at the foot of the bed pretending that the small gap between us makes everything hunky-dory and not a breach of every professional and standard that I swear I used to have.

"Ah, it's no big deal," I say, trying to fool myself as much as him. "I was clearing out wardrobes, and there it was looking all Zane-y."

That second bit is the truth, for what it's worth. I've given up asking Adam to start prepping for the renovation. His punishment is that half his possessions now grace the charity shop or the bin.

"Two hundred and thirty quid, though," he says, rubbing the

price tag like a rabbit's foot. "That's one big-ass goodbye present you got me. Although shouldn't it be me buying you one?" He pulls me into a hug before I can stop it. "God, you smell good."

I can't think what he's referring to. I certainly never wear perfume here; I barely wear make-up. Maybe I've carried the vanilla scent of the car air freshener in with me. I sincerely doubt it smells "good," but I suppose it smells different. An exotic female scent in a no-frills male domain.

I detach from the hug. "I told you yesterday, I'm not leaving."

"No, you *are*, Ellen. I've decided." He squares his shoulders, ready for conflict. I stare at him, confused. "It's just I've been thinking about this. About us." *Us.* "And the way I see it is, you get this job, you're gonna be crazy busy nine-to-five, yeah? So you don't need the hassle of me on top, and it ain't like I'm paying you. And anyway, I've got Frances from the LEA now." *Frarn-ces.* Not the way I'd expect him to say it. He points his nose upwards, standard code for *la-di-da*. "I mean, no way is she as hot as you, but she's good, she asks good questions." I should probably pull him up on *hot*, but that ship sailed a long time ago. "So you don't have to worry about me, OK? I'm gonna work hard. Go easy on the weed. Get my grades. Get out of here. All the things we talked about, yeah?"

So that's today's mood, is it? Hope over cynicism. Sardine stew over oven chips. I know I should play along, encourage him, enjoy Sunshine Zane while he lasts (he never lasts). But pathetic as it sounds, I'm feeling stung at being dismissed.

"Is she really a stuck-up cow then, this Frances?" I loathe myself for asking it. "That's what your dad called her," I add, quickly distancing myself from the dig.

"Nah, she's all right. Bit pleased with herself, but nothing major. Dad's just annoyed that he has to clear out of the flat when she's here."

"He's never bothered for me," I point out.

"Yeah, but you're different, you're . . ." He lets out a spiky laugh. "Actually, I really don't know what the fuck you are, Ellen."

I'm not sure *I* know anymore.

I deflect the conversation.

"Anyway, all this talk of me leaving is a bit premature," I say. "I don't even know if I've got the job yet."

"Be serious," he says softly. "Who in their right mind wouldn't want you?"

I sit down on the single bed, burying my blushes in my tote bag. The mattress sags beneath me. Everything in Zane's room—the bed, the clothes rail, the full-length mirror, and the busted beanbag—must be easily a decade old. Only his laptop is vaguely new.

"Right. Work," I say, whacking him on the arm with a copy of *The Changeling*. "And work means words. You know, sentences, paragraphs, pages. No shortcuts on YouTube."

"In a minute," he mutters, whipping off his worn grey T-shirt to try on his shiny new one. Then, after assessing himself favourably from every conceivable angle, he asks my reflection, "So, what do you think?"

I think that in hindsight Adam never really had the complexion to carry off pink day-glo. Zane's colouring, on the other hand, is very much day five in Tenerife.

"It suits you."

"Does, doesn't it?" He grins at himself. "Better believe I'm wearing it tonight. Might even leave the price tag on too."

I arch an eyebrow. "Date?"

"Better. My mate Anton's having a house party. He thinks he's, like, Giorgio Armani, just because he's got a few cool threads." Another grin. "Wait till he sees this is *limited-edition* Ralph. It'll proper eat him up. I'm talking weeping. Sick as a pig."

"And what are you going to say if he asks where you got it? If *anyone* asks, actually?" He ignores me, too busy appraising himself in the mirror (collar up, collar down, top button open, top button closed). "Zane." I raise my voice. "Are you listening? It's important."

He turns to me, glowering. As though I'm spoiling his fun, sullying his treat.

"Fuck's sake, stop stressing. I'll say I nicked it. No drama."

I give him a flat stare. "Nicked it."

"Yeah, nicked it. There's a Ralph Lauren store at Bicester Village. Perfect."

It's perfect and it's believable. And yet it does something to me that he's prepared to market himself so cheaply.

"I wish you wouldn't always be so ready to let people think the worst of you."

"Like I give a shit what Anton Keane thinks." He's never sounded more seventeen.

"Er, clearly you do." I laugh, perhaps a little meanly. "His opinion on a bloody T-shirt mattered a whole lot just a minute ago."

It could be the laugh or the fact I'm right, but in a flash the temperature changes.

Sunshine Zane, he never lasts.

"Fine," he says, ocean-calm and dead-eyed. "Shall I let them think the worst of *you* instead? Shall I say this posh forty-something teacher lady seems to have taken a bit of a shine to me, and she's got this dirty little fetish for dressing me up in her husband's clothes?"

It's not a threat, it's retaliation, I'm around eighty per cent sure of this. Which, of course, means I'm sure of nothing. The words are imprinted on my brain.

People have to learn there are consequences.

"Please don't speak to me in that tone, Zane," I say, the tension in my neck starting to build.

He gives me a look—*what tone?*—and really, I have no answer. Because he didn't shout or swear. He wasn't rude or overtly aggressive. The issue is *what* he said, and if what he said is what he thinks.

And I can't bring myself to ask him that.

"Anyway, I'm *hardly* posh," I say, homing in on the only part of his taunt I'm prepared to go within ten feet of. "I've never sat on a horse. I don't prefer dark chocolate to milk . . ."

The latter is our in-joke. The smile that follows is an olive branch. And when I feel like the temperature is at least on its way back up to cosy, I sneak in one final warning.

"I mean it, though. Don't even tell your dad it was me who gave it to you. It might seem . . ."

"Kind? Like someone actually thinks I deserve nice things." The hurt in his voice is quickly seasoned with self-pity. "But then I don't really, do I? You know I don't deserve shit."

We were mired in *King Lear* the day he first came out with it. I asked him if Lear deserved pity for his regrets over Cordelia, and he trotted out the naïve cliche about only regretting what you hadn't done, not what you had.

"Like, I blackmailed a girl once. Told her I'd videoed us— well, her—you know, sexually. Said I'd send it to everyone, put it on the internet an' that, if she didn't cough up three hundred quid."

This wasn't the crime that got Zane excluded from sixth form, but it was, he told me, the worst thing he'd ever done. But he'd had no choice, he insisted. He needed quick money. The old lady next door had been burgled three times already. The bastards kept coming back and what she needed was a front-door grille. And the girl's parents were doctors. She was loaded. She could afford it. And—and this was the crucial bit—it wasn't like he'd have gone through with it. He hadn't even taken any videos. He'd spun her a line. She coughed up the cash.

I said surely he felt guilty? He said that after his mum left, the old lady had taught him to cook, ironed his uniform.

"I saw an opportunity and I took it, Ellen. Don't hate the sinner, hate the sin."

I don't notice the tyre at first. I'm so busy cursing the pigeon that's shat on my recently cleaned windshield that it's not until I try to drive away from the Lomax and barely get ten juddering feet that I realise something's wrong.

I get out of the car and glance back to where I was parked, expecting to see a puddle of shattered glass, maybe the shards of a broken bottle. Nothing. The road into Lower Lawley is notoriously bumpy, so there's a chance I could have jarred the wheel if I hit a particularly treacherous pothole, but I'd have noticed that, surely?

I crouch by the driver-side wheel. The state of the tyre tips my world on its axis.

Five slashes in all. Clean and smooth and straight and even.

Hallmarks of human effort.

No question, they're deliberate.

With my heart thundering in my chest, I've no choice but to crank into mum gear. There's no way I'll make the boys' pickup now, and they take priority. My go-to is usually Gwen, but her phone goes straight to voicemail. Same with Kristy, then Orla. But good old Nush answers on the third ring.

"Are you free?" I ask, still crouched. I don't think I've the strength to stand yet.

"I'm hands-free, darling. Hold on a minute, let me pull over." The longest seconds pass, then, "Are you OK? You sound flustered."

Flustered. When there's a queue behind you at the supermarket and you've momentarily forgotten your PIN.

"Yeah, I'm fine," I say. "Well, no, not *fine*. I've got a flat. Drove straight over a broken bottle, can you believe that? Well done me." I make an apologetic face as though she's here and can see me. "Any chance you could pick the boys up? If you're not busy, that is. You're obviously out."

"I was, but I'm on my way back now." A brief pause. "So, wait, aren't you home? Don't you usually walk to nursery unless it's raining?"

"Doctor's," I tell her. The lie comes pretty easily. Nush waits for more detail; I'm a chronic over-sharer when it comes to anything health-related. "That mole at the top of my thigh—you know, the one I showed you the other week. But she thinks it's fine, probably just plain old hypochondria." I dredge up a laugh. "Bloody wish I hadn't bothered now. Christ knows how long I'll have to wait for the roadside assistance."

"You called them? I thought you'd be able to change a tyre, Ellen. Good feminist like you."

"I could if I had a spare." I ignore the snarky comment. "So can you pick them up? I've tried Gwen and Kristy but they're not answering. I can ask Susi Sands, but then I'll owe her a favour and . . ."

". . . that's not a life worth living. Of course I can. Am I right in thinking it's half past three?"

That isn't her last question. True to form, Nush approaches the collection of two toddlers the way she'd approach an annual shareholder meeting. Every timing, goal, and deliverable, all must be agreed.

But now, with the boys taken care of and panic free to engulf me, my overwhelming urge is to run. To abdicate all responsibility. I've no idea where I'd go. I don't much care where I'd end up, frankly. Anywhere is better than crouching on the road that runs the north perimeter of the Lomax, dealing with the irrefutable knowledge that someone knows I'm here.

Unless . . .

Clinging to one small hope, I stand and look around, praying that I'll spot a group of shifty-looking youths laughing at the rich bitch with the Audi. I swear, if it's just some bone-idle piece of shit who's slashed my front tyre out of bored envy, I won't trust myself not to kiss him. Right now, I'd happily hand him the keys.

But there's no one around. No credible suspects, anyway. Just a woman pushing a double buggy with a third child riding shotgun, and an old man with a walker, his tyre-slashing days long behind him. There is a sign on a lamp post: COUNCIL CCTV IN OPERATION. But CCTV means lengthy access requests, it means letters to the house, or if I want to bypass all that, it means police.

And police means the question And what brought you here today?

A coldness sweeps over me, starting in my core and spreading to each limb.

19

Nush

Rosy-cheeked in matching bobble hats. Oversized backpacks swamping tiny frames.

The children are edible. Nush feels it like a hunger. Although she's self-aware enough to know she wouldn't have felt like this last week. It's *that* pregnancy, of course. Or more accurately, it's Tom's happiness, nay, *euphoria* over it. That's the fairly important detail she couldn't bring herself to tell Ellen yesterday.

But yes, it's all *baby this* and *baby that*, according to her main source, Joanna Plimpton, whose husband, Josh, gets the same train to work as Tom every day. By way of Joanna-through-Josh, Nush has learned that the foetus is currently nicknamed Tiger, on account of it being both a boy and the size of a golf ball. And there's even talk of selling the Porsche Coupé. It won't be practical with a tiny tiger on board, *obviously*.

Nush feels bitter, but mainly sad, that the patience that generally only comes with age and life experience appears to be softening Tom into someone that Jasmine never had. Someone who'll dive into the ball pool without worrying about his Rolex. Someone who'll act the fool, roll in mud, put his phone down to play hide-and-seek. She always hoped she'd see that side of Tom as soon as they were blessed with grandchildren. Now her only hope is that her hypothetical grandchildren don't end up rolling in mud with Granny Jessie.

"Good afternoon, mums, dads, doggies, everyone." Mrs. O'Leary's reliably upbeat lilt rouses Nush from her glum reverie, and her reliable plumpness and Velcro loafers serve as a reminder that at least some things never change. "Well, I must say, we've been *very* busy today, haven't we, children? We've been painting and willow-weaving, and we've also learned about . . ." She cups one ear at her bobble-hatted charges.

"Otters!" they boom, with the exception of Max, who's scuffing the ground, clearly sulking.

Mums and dads beam. Doggies sniff the pavement. Nush gets a flash of a thousand happy memories.

Stepping Stones Pre-School is a bright lime and yellow building, famed locally for triggering migraines and nationally for banning glitter, after one of the UK's leading marine biologists gave the children an "age-appropriate" talk on the effects of microplastics on the sea. Stepping Stones is also where Jasmine went. Where she learned the days of the week in three different languages and helped prepare paella de verduras with vegetables picked from the school garden. Ellen likes to give the impression she finds the whole place faintly ridiculous. But, as Nush often thinks, she could send the boys to St Pete's church hall if all she wants is crowd control and ham sandwiches. She might be more suited there, too. It's unlikely St Pete's has such a strict lateness policy.

Although Nush was nearly late herself. She was a few miles from Thames Lawley when she received Ellen's distress call, and she'd forgotten how hard it is to get parked within two streets of the school after 3:15. She'd forgotten the whole hoopla of school pickup, really. The parking, the small talk, the bitching, the hierarchies. She was once the engine of it all, the Breton-striped ringmaster, but when Jasmine started cycling to school not long after her twelfth birthday, that was that. Enforced redundancy. Nush's heart was in her mouth the first time Jasmine set off on the two-mile journey. Tom scolded her, said it was high time she learned the difference between caring and catastrophising. But

Nush knows that to be a mother is to live in a permanent state of anxiety.

Unless you're Ellen, of course. Ellen wasn't even anxious about Nush not having child seats. "Ah, it's half a mile," she said, "they'll be fine. Just buckle them up, but not too tight. And tell them Santa won't come if they don't sit still."

"Nuss! Nuss! Look, Max! Hayo, Nuss!"

Kian has spotted her and her smile is automatic. His lisp and his pudginess, and the way he barrels through life as if every day is Mardi Gras, makes him indisputably her favourite of the two. Ellen claims not to have a favourite, but then Ellen claims a lot of things. And why did she have to make Nush godmother to the eternally morose Max?

"Mrs. Delaney, what a pleasure." Ellen said it would be their room leader, Faye, who would bring the boys over, but it's actually Mrs. O'Leary, a twin at either side. "How are you, and how is the lovely Jasmine?" After a few minutes of general wonder at how one minute they can't pronounce their R's and the next they're studying experimental linguistics at Cambridge, Mrs. O'Leary's face darkens slightly. "I was hoping to have a quick chat with Mrs. Walsh, actually. Max has been a little challenging today. Kicking, I'm afraid."

"Max," Nush says sternly. "Mummy's not going to be very happy."

"I said sowwy." Max looks up at her with gooey brown eyes. "And I hurt mine toe."

Good. Serves you right. Nush only feels marginally guilty.

"Perhaps you could ask Mrs. Walsh to give me a call," Mrs. O'Leary says quietly.

Nush nods. "Of course, but I can't promise it'll be this evening. She's got car trouble right now, and I know she's got a houseful for lunch tomorrow. She'll be flapping over that." She gives Mrs. O'Leary a sly smile. "Always something with Ellen. Drama morning, noon, and night."

Mrs. O'Leary looks uncomfortable, and Nush regrets the slight overstep.

"Oh, just my little joke," she says, laying a hand on Mrs. O'Leary's arm. "To be fair, there isn't always *something* with Ellen. It's usually just Max. Honestly, between the kicking and the meltdowns, she's at the end of her rope with him."

20

Ellen

Saturday starts badly, with Adam declaring, "Muriel advancing!" from the boys' bedroom window, followed by Kian shouting, "Take cover! Take cover!" even though he has no idea what it means. In the seconds before she lands, I quickly warn him that Muriel is a nice lady, who's feeling sad ("so be nice to her"), and that "Muriel advancing! Take cover!" is a secret thing that only Mummy and Daddy are allowed to say.

And anyway, given the past seventy-two hours, maybe a visit from Muriel isn't the worst thing. Compared to threatening letters and slashed tyres, it's almost light relief.

Almost.

"I was wondering, Ellen," she says, standing apron-clad in the kitchen doorway, casting furtive, judgy glances at a pile of ironing that's been there for two weeks. "Could you possibly speak to Val in the charity shop when you get a moment. I simply can't bring myself to do it, but those blazers of Dennis's you dropped off . . ."

"Ah look, Muriel, I told you, I've got no say over how they price them." She'd actually sent me in with a price list. I thought they'd laugh, but they felt sorry for me. Muriel's bossiness is the stuff of legend. As is my tendency to let her boss me. "And I know they're well made. But there's only so much people will pay for secondhand—"

"No, no, dear, it's not that." She pulls a tissue from her sleeve and dabs at her dry eyes. "It's . . . well, they're in the window, on mannequins. From a distance, it could be Dennis. I can't tell you how upsetting it is."

I give Adam hard eyes. *Don't you dare. She's an old lady.* There's nothing to be gained in pointing out that the mannequins are faceless and stop at the knees.

I wrap Muriel in a hug. She never reciprocates, but hey, I've done my bit. "That's horrible," I say. "Really insensitive. Leave it with me, I'll get it sorted."

She gives a weak—*satisfied?*—smile at the thought of someone getting their wrist slapped.

"Muh-reh-al." Kian can never say her name, so I taught it to him in basic phonics. "I be nice to you. Look." She gets a cuddle on the thigh from Brown Bear.

The gesture genuinely chokes her up—and me, too. So much so that instead of lying that we're on our way out, I pull a seat out at the breakfast table and ask if she'd like a cup of tea.

"No, I won't, Ellen, but thank you." *Huzzah.* "I'm making a cake this morning—an eighth birthday." *The poor lamb.* "But yes, it has been quite a while since we had a cup of tea and a decent chat."

Nine days. It's been *nine days.* And that chat wasn't remotely decent. Half an hour of how she'd prefer it if Adam didn't lace his shoe on her front wall.

"Definitely too long," I say brightly, my relief at her quick visit making me charitable. "Maybe during the week, then?"

"I'll bring some rock scones."

"That'd be lovely."

Behind her, Adam makes a vomiting gesture, and I've never so much appreciated normality.

Lunch starts well. All is fine for the first hour or so. Civilised, even, in a boisterous kind of way. Drinks flow and the chat is easy: the cost of replacement tyres, dodgy moles, whether

Mrs. O'Leary owns any other footwear except Velcro loafers (Gwen swears blind she once saw her in low-heeled slingbacks), and the boys and Bella take to Shay on sight, scaling him like a climbing frame and demanding to know if Kristy has stinky feet. Nush seems a little distant, and Esme keeps up her snobby habit of picking things up and putting them down as though browsing the wares at a particularly crap jumble sale. But that—*she*—is the only thing that grates on me during that first hour. Not bad for a room of six tipsy adults, two know-all teenagers, and three little kids wired to the moon on Fizzy Fish.

However, as sure as the sun will rise, lunchtime drinking only ever ends one of two ways: in a nap or an argument.

It's our fridge-mounted menu planner, of all things, that first gives rise to the friction. Shay takes against it in a big way. Puffed up with principle, and having sunk three beers before the pizzas came out, he declares menu planners to be a sign of everything that's wrong with the world. And I, as its tragic owner, to be "zombie-stepping through life."

"All I'm saying is, how can anyone know what they'll fancy eating in five days' time? Have you never heard of spontaneity?" He's rocking on the back legs of his chair and the twins are totally awestruck—any kind of messing on your chair is a breach of Mummy's rules. I should ask him to stop, but, God forgive me, it'd be funny if he toppled backwards. I don't want him to hurt himself, *obviously*. A bruised ego would do. "Like, what if it's Wednesday and you fancy chicken curry, but the planner says omelette. What happens then?"

His face is deadly serious as he waits for me to defend the system. I know he's mocking me, though. Everyone does. Only Gwen has the good grace to pretend not to notice, quietly sipping her Malbec at the far end of the table, her nose buried in my latest paint catalogue. I look to Nush, expecting support—it was Nush who bought me the bloody menu planner—but her face is impassive, verging on bored.

"Come back to me when you've got kids," I say, nodding towards Max, who's now whining that the mozzarella is "too bouncy" and he wants to watch *PAW Patrol*. "We'll chat about spontaneity then, OK?"

He grins as if to say *touché*, then squints towards the planner again. "Shame I wasn't here Tuesday. Can't beat spaghetti bolognese."

"So you don't loathe all Italian food, then?" Adam gives my thigh a solidarity squeeze under the table. "Just pizza."

The word wasn't *loathe*, it was *detest*. Shay *detests* pizza. Which is a shame, as I made nine of them. Three vegetarian, two gluten-free, one vegetarian *and* gluten-free, two exceptionally meaty, one emphatically vegan. All without mushrooms. In fairness, he subsequently downgraded *detest* to *dislike*. He also agreed that there's very little logic to it, given that he likes bread, he loves cheese, and he doesn't mind tomatoes and most toppings. But combined, it's all "too sloppy." Really not his thing.

"Insane," Orla says, shaking her head, still not quite over it. "Seriously, I reckon not liking pizza has got to be a sign of psychopathy."

Esme picks up her knife and makes a slashing motion through the air. "Ever slit your teddies' throats when you were little, Shay? Pull the wings off butterflies?"

Shay laughs. "Says the woman eating pizza with a knife and fork. *That's* psychopathic."

Esme preens at his use of *woman*, although she could be preening at *psychopath*.

Gwen looks up. "That's a misconception, you know—that psychopaths are always violent. And they're actually rarely insane. Not in the legal sense—that's what Jase says, anyway." And with that she drops her head again, keen to get back to satin versus matte.

"Jason—Gwen's brother—is police," Kristy explains to Shay.

"Sorry to hear that," he says, the front legs of his chair finally reacquainting with the floor.

"You're not a fan of the police?" I ask, trying for casual.

"If that's your way of asking if I've got a criminal record, Ellen, then no." That's something, I suppose, and must be a first for Kristy. Usually, as long as they're six foot minimum and Category C offence maximum, she's game. Shay twitches a half-smile. "I've had a few cautions here and there. But hey, we were all young and stupid once, right?"

"What did you do?" asks Orla, eyes ablaze. She's never seemed this fascinated by her uncles' extensive records. Her uncles on my side, obviously. Adam's brother still feels bad about the time he forgot to scan a pineapple at the self-checkout.

"Oh, you know, criminal damage mainly. Fighting. Threatening behaviour. Petty stuff."

"Basically, don't piss Shay off," says Esme.

I can make a scene about using inappropriate language in front of little ones, or I can dispatch said little ones into the living room to watch TV. I should go for the former, but the last thing I need is Orla having another reason to hate me.

I clap my hands. "Right, Bella, boys, take a slice of pizza and go into the living room. Daddy will switch on *PAW Patrol*." The kids are up out of their chairs and shimmying through the door within seconds. Adam looks briefly annoyed about being volunteered out of his seat until my glare reminds him that it was *me* who made nine pizzas, *me* who vacuumed the house, *me* who drove five miles to get a barrel of his favourite craft beer. "And be careful with crumbs," I shout, although it's futile; they're toddlers. "We don't want Attack of the Ants: The Sequel."

"So has Jason met many psychopaths?" Nush asks Gwen, twirling the stem of her wine glass. Gwen looks surprised by the question, but I know what Nush is doing. "It's just I thought uniformed police dealt mainly with burglars and vandals and . . ."

"The likes of me?" offers Shay.

"He's met a few," says Gwen. "Our parents, for a start." She gives a sharp laugh. "That was a joke, by the way. I mean, they were awful, but they weren't *that* bad. Just broken, damaged people. They should never have had kids."

"I know the feeling." Adam sits back down, having only caught the last line of the conversation.

"And working in London, he'd have met one or two psychopaths, I guess. His job was a bit more lively there." *And a lot more senior.* Nush is straining at the leash to say it. "He studied them at uni, too—psychology and criminology. He's always had this weird obsession."

"He should study Max," Adam says, shaking his head at some transgression or other.

"Actually, I don't think you're allowed to call children psychopaths," Gwen says, stretching for, and beating Esme to, the last slice of vegan pizza. "It's an adult condition, according to Jase." She makes a face suggesting that according to Jason, the earth could well be flat.

"I called Max 'Satan' the other day," I say. "Is that worse?"

"At least Jason put his degree to use," Orla interrupts, pouring herself a glass of Prosecco with a finesse that slightly shocks me. "Mum did art history. That was three years well spent."

"Ah, but uni was free back then," Kristy says, her voice laced with edge and three vodka tonics. "So you could just swan about studying underwater basket-weaving or whatever, and the state picked up the bill." She turns to Shay, pointing at me. "Can you believe *she* got into uni the year before they introduced tuition fees. I mean, is that typical or is that typical?"

Adam sighs. "So it's Ellen's fault when she was born now?"

Kristy gives him a hot stare. "I didn't say that—but, you know, top marks for the supportive spouse act, Ads." A sour beat passes between them before he looks away. "I'm just saying it's funny how things always work out for her."

Nush bites before I can. "Oh, and they don't for you? Living rent-free with a monsoon shower and a veranda. Designer dresses on tap."

Kristy's wearing one of my dresses today, although it's not designer, more £100 high-street. It was too mini on me. On Kristy, it's micro. But in trademark fashion, she couldn't give two hoots.

Spend one day in a wheelchair, Els, and you'll get some fucking perspective on cellulite, trust me.

"Yeah, well, some of us have to take our gift horses where we find them," Kristy replies. "We don't all have rich ex-husbands to feed off."

Tom isn't Nush's ex-husband—not yet—or in any way her financial feeder. Between her plumbing and aromatherapy businesses, she feeds herself exceptionally well.

But far be it from Kristy to let the facts ruin a good insult.

Orla grins at Shay. "Well, this is fun, isn't it? Bet you're glad you came to lunch now. Food you detest and everyone having a go at each other."

"I'd run for the hills if I were you," says Gwen with a smile. The weariness in her voice, however, suggests she'd gladly go too.

"Nah, no chance of that." Shay lays a hand over Kristy's, but his eyes are on me. "I'm staying right where I am. I know when I'm on to a good thing."

Attempting to change the subject, Adam asks Nush, "Any word on the Pelham grapevine?" He turns his head to me. "Thought you'd have heard something by now, didn't you?"

"Not necessarily," I say, defensive. Nush stares at her plate, seemingly transfixed by a sprig of basil. "These things take time. It's not just one person's decision. I get that."

"Thought you were the 'clear front-runner'?" Kristy says. "Doesn't sound that clear if they have to debate it."

"There might be internal candidates," I say. *But I'm sure they said there weren't?*

"Well, they'd definitely have to be dealt with first," says Gwen. "I remember that from when I recruited my maternity cover. It's frustrating—you know your external candidate's better, but you have to go through the motions."

"And it is a school holiday." The whole table, bar Nush, nods at Esme's surprisingly constructive input. Then she adds, "Oh, hold on, it might not be for them. Those schools have different calendars, I think."

"I suppose there could be another interview," I say. "Something less formal. Actually, that'd be nice . . ."

"You didn't get it."

Nush says it so quietly that even though the agitated tapping of her nail tells me everything, I still ask her to repeat it.

"You didn't get it. Sorry."

Orla mouths *ouch*. Kristy takes a triumphant bite of pizza. Although it's possible the triumph is entirely in my head.

"But you said . . . I thought it was as good as mine?" Adam gives my thigh another squeeze.

Nush shrugs. "That's what Joanna Plimpton said on Wednesday. Yesterday she said . . . well, that it wasn't."

"Yesterday?" So Nush had plenty of time to tell me before we had an audience.

She knows what I'm thinking. "Darling, with the letter and everything, and then you were dealing with the tyre yesterday . . . and I didn't want to ruin today's lunch." She pauses. "But, well, I couldn't let you sit there babbling on about internal candidates and second interviews."

"Did she say why?" I ask, too gutted to be offended by *babbling on*. "She must have given a reason?"

"Well, obviously they'll be in touch directly, but . . ." She heaves a huge martyr-ish sigh, as if she *really* doesn't want go there. "Truthfully, Ellen, the breathalyser." The local gossips have been busy then. It's been years since I've felt such a serious pang of *fuck this place*. "Word spreads, and it wasn't a great look, was it? Oh, and something about Facebook posts, too. I didn't quite catch the gist."

"God, yeah. Ciara Harkin." Gwen slides the Malbec towards me, an infinitely more helpful gesture than Adam's thigh clamps. "Who the hell was that, Els? And what letter?"

"Yeah, what letter, Mum?"

Adam stands and heads for the kitchen drawer. "Someone sent Ellen—"

"Leave it, Ads." I get up and quickly yank him back to the table. "Can we just forget about it for today?"

He acquiesces, but stares at me, confused. "Els, if this letter, this *campaign*, is the reason you've been turned down for a job, then this is big. We can't just forget it. I can't actually believe you'd want to."

"What letter?" repeats Orla. "What campaign?"

Shay strokes his beard, Confucius-style. "What I don't get is, why send a letter saying they're going to screw you? Why not just screw you?" He nudges Kristy. "We were talking about this last night, weren't we, babe?"

Orla's enraged. "Who's screwing who? What letter? Why does everyone know about this except me?"

Gwen adds a jolly "And me!"

I slam my hand down hard. "Omigod, can we stop talking about the bloody letter. I mean it. Can everyone just *please* shut up."

I'm no stranger to a bit of shouting, but I'm not usually a table-slammer. I'm embarrassed, though. *Cringing*. I honestly thought the job was as good as mine.

Seven faces stare back at me, their expressions a mix of shock, concern, and morbid fascination. After a moment, Gwen, always eager to recuse herself from anything remotely unpleasant, remarks, "It's a bit too quiet in there for my liking," and goes to check on the kids.

It's Kristy who breaks the stunned silence. "Oh well, Els—

back to teaching the fruit of millionaire loins, then. There's worse gigs, surely?"

"Not when you want to make the world a better place," says Orla, singing the last bit into the pepper-grinder.

"And is that wrong?" I fire back.

"To be fair, you do have a bit of a saviour complex," says Nush.

I glare at her across the table. "It's only a saviour complex, Nush, if you've only ever known privilege. I, *we*—me and Kristy—we were those Pelham kids once."

Kristy raises her vodka tonic. "Didn't do too badly, though, did we, sis? You in your Christmas movie house, planning your swanky renovation. Me travelling the world, walking for Westwood." She gives me a misty-eyed smile, so like Dad's. One more vodka tonic and she'll be crooning "Carrickfergus" for sure.

Not my finest admission, but I actually prefer Kristy slightly drunk.

Swallowing down my disappointment, I raise my glass to hers. "Yeah, we did well." I look at Nush. "But it doesn't mean I've forgotten how hard it is to thrive in a 'rough' school."

"Oh, here we go." Orla's eyebrows hit the ceiling. "'When I was your age I had to walk to school in my bare feet. I swept chimneys for half a shilling. I didn't get on a plane until I was twenty-one.'"

"I wouldn't call Pelham High rough," muses Esme. "It's not *that* bad. Chapel House or Tommy More's, now you're talking scummy."

St Thomas More's. Zane's old school.

My cheeks flush and beads of sweat start to gather on my forehead before a piercing scream from the living room turns my insides ice-cold. It's Max, that's for sure, and it's not a scream that signals a spider or a fight over the remote control. I make a dash for the door and bump into Gwen hurtling towards me.

She's holding my bleeding, sobbing boy. Her face is the colour of boiled cauliflower.

Air rushes from my lungs.

"It's his hand," she says quickly. "A bit of corn fell off his pizza and he said Mummy would be cross so he was going to get it . . . and then he screamed. I don't really know what happened, Els. I had my back to him, wiping Bella's nose."

OK, hands can be fixed. My relief is near nirvana. Max lunges into my arms as Gwen runs back the other way.

"Baby, what happened?" I ask, laying a kiss on his drenched cheek. He's too beside himself to tell me. The only word I can make out sounds like *night*. "Can you grab me a clean tea towel?" I shout to Orla, but it's Nush who springs into action. I sit Max on Adam's knee so I can get a proper look at the damage.

The cut is small, but so's his hand, and even at barely an inch, it runs almost the entire length of the soft, pudgy mound at the base of his precious thumb. It doesn't look too deep, but it's hard to tell when he won't let me touch it. As soon as Nush hands me the tea towel, I bite the bullet and grab him gently by the wrist, pressing the cloth firmly to stop the bleeding. Max looks at me like I'm his torturer. I sing "Maximoo is a brave boy" to the tune of "London Bridge is Falling Down."

"Jesus Christ," Adam says suddenly, gawping at something over my shoulder.

I turn around to look at the doorway, where Bella and Kian stand, and in the middle, Gwen, holding a knife.

Knife, not *night*.

Orla's eyes meet mine.

"It was down the side of the sofa cushion," Gwen says, voice quavering.

"*What?*"

I can't make sense of what I'm staring at. If it was a cutlery knife, sure, I could just about understand how it could wind up there—Adam and I sometimes eat dinner on the sofa, although we haven't done for weeks. But *this* knife is sharp. It's the one I use to chop vegetables and slice open parcels. If anything, Max is lucky to have got away with what I think is just a bad nick.

My stomach churns.

"How did it get there?" I ask Gwen, and even to my ears I sound witless.

Gwen gives me a roundly deserved look that says *you live here, not me*.

"What do you reckon?" I turn back to Adam. "Should we head to the hospital, just to be on the safe side? Although we'll have to get a taxi. We're all over the limit."

"Hospital? At five p.m. on a Saturday? Good luck with that," says Shay. "You'll have the football injuries piling in and the first lot of drinking casualties." He stands up and walks around the table, crouching beside me in front of a now fractionally less distraught Max. "Take the cloth off for a second," he says. "Let me look. I'm first-aid trained."

Sceptical, but hardly in a position to be choosy, I comply. The cut fills with blood again, but there's less now, no question.

Shay nods, satisfied. "Nah, there's no way that needs stitches. It's fairly narrow, and you've only been applying pressure for a few minutes and it's already drying up, see?" He chucks Max under the chin. "Want to come with me, big guy? We'll get that cleaned, get you sorted, yeah?" To me, he adds, "I assume you've got a first-aid kit, a little bandage or something?"

I don't have a first-aid *kit*. I have a first-aid depository. Four loosely organised shelves crammed with every "something" you could need. Gwen springs into action this time, putting the knife on the table in front of a disconcertingly quiet Orla.

Sadly, Esme isn't so quiet. "Wow, Shay—you can pull a pint *and* you're a first-aider. Gotta say, gimme a guy who's good with his hands over an office type any day." She twinkles in

Adam's direction. "No offence, Mr. Walsh. You're the exception, obviously."

I've got a bleeding toddler, and there's a teenage girl flirting with two grown men in my kitchen.

But it's Orla I can't take my eyes off.

And Orla can't take her eyes off the knife.

21

Orla

ESME: OMG how short was that dress ur aunt
was wearing??
Great legs tho.
ORLA: Model legs.
ESME: U get to the bottom of that letter thing?
Ur mum was so weird about it
ORLA: Nope. Asked Dad but he said forget it. He's so
under the thumb it's unreal
And I told u my mum's weird. Sketchy AF.
ESME: Baby bro ok?
ORLA: He cut his hand ffs!! People acting like he lost a leg
Little shit's milking it big time. Mum's like fawning
all over him.
Anyway serves him right
ESME: ???
ORLA: The knife didn't walk to the sofa did it?
He probably put it there himself and forgot. He's always
hoarding stuff. Little kids are weird like that.
ESME: Maybe Shay put it there? We established
he's a psycho.

Maybe he was leaving it there to come back and carve
up ur mum. He doesn't seem to like her much

ORLA: Which makes him totally sane.

ESME: He was properly taking the piss about that menu
planner thing. It was awks.

ORLA: It was funny!

Beat listening to my mum going on about her
moles. Zzzzzzzzz

ESME: I thought it was rude

Even I'm not that rude

ORLA: So u don't fancy him now?

ESME: Nope. 4 out of 10 would NOT recommend

ORLA: Er?? "Gimme a guy who's good with his hands . . ."

ESME: Can still flirt with someone I don't fancy!

But like the pizza thing!! Too weird.

Pizza is like sex—even when it's bad it's good. I mean even
that fig and fennel one that should have been gross was ok.

And fussy eater = crap in bed imo

ORLA: Not gonna ask u to explain logic. Might throw up
my fennel.

And since when has bad sex been good? Maybe for the
guy? About time we raised our standards I think.

ESME: Yeah ok, Michelle Obama.

ORLA: Fuck off 😊

Anyway, u know who is a psycho? Creepy Jason.

Weird loner—tick

Obsessed with psychopaths—tick

Lives with his sister—tick (Norman Bates lived
with his mum)

Spied on me thru bedroom door—tick

ESME: Who's Norman Bates?

22

Jason

Gwen stinks of the Walsh house. Wine, expensive handwash, and those menthol cigarettes she only ever smokes when she's with Ellen. There's a whiff of mints, too. Mints to mask the menthol. What's the point, Jason wonders, when they both smell the same? Like spraying shit with shite, as his old boss used to say. He should tell Gwen not to bother. Remind her that she's not thirteen and he couldn't care less what she fills her lungs with. If that's all he had to care about, he'd be a long way from here.

He thought she'd be later. Fifteen more minutes and he'd probably have left the house. Not that he had a date, or a destination, or a particular time he had to be anywhere. He was toying with the cinema, actually—the twelve-screener off the bypass, the one with the stadium-style seating and floor-shaking surround-sound. He can't stand the "picture house" in Thames Lawley, with its old-fashioned penny sweets and tubs of raspberry ripple ice cream. It might be perfect for reliving perfect childhoods. Not so perfect if yours was hell.

Anyway, it's immaterial now. They're back. Bella's playing upstairs and Gwen's in full debrief mode, sprawled across the opposite sofa, clearly wanting to chat. He could offer to put Bella to bed to avoid conversation, but he's not in the mood for bedtime stories, can't stomach the happy-ever-after. He's especially not in the mood for Bella asking if he can be her daddy.

"It's a shame you couldn't come," Gwen says casually, like it was simply a last-minute hitch that kept him absent, rather than disgust. "For the food, at least. She made pizzas, really unusual toppings. Figs! I've never had figs on a pizza before. Actually, I'm not sure I've ever had figs at all. Have you?"

She doesn't need an answer. She's not even looking at him. She's tapping on her phone like a bird pecking at a feeder, probably thanking Ellen for the hundredth time for her *ah-mazing* hospitality. And so he doesn't reply. Doesn't say that yes, actually, he *has* eaten figs. That Emma used to love them. That she'd throw them in salads and fruit cakes and wrap them in filo pastry for dinner parties. That the restaurant where he proposed did a mean ham and fig tartlet. That the last Christmas present he ever bought her was a £100 candle that supposedly smelled of spiced fig.

See, he used to have a life. A life a bit like Ellen's. Dinner parties. Christmas presents. Meaningful restaurants. Figs.

"One of the pizzas had that cheese you like." Gwen finishes tapping. "You know the one—quite crumbly, begins with G."

"Gorgonzola."

She points a finger—*correct*—then tilts her head back, eyes on the ceiling. After a moment, she says sleepily, "Anyway, it was nice. Really nice."

"The gorgonzola or the afternoon?"

The question seems to rouse her. "Oh, the gorgonzola." She lifts her head. "The afternoon was a bit of a disaster. Fine at first, but then Kristy's guy didn't like the food, Ellen found out she didn't get that job, and Adam was wound up about some letter. And of course, Kristy and Nush got into it, as usual." *As usual*. Like she's filling him in on the latest episode of their favourite soap. "I kept out of it mainly. Pretended to be interested in paint. I don't know why she bothers with those catalogues, you know. We all know she's going to go with white, white, and more white."

"Oh yeah, *big* disaster." Jason stands up. Honestly, reading

Llama Llama Red Pajama to Bella has got to be less tedious than this. "Some guy dissed the pizza and a couple of women bickered over what? Whose Botox looks better?"

Gwen heaves herself up. She's got something to say and she's not saying it horizontal.

"You know, it's no wonder Emma kicked you out if that's the kind of chauvinist tripe she had to listen to. I swear you didn't used to be like this."

He didn't. Emma would have drop-kicked him into next week. But it's this place. It's *her*. He's becoming more hateful, more hate-filled, with every passing day.

"And anyway, if you'd let me finish," Gwen carries on, "I would have got to the disaster."

"Save it," he says. "I'll go and bath Bella."

"Little Max had an accident."

Jason freezes at the foot of the stairs. "An accident? You mean like he wet himself?"

"No. He cut his hand on a knife that was down the side of the sofa. A sharp one, too. He was lucky, really. Can you imagine . . ." She breaks off mid shudder.

"How the hell did a sharp knife get there?"

"I don't know. How does anything get anywhere?"

To prove her point, she rummages between two sofa cushions, then presents him with half a packet of squashed Rolos and a membership card for a now-defunct gym.

"Hardly the same," he snaps, smacking her hand away.

"Oh, for God's sake, Jase. Bella got hold of a razor once, started trying to shave her legs because she'd seen me doing it. *And* she fell off a see-saw while I was looking for the back of an earring. We're parents, not cyborgs. We've only got one pair of eyes. I mean, I'm sure Ellen feels like shit, but these things happen."

Rage writhes in the pit of Jason's knotted stomach. "And

what's a scarred child between friends, hey, if she makes a demon fucking pizza?"

He shouldn't shout, but he's powerless; neglect has always been his trigger. He practically raised Gwen himself until Social Services cottoned on to the absence of a responsible adult, and "these things" never happened on his watch. He didn't even let her use the toaster. And if he had to leave her for any length of time, he always made sure he double-locked the door.

Jason knows for a fact that the Walshes rarely double-lock theirs.

23

Ellen

Today is declared Max Day. His rules. Mummy's demoted. It's both his reward for being a brave boy and my attempt to feel less shit. But while he's been in toddler heaven, mainlining sugar and monopolising the TV remote, I've remained in the horrors. Guilt is a frost coating my skin.

"These things happen," Gwen keeps insisting. "And it's Adam's sofa too, remember!" Contrast that with Nush's "helpful" admission that she vacuums under her cushions twice a week. Translation: if she was Max's mum, his hand wouldn't currently resemble a bandaged koala's after a bush fire.

And, oh, the what-ifs.

What if Gwen hadn't grabbed the knife?

What if Max hadn't cut himself and instead they'd started playing with it?

What if they'd been jumping on the sofa and someone had landed head-first . . . No, can't go there.

And now this afternoon, on an admittedly less hellish but still frustrating note, what if I'd had the sense to check the weather before declaring today Max Day?

Outside, it's cold and drizzly on and off. The sky is a slab of gloom and the air feels drained of energy, as though nature had a late one and can't be bothered getting up. It's a day for snuggling up indoors and making plans to move to Australia. It's not a day for making repeated muddied orbits of Proctor's Park, or

Pointless Park as it's known locally. Given that the world was Max's oyster—or a twenty-mile radius, realistically—it's baffling to us all why he chose this barren, boggy dump.

But such are the mysteries of toddlers, and even more mysteriously, Orla has deigned to join us. A bribe would be my guess. There's no way she's doing it for Max. I wonder how much Adam had to cough up to secure her attendance? Twenty? Thirty? He surely wouldn't stretch to fifty? Then again, I'm not sure what the going rate is for shivering side by side with the sworn enemy who birthed you while up ahead your dad and brothers pet an old lady's yappy dog.

"I suppose the boys will be getting a dog now."

Orla stares straight ahead as she says it, this statement full of subtext. The tenseness of her jaw suggests I should consider my answer carefully.

"You used to love dogs," I say simply, but there's every chance she'll find offence in it. Saying anything to Orla these days is like probing an electric fence.

"Wasn't allowed one, though, was I?" And there she goes, giving off sparks.

I'm about to point out that we lived in a third-floor flat for a large chunk of her childhood when my phone suddenly vibrates, letting out an outrageously loud beep.

An *offensively* loud beep, judging by Orla's evil eye.

"Bloody Max," I say, coming to a stop and fishing around in my handbag. "That's the last time he plays Pokémon Playhouse on my phone."

"Course it is, Mum." Orla gives a bitter, rueful laugh. Does she have any other? It makes me want to grab her and shake her and remind her that she once had a laugh repertoire. Hearty. Hysterical. Laughs reserved for funny dogs and fart jokes. She once snorted Sprite through her nose laughing at Adam attempt to do the splits. "You mean until the next time he turns on the waterworks and you cave in to him. You were *way* tougher on me."

Not tougher, more present. I was a better parent, no question. When it was just Orla, I had the time to say no. The patience to be unpopular. And I'm fairly sure I got around to cleaning under the sofa cushions once in a while.

I take my phone out of my bag, turn the volume down, then click on messages. It's probably just Gwen. Her *Not your fault!* pep texts have been coming thick and fast all day.

Ellen can u call me? Like now. Need ur help x

I stare unblinking, barely breathing, at the SOS before me.

Not Gwen.

Zane.

"Seriously, the boys get away with *way* more than I did." Orla continues her Cinderella spiel. "And I don't remember any Orla Day that time I split my chin."

Zane wants my help? With what? And what's he playing at, messaging me on a Sunday?

I look up slowly, punch-drunk. "That was different."

I'm not sure how it was different, but I have to say something to camouflage the shock I'm feeling. If that means picking a fight, so be it.

"The only difference is *I* hurt myself at Grandma's, so you didn't have to feel bad because it wasn't on your watch."

"I felt bad that you were in pain."

"You didn't have to feel *guilty*, then. Although I'm surprised you feel guilty now, about Max. We both know you're pretty good at parking guilt when it suits you." Her eyes bore into mine, challenging me to look away.

So we *could* do this now, me and Orla. Clear the air or poison it further. After all, Adam and the boys are out of range, and since all our old mum-and-daughter jaunts—shopping, theatre trips, bookshop browses—are now consigned to the annals of history, it's the first time we've been alone on neutral ground in several months.

"Oh, and by the way, I know you think it was me," she adds,

tightening her drizzle-dampened ponytail. "The knife in the sofa, I mean."

It comes out of nowhere. A nuclear blast of a statement.

Nerves jangling, I take a sharp breath. "Orla, I . . ."

I *what*?

My phone beeps again and I instantly look down at the message. It saves me from looking at the mess I made. The girl-woman I created.

Zane again.

My second mess.

Actually need air so gonna walk to Thames Lawley. Maybe see you there?

It could be my mood, but this reads less like an SOS and more like a threat.

24

Ellen

I know the worst thing he ever did. He knows that the theme from *The Deer Hunter* always floors me. And once, when I was executing a half-hearted downward dog next to Nush at Hot Pilates, it struck me how the calming blue of my yoga mat matched the exact shade of his eyes.

Observations, revelations, and yet I realise now I hardly know him. I've never seen him in the wild. I've never known him outside his flat.

With the drizzle still drizzling, the plan was that I'd call when I got here. I'd park up outside the Graps (the pub formerly called the Grapes until a storm dislodged the "e" a few years back), then Zane would grab his stuff and be with me in less than five. Instead he's here already, and he looks so young in natural daylight. Just a teenage boy in a soaked-through hoodie, taking his teenage angst out on his thumbnail.

I let down the window. "Ever heard of a coat? Or an umbrella? I thought you were going to wait inside?"

He shrugs. "S'only water. I ain't got rabies. And anyway, I had to get out of there."

I pop open the back and he tosses his bag in. Once in the car, he makes his presence felt, sliding the passenger seat forwards and backwards while filling the air with the scent of damp hoodie and stale weed.

"Seriously, you're a total legend for doing this," he says, as if the tone of his second message hadn't effectively been a summons. "I'd have got the bus, but you know me—broke as a joke, as usual. Don't know what I'd have done if you hadn't called back."

"Asked someone else?" I say, irritated. "I can't be the only person you know with wheels." I let out a small, huffy sigh. "So where are we going then?"

He pulls his hood down, revealing the right side of his face. "I couldn't ask anyone on the estate, 'cos I didn't want them seeing this, OK? Asking questions."

Within twenty-four hours, I've seen two wounds across perfect skin. A red gash forms a crescent around the curve of Zane's ear. It's no longer bleeding, but it's probably less than an hour old.

He puts a hand up before I can say anything. "And don't start freaking out. It's nothing. I just need to get away for a few days. I've got a cousin in Danesfield says I can kip on her sofa." He leans back, pulling his phone from his jeans pocket. "Gimme a sec, I'll put the address in Google Maps."

Forget freaking out about his face. Zane's got a cousin in affluent, bourgeois Danesfield? And when he said he needed a lift, I assumed he meant somewhere local, not Timbuktu. I promised Adam "forty minutes tops" after boring him into submission with my strategically dull tale of a student's mislaid study guide (best I could improvise), but Danesfield and back will easily take over an hour. If there's roadworks or hold-ups, maybe closer to two.

I clamp my jaw and start the engine. We need to go.

"So what happened?" I ask once we're a few streets clear of the Lomax. Zane is busy messaging someone, his thumbs a whirling blur. "Don't tell me, the other guy looks worse."

He looks up and out of the window, seemingly reluctant to

spill. I'm about to say *Hey, look, I was only making conversation* when he declares miserably, "Dad was the other guy. He was coked off his skull. We fell out."

"Paulo?" I wouldn't have thought he had it in him. He seems to love the bones of his boy, and physically he looks like he'd pack less of a punch than I would. "Fell out over what? The drugs?"

"The boiler." He gives an empty laugh, then checks his face in the visor mirror, tracing the jagged line of the cut with an angrily swollen finger. "It gave out earlier. It was freezing in the flat, like fucking Siberia, man. I couldn't concentrate, nothing." I flick on his heated seat; a lame gesture, but it's something. "So I figure I'll fix it myself. I mean, how hard can it be? I've been fixing everything else since I was tall enough to reach the toolbox."

Highly skilled through lack of options, like most of the kids I grew up with. The whole sorry lot of us mini tradesmen before we sprouted our first pube. I helped lay a carpet when I was eight. I was bleeding radiators by age eleven. Orla thinks she's worldly because she's swum with sea turtles on two different continents. But she wouldn't have a clue how to use a drill. Although I accept that's on me.

"So why the falling-out? Paulo thought you should call someone?"

A loud laugh this time, one hard crack. "Yeah, right. Nothing Dad likes more than handing over his coke money to plumbers. No, what he *thought* was, what's the point in studying A levels when I'm a 'thick useless twat' who can't even fix a boiler. But I swear, Ellen, I checked the pilot light, the pressure, the pipes . . ." His face is wreathed in hurt. His fist a ball of tension. I have to stop myself from reaching over and resting a kind hand on top of his. "Anyway, Dave from a few doors down said he'd take a look, but he wanted twenty quid, which was fair enough, I thought. Dad said fuck off, so I took it from his wallet. He hit me. I hit the corner of the table." A tiny shrug. *And so it is.*

"I'm so sorry." I glance over. "You know you didn't deserve that?"

"Course I know," he gruffs, but I'm not sure he feels it in his belly. He's still too young to grasp the chasm between showy confidence and self-worth. "He ain't an animal, though, Ellen. I don't want you thinking he is."

I consider this as I speed up to join the motorway. "My dad beat my brother once," I tell him eventually. "I hated him for it, but he wasn't an animal either. It's how he was raised. It's a shitty cycle."

But there *is* a crucial difference (or maybe I'm airbrushing history?): Dad was trying to teach Cahill a lesson before someone bigger and more batshit did—namely, don't steal from your neighbours. The only lesson Paulo taught Zane today is not to hassle cokeheads about boilers when they're down to their last twenty quid.

I could cry for him, I really could. Even with this "cousin in Danesfield," he seems so alone, so vulnerable. At least my lot had strength in numbers, our small sibling bloc. Zane's the kind of put-upon kid even *we* used to feel sorry for.

The next twenty minutes passes in short bursts of conversation and prolonged bouts of silence, the patter of the rain providing the bassline to our stilted chat. Then, just after we pass WELCOME TO DANESFIELD—an austere grey sign that looks like more of a warning than a welcome—Zane announces out of nowhere that his head "feels like shit."

Delayed concussion? It could be. He'd mentioned hitting his head and it might explain the silences. However, harsh as it sounds, that's going to have to be "cousin in Danesfield's" problem. Zane is undoubtedly my raw spot, but he's not my responsibility.

"There's a Tesco Express up here," he says, pointing ahead. "Any chance you could grab me some paracetamol? I'll pay you back when I see you next, obvs."

Obvs.

I take a fretful look at the clock, imagining Adam's face—worse, his questions. "Ah, come on, Zane. We'll be at your cousin's in a few minutes. I'm sure she'll have something."

"Don't think Ruby's the paracetamol sort. You know what poshos are like. It's all herbal remedies and crystals."

I snap, "Fine," and pull over, my *not*-fine-ness plain to see. Sensing my mood, he belatedly offers to venture in himself, but I'm already halfway out of the car. And in any case, I need to buy bribe beer for Adam and sweets for Max and Kian, and then maybe if I let Orla go to Frankfurt, she might dial down her disbelief ("A study guide? On a Sunday? They're either paying you top dollar or the dad's hot as hell").

Guilt gifts sorted, I pick up paracetamol, water, and a bottle of disinfectant for his cut—in case Ruby's not the antiseptic sort either—then I withdraw £20 from the cashpoint because I'm a woeful softie.

As I get back in the car, he's closing the glove compartment. The cut is now bleeding—not much, but he's obviously been picking at it.

"Got any tissues?" he asks, looking confused by the disinfectant.

He's less confused by the twenty and mutters a grateful, bashful *thanks*.

"There's baby wipes somewhere." I quickly buckle up and drive off—it's been thirty-seven minutes precisely since I abandoned Adam in Pointless Park. "Although good luck finding them. The car's a pigsty, if you hadn't noticed. Try under the seats."

He tries under his, then mine, grinning as he announces his numerous grubby finds. A flip-flop from summer. A wizened balloon from the twins' birthday. Three pounds, two lipsticks (one since discontinued), and the more recent remains of either a nectarine or a peach.

And finally some baby wipes.

"Yeah, OK, enough of the dirt-shaming," I say as he dabs at the cut. "Bless me, Father, for I have sinned. It's been six months since my last full-service valet." He laughs, his quarter-Italian-Catholic side instantly catching the joke. I shoot him a suspicious glance. "You know, you're pretty perky for someone with a headache. You haven't even opened the paracetamol."

"They say laughter's the best medicine. Then again, so's being with you." He gives me a coy, flirty smile that could probably break the internet.

Racked with unease, I roll my eyes and call him a cheeseball, then mercifully, two minutes later, Google Maps announces we're here. Trensale Row is at the very heart of suburban dead-zone Danesfield, and at this time on a Sunday, there's neither saint nor sinner in sight. It's also wider and leafier and even wealthier than I expected. Towering townhouses with neat gardens. Zero litter. Spanking-new cars.

Not the kind of road I ever imagined any cousin of Zane's living on. But then I never imagined I'd become such a presumptuous snob.

"Ruby actually lives off here," Zane says, pointing towards a side street halfway down. "But it's fine, just drop me on the corner. Her road's a dead end, really narrow. She reckons it's a nightmare turning her dinky little Polo around some days, so I wouldn't fancy your chances in this beast. Honestly, the corner's totally fine. S'hardly raining now. Thanks." Another smile. Less coy this time and more . . . I don't know . . . *sad*?

I pull over as requested. He gets out of the car.

So, that *thanks*—was that a preliminary *thanks* or the final *thanks*? Are we done? Can I go now? Or is another thanks coming after he's got his bag out of the back?

"Can't get it open," he shouts.

"It's definitely unlocked," I shout back, pressing the fob again to make sure.

A few seconds, then, "Nah. Still can't."

Give me strength. I get out and walk to the back of the car. Open the back, no bother.

"Well, would you look at that. I must be some sort of genius."

He hefts his bag over his shoulder. "You're definitely some sort of something."

I don't know what that's supposed to mean, but I know enough not to ask him. Instead, I crane my head forward to inspect his cut at closer range. "Well, I hope your cousin is some sort of Florence Nightingale, because that needs cleaning properly."

"Can't you kiss it better?" His eyes, no more than a hand-span from mine, blaze with mischief. "You know you want to, admit it."

I step back, my voice stern. "That's enough, Zane. I'm going now." I give an airy backwards wave as I walk away.

My hand's barely on the car door when he calls out.

"Hey, thanks again for the lift. Ruby would have got me, but why chose a Polo over a Q8?"

There was no need for him to say that. No need whatsoever. He must know it's going to rile me, but he doesn't care as long as it works. As long as it snatches another cube of time. He does this sometimes at the end of a session. Picks a fight or lands a bombshell on me—anything from ridiculing my earrings to *I'm worried I've got a brain tumour.* But like Max smashing Orla's iPad to try to stop me leaving the house, it's not calculated or malicious. He simply doesn't want me to go.

But Zane isn't Max.

Max is my baby. The boy I should be with right now.

I turn around slowly. "Ruby would have got you? You *are* fucking kidding me, right?"

If it's not the first time I've sworn in front of him, it's certainly the first time I've sworn *at* him. He jolts, then recovers quickly. "Kinda, I suppose. Yeah, I guess I am kidding. I mean, I did quite fancy a spin in an Audi, but it was more about you." The flirty look is back. I try to quell it with *severe face*. It doesn't work. "I wanted to spend a bit of time with you. And, well, to see if you'd show up, really. See how much you *actually* like me." He lifts his chin, victorious. "And lo, you came."

I stride back towards him. "Yes, because you practically threatened to turn up on my doorstep if I didn't."

He drops his bag to the floor. The dense thud suggests it contains more than clean pants and a toothbrush. Ruby might be expecting a drop-in, but I suspect she's getting a lodger.

"It was hardly a threat. And so what if I turned up?"

"Zane! This isn't fair. I do have a life, you know. Other people. Responsibilities. I'm not your . . ." I almost say *friend*, but even in the throes of rage, it feels callous. I let out a fed-up breath instead, leaving the sentence hanging in the air.

"My mum?" he says, intrigued, moving closer. "Is that what you were going to say? 'Cos trust me, I've given up trying to figure out what the actual fuck you are, Ellen, but I know you're not *that*."

The next thing I feel is a heavy velvet softness. The weight of his bottom lip cushioned perfectly on mine.

One.

Two.

Three.

"No." I step back, clear-eyed and emphatic. Now isn't the time to play the scandalised spinster, fanning herself and reaching for the smelling salts. I need to be calm. I need to be the grown-up. "Absolutely not, Zane. Just no."

Three seconds, though. Recoiling at *one* would have been honourable. *Two* perhaps forgivable. But *three* is questionable. Probably inexcusable. And I can blame shock all I like, and in the days and weeks to come, I probably will. But it was also the sheer thrill of novelty—lips lingering on mine that don't belong to Adam or the kids.

"I'm . . . I'm sorry. I just thought that maybe . . ." He dips his head, crestfallen. "Oh God, look, I don't know what I thought. I'm such a twat. I mean, why would you . . ."

One look at his forlorn face and I slip into *make-it-better* mode. "No. No you're not, Zane. Don't call yourself things like that. After what happened with your dad today, you're just a bit confused and emotional, that's all." His eyes stay on the floor. "Listen to me—you're bright and you're brilliant, and I know saying 'if I was twenty years younger' makes me sound like a terrible old lech, but if I *was*, then definitely. But I'm not, so no. OK?"

He manages a nod and a quiet "'K" before picking up his bag again.

"And don't be wasting your kisses on old birds. Not unless you've got a thing for random chin hairs."

That gets a smile at least.

"S'pose I better get going then, beardy." He chucks me under the chin, his finger grazing my bottom lip, the scene of the crime not two minutes ago. "Seriously, I really am sorry, Ellen. You've no idea how sorry I am."

I take a quick glance around, but the street bears no witnesses.

25

Ellen

I flirt with the speed limit all the way back to Thames Lawley, experiencing a love for my family so strong it could bend iron. I feel like I've been gone for days, *weeks*, not the mere hour and twenty-five minutes I'll package as "an hour, roughly" to Adam, and as I turn my key in the front door, all I want is familiarity: Adam's grumbles, Orla's glowers, and most of all, Max and Kian's tiny, slobbery, puckered, yoghurt-breathed lips on mine.

And a scalding hot shower. The damp of the afternoon and the shock of Zane's mouth—I can't think of it as a kiss—has seeped into my every pore, every joint, every bone.

So that's what I *want*: family, kisses, the healing power of water.

What I *get* is Shay, alone, singing along to Tom Jones in my kitchen. He appears to be performing surgery on a potato with the knife that cut Max.

I stop dead in the doorway. "What on earth are you doing?"

"Hasselbacks," he says, not even looking up. "They're a bit like roasties, except they're a lot more fiddly. You have to partially slice them into *veeeerrry* thin—"

"Yeah, I know what a Hasselback is, thanks." I haven't the faintest idea. "I meant what are you doing in here, *alone*? Where's Kristy?" I put my bag on the table, then switch off "Delilah." The house falls silent. "Is Adam not back? Orla? Where is everyone?"

"Orla—no idea. Adam came back, but he went out again with

what's-her-name from yesterday. Not the posh one, the pixie."
He finally looks up from the kitchen counter, the knife resting
on the potato. His man-bun lolls precariously, threatening to
capsize. "Hey, is she single? Because I've got this mate—"

"You mean Gwen? Where'd they go?"

"Dunno. She came over with her kid. There was a lot of
whooping about ice cream, then they all went out." They'll have
gone to the Frozen Spoon, then, for a Spectacular Sunday Sun-
dae. I hope Adam took out a second mortgage. "The kid made a
get-well thing for Max." He points the knife towards the fridge,
grinning. "It's next to your menu planner, look. Sweet, huh?"

A sweet thought, yes, but my God, it isn't staying there. Bless
Bella, but her depiction of Max is a Dalí-esque nightmare. The stick
man's face is twisted in the most appalling agony. Splodges of tears
litter the page, and then there's the horror of the mangled hand.

Not something I want to see every time I take the milk out.

Loved ones located, I turn my focus back to the interloper.
"So, er, sorry, Shay, I didn't quite catch what you're doing here?"

"Making a roast for me and Kris." He squints at the oven
clock. "Actually, I better get the beef in." I try to blink away my
irritation, but he sees through me easily. "Ah, look, Kris said you
wouldn't mind. Adam didn't seem to."

"And where is Kris-who-said-I-wouldn't-mind?"

I doubt she's tagged along to the Frozen Spoon, having always
insisted—I suspect for the sole purpose of being contrary—that
she doesn't "get" ice cream. *Don't you find it weird watching
people lick?*

"You tell me! She only went to get to horseradish sauce, but
that was nearly an hour ago. She's probably in the pub, spending
the tenner I gave her. Some sous chef, ha!"

Where does she find this endless conga line of men who find
her selfishness endearing?

I open the fridge and forage through the shelves. "We have

horseradish sauce. We must have, we've got everything else."
Including a jar of chutney whose sell-by date pre-dates the twins.

He comes and stands beside me, nearly as broad as the
fridge (but not the stainless-steel goliath I'm slightly regretting
ordering for the new kitchen). "Nah, you were all out. Low on
ketchup, too, and mint sauce. I told Kris to get both." He takes
a small joint of beef off the top shelf.

"Thanks. Max doesn't cope well without ketchup." I grab my
purse from my bag and scrape together £4.60. "Here." I give him
an apologetic look. "That's all I've got. Sorry, I thought I had another fiver . . ."

"Are you for real?" He looks offended. "I don't want your
money."

"No, no, I insist." It's all too much. Shay appeared less than
seventy-two hours ago and he's already replenishing our bloody
sauces. I don't like it. I feel ambushed, manipulated. "Look, if
you don't take it, I'll give it to Kris, and believe me, she will—"

Our stand-off is broken by Adam's key in the front door.

"Oh, hello," he says with a plainness I can read absolutely
nothing into.

Gwen's behind him, waving over his shoulder. "Hey, Els, did
you get everything sorted? I was just telling Ads you should be
up for Teacher of the Year, delivering textbooks on a Sunday.
Pelham High's loss, I say."

Kian and Bella veer off into the living room. Gwen follows,
warning Bella that she's allowed one *Peppa Pig*, not a *PAW
Patrol*. Rough translation: *You've got five minutes, not fifteen.*

Max hares towards me, tearing off his coat and tossing it on
the floor. "We had ice cream, Mummy! Kian had choc-late and
my had stwa-bewwy."

I crouch down. Jesus, the state of him. "I can tell that from
your t-shirt, baby. Did Daddy have anything?"

Adam scoops up Max's coat. "Only a cardiac arrest when
they handed me the bill."

Gwen comes back. "Right. Peppa's gone birdwatching, which means I'm going for a quick ciggy." Shay watches her as she walks to the back door—storing details for his mate, maybe? (*Smokes. One daughter. Slightly weird purple dungarees, but her arse still looks great in them.*) "Although, have you got any mints, Els? Jase is home and I can do without the guilt trip."

I shake my head.

"Kris should be back with some mint sauce soon," Shay says, joking of course, but Gwen looks like she's considering it. He waits until Max toddles off, then adds, "You should tell your brother to fuck off, though."

I try to formulate a more moderate view, but I can't, so I say, "God, Ads, can you imagine me taking that from Cahill or Mikey?"

"You'd take it from Sylvia," Gwen says, opening the back door.

"She's my mother-in-law. You have *no* idea how different that is."

"Oh, speaking of . . ." It's a sheepish *oh* from Adam. An *oh* that suggests he's pimped me out to Sylvia *again*, and I'm going to end up manning a cake stall at a church fete sometime soon. "Those flowers—were they from my mum?"

Flowers? "What flowers?"

"Over there on the windowsill. They were on the doorstep when we got back from the park."

I turn around. Jesus. How did I miss them? The bouquet is the size of a small oak and an assault of bright colour—pink and yellow and orange and blue.

"Why would your mum be sending me flowers?" I ask, heading to inspect them.

Adam's sheepish look intensifies. "I might have told her the Pelham job was as good as yours." He toughens up quickly. "But only because *you* gave me that impression. I was only repeating what you said."

Sylvia sending me flowers, though? I doubt it. She'd be far too busy making her presence felt on her luxury cruise ship to be bothering her blow-dried head about me.

Nush maybe? A thanks for lunch yesterday (slightly over-the-top, but that's breeding for you). Or maybe just something to cheer me up after my Pelham kick in the teeth.

Although they're a bit tacky for Nush, I think as I fish the small card from its envelope.

The fun starts now, Ellen. Things are about to get worse.

I stare silently at the words, battling to keep the tremor in my hand under control.

Gwen, previously watching through the window, opens the back door. "Who're they from, Els?"

Think.

I need a name. But not just any name. I need someone who makes sense, but someone neither Gwen nor Adam is likely to talk to. (I'm not worried about Shay.)

Drawing a blank, I keep it vague.

"Oh, just another satisfied customer." Somehow I manage a smile. "The mum of a student who aced her exams. Teacher of the Year, remember?"

I excuse myself on the basis that I need a bath after being in damp clothes for three hours. Then I head up to our en suite bathroom, where I quietly throw up.

I resolve to tell Adam about the note in bed, then to really ramp up the sexy pillow talk by suggesting a new security system. Unsurprisingly, the Merricks had an alarm fitted not long after they were attacked here. But alarms are *so* fifteen years ago. I want motion sensors. CCTV.

My plans are scuppered by a row with Orla, who saunters in late, smelling of Prada Candy and white wine. "Esme's," she says, although her blatant smirk suggests otherwise. There's little point in checking, though. Esme will be well briefed and Esme's mum well oiled by this hour.

And actually, it isn't the hour, or the lying, or the probable secret boyfriend that ignites things—that's the kind of stuff you sign up to the second you hear *Congrats, it's a girl!* No, it's the fact that she's wearing one of my earrings. *One*, because she's lost the other. And what bothers me isn't the loss, it's that she couldn't care less.

"Can't believe you're shitting the bed over some cheap plastic earrings that don't even suit you."

Of course, what I'm really "shitting the bed" over is her accusing me earlier of believing she left the knife under the sofa cushion. But as we can't go there now, I'm going to have to make it about this.

"Were they expensive?" Adam asks after Orla retreats to her lair.

I plump my pillow aggressively. "No, but that's not the point. If she's going to help herself to my stuff, she could at least feel bad if she loses something. I still can't find that charm bracelet, you know."

"No offence, but I don't think charm bracelets are her thing."

"Wouldn't stop her pawning it."

I wait for it. The outrage, then the defence. The insistence that "she's not *that* bad."

He lets it go, though, which means there's something else on his mind. Now that I think of it, he's been quiet all evening.

Maybe an apology will open him up, then I'll tell him about the latest note.

"Ads, I'm sorry . . . earlier, at the park. It's just she's one of my highest-paying clients. It was presumptuous of her, but it's hard to say no."

Ain't that the truth.

He nods. "And money's tight, right?"

"Too right." God, that was easy.

He turns to me, propped on one arm. "Look, I was thinking . . . What with you not getting the Pelham job . . . and this whole letter business . . ."

"What about it?"

"Well, I thought . . ." He lets out a sharp *here goes* breath. "I was wondering if we should we postpone the renovation. Just for a bit. Maybe another year, even just six months." I stare at him, agog. I don't know what I expected him to say, but not this. "I called Steve, the builder, earlier—"

"Er, excuse me? You did what? When?"

"When you were in the bath—you know, that *full hour* you were in the bath." Adam has a deep distrust of my baths. He views my love of a long soak as a blatant dereliction of kid duty. Today it was more, though. A dereliction of my whole life. In the words of Max, when I'm trying to get him to do anything, *I just want to be leaved alone.* "Anyway, it was just a chat, getting the facts, that was all. But ultimately he said it's fine, happens all the time. Obviously he'll keep the deposit, but he's happy to push the date back. Book us in for next summer, maybe? I mean, you're the one who's always saying Orla needs stability for her exam year." He's pleased with that last point.

"Yeah, but the work will be done by spring, and it's not like we're going to be camped out in the middle of it. We've got your folks' place in Coombe for as long as we need." I sigh. It's either that or cry. "Adam, you know what this means to me. I'm in my bloody forties, and I've never, *ever* had a home I've loved, or even one that felt like *mine.*"

He's confused. "So what was the Streatham flat, then? We were there seven years—how could that not feel like *yours*? Or Lawley Old Road? We'd have murdered someone for a place like that in London."

"But both were a compromise. Streatham was a first flat—it was what we could afford at the time. And we never really put our stamp on it because, well, money, but also 'cos we knew we'd probably leave eventually. So no, Ads, it didn't feel like *mine*, not totally. Not when I was cooking in the previous owners' kitchen, walking on *their* carpets, staring at *their* botched DIY jobs." I shrug. "And we panic-bought Lawley Old Road. It always felt like a stopgap."

"Maybe we panic-bought this place. It was a bit frantic at the end."

"You move fast when it feels right." I tap my heart. "When it's your forever family home. Something you design, mould around you. *Your* family."

"But now, with this letter and the other stuff . . ."

"We need something positive to focus on." No way am I telling him about the latest note now. I need something to hold on to. Something I can control. "And anyway, this isn't just about open-plan kitchens, or monsoon showers, or aesthetics. What about the rattling windows, the leaky roof, the faulty wiring? The *asbestos*, if bloody Shay's right? Are we postponing all that too?" He stares at me, out-argued. "Seriously, Ads, what's this really about?"

"Nothing," he huffs. "It was an idea, that's all. I just thought I'll have a better idea of my bonus by March, and you might be back working full-time by then." I can't help hearing: *And if you'd done a better Pelham interview, we wouldn't be having this talk at all.* It obviously shows on my face. "Oh, and don't look at me like that, Els. You know I've always been a bit nervous about this. We already paid over the asking price for the place. One knock to the economy and we're in negative-equity hell."

No, hell is an ice-cold flat and a coked-up dad who thinks you're a punchbag.

"Negative equity only matters if you're planning to move again at some point. And we're not, so stop stressing." I switch the light off. "Trust me, Ads, we're going to die in this house."

26

Nush

Nush has been out all day. Here, there, and everywhere. She likes to keep busy on a Sunday. It stops her from going mad. So first the gym, then the farmers' market, then to Oxford in a quest to buy a teapot. Tom took the old teapot, a wedding gift from his grandmother, and until this week holding off on buying a new one felt like an act of hopeful defiance. A warning finger to the universe: *Hold your horses, he might come back*.

Well, the pregnancy has eliminated to that foolish notion, so one teapot purchased, and a very un-Tom one at that. She chose a gaudy piece of kitsch emblazoned with *Tea-Riffic!!* and purple polka dots. His racist old granny would have hated it too. It's the best £5.99 she ever spent.

"Oh, it's hideous, just perfect," her mother agreed as she hurried Nush through a light lunch of salmon and wilted spinach. "Now remember, my book club is at three, so no loitering, darling. Anyway, I expect you've got places to be . . ."

Not really, she should have said. She'd have enjoyed nestling in the bosom of her mother's book coven. Because despite all her friends and connections and commitments and meetings, since Tom left, Nush rarely feels like she belongs anywhere on a Sunday. These days, her plan of action is simply "kill time until bath-and-bed."

She went for a drive after her mother's, although exactly where, she couldn't tell you. Countless villages passed by in one long Cotswold-stone blur. She doesn't get the appeal of recreational driving, taking the wheel always having been an A-to-B activity for her. But when you've got time on your hands and there's a good chance your ex is currently toasting his virility with the same people *you* used to lunch with, aimless driving seems a better option than festering home alone.

(Actually, she realises now, Tom wouldn't have been lunching with anyone. He'd have been in the air as she drove around, probably somewhere over France. His flight back to Heathrow from Zurich was due to leave at 11:30. But Nush checked the BA website—delayed until 2:15.)

Jasmine suggested coming home today. Such a heavenly, thoughtful daughter. Earlier in the year, she also offered to defer her Cambridge place so that she could be at home with her mother. Tempting though the offer was, Nush obviously wouldn't hear of it. Quite apart from the fact that she doubts Cambridge approves deferrals on the basis of parental separation, there was no way she'd jeopardise Jasmine's future. Nush, as always, put her child first.

Not like Ellen, she thinks, as she pours lavender oil into her spa bath. Yesterday Ellen took the word of a *barman* to save herself a trip to the hospital with Max.

Now, Nush *knows* she has a reputation for firm and exacting standards, but truthfully, until a year ago, she'd never judged Ellen that harshly as a mum. If pushed, she'd have said *decent*. Loving, if slightly scattered. And who cared if a week barely passed without a raisin up someone's nostril or a nosedive off the sofa. Boys are boisterous, Nush understood that. Ellen was doing the best she could.

Of course, this doesn't mean that she *never* found fault with Ellen's parenting. She always felt Ellen pandered too much to Max; then there was the rigmarole of the boys' potty training (she started them too young, no question). But these were private observations. Nush only offered advice when it was asked for.

And it's not like she revelled in Ellen's shortcomings, or particularly relished the chance to judge.

Oh, but she does now. Has done, in fact, ever since that conversation a year ago, when Ellen's judgement on *her* parenting led Nush to act too rashly.

"Seriously," Ellen had said. "How would you feel if someone treated Jasmine the way Tom treats you? Don't you think you should be setting a better example?"

Nush *knows* Tom would still be here now, and she wouldn't be the owner of a truly tasteless teapot, if she'd only told Ellen where to stick her holier-than-thou advice.

27

Kristy

Kristy's staying at Shay's tonight. Living every girl's dream in a poky room above a pub. Shay takes up two thirds of the double bed that takes up two thirds of the sticky carpet, and as the TV has no remote, when they're lying in bed—as they often are—they have to use a pool cue to change the channel, turn the sound up, or switch it off.

The Four Seasons it is not.

And yet she'd rather be here than within a thousand miles of the Meadowhouse.

Cooking the roast didn't go down well. Kristy knew that it wouldn't as soon as Shay suggested it. It's why she'd made herself scarce, jumping at the chance to escape in pursuit of horseradish, her thinking being: *It was his idea, let him deal with her. I'll waltz back in later when things have calmed down.*

It didn't quite work out that way.

At first, according to Shay, Ellen seemed a bit thrown but not angry. More concerned with Adam's whereabouts and Gwen's brother hassling her for having a smoke. It was after she'd come down from having a bath that the mega-mood started, apparently. Snapping, tutting, finding fault with virtually everything. Pointedly wiping down surfaces he knew for a fact he'd already cleaned.

And then serious stink-eye for Kristy as soon as she got back.

"Menopause, *definitely*," Shay says now, using the pool cue to turn the TV up, having turned down *Die Hard 2* for another round of Sunday sex. "Mood swings—classic symptom."

Kristy stops twiddling his chest hair and thumps the sexist oaf.

"No, listen," he says, laughing, rubbing his arm like she actually hurt him. "What about her freak-out in the pub the other day, just because I was talking—like, *talking*—to Orla? That wasn't exactly rational, was it? I'm telling you—*men-o-pause*." He looks at her expectantly. All he gets are contemptuous eyebrows. "Seriously, Kris, that group, 'the mums'—the pack of hyenas who reserve the big table every Thursday. That's *all* they ever talk about. I'm an expert now, I swear."

Hmm, no he isn't. And it's not *all* they talk about either. She overheard them on Thursday when she popped in to steal a kiss and a packet of peanuts. They were in full flow that day, and the topic was Ellen, not HRT.

Some were sympathetic: "Oh God, I couldn't watch when he got the breathalyser thingy out. I can't bear seeing people humiliated. It's why I can't watch those talent shows. I'm typical Pisces, too much empathy."

Some stirred the pot: "I'm surprised she passed, to be honest. Remember her at the Foxton summer fundraiser? I've said it before and I'll say it again—tequila is a young woman's game."

"It's called *peri*-menopause at Els's age, actually," Kristy says now, correcting the supposed *expert*. "And anyway, it isn't that. She's just a moody cow. Always has been. Not in front of most people. But the people who know, they *know*."

"*Still* can't believe she offered me four pounds sixty," Shay says, shaking his head for what must be the hundredth time. Kristy honestly doesn't know what his problem is. She'd have taken it. She's never been one to look a gift horse in the mouth. "Like, if it was a fiver, it'd be less insulting. Even if it was four pounds. It's the sixty pee that gets me."

Kristy grins up at him, her chin on his chest. "I'm sensing now isn't the time to tell you she gave an ex-boyfriend of mine two grand." His mouth falls open so wide she can see the metallic crown on his back molar. "Oh, not as a gift—to get rid of him. I wasn't supposed to know, but I found out years ago. I can't even be mad anymore. I just think she's an idiot, because he'd have taken a quarter of that. Less, probably. She's got no money smarts at all. No sense of proportion."

For instance, Ellen thinks Kristy dislikes Nush because she's jealous of her wealth. And of course she's jealous. Who wouldn't be? But only in an abstract kind of way—the way you're jealous of film stars and royalty, cooing over the perks but not envying them the pressure. When it comes to Nush, Kristy isn't even sure what she's supposed to be jealous of. It's all double Dutch. Businesses and property portfolios. Stocks, bonds, and pension pots. She's welcome to it.

No, what really pokes Kristy's green-eyed monster is Ellen's casual, everyday squandering. Boxes of macaroons from the pricey bakery, an express-mani here, a £50 candle there. Memory-foam pillows. Being able to pay bills on time. Buying a new pair of boots just because.

That's the life Kristy had. And is it so bad of her to want it back?

"Depends what you'd do to get it," her old flatmate, the therapist, had warned. "Because there's what we call 'normal' jealousy then there's 'harmful' jealousy."

"So, OK, this ex-boyfriend . . ." says Shay, without a hint of jealousy (Kristy's not sure how she feels about that). "What did he do to be worth two grand? Actually, I'll rephrase that: What do *I* need to do?"

"Lock me in the house. Cut all my hair off while I'm asleep."

"Oh, right. Maybe I'll pass, then."

He strokes her nose, the line of her scar. It tickles a bit, and she's not mad about the sensation, but it communicates something worth having. Something she doesn't think she's ever had.

"You must have pulled in that sort of money regularly when

you were an electrician," she says, grabbing his finger. "And you'd earn more around here. Big houses, deep pockets."

"And bored housewives." He smiles, pretending to be tempted by the prospect, then, "Nah, not for me. Not anymore. I'm all about the life change now." Here it comes, the Cornwall pipe dream. The two of them cosy in their little pub, herring gulls swooping over the vast Atlantic Ocean. Shay in the back, working on experimental menus. Kristy out the front, doing the chat, charming the regulars. "I'm serious, Kris. I've told my mate in Port Isaac I'll be there by next March latest. But I want you with me. I want to take care of you."

Kristy's hard-wired reflex is usually *I don't need taking care of*, which she knows is a bit rich as she's literally living off Ellen's grace. But it's different with Shay. He doesn't pity her, or patronise her, or make her feel like she's helpless. He makes it sound like taking care of her would be his life's greatest honour. She's not really sure what she did to deserve him. How the universe conspired to draw them here at the same time.

"I'll come," she says suddenly, surfing on post-coital pheromones and raw, reckless instinct. And then he's kissing her, and they're smiling, and saying lots of weighty things that stop short of *love*. "I mean, sod it, why not?" she laughs, dampening things down before they go there. "I did enough bar work in Ibiza." She adds a note of caution. "Though I've got a dodgy back, remember. I can pull a pint and I make a mean porn star martini, but I can't be hefting crates."

"Don't worry about that, Sicknote. You can leave the hard work to me."

Another warm, lingering kiss, finer than any suite in the Four Seasons. When he pulls away, his eyes are shining. Don't say the L word, she thinks; then, *Oh, go on.*

"So have you got any savings?"

Talk about putting a damper on things.

"It's just the place needs doing up," he goes on while Kristy tries to recalibrate. "Smithy's throwing in eight grand, and I said I'd more or less match it." She says nothing. "I mean, why do you think I'm living here? It sure as shit isn't for the vibe. It's to save cash."

"Whereas I'm staying at Ellen's because I don't want to touch my trust fund." She gives him a flat-eyed stare. "No, Shay, I *don't* have savings."

He nods. "OK, that's fine, completely fine. I just wasn't sure. I mean, you've got your eBay business."

She regrets telling him about that now. Fucking vodka.

"Yeah, which just about covers my minimum credit-card payments."

He thinks. "Can't you ask Ellen?"

"To pay off ten thousand pounds of debt?" She pretends to think. "Hmm, let me see—a financial lecture from Ellen or cut my own arm off? Anyone got a saw?"

"I meant ask her for a few thousand for the pub."

"No chance."

"Of you asking or her giving?"

She sighs. It was so much easier when they were discussing the £4.60 and Ellen's "menopause."

"Both. I've never asked her outright for money *and* the thought makes me want to spew. Anyway, they've got the renovation coming up. It's not a good time."

"Fuck 'a good time.' After everything you gave her?" He sits up, shifting her off him, shaking his head like she totally baffles him. "You forget, Kris, she owes you. I don't understand why you don't hate her. I would if I were you."

Second Bad Deed

The Money

Kristy

When me and Ellen were kids, we had a physical fight. A real humdinger. She was nine and I was seven, and it had been brewing for some time. The heart of the issue was her refusal to grant me access to our shared Teddy Ruxpin. Honestly, you'd have sworn he was the Pope and she a member of the Swiss Guard.

I was the aggressor. I don't deny that. I slapped her hard across the face, the way wronged women did on *Dallas*. And do you know what it did? It cleared the air. It was as though a fog of resentment lifted as soon as her cheek stopped smarting. For years after, we'd talk about it, laugh about it, sometimes reenact the scene for pure entertainment.

Now I often wonder, if I'd just given Ellen one hard slap the day she came back from Courchevel, would we be where are now?

Could I have found a way to forgive her?

I guess the signs were always there that Ellen was destined to have a better life than me. "I'm telling you now, that one has one notions," Mum would say when Ellen diligently did her homework and complained that all our stuff was nicked. That's not to say I was in her shadow, though. Not at all. Pushing five foot ten by sixteen, and with a bleached bob that earned me the nickname Marilyn, *I* was the popular one growing up. The striking one. The cool one. The first name on any guest list and invariably the last to leave. But while I got all the headlines, Ellen got all the affection. I might have pulled in bigger crowds on my birthday, but Ellen got better, more thoughtful gifts.

People *liked* her.

And so it was only natural that handsome, well-educated, all-round-quite-the-catch Adam liked her too.

The meeting of Adam and Ellen, or at least the version they trot out at dinner parties, has Adam knocking over Ellen's pint of Guinness and replacing it with a glass of Moët. Ellen's always been at pains to give the impression that she thought it a wankerish gesture, and that the Moët was flat anyway. And yet I knew instantly, as did anyone who'd spent more than an hour in Ellen's company, that she'd have been impressed by the gesture, *fuelled* by it, planning a repeat of it. She'd just tasted champagne, literally and metaphorically. There was no way she was going back to beer.

There was no doubt in my mind that it *was* a wankerish gesture. Cocky and presumptuous and, as I learned later, not typical of who Adam is. But I suspected he'd recognised "notions" in Ellen that he was only too happy to accommodate. And that was the extent of my thoughts at that point. Basically, good luck to her and him.

It was around six months later that I really noticed the "uplevelling" in Ellen. She'd just come back from Christmas at Adam's parents enchanted with everyone and everything.

They listened to carols on Christmas Eve; we went down to the pub for the usual lock-in.

They grazed on nuts and dark chocolate dates; we gorged on Twiglets and Quality Street.

They opened their presents in the evening ("I know, Kris! I couldn't believe it!"); we descended on ours at 6 a.m. like a pack of tigers on fresh meat.

There was no *Top of the Pops*. And the Queen's Speech—*they* actually listened to it!

So was our way wrong now? I didn't think so. The Walshes'

Christmas wasn't "right," it was just different. However, where I saw difference, Ellen saw improvement. Never mind that prior to boarding the coach to Oxford on Christmas Eve morning, she couldn't stand carols, dark chocolate, delayed gratification, or royalty.

But see, Ellen always had a roadmap. I didn't need one. I had beauty. Beauty wakes up in the morning and sees where the day takes it. It rarely has to strategise or manipulate, reassess or plan ahead.

I mean, I hadn't planned to be in Topshop the same day as a modelling scout from Glow Management. I was only there because I'd wanted to steal a crop top ever since some guy had shouted, "Look out, it's Gwen Stefani" from a passing van.

Thomasine, the scout, didn't agree about Gwen Stefani. "Sure, she's pretty," she said, looking around. "But so are half the girls in here. You've got that 'something,' Kristy. An aura. Take it from me, it's a very rare thing."

"You sure they're kosher?" Mum said later, predictably raining on my parade. "Bound to be some sort of scam. Next thing they'll want money, or they'll be getting you to take your bra off."

But it wasn't a scam, and the only time I took my bra off was for a tasteful black-and-white *Dazed* shoot, and even then no nipples. Glow were categorically, head-spinningly, life-changingly kosher, and after eighteen months of going back and forth to London for shoots, castings, and fittings, I was getting enough work to justify moving there.

For years, I lived with three equally gorgeous creatures in a flat in Camden Town, just a five-minute stroll from Glow's head office. Founded in the early nineties, Glow had chosen Camden because of its "embracement of subculture and deep personal freedom," which was another way of saying to rival agencies, *We're just a bit cooler than you.*

In line with Glow's values, I took the "freedom" bit *very* seriously, and London was everything you'd expect it to be for a nineteen-year-old with no boundaries, whose "walking for Vivienne Westwood" credentials had given her the keys to the city. Not that it was all shits and giggles. While the nights were glamorous, the days could be gruelling. Nine-hour shoots in the freezing cold, your body contorted into all manner of positions. Your dignity evaporating as someone manhandled your head and shouted, "Any way we can pin her ears back?" Yes, the money could be great, sometimes embarrassingly so. But for every job you landed, you were rejected from twenty others, and then there was the insufferably boring burden of having to constantly watch your weight.

When it came to weight regulation, each of my housemates took a different approach. Lena, the most homesick and least starstruck of us all, announced after two years, "Zis is bullshit," and high-tailed it back to Hungary. Sadie and Bex chose disordered eating (respectively laxatives and a stupidly low-calorie diet designed for recovering heart patients). I chose drugs.

And that's all cocaine was to begin with—a great appetite suppressor and confidence booster to boot.

A great career-wrecker, too, but ain't hindsight a wonderful thing.

Not long after I'd settled, Ellen and Adam also moved to London (Edgware, though, hardly Camden), and we'd meet up every few weeks and I'd regale her with my impressive life. It felt good. While she'd never admit it, I knew Ellen had always assumed I'd follow the pattern of every Best-Looking Girl on The Estate and get knocked up by the Best-Looking Boy before my twenty-first birthday, and until Thomasine approached me in Topshop, I probably wouldn't have considered that a bad fate.

But like Ellen, I'd gotten out. Out of the Highfield, out of lack (Ellen wrongly insists on calling it "poverty"), and there I was in

London, exceeding expectations and paying for her drinks. And so I never talked about the downsides: the aches, the gropes, the getting changed in public toilets. Ellen had enough stresses of her own, trying to teach Chaucer to couldn't-give-a-shit kids in some failing inner-city comprehensive. No, when we met up, she wanted glitter, I told myself. She didn't want to hear my gripes.

Or more to the point, *I* didn't want to share them. It would spoil the illusion, diffuse her envy. And for reasons I've never quite understood, and probably never will now, Ellen's envy was my motivator, my toxic rocket fuel.

I needed her to believe I was living a *deeply* fulfilled, moneyed life.

And I *did* have money for a while. It was the deep fulfilment that eluded me. While I couldn't exactly claim I wouldn't get out of bed for less than ten grand, I did get out of bed most mornings because I had a job or meeting to go to, and most models can't say the same. Ninety per cent have side hustles or second jobs. Being in the lucky ten per cent didn't make me rich, but I was comfortable. Before Ellen had Orla, it was me, not Adam, who took her to Cowley Manor for a "babymoon." After Orla came along, I single-handedly pushed up the share price of JoJo Maman Bébé clothing. And on top of all this, I supported a trail of sexy-but-unsuccessful actor-singer-dancer-model types. The only guy with money I ever dated was Alfie.

But suddenly I was twenty-six and staring down the barrel of my late twenties. Hardly old by normal standards, but fashion is fickle and it thrives on a new face. It didn't help that my look had been growing gradually more edgy. In what I now recognise to be an attempt to wrest back some control of my own body, I'd been adding more tattoos and facial piercings, testing the patience of my agency. It wouldn't matter so much these days, now that originality is a meal ticket, but back in 2010, even a left-field agency like Glow liked their models to keep a toe within the bounds of conformity.

It also didn't help that by then I was doing a couple of grams of coke most days. I thought they'd be happy I was at my thinnest. Turns out that sleeping through your alarm and missing shoots doesn't make them happy. Nor does being rude to make-up artists or being hospitalised on the eve of London Fashion Week after a minor OD.

But as bad as the situation was, doing drugs wasn't my downfall. It was selling them that sealed my fate.

That, and Ellen's greed.

The reality was that the year leading up to my "accident," I was broke and hardly working. First I blamed Glow, then the industry, then I turned my rage on consumers, who with their flat-ironed hair and skinny jeans were perpetuating this boring brand of beauty. The models who earned the most, I'd rant, were women you'd barely look twice at in the street.

But I said none of this to Ellen, or to any of my family. As far as they were concerned, the cameras were still snapping, the good times were still rolling. No need to suspend their bragging rights. I was still very much the Big Success. So if I was seeing Ellen, I'd buy a designer dress online, knowing full well I'd return it. Then I'd "borrow" a couple of hundred off Alfie to keep the mai tais coming and the *everything's great!* pretence alive.

Alfie.

I think at the time I called him my boyfriend. I still remember every terrible name he ever called me. We'd started out as friends, in the sense that he was my friendly local drug dealer. Quick, reliable, and reasonably priced for central London, and with the kind of jovial, bumbling manner that masked the fact that he is to this day the most vicious person I've ever encountered. Devoid of any conscience. Completely lacking empathy.

One day in bed, Alfie said he knew I was a "shrewd little cookie" and that he'd given it some thought and he had a business proposition for me. Basically, he had contacts in several modelling agencies who'd point "clients" in his direction. Did I fancy being his eyes and ears at Glow? I think he actually used the word "emissary." He made a point of saying he was aware my career "had stuttered slightly" (which managed to be cutting but kind of gracious) but he knew I was still "a face"—the ever-present party girl—and there was five per cent on offer for just spreading the word, working the scene.

Being a shrewder little cookie than anyone gave me credit for, I countered, arguing that he'd sell a whole lot more if the girls could buy direct from me. He resisted, then we haggled, then we had bizarre power-struggle sex for the best part of an hour (we'd done *a lot* of coke that day), before finally settling on twenty per cent and collection of the money every Friday.

Everyone, in the most soulless sense of the word, was happy.

As soon as Ellen whined the words "Zara's hen," I just knew it was going to cost me. It had already cost me, in fact. Several months before, when I'd been temporarily flush during a secret—and short-lived—dabble into escorting, I'd given Ellen £900 to cover her share of the chalet, plus £500 for the business-class flight ("I know it's only ninety minutes, Kris, but I can't be the only one in economy!").

But now, with just under a week to go, Ellen had received another email from the chief bridesmaid, "Fenners." It was an invoice, essentially, detailing the full lunacy of the itinerary. There were in-chalet spa treatments to be paid for, VIP reservations, a private chef for three nights, not to mention all the "additional bits and bobs" Fenners thought "the Z-ster totally deserves." *I think £1,200 each should cover it.*

"And that doesn't even include everyday spends," a frazzled Ellen explained over her £5 ginger and elderflower smoothie—the most expensive on the menu. "Taxis, bottles of water, hangover breakfasts. All those things add up too."

I knew where this was heading, but I wasn't going to make

it easy. Not least because, despite what my exquisite fake of a Bottega Veneta bag suggested, laying my hands on £1,200—once a couple of days' work—was now a very big ask. I might have been dealing regularly across Glow and bringing in over two grand a week for Alfie, but my twenty per cent cut went to things like rent and food and heat.

"I take it Adam's bonus wasn't brilliant," I said.

"Bonus? He dodged the last round of layoffs—that was his bonus." She twiddled her straw in silence.

After a minute, I said, "Look, can't you drop out? Say you've got a highly contagious fungal infection or something? No way the Sloane Rangers would want you within ten miles with that. I know you'd lose the chalet and the flight, but I gave you that money and I honestly don't mind."

Obviously I did mind, but if it was a toss-up between losing *that* £1,400 and having to admit I couldn't cough up *this* £1,200, I'd choose my pride every time.

She gave me a soft smile. "You're the best, you know that?" Oh hello! I might have got away with this, I thought. "But I actually *want* to go, Kris. Seriously, I know they're snobs, and I'll probably break both legs just trying to put my ski boots on, but I haven't had one night away, never mind *five*, since Orla. And I want to feel like me again, you know? Not just some tired, frumpy Pom-Bear dispenser."

I felt sorry for her, I did. And I *loved* feeling sorry for Ellen. But it meant nothing, really, if I couldn't bail her out. If I couldn't play the White Knight.

"And the thing is," she went on, "I'm getting paid next Friday, the day *after* we get to Courchevel, so I could cover it then, *just*. But Fenners insists she wants it now." I raised an eyebrow. This Fenners really did sound like a colossal pain in the hole. "Apparently there was this massive falling-out last year over someone else's hen—people paying late, or not at all, then someone called Flops ending up footing half the bill."

Poor old Flops. But with a nickname like that, my guess is she could afford it.

And if all Ellen wanted was a short-term loan, maybe I could afford it too, I thought. All that was required was some creative accounting and an ability to hold my nerve.

See, it was Saturday lunchtime. Alfie had collected last week's money the day before, and I'd made the bulk of *this* week's at a friend's birthday shindig the previous night. So I had funds. Technically they weren't my funds, but with Alfie away in Rotterdam for the week, "teaching some greedy pricks a lesson," to all intents and purposes they were for now. Which gave me the chance to save face.

I sat up straight, popping on my sanctimonious hat—a hat that rarely got an outing, but was perfect for what I was about to do.

"Look, I'll give you the twelve hundred in cash, but I *do* want it back next Friday, so you'll have to transfer it, OK?" Maybe I should have said "need it back" but "need" sounded too, well, needy. "Obviously it's no problem," I added with a cool, money-schmoney air. "But I'm starting to think about buying a place, see." Ellen's eyes lit up, thoughts of spacious Soho lofts flooding her sweetly deluded head. "So I need to start being more sensible with money. Setting more boundaries, you know?" She looked impressed.

"Next Friday," she said, blowing me a kiss across the table. "It'll be in your account before you've poured your cornflakes, promise. Have I ever told you you're *the* best sister? What would I do without you, eh?"

The White Knight rode again.

I had no reason not to trust her—she'd always been so reliable. My mistake was not realising that Regular Ellen and Holiday Ellen might be slightly different beasts. Regular Ellen remembered everything—birthdays, anniversaries, the approximate date of your last pap smear. Holiday Ellen was the same as every other nine-to-fiver—detached from real life and out of routine.

Still, I wasn't *too* anxious as I poured my cornflakes on Friday morning. The money wasn't in, but Alfie wasn't due back until the evening, and I had nothing at all planned that day except a trip to the bank once it had been transferred.

I called Ellen a bit later, but when she didn't answer, I didn't panic. Proud fool that I was, I hoped my sunny *How's it going?* message would be enough to remind her to move the cash. But then another hour passed—no reply and no money. By midday I was raging, although I tried to keep up a casual tone.

Any chance of my moolah, Els-Bels?

Just over an hour later, I was starting to lose my mind.

Hello? Money? Getting a bit fecked off now.

And an hour after that:

See this is what I mean about boundaries—people thinking they can take liberties. Call me.

Nothing. No contact, no transfer. I called the bank to ask if there was anything showing under "pending," but the only pending payments were things going out, not coming in. Running out of time, I bit the bullet and called Adam, thinking surely Ellen would have been in touch to check he hadn't burned the house down or poisoned Orla. But I got no answer however many times I tried, and I couldn't bring myself to leave the sordid truth on his voicemail.

"Hey there, Ellen owes me money, but I'm afraid you're going to have to give it to me. Because far from being the toast of London, I'm just an out-of-work loser who owes a drug dealer twelve hundred pounds."

By then, I'd stopped viewing Alfie as my boyfriend, or even a friend. But before he returned that night, I'd still considered him broadly human.

He was understanding at first, supposedly outraged at my "mugging." Two of them "pounced," I told him. It was over so quickly. Robbed of £1,200 outside Sketch while I was trying to flag a taxi. I should have known he was faking concern. As if he'd give a shit about my welfare. But I wanted to believe I could relax, that he really wanted to make me "a nice cup of tea."

I was lucky he didn't throw it in my face. Just a few drops of boiling water to the groin—hardly pleasant, but I'd survive. It was a warning, he said. Child's play compared with what he'd do if I didn't have his money within twelve hours.

I phoned Ellen constantly that night. Every time, the same message—"The mobile phone you are calling is currently unavailable." In desperation, I went over to their place to find Adam gone and the house in darkness (I later found out he'd taken Orla to visit his parents in Thames Lawley, then known for its patchy phone coverage). And every crappy friend I called—because I'd burned bridges with the good ones—"Would love to help but can't, but let's catch up for drinks soon, K?"

But still I didn't run. I assumed that for all his menace, Alfie was probably bluffing about timescales, and that in order to get his money, he'd give me a few days.

However, in contrast to Ellen, Alfie was at least true to his promise. Exactly twelve hours after he made his threat with boiling water, he threw me down the stairs, breaking my spine and one of my knees.

My nose was broken, too. It was never properly reset—I could breathe, that was all the doctors cared about. And frankly, when you have to relearn how to walk, people assume that a slightly wonky nose is the least of your concerns. I wouldn't mind if they weren't so obsessed with their own faces—their endless supposed flaws and the futile fight against ageing. But, see, at least flaws and ageing are things you have time to come to terms with. The end of my "beauty" was as quick as it was brutal. It felt like the end of me.

The next time I saw Ellen was at my bedside in the Royal Free

Hospital. She was snivelling to Mum that she'd tried everything to get an earlier flight.

I thought, *Seriously, that's what you feel bad about?* but I couldn't bring myself to speak to her. I couldn't bring myself to speak to anyone. I figured the less I said, the less chance they'd find holes in my story, which was that I was about to run down the stairs to grab my phone charger and the next thing, I was here.

See, I was happy to be the klutz, the bonehead who couldn't use a banister. I didn't care if they thought I was clumsy. Better that than a coke-dealing mess.

I don't know if the doctors believed me. I didn't care about that either. And it's not like Mum asked lots of questions. All Mum cared about was that Dad was AWOL and she'd been "left to deal with the shit, as usual," and when it was clear that Ellen wasn't going anywhere and was better at "all this" than she was (talking to doctors, taking an interest), she left and went back to Leicester. No point hanging around a boring spine unit when she could be down at her local pub, accepting drinks and garnering sympathy.

It was when we were alone that I finally rasped to Ellen, "I called you on Friday."

To me, this statement felt colossal. It was all I'd thought about. Even deep in the throes of morphine, it was still there, my North Star. To Ellen, of course, it was just a throwaway comment. Better still, a sign of recovery.

"Friday? Oh, of course, you wouldn't have heard. I really excelled myself, Kris—I dropped my phone out of a ski lift on the Thursday. Yep, the *day* we got there. First time away from Orla, and I didn't even have a phone." My finger hovered over the nurse call button—*can you please get this bitch out of here.* "Well, I mean, I had Zara's for emergencies, but I could tell she was getting pissed off with me using it." She gave a tiny shrug. Even now, I can still see the flippancy of the gesture. "So yeah, sorry. I didn't end up transferring that money until this morning.

It was bad enough Ads texting Zara's phone every five minutes. I think she'd have flipped her lid if I'd started messing around with online banking. All done now, though." She smiled sadly. "Not that money seems important anymore."

I let her rattle on a bit more, the thrust of her rattle being how lucky I was that the spinal fracture was in my lower back, not the cord. Funny, I didn't feel that lucky.

I asked her to leave. Said I needed to sleep.

For hours after, while nurses bustled in and out, I lay there ruminating over whether it was fair of me to blame her. After all, she'd had years of me indulging her and being completely casual about money. She didn't know that this time was different. Yes, I'd said I wanted the money back when she got paid the following Friday, but had I properly stressed *on* Friday? Had my desperate need to hide the truth of my situation meant I hadn't been crystal clear?

But try as I might, I just couldn't go there. I needed *someone* to aim my anger at, and I couldn't aim it at that remorseless amoeba Alfie. That would only lead to trouble. Maybe even in death.

So I chose to blame Ellen.

For her greed. Her "notions." For being more worried about Zara's flipped lid than transferring my money. For the end of my modelling career, and the start of a series of low-paid, dead-end jobs. For the five years I lost to weed as I struggled with pain management. For the scars and the disappointments.

For my car crash of an adult life.

Hers, in comparison, has been a smooth and pleasant drive. *You forget, Kris, she owes you.*

While Shay was referring to how I used to spoil her (I've never told him, or anyone, the full story), he is right about one thing—she *does* owe me.

He's wrong to think for a second, though, that it's something I forget.

28

Ellen

On Monday, I relay the saga of Max's hand to Faye, his room leader. She repeats "oh dear" on a loop, then asks if "Mrs. O-L" has been in touch. Max kicked someone on Friday—it was mentioned to Nush, but it's the first I've heard of it—and Mrs. O'Leary would like "an urgent sit-down," which sounds like a Mafioso request. Luckily, though, the Godmother is at an Early Years conference in Bristol today, so I'm granted a short reprieve before I'm officially anointed World's Worst Mum. After drop-off, I head home to meet Bert about the wiring (he doesn't turn up), then I pay a visit to Buds & Blooms on the high street to see if yesterday's flowers came from there. The answer is a resounding no. One look at the loose, drooping petals, and the owner, Lynn, declares that they were probably cut several weeks ago and placed in cold storage, which means a supermarket or a petrol station. Needles and haystacks spring to mind.

Tuesday rolls in. I get a frosty voicemail informing me that Pelham High have gone with another candidate, and I think about Zane as I go through the motions, teaching *Othello* and cleaning the house.

In a nutshell, a couple of days pass comparatively quietly and uneventfully, and the only thing that "gets worse" is Orla's attitude. I can accept her being secretive, I'm well used to her being surly. But I'm getting sick of the stealing. My Tiffany circle necklace is nowhere to be seen.

"Look, what's mine is yours," I tell her, attempting a pacifist approach instead of shouting. "Jewellery, dresses, kidneys, you name it. But you ask first, OK? You do *not* just take."

"I don't know what you're talking about," she says. "No one my age cares about Tiffany." Then, "Have you tried under the sofa cushions? It's mad what ends up there."

And now it's Wednesday morning. The bin men have come and gone and they've taken the stinking flowers with them, and I'm dithering in the vegetable section of the supermarket when suddenly my phone rings. Unknown number.

"Good morning, am I speaking to Mrs. Walsh? Ellen Walsh?"

"You are," I say, readying myself to tell a salesperson to bugger off. Politely, of course. We've all gotta make rent.

"Ah, good. Well, my name is Cathy Grantham. I'm calling from Oxfordshire County Council Children's Services."

The words are as sharp and disorientating as a blow to the back of the knee.

"Okaaay . . ."

She gets straight to the point, although her tone is cordial, almost sympathetic. "I'm following up on an anonymous call referred to us recently. Several safety concerns were raised, and while I assure you we keep a *very* open mind at these early stages, you'll understand that we have to take any allegations regarding the welfare of a child seriously."

"What allegations?" I say, quietly hysterical. "What child, for that matter?"

"Specifically your son, Max." She pauses as an announcement comes over the loudspeaker. A Halloween promotion. *Savings to make you scream!* "Listen, it sounds like you're out somewhere at the moment, Mrs. Walsh."

"I'm in the supermarket."

Buying green lettuce, red peppers, black olives, and bananas, so I can make a Ninja Turtle salad that there's a slim chance Max might eat.

"OK, well I think it might be better for me to fill you in further when you're somewhere a bit quieter."

"Give me two minutes, I'm just walking to the car."

Things are about to get worse.

29

Jason

Jason looked her up on the PNC once, not too long before he came here. He knew that "improper use of the Police National Computer" was a violation that could result in instant dismissal, but he had to know what he was dealing with, so he decided it was worth the risk.

He was shocked by the results. The *lack* of them, basically. He couldn't believe that over the years she hadn't been up to her old tricks.

But then the worst things people do don't always end up on the police computer.

Her problem, he's always thought, is that she always got what she wanted. Although now that he thinks of it, the same is true of most of the women in his life. Their mum was a total leech, so is it any wonder Gwen turned out needy? And then there's Emma, who "doesn't need his baggage" but *does* need him pretty quick when the fence blows down or the toilet tank needs replacing. *Then* she isn't quite so keen for him to "learn to let things go" and "move on."

But Ellen Walsh. If *ever* a woman got exactly what she wanted, it's her. His bet is that she was overindulged as a child. Everyone saying they loved her. No one saying "no."

He watched her the other day from the side of the station, trying to pull into what wasn't a particularly tight space outside the florist. Multiple attempts, in and out. Why do people buy big cars when they can't handle them? Some guy walking past shouted that she'd be better off reverse-parking. Jason assumed she'd give him a mouthful, but instead she threw him the keys and said, "Be my guest."

The fool did it, as well.

Is it any wonder she's how she is?

PC Lizzy Allen, on her way back from the chocolate run, spotted him watching Ellen. She said she knew *exactly* what he was thinking and that it was obvious he was "anti-women."

"Don't have to be bitter towards all of us, Jase, just because your wife gave you the elbow. I mean, 'women can't park'— thought you'd be a bit more enlightened than that, coming from mighty cosmopolitan London an' all."

Jason isn't anti-women, but Lizzy Allen sure is anti-London.

She's also wrong about his bitterness. He's doesn't feel bitter towards *all* women. He doesn't feel bitter towards her, for example, even though she's walking towards him right now wearing that self-satisfied side-smirk that suggests she's about to land him with some tiresome, small-fry shit.

"You free?" she asks, and he can hardly say he isn't. Not when he's lazing back in his chair, scraping up his last bit of porridge. "There's a woman downstairs screaming blue murder about her son. I can't get much sense out of her. She doesn't seem to like me. She wants to talk to 'someone with a brain.' I said you'd have to do." She waits for him to laugh. He never does, but he admires her persistence. "Anyway, she says he's gone missing. And she wants answers."

Women and their *wants*.

Some of them scream them.

Others go after them silently, stealthily.

Those are the ones you have to watch out for.

30

Ellen

While shock tends to freeze you, righteous fury propels you forward, which means I'm striding towards Stepping Stones' entrance before I've really considered if it's a good idea. The drive over here was a blur. The radio was on, but I didn't hear it. My last clear memory is of sitting outside Tesco, staring at the distant glowing arches of a McDonald's, while someone I've never met explained that someone else (whose name they couldn't give me) has concerns about my parenting. Thinks I'm a danger to Max. His hand was the last straw.

That's my last *clear* memory. I do have a fuzzier one of phoning Stepping Stones in a blinkered rage. Of telling Amma at reception that I'd be there in fifteen minutes, and that Mrs. O'Leary was in luck because I fancied an "urgent sit-down" myself.

Now, sitting straight-backed outside her office, I still can't compute it. Someone thinks I'm a *danger*? To *Max*? My bonus baby. The child I birthed for twenty-seven hours, then fed and bathed and loved. It's a loony accusation. Beyond contempt. Beyond conceivable. I'd have been less shocked if I'd been accused of armed robbery or ritually sacrificing sheep.

Although could the call have been a hoax, someone impersonating a social worker? The same person who's been harassing me. My inner voice says: *Ellen. Go. To. The. Police.*

I drown out the voice by googling Cathy Grantham, who according to her extensive LinkedIn profile is unfortunately legit. Her hair is a brown shapeless splat that looks like it fell from the sky and landed awkwardly on her skull, but she's worked across four different councils in a career spanning thirty years. She also has a master's in applied social care. Christ, she's even got an MBE.

So the allegations levelled against me aren't Cathy Grantham's first rodeo. I think that makes me feel worse, not better. At least it'd be a sign that they weren't taking it *too* seriously if the complaint had been palmed off on some recently graduated kid.

"Mrs. Walsh, would you like to follow me?" If I had to guess, I'd say this *is* Max's room leader's first rodeo. Faye seems uneasy as she leads me down the corridor, as though she only signed up for forest trails and finger-painting, not managing hostility. "We thought Little Ducklings might be a better room for our chat," she explains. "It'll be outside time soon and the children can see directly into Mrs. O'Leary's office from the playground. We wouldn't want Max or Kian to be confused if they spotted you."

Mrs. O'Leary stands as I walk in. Not that her standing makes much difference. As Dad used to say about Gran, "It'd be easier to jump over her than go round her." At five foot seven, I feel like King Kong.

I don't bother beating around the bush. "I need to know if it was you who reported me to Children's Services."

"No, I did not." Her answer is firm but serene; she'd make a perfect Crown witness. She gestures for me to take a seat on one of the duck-patterned chairs. "But perhaps you'd like to tell us what's happened?"

"Did you?" I ask Faye, who's looking deathly, *guiltily* pale. In her defence, she is pregnant. Kian's already suggested that the baby should be called Chickaletta, after the pet chicken in *PAW Patrol*. "Because I explained about Max's hand. It's literally nothing. If anything, I probably made it look worse by dressing it with a bandage. But where it was on his hand, you know, I didn't think a band-aid would stay put . . ." I ask the question again. "Well, did you?"

She glances at her boss for moral support, then takes a deep breath. "No, Mrs. Walsh, I didn't. I did raise some concerns with Mrs. O'Leary, but that was all."

"Concerns about *what*?"

If she could climb out of the window, she would. "Just a few things I'd overheard at the gate."

"Like *what*?"

I'm not sure why I'm enunciating my T's. Do I think precise elocution makes me sound like a better parent?

She shifts awkwardly. "Well, the breathalyser, of course."

"The breathalyser *I passed*."

"Well, yes. But someone had also seen some . . . unfortunate photos on Facebook." I open my mouth to explain. "And then there's been some general chatter about, well, *incidents* in the supermarket."

"And do these chatterers have names, because I—"

Mrs. O'Leary interjects. "We can't divulge that. I'm sure you understand. Several people, though."

"Saying *what*?"

I mean, "incidents." What's an "incident." You tell a three-year-old child they can't eat the toothpaste or push the trolley, then you're going to have an "incident."

Faye flushes. "Well, that you've been seen . . . um . . . shouting at them—Max, specifically—on several occasions."

In a move that *really* doesn't help, I laugh. I can't help it.

"How far gone are you now, Faye? Four months, right?"

She smiles nervously, says, "Nineteen weeks."

"Well, when I was nineteen weeks with my eldest, I thought I'd never shout at my kids in the supermarket either. Never shout at them at all, actually. Oh yeah, I was going to *reason* with them. Tell them how their behaviour made mummy *feel*. All that perfectly sensible, idealistic stuff. But life isn't like that. Patience isn't like that." Mrs. O'Leary issues a warning cough, but I'm damned if I'm done yet. "Do you know what else I thought? That I'd never swear in front of them, or let them watch too much TV, or feed them anything not organic. Oh, and they were going to have handmade wooden toys, too. No cheap, ocean-destroying bits of plastic. Sound familiar?" I know I'm being unbearably patronising, but a) she started it, and b) *someone* has claimed I could be a danger to my child, and if I can't rain hell on them, then I'm going to have to take another scalp. "Well, trust me, Faye, you'll end up like most of us—shoving the kids in front of the telly with a bowl of chicken nuggets and a Trans-former, because Mummy has had her fill and she just needs ten minutes of bloody peace."

I feel like taking a bow. Or a Valium.

Mrs. O'Leary, mildly mortified, ignores my outburst. "Also, I have to say, Mrs. Walsh, the 'Satan' comment you made last week rather concerned me." *Do not roll your eyes, Ellen. Do not roll your eyes.* "Max's behaviour *can* be challenging, and—"

"Look, I'm sorry, I shouldn't have said that. But it was just a bad joke. And it's not like he heard or that he'd have even understood if he did."

Her expression is tender, almost motherly. It jabs me in the solar plexus: the semi-grief of only ever knowing a mother's baseline love, never her care.

"My concern isn't just for Max, Mrs. Walsh. It's for you. How you're feeling."

"Me?" I say, not following. "I'm fine."

"Really?" Her smile seems to say, *we're on the same side here*, but it sure doesn't feel like it. "Because that slightly contradicts something a friend of yours said . . ."

31

Gwen

"I reckon she's having an affair, you know. She's shady, Gwen, I keep telling you."

Orla *does* keep telling Gwen this, and Gwen *does* keep feeling awkward. Sometimes she'll say, "Enough!" or something like "That's probably not fair, Orla," but right now, she's not sure whether to defend Ellen or to encourage a clearly het-up Orla to talk.

See, when Gwen told Ellen the other day that she and Orla often chat when she comes to babysit, what she didn't mention was Orla's habit of dropping in at other times, principally to trash her mum. It could be anything. Sometimes it's petty, and admittedly quite funny—ten-minute rants about Ellen thinking she invented Hot Pilates, or how she's at least a decade too old to wear cuffed joggers with stiletto heels. Mostly, though, it's the twins, specifically Ellen's "blatant" favouritism toward them. Lately, it's been the Meadowhouse, and how all the money they're spending should be spent on Orla, obviously.

Orla's drop-ins are kind of Gwen's fault, although to be clear, what happened wasn't intentional. As with a lot of things in life, Gwen blames being *slightly* drunk.

It was a few months ago, early summer, when after sharing a jug of Pimm's with an ex-colleague, Gwen came home to relieve Orla of her babysitting duties and made a comment about Ellen as Orla was about to leave. It wasn't even *that* bitchy, more of an eye-roll at Ellen's recent Facebook post: *Don't scrub up too bad for an old bird!* alongside a photo of herself in a slip dress, looking obviously, *knowingly* hot.

Gwen can't stand a blatant humblebrag, so what she was thinking *was* bitchy. But to Orla, she merely said, "She looks incredible, but she should ditch the 'little ol' me' routine."

Really, it was a compliment.

But that was it.

That was the moment Orla realised Gwen sometimes found Ellen irritating. And then she began to see her as an ally, occasionally popping in to test boundaries, dropping casual little snide-bombs designed to tempt Gwen into slagging Ellen again.

"She wants a wine fridge now. Course, it's only because Nush's got one."

Or:

"Some people can carry off sequin jackets. Mum looks like a magician."

Actually Gwen thought the jacket was great. In fact she told Orla she'd love to borrow it. She thought that Ellen had styled it perfectly, with a plain white tee and mom jeans.

This affair thing, though. She's not sure how she should play it. And if she's honest, she's not in the mood for Orla.

Bella, on the other hand, is ecstatic that Orla's here.

"La-la, can we play hair? Or do puzzle?"

She's hitting Orla with the lid of a jigsaw puzzle. It amazes Gwen how Orla sits there and takes it. If it was her one of her brothers, there'd be murder. In fact, she'd probably hit them back and twice as hard.

Gwen gives Bella her iPad. "No, Belles, La-la is talking to Mummy. Watch YouTube for a bit, then she'll play." She turns her focus back to Orla. "Look, I'm a bloodhound when it comes to sniffing out affairs, hon. Ex-boyfriends, ex-bosses, other people's partners, you name it. So trust my expertise here—your mum is *definitely* not having an affair."

She doesn't *know* that, of course, but all things considered, she doubts it. For a start, Ellen's always been so vocal in her complete loathing of Nush's Tom.

But then again, most people are fucking hypocrites. Ellen Walsh is no exception.

"You sure about that?" Orla says, reaching for the tiny splash of wine she browbeat Gwen into giving her. "Why? Because her shit doesn't stink? Because she not the type? She's *exactly* the type. *And* she keeps going AWOL. Dumping the boys on you so she can 'do errands'—she was *so* cagey when I asked her about that, too. Then that thing in the park on Sunday—running off to deliver a textbook. Yeah, *as if*." She takes a pinched sip of wine. It's Chardonnay. She doesn't like it. But Gwen knows there's no way she'll admit it, because she wants to be a big girl, and big girls drink wine. "I caught a glimpse of that message. Couldn't read what it said, but it was short, like *really* short." She prods the arm of the sofa, making a point. "Now, if *you* were asking your tutor to go out of their way on a Sunday afternoon to bring you a textbook, you'd write more than a few words, wouldn't you? It'd be long-winded, kind of grovelling."

That's perceptive, to be fair. Maybe Orla's not as self-absorbed as everyone thinks.

"Who with, then?" says Gwen, deciding to humour her. "I mean, where would she meet this hypothetical guy? Are we talking Tinder?"

Orla scoffs. "Get real. She can barely use Facebook. And there *are* men in Thames Lawley, you know. Not many fit ones, granted, but then she's not all that either." She laughs, but Gwen doesn't. There's indulging Orla and there's encouraging her. And anyway, it isn't true. With her great curls, great tits, and that Cupid's bow mouth, Ellen's undeniably attractive. "I don't know, but there's been builders and plumbers, loads of guys coming and going, giving quotes. Maybe she's shagging one of them. Or one of her students' dads. Could be anyone."

"And when would she find the time?"

"Fridays."

Gwen laughs. "Whoa, that's very precise."

Bella toddles over with the iPad, demands, "Mumma, my want *Mickey Mouse Clubhouse.*"

The theme tune is worse than a lobotomy, but at least it'll keep her quiet.

And Gwen wants quiet.

This is getting interesting.

"Answer me this, then," Orla says. "She's always saying we're broke—'cos of the renovation, *obviously*—but she's got the boys in nursery for a full day on Friday. Why?"

"Admin? Appointments? Trust me, everything's easier when you don't have little kids hanging off you."

"Yep, especially shagging someone's brains out." Orla swishes her wine around the glass—an elegant way of avoiding drinking it. "I've thought about bunking off school. Watching her, seeing if she leaves the house, following her if she does. Not sure *how* I'd follow her, to be fair."

Gwen shakes her head. "It's a bad path to go down. The minute you start watching someone, checking their phone, reading their diary, you'll see *something* you don't want to see, guaranteed." She gives Orla a kind smile. "Look, hon, I know things haven't been great between you two for a while—and for the record, I'm aware she's not perfect. She makes shit decisions, same as everyone. But I really, *really* don't think she's having an affair. So go easy, yeah? She's got a lot on."

Did she pitch that about right? It's such a fine line to tread. Because while it's good that Orla opens up to her, and she doesn't want to ruin that by being *too* pro-Ellen, she also doesn't trust Orla as far as she could throw her. Anything she says could well get back.

"I assume by 'a lot on,' you mean the renovation?"

"Well, not just that, but yeah. It's a big job. And it's not long until they start."

Orla sits forward, suddenly animated. *Irritated.* "Fucksake, she's not knocking down the walls herself! She's choosing tiles and ordering furniture."

"But it's important to her, Orla. Houses get under people's skin. They're part of your identity. And your mum wants to get it right. You're lucky she wants that for you, the perfect family home." Gwen grins, she can't stop herself. "Well, the perfect astronaut's home. It's all a bit NASA HQ for me."

This seems to rile Orla more, which wasn't Gwen's intention.

"See, she didn't consult anyone about that either. Well, maybe Dad, but like *he'd* have an opinion on interiors. But *I* live there too. Maybe I like all the chintzy crap—obviously I don't, but that's not the point. Shouldn't I get a say in what it looks like? No, of course not. Because it's *her* perfect home, not mine or anyone else's. Although I bet she ends up letting the boys draw fucking dinosaurs all over the walls."

"Fucking dinosaurs," says Bella, although her eyes don't leave the iPad.

"Hey—naughty word," Gwen tells her sternly; then, looking at Orla, "You need to be careful, she's like a parrot."

Bella looks up. "Will gumpy goblins get me, Mumma?"

Gwen says no, then pulls a face at Orla that says, *Your guess is as good as mine.*

Orla smiles, sets her wine glass on the table. "Anyway, where were we, before that sweary toddler interlude?"

Where we always bloody are, Gwen thinks. Ellen's supposed rejection of Orla and Orla's belief that she's *so* hard done by.

And as always, Gwen's stuck between wanting to shake

Orla senseless because she has no clue about real hardship, and wanting to cut her a bit of slack because she remembers what it's like to be sixteen.

And she knows—as does Jason—how it feels to be rejected by a parent.

The hole it leaves.

The damage it can do.

32

Adam

Ellen was in such a state when she called, Adam thought he'd heard her wrong at first. She was making so little sense that he had to keep repeating things back. "Cathy *Who* is visiting?" "Nush said *what*?" "Children's Services?" In fact, it wasn't until she bawled, "For Christ's sake, Ads—*Social Services*!" that he properly understood the full weight of the road ahead.

Social Services. For Christ's sake indeed.

And now, here. *Her.* A lime and soda for the lady. A pint of Carlsberg for him.

"Listen, you've got this all wrong. It wasn't me. I didn't report her." Nush's hand on his arm makes him shiver, and not in the good way. "Think about what you're saying. Remember, Walshy, this is *me*."

But who exactly is *me*? Adam wonders now. Is she the Nush who sat beside him in Latin and always shared her Fruit Pastilles? Or is she the Nush who blithely went shoe shopping with his wife the morning after she'd become reacquainted with his tongue?

It happened—the kiss—in this exact same pub, the Fox & Angel, a safe ten miles from Thames Lawley. It was this exact same booth, in fact. He thinks it was the same barman. He should never have agreed to meet here. After the events of today, it feels hugely inappropriate. Preferable to meeting at her house, though, he supposes. He can just imagine the scene if Ellen turned up and he was there.

He should have gone straight home after work, but he *had* to see her. Had to ask her. He desperately needed to know if this was all his stupid fault. Of course, he knows things will never be the same after this—you can't essentially accuse someone of treason, then invite them to your next barbecue. But things changed anyway the second their lips touched, and there's undoubtedly been a shift in her friendship with Ellen. He's not sure if Ellen's noticed, but he certainly has. The subtle slights, the snips. The fact she clearly doesn't seem as supportive of Ellen as she once was.

"I just can't get my head around any of this, around *you*," he says, shoving her hand off his arm. "I mean, that stunt on Saturday was cruel enough, but I never *ever* thought you'd stoop to this."

"To what? I told you, *I* didn't report her." So she keeps insisting, but she doesn't seem nearly outraged enough for Adam's liking. Defensive—yes. Offended by the accusation—not particularly. That said, she did once tell him, two thirds into a bottle of Merlot, that all her feelings seemed to have dulled since Tom left. Maybe that explains the glibness. "And what do you mean? What 'stunt' on Saturday?"

"Announcing in front of everyone that she didn't get the Pelham job. It's not like you couldn't have grabbed her beforehand—you came over early enough."

A wisp of a smile. "Desperate to see you, is that what you thought?"

Was that scorn or flirtation? And *is* that what he thought? What he hoped?

Probably, if he's honest. Although oddly enough, it's not the thrill of the secrecy or the unspoken possibility of extramarital sex that he most misses about their *thing*. It's having a listener on tap, and an attractive one at that. One largely free of kids and routine and therefore always there for him at a moment's whim.

God, their affair-that-wasn't-an-affair was so damn convenient.

But he needs to stop this train of thought. That was all put to bed—or actually *not* put to bed—months ago. This is now. And *now* is a terrified wife and a visit from Social Services.

"Look, I want to believe you," he says. "I really do. But Ellen seems sure it wasn't the nursery, and it's all a bit coincidental, don't you think? You tell Mrs. O'Leary that Ellen's 'at the end of her rope' with Max. Next thing, a social worker's calling."

She sighs, but again it's lacking enough bite to convince him.

"For heaven's sake, it was a turn of phrase. I didn't *mean* anything by it. Max had kicked another child and I knew Ellen would be upset, that's all. If what I said created an issue, then I'm sorry." She takes a pointed sip of her drink, eyes scouring his. "But Ellen hardly helps herself. Calling Max 'Satan.' Always being late to pickup . . ."

"Always! She's been two minutes late, twice."

Adam isn't a shouter. He wasn't raised that way. The Walsh siblings were taught from a very young age that the worst thing you can do in life is "cause a scene." But God, how he'd love to cause one right now. He'd love to scream in Nush's face. Get thrown out of the pub. Maybe even written up for breach of the peace.

But because he's Adam, he goes the opposite way.

"Look, I know you were hurt," he says softly, swirling the dregs of his Carlsberg. "When I didn't . . . well, when *we* didn't, you know. But taking it out on Ellen . . ."

She reaches for his arm again. Her firm grip suggests she's not prepared to be shoved off this time. "Seriously, Adam—*Social Services*. Do you honestly think I'd do that to *you*?"

And there's the rub.

To Ellen, who knows? To him? He doesn't think so.

"So who was it then?" he asks, desperate.

Nush shrugs, smooths her hair. "It could have been anyone. One of the nursery mums? Maybe the mum of the child Max kicked."

"Yeah, but it's got to be linked to the other stuff—the breathalyser, the letter, that puerile crap on Facebook." He's wondered about the tyre, too, but Ellen insists it was an accident. "That's *some* vendetta, Nush. And it just doesn't make sense. Whatever's gone on between us, you know she's a good person."

"Do I?"

Winded, Adam looks at her, *really* looks at her, for a few seconds. There was no petulance in her voice. He can't see it on her face either. That "Do I?" was genuine.

Catching the barman's eye, Nush points at Adam's empty glass—the universal sign for *another*.

"I can't," he says. "I've got to get home. And I've already had one."

"Drink half, then. You're going to need it." She sits back, arms folded, her expression fighting a battle between resolve and regret. "There's something I need to tell you about why Ellen didn't get the Pelham job."

33

Ellen

Adam isn't home. His phone is off. My mood is filthy. He sometimes plays squash on a Wednesday, but *surely* he wouldn't today? Lord knows I admire a bit of stoicism in the face of adversity, but I'd have thought the welfare of our kids was more important than whacking a rubber ball against a wall.

But hey, at least I have Kristy, who, having not been seen since Sunday, ambled in half an hour ago and is now warming my cockles with her sage, sisterly advice.

"Straight up, I would lay that bitch out, Els."

And I might have done too if Nush had been home when I'd driven over to her place. I fully planned to go back until Adam talked me out of it. "Wait till I get home, then we'll decide."

Well here I am, Adam. Still waiting.

Where is he?

Kristy's at the oven, stirring soup. "Look, I know you'll say hindsight is twenty/twenty, but she's always been weird with you, if you ask me." She dips a finger in the soup. It burns. She flinches. "I mean, it's *really* subtle, but it's there. Doesn't surprise me that she's dropped you in the shit."

"I don't know for sure that she did."

"Not with Social Services, no. But she definitely did at nursery. That little dig to the head honcho—she knew what she was doing."

"I don't know if claiming I'm at the end of my rope is what

I'd call a 'little dig,' Kris." I flop down at the breakfast table. "I just don't get it. What did I ever do to her except be a good friend?" Each time, it wounds. All the hours I spent counselling her, cajoling her, trying to convince her she was worth more than him. "I think since Tom left—"

Kristy pounces. "And *that*—that drives me nuts. So her marriage broke down. Boo-fucking-hoo. Get over it. She's *obsessed*." She brings the soup over to the table, starts eating it directly from the pot. "And anyway, unless I've picked the story up wrong—and I doubt it, I've heard it, like, five million times—*she* kicked him out. She was cheated on, sure. But she wasn't 'left.'"

I've often thought this myself, but I followed Nush's lead when it came to semantics. However she needed to frame it, that was good with me.

Except she hasn't got over it, and I can't see anything ever being good between us again.

"You know, she was supposed to tell me to call Mrs. O'Leary— Max was up to his old tricks again last Friday," I say. Kristy mimes a bite. "No, kicking," I tell her. "But I didn't even realise until I dropped them off on Monday and Faye collared me."

"And what did Nush say?"

I shrug. "I called her Monday afternoon—she said it slipped her mind. She didn't even apologise. Not that she had to; she was doing me a big favour picking them up. But you *would*, wouldn't you? Most people would."

Kristy makes a gesture with the pan and spoon: *I rest my case.*

"Yeah, well, don't look so smug," I say. "It won't look great to the social worker, will it? I can hardly say, 'Yep, that's true. I didn't call the nursery about my aggressive child, but it was my friend's fault. Blame her.' It makes me look irresponsible. Unengaged. And then there's his hand . . ."

"Oh, give it a rest, Els." She throws the spoon down, losing interest, as though she can only stomach being on my side for so long. "How 'engaged' were Mum and Dad? How many parents' evenings did they go to? One. And the less said about that, the better. And as for Maximoo's hand—do you remember the time Mikey jumped out of the window because he thought his Superman pyjamas would make him fly? I think if Mum and Dad survived *that* Social Services visit, you'll survive this one. You're just creating a big fucking drama out of nothing, as usual."

An hour later, and I'm arguably creating another "big fucking drama" by insisting to Gwen that even though Nush is a back-stabber, maybe she did get something right.

Maybe the Meadowhouse *is* cursed.

Maybe it *does* have "bad energy."

"OK, why?" Gwen asks levelly, blending compassion with a *get-a-grip* tone. "Because the Merricks got beaten up, that other couple divorced, and your week's been a stinker? Obviously none of that's nice, but I wouldn't go planning an exorcism. Violence happens, marriages break up . . ."

"People get reported to Social Services."

"Every day of the week. So relax, hon, it'll all be fine."

I knew as soon as I mentioned Social Services that Gwen would be across the village green like a freight train. What I hadn't realised was how reassuring and knowledgeable she'd prove to be. I mean, I'm aware she had a rough childhood—"crap parents, crap children's home, then the crappiest of crap foster care"—but I didn't know she was such an expert, so clued up on how to handle things. In the glaring absence of a supportive husband, she's just what I need.

"So tell me again—what are the allegations *exactly*?" she says. "And remember, that's all they are to Social Services at the moment—allegations, not facts."

Cathy Grantham said the same, but it sounded rehearsed. *Your call is important to us.* Gwen's words scorch with conviction, and for the first time in hours, I feel *slight* relief.

"Well, it's mainly Max's hand—that the house isn't a safe

environment. But I'm also apparently 'never without a glass of wine,' and I'm always screaming at him, and he never looks happy."

"Oh, hon."

Her eyes fill. She gets it. Of all the accusations, my little boy's supposed misery is the lowest blow of all.

"And who knows about Max's hand?" she asks, thankfully getting back to business quickly. It's almost 7:30, and I'm all cried out for one day.

"God, who doesn't? All of us, obviously. Nursery—a lot of the parents, too, because I was explaining to Faye at drop-off in front of everyone. And then we went to the park on Sunday, and you guys went for ice cream." Gwen cocks her head, presumably trying to recall who they saw. "I think I mentioned it to Lynn in the florist's. Oh yeah, and I took them to Crazy Crocs on Monday after nursery." I sigh. "I mean, *everyone* knows, G. It's not like I'm hiding anything."

"OK." She thinks for a minute. "Look, it's none of my business, and I didn't want to bring it up again, because, well, you hadn't . . . but that Facebook thing. The photos of you drinking and the bitchy hashtags. Did you screenshot any of it?"

I frown. "No." I just wanted it gone. Expunged from the universe. "Why?"

"Because Social Services get malicious calls *all* the time, and if you can prove that someone has it in for you, they'll still have to investigate, but they'll take it into account, definitely. It happened to me with my ex, Marc—Bella's dad. He made a complaint about me when Bella was a baby."

"You're joking? What an absolute shitstain."

She shrugs. "I was trying to get him to up his child support, and it all turned a bit nasty. Anyway, they could see it for what it was. Like they will with this, I promise."

"Well, there's the letter. That's proof," I tell her. She looks at me blankly. "You know, the nasty letter Adam mentioned at lunch. The thing I didn't want to talk about." I think about showing it to her now, but I'm reluctant to breathe new life into it. "It came last week, postmarked High Wycombe. Someone wants to 'teach me a lesson,' apparently."

I expect her first question to be *And why didn't you tell me?* but she stays rooted in practical mode. "So you've still got it then, this letter?" I give a thumbs-up. "Well, that's good. That's great. Don't suppose you made a police report, too? That would be gold."

"Oh Christ, don't tell Adam that. He's been on my case about the police." I glance at the oven clock. "Although I'm going to be on *his* bloody case if he isn't home soon."

"Hey, you guys need to be pulling together right now, not fighting, OK?"

"I know, I know." I let out a cathartic "*Gaaaaaaah*" and rub both sides of my face. "Seriously, who would do this, G?"

She gives it some thought, then, "I don't know, Els. I honestly don't. What I do know is that for now, you need to pause thinking about who it is and start focusing on what's happening. The social worker's coming Friday, right?" I nod. "OK, well just focus on Friday. Then after that, we smoke this fucker out."

I laugh. It feels good and wrong in equal measure.

"Speaking of." I mime a smoke. "Are you carrying? The boys should be out for the count by now."

"Always." She waggles a packet of Marlboro Menthols.

"Hold on. Lemme grab the keys."

Turns out I don't need them. As Gwen waits for me to finish my customary where's-the-key? kitchen waltz, she leans heavily on the handle and the back door falls open. Her stumble would be comical if it wasn't for the fact that I could have sworn I locked it earlier. And Orla's been over at Esme's for hours, and Kristy and Gwen both came in through the front door.

Gwen starts talking again before I have much time to process it.

"I'm assuming you've given her permission to speak to nursery and your GP?" I nod as she lights my cigarette. "And Soccertots?"

"Soccertots too?" I whine through a plume of smoke. "I might as well take out an ad in *The Echo* at this rate."

"She probably won't contact them—Children's Services are massively overworked as it is. But the more open you are, the better. 'Amenable' is the name of the game here." Something else occurs to her, something I'm not going to be too *amenable* to, based on her expression. "You know she'll want to speak to Orla, too—have you told *her* what's happening?"

I have, and I've never been more grateful for her indifference. I was dreading questions, or worse, opinions. But a few seconds pondering and one "whoa" was about it.

"Yeah, she knows." I take a short drag of my cigarette, which I didn't really want. I just liked the idea of it. "She's probably hoping they'll take her away instead of Max."

"They're not taking Max anywhere, Els." Gwen frowns, choosing her words carefully. "Look, I was classed as an at-risk kid for my most of my childhood—get the violins out—and I had more social workers than you've had leg waxes, and well . . . I suppose what I'm trying to say is, you need to be careful with social workers, obviously, but don't demonise them, OK? Remember Cathy Whatsit is just doing her job. And her job is to help if you do have any parenting issues . . ." She shoots a hand up, lightning quick. "And *I* know you don't, but I'm just making the point that her intentions aren't bad, so don't see her as the enemy. Work with her and you'll be fine. You'll sail through, trust me."

I could kiss her. I *have* kissed her once, in a dream that left me nine parts mortified, one part horny. Adam's ratio was the exact reverse.

Speaking of Adam, he's back.

As if out of nowhere, he's standing in the centre of the kitchen. I open the back door and mumble a lukewarm "hi" (Gwen's right, we need harmony).

But he's looking far from harmonious. He looks like a six-foot-two throbbing artery.

"Gwen, I'm sorry to be rude," he says. "But can you leave, please. Like, now."

34

Ellen

I'm still reeling from the fact that Adam has been talking to Nush without me when he drops the main bombshell.

"*Theft?*" The word is as welcome in my kitchen as dogshit on a shoe. "What do you mean, theft?"

Adam's voice is flat. "Someone emailed Pelham anonymously— a 'concerned parent.' They said they'd heard you were interviewing there and felt duty-bound to report that they'd suspected you of theft when you were tutoring their child. They said they'd had money and valuables go missing, and it was always after you'd been in the house."

I mentally file through my clients, past and present, but of course there's no "concerned parent." Miniature bottles of hotel shampoo aside, I've never stolen a thing in my life.

"So that's it? I'm a thief because of one anonymous, unsubstantiated email? Well, fuck them."

Shame *soaks* me and instantly I feel small yet incredibly heavy, my body burdened by a bag of emotions I haven't carried in over twenty years. In the blink of an eye, I'm Ellen Hennessey again. The one who thinks she's a cut above, even though her family is a pack of thieves.

"They had a second-choice candidate, Els. And *that* candidate hadn't been breathalysed or accused of stealing." He splays his hands wide—*what can I do?*

I start pacing, burning off the shame. "And why am I hearing this from you? Why didn't Nush tell me?"

"She only found out today, and after I said I wanted to meet to talk about . . . well, all this . . ." He shrugs. "I guess she thought it'd be easier to break it to me. She'd have felt awkward telling you."

I stand stock still.

"Oh. My. God. She *actually* believes it, doesn't she? What does she think? It's in the genes or something?"

Nush has always *loved* being regaled with dispatches from my dysfunctional childhood, but while I knew she was privately appalled, I never thought she'd use it against me.

"Of course she doesn't believe it," Adam says. "Any more than I believe she called Social Services." He goes over to the sink and fills a glass with water, turning his back to me. "And, look, what she said to Mrs. O'Leary was clumsy, but it was just a turn of phrase, OK."

There's a finality to his *OK* that he can stick up his arse.

"A 'turn of phrase' that made Mrs. O-L concerned about Max's welfare—and I've had to agree to let this social worker woman speak to Mrs. O-L, so actually, no, Adam, it's very *not* OK."

He turns around, eyes flinty. "Do you know what I want to know?" *Not really.* "What did you do to upset someone this badly?"

I don't answer, because I can't. I honestly don't know. I know I'm far from perfect. I've made some questionable decisions in my life, and some truly terrible ones this year. But they don't explain *this*. This attack on my name, my job, my family. My bloody *tyre*.

"Adam, I'm scared," I say. "This is some serious shit now. I mean, Social Services, accusations of theft . . . Someone wants to hurt us. *Properly* hurt us.

"*You*, Els, not me."

Right in the jugular. It's so wildly un-Adam, I actually gasp.

He's on me in seconds, all desperate hugs and hair-nuzzles. "Didn't mean it. Shouldn't have said it. I'm an idiot. I'm sorry."

I almost tell him what to do with his *sorry*, but Gwen's right. We shouldn't be fighting. Cathy Grantham arrives in less than thirty-six hours, and I can't have Adam acting all mopey and chastised.

"It's fine," I say. "I get it. This is rough on you too. Let's just focus on Friday, hey?" I wriggle out of his arms and walk over to the kitchen drawer. "Listen, Gwen said the letter actually works in our favour. It's proof that the call could have been malicious."

I'd shoved the letter in the junk drawer. The Drawer of No Specific Purpose. Home to everything from crumpled euros to handheld face-fans, from long-expired driving licences to long-defunct pens. I'll tip the entire contents in the bin when they come to rip the kitchen out.

The letter is gone.

"What the hell . . .?" I rummage deeper with both hands, checking inside leaflets and takeaway menus. "Ads, it isn't here."

"You must have moved it, then."

"I haven't touched it. I couldn't bring myself to. I brought it to show Nush on Thursday evening, then when I came back, I shoved it in here." A sudden memory brings faint hope. "Saturday lunch—you went to get it . . ."

"And you pulled me back before I got the chance." He hip-barges me out of the way. "Here, let me—you're notoriously bad at looking for things."

I'm not, but I want to be. I want Adam to find it instantly and give a condescending sigh.

He doesn't. It isn't in there.

"Orla?" I suggest.

He raises an eyebrow. "There's nearly fifty euros in here. You seriously think she'd take the letter and leave that?" He slams the drawer shut. "Who else has been in the house since then?"

"Just everyone who was at lunch." I count them off. "Us, Orla, Esme, Gwen, Nush, Kristy, Shay." I pause. "You know, *you* left Shay in the house on his own on Sunday. Someone we barely know."

Adam's quick. "He wasn't on his own when I left. Kristy was here. And anyway, why would he move the letter? Can't say I warmed to the guy, but—"

"I don't know! I don't have reasons for any of this. Maybe he was looking for something when he was cooking and then he opened the junk drawer, saw the letter, and . . ." And *what*? I don't know where I'm going with this. Nothing makes sense. "Or maybe he's just a complete psycho who gets off on wheedling his way into people's lives and totally freaking them out. I mean, the timing *is* interesting—all of this started happening right after I met him last week."

"It's a hell of a stretch, Els." Adam looks out the window, towards the cabin. "My money'd be on Kristy before Shay. She's always been jealous of you."

"On her doing *what*, though?" It's not true she's *always* been jealous, but now really isn't the time. "Moving the letter? Everything else?" I'm so frustrated I could kick something; Max must get it from me. "Anyway, all that matters *right* now is that that letter was proof for Social Services, and we don't have it."

We stand, gawping at each other, not knowing what else to say. And that's when I remember.

"The back door was unlocked."

"What?"

"When me and Gwen went out for a cigarette. And I'm *almost* sure I locked it before I drove over to Nush's earlier."

"You're sure, or you're *almost* sure?"

I try to retrace my steps, but it's hard. I was on rage-powered autopilot. I definitely remember thinking, *I must lock the back door*, I remember picking up the keys, I remember standing in front of it. But did one of the boys come running in? Did my phone ping? Another distraction?

The doorbell drags me out of my reconstruction. Adam goes to answer it, blasting Orla for never having keys. But when he returns, it's not with Orla, it's with Jason—looking sombre, which is standard, but also looking official.

My stomach lurches.

Orla. Something's happened. *Please no please no please no.*

"Jason wants a quick word with you," Adam says, giving me puzzled eyes.

A quick word suggests nothing terrible, *thank you thank you thank you.* So my bet is Gwen's told him what's been happening, and he's come to . . . what? Help? Provide advice?

God, he isn't here about the "theft," is he?

"Ellen," he says, deadpan, "I need to speak to you about Zane Jackson."

My brain short-circuits. For a moment, it actually hurts to breathe.

"He hasn't been seen since Sunday. He was reported missing yesterday. We got his phone records this afternoon, and you appear to have been the last person to speak to him."

Things are about to get worse.

35

Nush

When her mother is taking her meds, she's an astute and practical woman, and Nush dearly wishes she'd listened to her, not Ellen, when it came to matters of the heart. It was Shani who told Nush, age sixteen, that she'd never be happy with Adam ("delightful, but a lapdog—you'll be bored within a fortnight"). It was also Shani who advised her strongly to close her eyes to Tom's "carrying on." During a conversation that she could have happily lived her whole life without having, Shani revealed that Nush's father had been a "keen swordsman" himself, but that his extramarital "fumblings" had waned to nothing by his late fifties.

"Don't sacrifice the later years for the younger years, darling" was her uniquely sensible advice.

Not that Shani got many of those years. Nush's father died at sixty-two of a massive heart attack, while kayaking on the Kalu river.

Men can be *so* unreliable.

Even, as it turns out, Lapdog Adam.

His cologne had smelled fresh earlier. Nush wonders if he topped it up on her account. She also wonders if Ellen knows that it was her who gave Adam his first bottle of his signature scent (Givenchy Gentleman, Christmas 1996). She spritzed it on Tom once in a luxury department store in Athens, but it was too sweet on his skin. It was probably the heat.

Athens was magical. Luxury holidays had been a staple of their relationship. No one warns you they'll fall by the wayside when you're of a certain age and on your own. Nush has girlfriends, of course, but most with children too young to leave for more than a night or two, and she can't see herself as a solo traveller—or worse, in a "singles" group. For her, the best part of any holiday was always sipping sundowners with Tom, idling over well-worn topics and familiar people. She has no desire to make new friends, but she hates the idea of solitude equally.

When she and Adam were in the throes of whatever *it* was or wasn't, they had this fantasy about her joining him on a work trip overseas. Cape Town was bandied about. They spent time researching the place on Google. Wine-tasting in Constantia. White sands and sapphire sea. They were going to ride horses along Noordhoek Beach. Then after the kiss, Adam got cold feet.

As it happened, they wouldn't have gone anyway. The night before Adam's flight, Kian was hospitalised with croup as a precaution. So it was probably good that they'd cooled things. The disappointment, while she'd have got over it, would have been moderately tough.

Nush often thinks that if it wasn't for the boys, she could probably prise Adam away from Ellen. It wouldn't be the quickest process—he's a good man—but the sweetest victories seldom are.

But the biggest issue isn't the boys. It's the fact she doesn't want him.

The thing with Adam was never about Adam. It was always about *her*.

And she knows deep down she *shouldn't* blame her, but "shouldn't" is such a pointless word. People *shouldn't* break the law. They *shouldn't* announce they're going to the toilet. Nush *shouldn't* be sitting alone scrolling Instagram, waiting for the next instalment of Tom's brave new world.

Pram purchased! Next up, large Merlot, methinks!!
At least teach him a lesson, Ellen said.

Why in God's name didn't she listen to Shani?

Still, it's comforting—actually, it's fun—to watch Ellen get taught a lesson of her own.

36

Ellen

Gouging my nails into my palms, I land back in my body facing two stark options: fight or flight. The urge to fight, to lie—*Zane who?*—is beyond all-consuming, but I've watched enough crime dramas to know that would be my undoing, and crucially, he's *missing*. What if he's come to harm? Failing to help would mean failing him, and I've failed Zane Jackson too many times already.

So I choose flight. Momentarily. Just a brief step away to allow myself a mental count to ten.

"Two secs," I say to Jason, already on my way out of the kitchen. "I'll just go and close the boys' bedroom door. If they hear a different voice, they might come down."

I *do* close their door, but not before taking a moment to watch them breathing. Max's mouth is tightly closed, his arms folded across his little body. Kian's arms are flung wide, embracing the night, always ready for a hug. I drink them both in. My slumbering heaps of goodness. Proof, if I ever needed it, that I've done some things right in my life.

I walk into the bathroom and smooth my hair down in the mirror. Then, as a silent thank-you to the universe for the fact that Orla is ensconced at Esme's, I make the only vow I'm confident I can honour: *I will lie as little as possible.*

I will tell the truth about anything that might help locate him. Everything else is out of bounds.

*

Adam is making Jason a cup of tea—fight, flight, or put the kettle on—while Jason sits at the table, flicking his pen impatiently.

"Sorry about that," I say, choosing the seat furthest away from him. "If either of them came down and saw you in your full regalia, I think I'd probably have to sedate them." *Great choice of words, Ellen!* "So, um, you said Zane Jackson's missing. What do you mean by missing?"

"There's been no confirmed sighting of him since around eight o'clock on Sunday morning, when a neighbour saw him going into the Costcutter on the south perimeter of the Lomax. And his phone has been dead since Sunday evening." He looks down briefly at his notebook. "But as I mentioned, we got his phone records earlier today and saw that he received a call from you just after two thirty p.m. that day. Can you tell me what that was about?"

"He'd sent me a couple of WhatsApp messages asking for my help with something. So I called him."

"Messages? Can I see those, please?"

"Of course."

I can hardly say no, and in any case, there's no real reason to. There's nothing particularly untoward or incriminating in them. I take my phone out and casually present it to him. Jason reads the messages, then snaps a photo, reassuringly unmoved.

"So what did he need help with?"

"A lift to his cousin Ruby's place in Danesfield." *Lie as little as possible.* "Which I gave him—so there's a later confirmed sighting for you. I dropped him off around four-ish."

I can't bear to look at Adam. Partly it's shame, but I also don't want to drag Jason's gaze towards him. I don't want him to see Adam's obvious shock. *What, no mercy dash with a study guide?*

"So, mystery solved—he's probably still there, right?" I say, genuinely glad to be of assistance. *And now please leave my kitchen.* "I know he said he wanted to lie low for a few days, but God, I didn't realise he meant completely off grid."

Adam puts a mug in front of Jason and sits down. The mug is Mr. Happy. He obviously chose it to make me smile before finding out I'd lied.

"Ruby, Ruby . . ." Jason flips back through his notebook, a deep crease across his brow. "Ah, there." He looks up. "Zane's mother gave us a list of his friends and family, and there *was* a cousin called Ruby mentioned . . ."

I can't stop myself. "His mother? That's a joke. I doubt she'd recognise him in the street, never mind know who his friends are."

"She's frantic, Ellen. She might not lead the most stable life, but she makes sure she sees him regularly. *She* was the one who reported him missing yesterday." He cuts me an odd glance. "And she knows all his friends, actually. She knew about you, how you've been tutoring him every Friday. You were on our list to speak to even before the phone records came in."

Zane told *me* his mum was long gone.

He told *her* about me?

Adrenaline floods my body. I need to move, but it would look suspicious. I settle for twinkling my toes furiously under the table where Jason can't see.

"So, sorry, you were saying about Ruby?" I say lightly. My cheeks feel red hot. "You're aware of her, then?"

"We're aware of *a* Ruby, yes. But she told my colleague that she hasn't seen or heard from Zane in months. And she certainly doesn't live in Danesfield."

"I don't . . ." I'm at a loss. I instinctively look to Adam, because that's what I do when I can't explain things. But clearly he can't help, and by the look on his face, he wouldn't even if he could. "Well, um, look, I can't tell you the exact house, because I dropped him off on the corner. But it's a cul-de-sac off Trensale Row. That's the last time I saw him."

Jason goes into the hall. I hear the crackle of his radio as he repeats my information. Adam and I eyeball each other across the kitchen. I go to speak, but he says, "Just don't."

When Jason comes back, I stand up, assuming we're done here.

I assume wrong. He sits down again.

"So why did he ask you for this lift?"

His tone is less formal than before, more curious, perhaps even accusatory. He picks up his tea, looking at me in a way that says, *Settle in, we've only just begun.*

"He didn't have any money for the bus." I know that won't be good enough.

"Yes, but why you specifically? His tutor. Seems a bit over-familiar to me."

Lie as little as possible. I don't have to tell him about the kiss, or Zane craving proof that I genuinely liked him. I just need to stick to the facts—the relevant ones, as I see them.

"Look, he'd had a row with his dad and I think he wanted someone to feel sorry for him, not a mate who'd probably laugh at him." A thought strikes me. "Actually, that's a point—his dad would have seen him later on the Sunday," I say, confused. "It was three-ish by the time I picked him up, and I got the impression the row was pretty recent." I don't mention the fresh cut; I'm pretty sure Zane wouldn't want me to. "What has his dad said?"

"We haven't been able to locate Paulo Jackson over the past thirty-six hours." He puts his mug down and leans forward: *Now you've got my attention.* "But carry on. They'd had a row . . ."

"Yeah, a pretty big one, I think." I *know*—but being vague isn't lying. "Their boiler was broken, and Zane wanted money off Paulo to pay Dave from a few doors down to fix it. Paulo said no—or words to that effect."

Jason consults his notebook. "Dave—is that Dave McDaid?"

I shrug. "Possibly."

"Because Dave McDaid is the neighbour who saw Zane early Sunday morning. I spoke with him today, and he didn't mention anything about a boiler."

"I'm only telling you what Zane told me." I raise my hands in casual confusion, but I feel anything but casual. I feel like I'm drifting, unanchored. Not sure what to believe.

"And what you said earlier," Jason says, pen poised over the notebook. "About Zane saying he wanted to lie low for a few days. What did you think he meant by that?

I shrug again. "I assumed he meant he wanted to stay out of his dad's way."

He writes something down, then, "What else did you talk about on that car journey?"

"Not much," I say, telling the truth. It was at the back of the car afterwards that so much was said. "He was quiet, really. Upset about the row, I thought. So I just let him sit in silence. And then he got out of the car on Trensale Row and . . ."

My gesture says, *I don't know.* My head screams, *And then he kissed me.*

Pen still poised, Jason bites his thin, smudgy lip. "Did he ever seem troubled—prior to the row with Paulo, I mean?"

"Troubled?"

"Depressed? Suicidal ideation?" Nausea jolts me. My hand flies to my stomach. "I appreciate that's a deeply unpleasant question," he says without one molecule of empathy. "And I would stress that it's not something anyone else has signalled, but as the two of you are obviously quite close, I'd be interested to get your take."

Adam shifts at the word *close.* I repeat it back to Jason with a perplexed stare.

"Well, giving him a lift—on a Sunday, of all days—suggests a more personal relationship than just tutor and student." He pauses, eyes glued on mine. "He obviously felt he could rely on you. You must have earned that trust somehow."

I take a deep inner breath. "If any of my students—in fact, any distressed teen—needed my help, it wouldn't matter if it was Sunday or Christmas Day." He's unmoved by my declaration. I don't care. I said it for Adam as much as him. "And no, no suicidal ideation. Quite the opposite. Zane's full of plans and ambitions. And he'll fulfil them too, if he applies himself and gets the A-level results he's capable of."

Jason glances down, turns a new page in his notebook. "Can you tell me how you came to be Zane's tutor? I understand from his mother that you were tutoring him for free."

Adam walks out of the room, but because he has manners, he says, "Excuse me." There'll be a row when Jason leaves, though. I should count myself lucky he hasn't caused a scene.

"I *think* he contacted me through my website," I say, all vague and unflustered. I knew this question might come up, and I made my peace with my lie in front of the bathroom mirror. It's not relevant to where Zane is now, so Jason doesn't need the whole truth. "And I was impressed, you know? He'd been excluded from school, and as usual it was taking the LEA forever to sort out tutoring, and there he was, taking the initiative. So I agreed to meet him, and I liked him. I could see straight away that he was very bright." I give a tiny laugh. "Turns out he was pretty brazen, too—he asked if I fancied taking on a charity case within twenty minutes of us meeting."

"And you said yes—is that common?"

"It's not unheard of. And I've been a bit bored coaching rich kids, so I thought, why not? Someone I can actually make a difference to, maybe? See, I didn't exactly grow up in the best environment myself, so I know how easy it is for kids like Zane to slip through the cracks—I was in a position to make sure that didn't happen." He hasn't written anything down, which reassures me it's not relevant. "He does have an official LEA tutor now, by the way. Frances something. Have you spoken to her?"

He ignores the question, asks another of his own. "And you carried on tutoring him for free? Even after the LEA came through."

"She only came on board around a month ago, and I wanted to wait and see that he was making progress with her. A tutor's a bit like a therapist, see—there's no guarantee you'll be a match."

"OK." I'm not sure what's *OK*, but rather abruptly, he flips his notebook shut and stands up. "That should do for now, thanks. And if you do hear from him . . ."

"Of course, I'll let you know."

I lead him out into the hallway and open the front door.

Then I make a split-second decision. A sensible one.

"Actually, before you go," I say, stepping outside, "can I ask you something off the record?" He couldn't look more displeased, clearly not an off-the-record kinda guy. "Look, I don't know if Gwen's mentioned anything, but I've been having some issues." I laugh nervously. "I won't bore you with the gory details, but I found out today that someone made a malicious call to Children's Services about me. And I wondered if that was a police matter. If I should at least log it with you."

"How do you mean 'malicious'?" There's something in his tone I don't like—or crucially, there's something missing from it. Basic sympathy. *Interest*, even. "What exactly did they say?"

"Oh, a few different things, but my boy, Max, cut his hand last weekend. It was mainly about that."

"Doesn't sound malicious to me, then. It sounds responsible." His chin lifts. "I'm sorry, but a child was hurt. I'd probably have done the same. Speak to one of my colleagues, by all means, but I doubt they'll be able to help."

*

Stung to my core and needing a minute alone to punch a pillow,

I shoot straight up the stairs, assuming that Adam will be in the living room, hating me in front of Sky Sports.

No such luck. A grim-faced Adam is waiting for me in our bedroom. I almost turn and run.

"Working for nothing now, are we?" He's half lying, half sitting on the bed, one long leg planted on the floor. His expression is tight, anger pinching every feature. "So while I'm guzzling antacids morning, noon, and night, stressing about the cost of this renovation, you're doing your Mother Teresa act, working for free." He's entirely still. "Ellen, who *is* this boy?"

I sit down with a light laugh. "Jesus, Ads, you've just listened to me answering questions about him for half an hour. What more do you need to know?"

He pushes himself upright, moves his face closer to mine. "Oh, but you left an awful lot out, Ellen. You didn't mention you left a *family* outing to go and help him. I mean, 'Max Day' went out the window fairly quick, didn't it, as soon as your 'charity case' clicked his fingers." So he was listening at the door, then. "And all that crap about the textbook?"

I sigh. "Look, I didn't have time to go into it; he sounded pretty desperate. If I'd given you the background, I'd have been there all day." It's weak and we both know it. I pause for a moment, scrabbling around for something stronger. Eventually I hit on something that, in retrospect, is partly true. "And as for why I left the park to help him? Orla. She'd been whining on about how she was never allowed a dog, and then after the Frankfurt strop, too, I just thought . . . this boy hasn't even got *heat* at home, you know? Orla has *everything*, and she still thinks she's oppressed. All he wanted was a bloody lift." I pause again. I don't think he's softened, but I don't appear to have stoked the fire, at least. "And yeah, working for free . . . I wasn't going to, but when I met him, it was like . . . I don't know . . . like I saw *myself* in him. A bright kid hampered by parents who don't give a toss about education. I wanted to help him." Silence follows, which is unfortunate, as I don't know what else I can say. "And *of course* I hope they find him. And that he's OK, obviously." I lay my hand on Adam's leg. "But frankly, I've got my own kids to worry about. This Social Services thing—*that's* my priority."

It's the truth. One week ago—hell, one day ago—I'd have been knocked sideways by this Zane news. But now, while I'm obviously concerned, all I care about is *my* children. *My* children, Cathy Grantham, and what she's going to say in her report.

Adam nods. "See, I hear you, Els, and I even understand what you're saying. But why I do still feel like you're lying about something?"

He's wrong—or at least he's not entirely right. Because *lying* suggests a collection of lies. One untruth following hot on the heels of another.

But actually, I've only told one bare-faced lie this evening.

Zane didn't contact me through my website.

I purposely sought him out.

37

Kristy

High drama at the Meadowhouse! A copper in the kitchen (or at least she *thinks* it was a copper; her long-distance vision is shot to shit like the rest of her), and now Ellen's outside chain-smoking, puffing away on the back step. She's been there almost an hour—Kristy knows this for sure, as she'd just put on a new episode of *Ozark* when the back door opened—and even though it's late and it's chilly, she hasn't bothered with a coat.

Obviously, the done thing, the *nice* thing, would be for Kristy to go and check on her. But that would mean bending down and lacing her boots again, and her back's been spasming like a bitch all day. And anyway, she wants to watch the next *Ozark*, then do some proper research on North Cornwall. And she already used up her *nice* quota earlier, talking Ellen back from the Social Services ledge.

She also can't stop thinking about what Shay said a few nights ago. Not his suggestion that they have a threesome with the Aussie barmaid from the Cricketers (Kristy's game, even though the other woman's a bit skinny for her liking—her tendencies that way generally lean towards robust and well stacked). No, it's the thing he said about Ellen that's being playing on a loop since Sunday evening. *I don't understand why you don't hate her. I would if I were you.*

The weird thing is, Kristy *didn't* in the years they were apart. When she was partying hard in Ibiza and Ellen was menu planning in Thames Lawley. It was as though the distance had created a space where happier memories could creep back in.

The roller skates that came from Santa with the note that they had to share them. They hadn't understood that meant taking turns, so they'd skated around the estate wearing one each.

Baking a birthday cake for Dad and forgetting to put the eggs in. He'd laughed like a loon, then given them £2 to buy him one "that doesn't taste like fecking shite."

So many other pre-"accident" memories—teenage exploits, nights out in London. And while she wouldn't go so far as to say her heart grew fonder while she was in Ibiza, there was definitely a mild thawing. Ellen went from being a toxin to just an irritant.

But since Kristy's been here, wearing Ellen's clothes, accepting her charity, it's as though the hate has been reactivated, stirred from its sleeper cell. And she can't help the way she feels, because unless you're a corpse or the Dalai Lama, you're basically a slave to your darkest feelings. And in Kristy's experience, it's pointless—and usually expensive—to try to bring those feelings under control.

Although she *has* tried. Earlier this year, after years of smoking weed, occasional therapy, and learning to crochet (of all things), Kristy turned, along with half of the Western world, it seemed, to "mindfulness" to calm her brain. It was an ex who introduced her to it. The same ex who introduced her to his fist on more than one occasion, eventually causing her to flee Ibiza and take up residence in Ellen's home.

Anyway, her point is that mindfulness *clearly* didn't work for him. Does it *really* work for anyone?

Maybe some people are destined to be the ocean. Others to be the storm.

A while later, there's a knock on the cabin door while Kristy's busy tweezing her eyebrows. She checks her phone: 11:15 p.m. A bit early for it to be Shay.

It's Ellen, looking awful. And not in the sense that she looks stricken, but rather that she's wearing red flannelette pyjamas. Kristy doubts she's bothered with sexy nightwear since the night they conceived the twins.

"Can I come in for a minute?"

She thinks about saying no, just to see her sister's reaction, but instead she steps aside and says, "Bit late for a tenancy inspection, don't you think?"

Ellen rolls her eyes, but Kristy knows she'll be making mental notes, clocking everything. She kind of wishes she'd washed up now. That she'd tried harder to get that red wine stain out of the quilt.

"Did either you or Shay move the letter?" Ellen says, straight to the nitty-gritty.

"Letter?" Kristy catches on as she sits down. "Oh, *the* letter, you mean? No. Why would we do that?"

Ellen's perching on the very edge of the arm of the small sofa. She reminds Kristy of a nervous cat, ready to spring, ready to scratch. "I don't know, Kris, but it's vanished, and I'm having a hard time making sense of it. All I keep coming back to is that Shay was in the house on his own, doing his Jamie Oliver thing on Sunday . . ."

"Oh, come on, Els—if he was going to take anything, surely it'd be a pair of your dirty knickers for his shrine."

Ellen doesn't react. ". . . and *also* that, basically, I met him for the first time in the Cricketers last week, and it's been non-stop trouble ever since."

It would barely take a tap to knock her off the edge and onto the floor.

"So you're accusing of him of what exactly?" Kristy says, grabbing her mirror off the table and getting to work on her left eyebrow. It'll wind Ellen up more if she thinks Kristy couldn't give a shit, that she's bored. "Being the phantom letter-writer? Facebook-poster? Social Services–caller? Anything else I've missed?"

Seriously, Ellen's always been self-absorbed, but this is weapons-grade narcissism. The idea that every single fucking thing—even who Kristy's fucking—has got to be somehow connected to her.

Ellen sighs and closes her eyes, then like clockwork, the pious pout. "I'm not accusing him of anything," she says, which is an absolute joke, really. "All I know is that someone has it in for me, and I feel scared and unsettled, and I don't want *anyone* I don't know well hanging around the house until this Social Services thing gets sorted." She waits for Kristy to look up and behold her shrewd stare. "Be honest, Kris, what do *you* know about him, really? Why is he even here? One minute he's an electrician in London, next he's pulling pints in a village pub?"

"He's always dreamed of running his own pub. He's building up experience."

"Oh, and there are no pubs in London?"

Kristy asked the same once. Shay said, "London pubs are a different animal," and it didn't seem much of an answer, but then he did that thing with his middle finger that made her forget her own name.

"So is Lady Nush allowed round?" Kristy asks, swiftly changing the subject. "I mean, you know *her*, but only a few hours ago you were wondering if she was behind the Social Services 'thing.' So maybe *knowing* someone isn't exactly the best criteria."

"But it's *my* criteria. And in case you've forgotten, this is *my* house."

It was only a matter of time, although Ellen's usually a bit subtler when it comes to pulling rank.

It's then that Kristy realises she'll never have a better "in."

"Hey, I'll tell you how you can get Shay out of your hair pretty quick," she says, putting the mirror and tweezers on the floor. "And me, actually—two for the price of one." Ellen cuts in, saying she doesn't want Kristy out of her hair, but Kristy speaks over her. "Four thousand quid. A sort of long-term loan."

"What do you need four thousand quid for?" Ellen's forehead crumples as she takes in the request. A second later, the penny drops. "Or what does *he* need it for, more like. Jesus, Kris, you sure know how to pick 'em."

Kristy swallows down *fuck off*—it's not in her best interest. "Shay's got a mate in Cornwall who wants us to help run a pub. The place needs sprucing up, though."

"Wow, that's . . . commitment." Ellen's quiet for a moment. Kristy awaits the lecture on moving too fast, look where that's got her in the past, *yada yada*. Instead Ellen says, "Four thousand quid isn't a lot of sprucing. Not for a pub."

Not an outright no, then.

"The idea is we put in eight, his mate puts in eight. That's a decent spruce."

"But who came up with that figure? Shay's mate? Have you met him? Has he actually priced things up, or has he just—"

Kristy puts a hand up, already wishing she hadn't asked. "You know, I don't recall requesting an itemised breakdown when you asked me for that cash for Zara's hen weekend. What was that in total, with the flight? A few thousand?"

"Yeah, but you could afford it. *And* I paid you back within a week." A week and two days, and, God, hadn't Kristy paid for it. Ellen brings her hand to her chest. "I'm sorry, Kris, it's just really bad timing. We're trying to save every penny. Rog and Sylv might have stumped up the money for the actual work, but, you know, there's the furnishings, the appliances, all the other stuff."

"Oh yeah, I meant to ask, did you go with the LG double fridge in the end?"

Ellen quickly looks away. She knows that wasn't a friendly enquiry. It was a point made. A point scored.

Two grand on a fridge-freezer. Four grand could change my life.

"Look, maybe next year?" she says, all hopeful and heartfelt. "By next summer, we should be in a better position—over the financial shock, you know?"

Kristy shrugs. "Next year's too late, but honestly, just forget it."

As their dad always said, there's more than one way to crack an egg.

38

Ellen

I was obviously lying to myself that Zane's vanishing act hadn't floored me, because my first thought upon waking at 4 a.m. is: *I wonder if Cathy Grantham or her ilk were ever made aware of him?* I mean, Paulo is, well, Paulo, and Jason implied his mum isn't the most stable. So did anyone ever tell Social Services that *his* home might not be a safe place?

Is he safe now?

The dead-of-night darkness fires question after question.

Where are you? And where's Paulo? Why did you lie about your mum, and who are they going to find you with in Danes-field? A girlfriend? (But you kissed me.) Or did I deliver you to a bad person? Are you hurt? Why's your phone off? Do you remember asking me that day—the day you confessed about the blackmail—if I'd done things I'm ashamed of? What's the worst thing I ever did?

I can't remember exactly what I said, but I remember Zane *howling* laughing because it was pitifully boring. And then I laughed too, because Sunshine Zane is *so* infectious, and all the time I was thinking: *God, if you only knew.*

Orla's out the door by seven, something to do with cross-country time trials, and Adam gets ready for work without speaking, except to say that he'll be home late—team drinks. I swear it's the first time he's mentioned them, so I ask politely who they're for. He says, "Dunno, just drinks," and offers no more information. Deliberate caginess doesn't suit him, but then I'm in no position to speak.

It's not long after I've dropped the boys at nursery that the cancellation comes in.

I can't decide whether it's kind or plain spineless, but my student Piper Lewis's mum (whose sister-in-law, incidentally, is pastoral lead at Pelham) frames my instant dismissal as a compliment. A big success story.

"Piper's doing so well now, and it's all thanks to you, Ellen. I don't think we need to trouble you any further, ha ha. You've got her exactly where she needs to be."

If "slightly below average" is where she needs to be, then agreed, I'm a genius. I suggest one last *Brighton Rock* session as we're so close to finishing, but she says she'd like to terminate things immediately, although, *of course* she'll pay me for the session we've already got booked for next week.

She might as well add, *Because rumour has it you need the money, you nasty little thief.*

Afternoon descends and I go to the charity shop to ask them to take Muriel's dead husband out of the window, then I head to Tesco, where I spend a whole ten minutes wondering what kind of biscuits social workers eat.

I call Nush three times. She doesn't answer. The ball's in her court now.

And I haven't seen Kristy all day. This, at least, is a blessed relief.

I've just finished mopping up the flood after the boys' typically rollicking bath time when Jason Bale arrives on my doorstep again, looking his typically pissed-off self. Thank God Orla's in her room, AirPods in, as she bashes away on WhatsApp. It used to annoy me how long she'd happily stay like this, but now I'm mainly glad of the peace.

"Any news?" I ask as I usher him into the living room. I don't offer him tea or a glass of water. I don't even offer him a seat.

"Paulo Jackson has turned up." I assume this is good news, but Jason's face suggests different. "He's incredibly stressed about Zane and denies that any argument took place on Sunday."

OK.

"And do you believe him?" I may have a soft spot for Paulo, but he's hardly a man of honour.

Jason gives a satisfied nod. "The last time Paulo saw Zane was on Saturday morning. He then went to London to stay with friends. By Saturday evening he'd been admitted to Ealing Hospital, and he wasn't discharged until this morning. This has all been checked and verified. He had no idea Zane was even missing."

"Hospital? Is he OK?"

Zane lied. Again.

"He is now, just. He fell in front of a car while severely intoxicated. When he got to hospital, he had no phone, no wallet, no ID, but once he was compos mentis, he provided a next-of-kin—the friend he was staying with. He said he hadn't wanted to worry Zane unduly ahead of his A-level mock exams. I said surely Zane would be worried when he didn't come home for four days, didn't make contact." His face clouds. "But apparently that's not an entirely irregular thing."

But the cut on Zane's face was fresh. *Someone* had hit him.

And I *know* I should tell Jason this. And I will, I *will*, tomorrow. Just as soon as Cathy Grantham has skipped away from our happy, risk-free home, I will honour my vow to tell the truth about anything that could help find him, and I will drive to the station and tell Jason—or whoever—that Zane had a fresh cut, and that I didn't mention it before out of misguided loyalty towards Paulo, who I believe loves his son immensely, even if it's a dysfunctional love that the lucky majority don't understand.

I *will* say all this tomorrow. But right now, less than twenty-four hours ahead of a Social Services visit, I simply can't risk the consequences of getting further embroiled.

I mean, can you imagine? *'Fraid I'm gonna have to reschedule, Cathy. I'm a little bit busy today, answering police questions about a missing lad.*

Jason carries on. "Also, we've now canvassed Trensale Row and the cul-de-sac leading off it, as you indicated. No one had heard of Zane or recognised him, and both his mother and Paulo have confirmed that they know of no links whatsoever to Danesfield."

In confusion and fear, I lash out. "Well, I'm not lying, if that's what you're thinking."

At best, I sound petulant. Worse, defensive. Worst, guilty.

Jason stares at me for two seconds longer than feels comfortable.

"Not at all," he says finally, but I don't think I believe him. "Regarding Paulo—as you said yesterday, you can only go on what Zane told you. And we know you drove him to Danesfield, because ANPR—that's Automatic Number Plate Recognition—picked you up on Kenpas High Road and tracked you turning onto Trensale Row." A coldness hits my core. "We lose you then, obviously, because you're entering a residential area. Unfortunately, for that same reason, we have no way of tracking what Zane did once he got out of your car."

I'm caught between momentarily sharing the disappointment, because I want to know what's happened to him, and instinctively thanking the heavens for proving there is a God.

39

Jason

"Bloke downstairs says he's got info on the Jackson kid."
Jason is sure that Stu Bartlett, the front counter officer, doesn't
like him. Everyone says Stu's great with the public, from calming
terrified old ladies to defusing drunken, mouthy teenagers, but
in over a year, he's yet to offer Jason a mere hello.

Still, while Jason isn't here to make friends, he doesn't have
the headspace for more enemies, so he says a chummy "Great,
thanks, mate" and tells Stu he'll be down in five.

The "bloke" has arrived while Jason is trawling through a
load of hearsay on Facebook. Zane Jackson doesn't have an account himself—like a lot of kids, he probably thinks Facebook is
the online equivalent of an old folk's home—but some guy who
seems to live on the Lomax, Baz Harris, has set up a *MISSING!*
post. There's a photo of a pouting Zane wearing a blue coat and
making a sideways peace sign.

*** PLEASE SHARE!!! HAVE YOU
SEEN ZANE JACKSON??? ***

Zane is 17 and has been missing since Sunday around
4 p.m. Last seen in the Danesfield area. He is 6ft, slim build,
and was last seen wearing a yellow North Face hoody. Zane
if ur reading this pal, please get in touch with ur mum or dad

or contact the police. If you don't wanna come home that's fine but just let someone know ur safe.

Underneath, the Facebook army are out in force.

Angela Burnby: Well done on setting this up Baz. You're a diamond.

Remi Hale: Not being funny but really??

Angela Burnby: What?

Remi Hale: Who says he's missing?? Bro might just want a bit of time out.

Angela Burnby: His phone has been off since Sunday.

Remi Hale: Maybe he's got another phone?? You people chasing drama . . .

Stevie Su: Yes well done Baz. Hope he's OK. Don't know Zane well but seemed a decent kid.

Remi Hale: Seemed? Past tense!! You wanna confess something Stevie Su??

Angela Burnby: Ignore him Stevie Su. Don't even know who Remi Hale is.

Remi Hale: Zane's mate. Who are YOU?? Just the usual FB rubbernecker.

Baz Harris: Go easy pal. Got any ideas that might help?

Remi Hale: Yeah, here's an idea—Zane's currently balls deep in some sweet piece and laughing at this post

Dean Frederick: He'll come back when he's hungry. That's what my old man used to say.

Belinda Quinn: Helpful as ever, Deano. Paulo is well cut up.

Dean Frederick: Sorry. Hope kid is OK.

Jada Uzoka: I saw him at Anton Keane's party on Friday night wearing this savage Ralph Lauren top. Said his girlfriend bought it for him. Anyone know who girlfriend is?? Thought he was single since Frankie??

Remi Hale: Sofia Luz wishes she was his gf

Sofia Luz: Fuck off Remi Hale

Chloe Downham: Wasn't he seeing that girl from Chapel House? Can't remember her name. Looks like a fatter Sommer Ray (not fat but u know what I mean)

Remi Hale: Nah they hooked up but he wasn't seeing her. And yeah Jada Uzoka that RL T-shirt was sick. £230 notes he reckons. Be just like Zane to bag a rich gf.

Sofia Luz: My brother is tight with Zane and he reckons he was seeing an older woman.

Remi Hale: Sounds like something the lucky bastard would do.

Sofia Luz: Yeah but like OLDER older.

Remi Hale: Can I just say that if any sexy older woman wants to sit on my face, I am HERE FOR IT.

Baz Harris: Who's your brother Sofia Luz? Has he spoken to police?

Sofia Luz : He ain't on Facebook. Don't know if he's spoken to police. He don't really like police.

Belinda Quinn: Sofia Luz if your brother has information he must go to the police. Zane's dad is going through hell.

Angela Burnby: And his mum!

Belinda Quinn: Yeah sorry, Ange. And his mum

Stevie Su: I saw him and his mum in Aldi the other week. He was helping her with her shopping. Nice lad.

Remi Hale: Good story Stevie Su. Got any more?

Anton Keane: Me and Sofia Luz's bro got all the deets about the older woman!!!

Belinda Quinn: You know who she is?

Baz Harris: Anton Keane don't know you pal, but if you know who this woman is and you think Zane might be with her you need to tell Zane's family at least if you won't go to police. Zane is 17 so there don't need to be any big fallout from it but at least we'd know he's safe.

Ciara Harkin: I heard he was smashing his tutor.

Angela Burnby: Who is this?

Angela Burnby: I mean who are you?

Belinda Quinn: No profile pic, looks like a fake account
Angela Burnby

Chloe Downham: OMG who??? What's her name?

Where to start, thinks Jason, as he rhythmically circles his finger over the boil that's recently sprouted on his chin. It's hard enough to get a handle on Facebook at the best of times, never mind when his brain feels like mush. He's barely slept a wink for weeks and can't remember the last time he got a solid six hours. It must have been over a year ago, because he's never slept well in Thames Lawley. Too much on his mind. The past that he can't change and the present that needs constant vigilance. He doesn't think too much about the future.

One step at a time.

"Ciara Harkin" doesn't reply, and five minutes pass without any new info. It looks like the comments section might have burned itself out for now. He'll check back later. Pick his way through more half-truths. He definitely needs to speak to Anton Keane again. He met the kid yesterday and he didn't mention a thing about an older woman. Sofia Luz's brother will be getting a visit, too.

And Ellen. His tutor.

He only left her house a couple of hours ago. He needs to have a cold, hard think about Ellen.

But first, "bloke" in reception. Stu Bartlett's bound to be moaning that he's been more than five.

40

Ellen

With a kind of do-or-die energy, and to the obvious confusion of passing dog-walkers, I decide it's imperative to tidy the front garden not long after 7 a.m. Of course I know that Cathy Grantham is coming to assess the boys, not my chances at Chelsea Flower Show, but I need to do *something* to burn off the nervous tension, and scowling at a sleeping Adam just wasn't cutting it.

It's good to be outside. It's a beautiful autumn morning. The air is fresh, and the rim of a just-risen sun shines through the bare branches of the cherry blossom, glittering off the sash windows and dappling the golden brick. And once I've finished raking and weeding and dead-heading my perennials, from the outside at least it looks like nothing bad could happen here.

I wonder if the Merricks felt the same before their attack all those years ago. Or the Sharps, who we bought the house from, whose marriage ended in bitter divorce.

What did Nush say? *Nothing good ever came from living in that house.*

Something good has arrived, though, by the time I'm back from the supermarket (after a sudden impulse that I should be able to offer Cathy Grantham decaf tea). Gwen is on her throne, cross-legged on the window seat, wearing a vintage Britney T-shirt, ripped jeans, and a gingham headscarf. She could pass for eighteen, if not younger, and yet she has an air of calm authority that makes me want to melt her down and bottle her.

"That reed diffuser thing on the hall table," she says before I've even got my coat off. "I'd put it up somewhere higher if I were you. Give it another month and the boys will be able to reach it. And you know what Kian's like—he'll think bergamot oil makes a nice drink."

"OK. Hey, do you know if Orla's still here?" I ask, slightly panicked. "I need to grab her before she leaves. Make sure she understands how important this visit is."

"She's in her room. And the boys are watching *Octonauts* and Adam's upstairs taking a work call." She gives me a military salute. "And I, Gwendoline Bale, am reporting for duty." I smile, pleased that she seems normal. I'm assuming Jason hasn't mentioned the Zane business to her. Would he even be allowed? I've no idea. "Thought I'd roll up my sleeves. Give you a hand with whatever."

I put the decaf on the table. "God, she isn't coming until three. The house isn't that bad, is it?"

"Well, no. The opposite, in fact." She smiles coyly. "I actually came over to check you weren't going overboard."

"In what way?"

"Oh, I dunno—dusting the blinds, baking cookies." I hadn't thought of the blinds, but I have wiped down the light switches. Gwen gestures around the kitchen. "I mean, it's kind of pristine in here."

As it bloody well should be. I was up until eleven decluttering and disinfecting *everything*. Gwen's tone, however, suggests "pristine" isn't good.

"She's a social worker, Els, not a real estate agent. You don't have to 'stage' the house. They're wise to all that freshly baked bread crap." She points to an empty shelf. "*And* you've hidden the booze."

"I'm 'never without a glass,' remember?"

"Yeah, and she's going to want to see that the boys aren't in the care of Keith Richards. She's not going to care if you like a glass of red now and again. No booze at all looks suspicious." She looks me up and down. "And really, a *tea dress*. Where'd you panic-buy that from?"

"I think it's nice," I say, giving a twirl.

"It *is* nice, but it's not you. You're not a vicar's wife. You're Ellen Walsh. And you're amazing as you are."

She's right, it isn't me. But then I don't want to be me today.

I change the subject. "Hey, is Bella with the boys? I'm going to make them waffles." *So they'll love me in front of Cathy Grantham.* "I take it she'll want one?"

"She's at home. I left her with Jase—he's off sick today. Migraine, apparently. He seems fine to me, though." She shifts on the window seat, groaning at having been sitting cross-legged for too long. Give it ten years, I think. "It's weird, he's never sick. Even as a kid, he was like a robot. I was like Bella—always picking up germs."

If Jason's off sick, does that mean Zane goes on the back burner? Or is there a whole team of people looking for him? I wish I could pay Paulo a quick visit to check in.

I put the kettle on. I need caffeine on a drip to get through what already feels like the longest morning. I'll stop by lunchtime, though. I can't be wired to the eyeballs for the royal visit. And definitely when she's here, I'm going to force down herbal tea.

When I turn around again, Gwen looks concerned, kind of twitchy. Like she needs to say something else but would rather drink bleach.

"Out with it, Gwendoline Bale." She frowns, surprised. "It's the earlobe thing," I say, tugging my own. "Dead giveaway."

"It's just . . ." Her mouth twists side to side, as though she's trying to trap the words in. "I was talking to Adam before— well, he was talking to me . . ." She stops again, giving a sharp, purposeful sigh. "And look, I don't know the ins and outs of what's gone on, and I don't need to, but you guys *have* to mount a united front for Social Services, you hear me?"

"What's he been saying?" I snap. Surely it wasn't about Zane?

She rolls her eyes. "Oh, just stressing about the renovation. He wants to postpone, but you said no, apparently." *This again? Seriously?* "I mean, I don't get his problem—it's not like his folks are going to kneecap him if you don't pay the loan back. But it got me thinking . . ." She hesitates again, lips pressed together. "Look, it's up to you, but if it was me, I wouldn't mention the renovation in front of the social worker."

I wasn't going to—it's hardly relevant—but now she has me intrigued.

"It's just . . . it *could* create concerns about the kids living on a building site. And obviously *we* know that's not going to happen, but you don't want to give her any excuse to think she needs to come back." Her voice wavers. "Because, you know, those floating stairs you've got planned, for example—I know you've had them safety-checked, but they don't *look* the most child-friendly. A country bumpkin farmhouse is a much better 'optic,' as we say in PR."

"I thought you said she'd be wise to all that bullshit. Homemade scones, tea dresses . . ."

"Yeah, but *they're* obviously staged. Your house is . . . well, kinda fixed. You can't conjure up a house straight out of an Enid Blyton novel just for a Social Services visit, can you? And I know you think it's ugly and a bit dated . . ."

"A *bit*?"

"OK, a lot. But in this instance, dated is good. Or at least it is through the eyes of a social worker. It says lived-in. And lived-in says stability, and stability says safety. Trust me, Els, I know how they think." She pauses, swallowing hard. "So honestly, that's the *only* reason I think it might be worth considering what Adam's suggesting. Then, as soon as you know Social Services are *definitely* out of your hair, you can crack on with Project Space Age."

Adam's put her up to this. I'd bet the ugly, dated house on it. The thought of him pressuring her to "have a quiet word" makes me seethe.

United front, Ellen, united front . . .

Conveniently, the kettle whistles. Glad of something to do, Gwen swings into action, shifting it from the stove to the stand, then bustling me out of my own kitchen.

"Orla," she says, pointing upstairs. "Go and have your chat with her, and I'll give the house another once-over for the kind of things they look for." She smiles. "And then when we're both done, I'll make us a joyless cup of decaf tea."

I watch Orla from the doorway. She's contouring her perfectly perfect face in the bathroom mirror that I finally managed to get smear-free using distilled white vinegar.

Cathy Grantham will be impressed.

"Why are you looking at me?" she demands, dotting liquid bronzer down her temples.

One minute she was all marshmallow cheeks, baby wrist fat, and Iggle Piggle. Now she's long limbs and attitude, contours and constant grief.

"I'm looking at you because you're my daughter, and you're beautiful, and because I love you." She arches a fashionably fluffy eyebrow. For once, I ignore the disdain. "You *could* be a model, you know. Auntie Kris told Shay that's what you want to be. Is that right?"

"I don't want to *be* a model, Mum. I'd like *to* model. There's a difference."

I'd ask what the difference is, but she'll inevitably find the question tedious.

"Remember, I need you home straight after school today."

"I remember."

"You'll miss the start of the visit, but I want you here for some of it. And I want you to be nice in front of Cathy, OK?"

"I'm always nice when the person warrants it."

I don't bite. "So no spinning by Esme's."

"No spinning by Esme's."

"Because you've been doing that a lot lately, and your spins turn into four hours." I grin at her in the mirror. "Her mum must be getting fed up with you."

She turns around. "Well, *obviously* she isn't, Mum, because as you well know, she's got zero interest in Esme and wouldn't care if she brought Ted Bundy home." She smirks. "But good work, though. Smoothly done."

I say nothing, waiting to be enlightened.

"Well, that's what you were doing, right? Digging for dirt on Esme's mum to feel better about yourself. Kinda 'See, I might be bad, but I'm not *that* bad.'"

Bad. While it's abundantly clear she's thought it, she's actually never said it before.

"Is that what you think? That I'm a bad mum?" She opens her mouth but struggles to answer. Maybe she hasn't *totally* erased all the years of loving me, then. All the fun and the cuddles and the ganging-up on Adam. "Because, Orla, I love you so, so much that when you leave the house, it's like my own heart is stapled to your jacket." She wrinkles her nose at the image, but there's a softening around her eyes. "And it kills me that you seem to . . . I don't know . . . *hate* me."

"I don't hate you." She shakes her head, her voice cracking. "I hate *myself* sometimes, and I kind of blame you for that, I guess. And I hate that you're not the goodest person in the world anymore. Do you remember when I used to call you that?" I do. I was the "goodest" and the "beautifulest." "Mainly I hate that I always trusted you to do the right thing, but when it really mattered, you didn't."

"*Ellen!*" Gwen is suddenly hollering from the kitchen. "*El-len!*"

I look at Orla, desperate. "La-la, *please*, let's talk about this later—thrash it all out, yeah?" I kiss my fingers, then touch her face. For the first time in months, while she doesn't exactly welcome it, she doesn't flinch. "But you should know, for the record, I still think I did the right thing."

As I come down the stairs, I see Gwen standing at the bottom, holding the remains of a joint and the jagged stem of a broken wine glass.

"Um . . . I think you're going to have to talk to Kristy," she says, wincing. "These were at the back of the cabin, in front of the veranda. Damn lucky I spotted them."

Damn lucky for Kristy that she's at Shay's, or at least I assume she is.

I hope for both our sakes she stays gone.

If I saw her right now, I might kill her.

41

Orla

ESME: OMFG!!

Need to speak. Where you at?? I'll come find you.

ORLA: No can do—cello in ten.

ESME: Fuck cello, La-la! I have news!!!

ORLA: Can't hun. Winter concert coming up—afraid cello is unfuckable.

ESME: It's only October.

ORLA: It's nearly November.

So come on?

I've got to go straight home tonight and we've got no classes together this aft. So spill??

ESME: Shit. This was face to face news really.

Drum roll . . .

ZANE JACKSON HAS GONE MISSING!!!!

It's all over Facebook. No one's seen him since Sunday.

ESME: So??? Paging Orla??

Hello??

What's with the silence, bitch?

ESME: Serious? Two hours, La-la?? U must have finished fucking cello by now

ESME: Oh look whatever. Just call me

42

Ellen

Adam's playing football with the boys—a toddler approxima-
tion of football, anyhow—when Cathy Grantham arrives fifteen
minutes early, saying she can't believe the traffic was so light.
I'd be lying if I said I'm not pleased with the sweet family scene
she's walked into, but it wasn't at all staged on our part. Simply
an attempt to subdue the boys by wearing them out a little bit.

But was her earliness staged, I wonder, as I welcome her
effusively to the Meadowhouse? Was it an attempt to catch us
unawares: Me downing a glass of wine while a starving Kian
tucks into a tin of shoe polish? Max playing with a cigarette
while Adam screams at the horse-racing on TV?

The very thought.

We are caught *slightly* unawares, though. Despite my best
efforts at bribery, Max still isn't wearing a jumper, and making
sure your child is in weather-appropriate clothing is very important, according to @silenceoftheprams on Mumsnet. Also,
Adam was meant to be putting a smart shirt on so I didn't feel
too OTT in my cutesy tea dress. But he's still dressed for toddler
football, so let's hope Cathy Grantham doesn't have an issue
with Chelsea FC.

Not that I imagine she cares much for aesthetics. Her hair, the
colour of Weetabix, is the same formless splat as on her LinkedIn
page, and her frumpy brown coat has a splotch on the lapel that
looks like mayonnaise.

The mayonnaise calms me somehow. It says, *Yes, I have power, but I'm also messy, clumsy, and human.*

"*Beautiful* African marigolds," she says, as she settles herself on the leather sofa (aka "the knife sofa"). "You have quite the front garden. My other half would be very jealous."

I beam inwardly and outwardly, taking the compliment oh-so-graciously. She doesn't need to know I didn't plant them. I don't even know what one is.

The boys are introduced, and honestly, they couldn't do me prouder. They're intrigued by the strange lady, but in a wholly charming way. Max announces quite urgently that "Jared's mummy is called Caffy" and Kian shows her his *CoComelon* puzzle then asks her if she wants an ice cream.

After I've made tea and she's rejected three different types of biscuit ("If I eat one, I'll eat the packet"), I immediately get out ahead of things and calmly assert that the anonymous call was malicious. I tell her about the letter and the Facebook posts—both things, regrettably, I can't provide proof of. However, I suggest that the police might have a recording of the call that led to me being breathalysed then inform her that Pelham would be happy to send her the anonymous email they received about my supposed theft (after an *excruciatingly* honest chat with the head about the whole debacle).

"Good. That would be very helpful, yes," she says, nodding. "It shows a pattern, gives the bigger picture. Sadly, malicious reports are more common than you might think."

"And are they always anonymous?" Adam asks, keen to understand this bleak world that's opened up to him. There's a slight snippiness to his voice. If I wasn't worried she'd notice, I'd give him a tiny kick.

"Not always, no. But you must remember, Mr. Wal—sorry, Adam, that we rely heavily on the public to alert us to children who might be suffering. Without respecting anonymity, many genuine cases would be missed."

Then between sips of tea, which she praises (despite being famed for her apparent fussiness), she lays out the list of allegations against me while Max and Kian watch *SpongeBob* on the TV.

The house is chaotic and small children have access to sharp objects.

I drink excessively and was recently breathalysed when I had the children with me.

I lose my temper disproportionately, and Max, in particular, looks withdrawn and unhappy.

"They might as well name a wing after that family," because the boys are never out of the hospital.

We talk about the Max "incident." I explain that the cut was small, and after a look herself, she agrees that his "ouchie" is minor. She records her findings in a tartan-covered notepad, then asks us if we got to the bottom of how the knife ended up down the side of the sofa.

I clear my throat. Of all the allegations, this is the one that I can try to explain but can't defend.

"See, I've thought and thought about it, Cathy, and the honest answer is that I really don't know."

And it is. While the craziest, darkest thoughts have occurred to me—from a psychopath breaking in and leaving the knife there for a future slaughter, to Orla self-harming in front of Netflix—none of them really make sense.

"The *only* thing I can think," I say, "is that maybe someone brought it in here to open a parcel, then got distracted. It's hard to believe, though, because we're usually so careful about stuff like that, I promise. But the only logical explanation is that someone left it behind mistakenly."

"And who are the 'someones' in this house?"

"Erm...me, Adam, my daughter, Orla, and my sister, Kristy."

"Orla should be home soon," Adam says brightly, although to

the well-trained marital ear it has strains of *at least she bloody well better be.*

I sail through the other allegations. We've been to the hospital *twice*—once for croup with Kian (and in hindsight, I overreacted) and once when Max developed a suspicious bump on his head, which turned out to be an insect bite. And yes, I lose my temper occasionally, but show me a parent who doesn't. And yes, Max can be challenging, certainly in comparison to his sunbeam brother, but "withdrawn" is wildly inaccurate, and I know in my heart that he's a happy soul. As for drinking "excessively," I tell her I like a glass of wine at weekends and *very* occasionally with dinner, but overdoing it just isn't worth the hangover when you've got two small boys who want to talk dinosaurs at 5:30 a.m.

Next—and quite quickly—she files through what I sense are standard questions. When did they last visit their GP, the dentist? A few questions on extended family. All the time, she's making notes, her spidery scrawl already filling two pages. Then suddenly she flips the book shut and says, "Max and Kian, do you know what I'd love to see?"

The answer is their bedroom, which she'd love them to show her round. A chance to chat to them on her own, no doubt, while having a nose at where they play and sleep. Unsurprisingly, Kian is game. Max is hesitant until I tell him Cathy's never played Zingo Bingo. Then, as they're marching her out of the room, she announces to Adam and me with a whirly finger, "And then I'll just have a general peek around the house."

As soon as we hear footsteps upstairs and Cathy Grantham marvelling at Brown Bear, Adam turns and hisses, "I thought you said Orla was coming straight home? I bet she's at Esme's."

It's almost 4 p.m. Orla finishes at 3:15, and we're only a twenty-minute walk from Foxton Grammar. Maybe twenty-five if you're dawdling and messaging, as Orla inevitably will be. I roll my eyes and dial her number, ready to whisper-rant down the phone about how she promised me.

She doesn't answer.

It rings out and goes to voicemail. "*Hey, leave a message, but WhatsApp's better.*"

I try again and again until I'm actually fit to kill her. I thought we had some sort of microscopic-but-meaningful breakthrough this morning, but as usual, I'm the fool.

Adam's scrolling his phone. "I think I've still got Esme's mum's number—you know, from when we took the girls to *Britain's Got Talent* a few years ago."

"You should mention that in front of Cathy. If that doesn't convince her we're selfless parents, nothing will."

I pick up the mugs and the biscuits and go and distract myself in the kitchen. Idly, I check the fridge (still full) and the cleaning cupboard (still padlocked), then make a start on the plate of biscuits. I'm on my third when Adam walks in.

He's staring at his phone, bewildered. Looking like a time-traveller from the 1820s.

"Esme's mum's at work, so she couldn't say for sure whether Orla's at her house." He looks up, brow furrowed. "But she said she doubts it, as she hasn't seen Orla in weeks, maybe months. I mean, I know she's not the most observant, but still?"

"I had a feeling," I admit, angry but unsurprised. "That night she came home and she'd lost my earring—I had a feeling she hadn't been at Esme's."

"So where?" he says. His face is a woeful mask. *No one ever tells me anything.*

"Boyfriend, I suppose."

"You *suppose*? Seriously, it's like you've given up on her, Els. She's been lying to us for possibly months and . . . and it's like you don't even care."

"Keep your voice down," I snap, suddenly aware of descending footsteps on the stairs. "And it's not that I don't care, but I was a teenage girl once . . ."

"You still have a top stair gate?" Cathy Grantham appears in the kitchen doorway, wearing a warm smile and a Pokémon sticker—Max's way of saying *I like this one*. "It's not a criticism, by the way, more an observation."

"Oh, it's probably just me being over-cautious," I say, delighted to have been handed the opportunity to show off my over-cautious credentials. "If one of them wakes in the night, they usually head for our bed, and they have to walk past the stairs, see. And while I do leave a small lamp on . . ."

"I understand," she cuts in, clearly pleased with the answer. Then she goes back into the living room and returns with a form for me to sign. "Just to say you're fine for me to contact your GP and a have quick chat with the nursery." She smiles again. "Then, assuming I'm satisfied with those conversations, I'll be suggesting no further action. The house is very safe and secure"—*thanks, Gwen!*—"and the boys seem happy and well cared for . . ."

There's a hammering on the front door. The type of blunt, insistent force that can only spell trouble.

Adam's eyes spear mine, as if he knows instinctively that this is my doing. I shoot a look at Cathy Grantham. The shock blanched across her face undoes every preparation I made and every truth I told today about how much my kids mean to me.

While Adam is closer, and physically stronger, to deal with whatever destruction awaits on the doorstep, I fly past him before he gets the chance, only stopping to bundle the boys back up the stairs.

When I open the door, recognition is instant, even though she's a total stranger.

The dark curls and the blue eyes. She even has his way of seeming to smile as she unleashes catastrophe.

"You fucking bitch. Get him out here."

From behind me Adam says, "Now hold on there . . ."

Zane's mum ignores him, moving forward. "And don't even think about lying, you dirty paedo scum."

I tell her to take a breath and calm down.

And that's when she flies at me.

43

Ellen

My nose is bleeding, and heat blooms across my cheeks. Advance warning of a bruise, maybe? Or just a natural physical reaction to deep, oceanic shame.

I pinch both nostrils. "Do you know what time it is in the Galapagos Islands?"

It's the first thing I've said since Adam manhandled Zane's mum out the door and Cathy Grantham rushed me to the kitchen sink. And as Cathy has no context, I know the question must sound quite mad.

To her credit, she humours me, albeit with concerned eyes. "Mid morning, I think. South America is generally five or six hours behind." She presses a gentle hand on my upper back; I keep forgetting to lean forward. I don't think I've ever had a nosebleed. I've certainly never been punched. "Listen, is your head OK, Ellen? Do you feel dizzy or disorientated?"

I mouth *no*, my head is fine, which is more than will be said for Sylvia's once news reaches her over her mid-morning Darjeeling. She might be over six thousand miles away, taking out-of-focus photographs of Galapagos reef octopuses, but the Thames Lawley grapevine has equally long tentacles, and the constant pinging of my phone suggests I'm already making waves.

I'm not sure why, amid everything, I'm fixating on this image: Sylvia's ageing manicured hands clutching her silk paisley neckscarf. Her expensively moisturised jowls quivering with I-told-you-so rage.

"*I always knew she'd bring trouble,*" she'll seethe while Rog nods non-committally. "*You can take the girl out of the council estate, but you can't take the council estate out of the girl.*"

"Well, I don't think it's broken." Cathy Grantham's feather-light prod of my nose brings me back to even grimmer reality. "I'm something of an expert on broken noses. Both my sons do amateur boxing."

I turn my head and smile faintly—the polite thing to do in the face of kindness. Then I wonder where Adam is, and Orla, and why I can't hear the boys rioting, and how Cathy Grantham reconciles judging the safety of other people's children while her own get bashed around in a ring.

"Where's Adam?" I croak, dabbing my nose with my bloodied tissue.

She cups the back of my neck, dips my head down again. "He thought it best to get the boys out of the way. He's taken them to a friend's. He said he'd back in a few minutes."

A *few*. Must be Gwen, then. A quick frogmarch across the village green. Kian waving to the early evening t'ai-chi-ers, full of beans as usual. Max repeatedly asking Adam about *the mean lady who did shout.*

"What's going to happen now?" I ask, blinking back tears. "I mean, with your report . . . all *this*, that woman. God knows what you must be thinking."

She raises a hand; a shush. "Hold on, 'that woman'? Are you saying you don't know her?"

"No. Well, yes." I turn away from the sink; the flow of blood is now barely a trickle. "I know who she is, but I've never met her before today. Her son is a student of mine. I've no idea why she thinks he's here. I don't understand anything, to be honest."

"Could she be the person who's been making the anonymous complaints?"

"I don't know. Maybe . . ."

There's a knock at the front door. Robust, insistent, but notably less warlike than last time. Not taking any chances, though, Cathy Grantham says in the kind of point-blank tone I guess you'd need to parent two boxers, "Do *not* move a muscle, you hear? You absolutely stay right there."

Less than a minute of low murmurs and she returns with two people. Two police officers, at a guess—I told Adam not to call them, but I suspect my opinion holds little weight right now. One is a hulking great wardrobe of a man who takes up the entire doorway, his blue suit and grey shirt practically straining at every stitch. The other a small black woman who I'd put around my age despite her grey buzz cut. It's clear she's running the show. While her stature may be slight, her whole demeanour screams purpose. The Hulk keeps a respectful distance, as if giving her space to do her thing.

"Ellen Walsh?" she says with a half-smile I can't decipher. "My name is Detective Sergeant Roberta Knowles, and this is DC Damien Flint."

A *sergeant*? For what amounts to a few spots on a tissue and a nose that isn't broken? My urge is to shoo them out of here, but I settle for being firm and clear when I speak.

"Look, I'm sorry if my husband called you, but you've had a wasted journey. I'm not pressing charges. She was upset and confused. I don't want to make things any worse."

The sergeant takes a step closer. A stream of late sun through the kitchen window hits her face, putting her closer to fifty than my age. "Nobody called us, Mrs. Walsh, and I'm not exactly sure what you're referring to. But clearly you've been assaulted—we can get a doctor to check you out at the station."

"Station? For what? I told you, I'm not pressing charges."

The front door opens, followed by a hollered "What the actual fuck, Mum?"

The sergeant turns briefly but doesn't let it throw her off her stride. "We need you to accompany us to the station so that we can question you further regarding the disappearance of Zane Jackson."

"*What?*" I cast a desperate look at Orla through the gap between the Hulk's shoulder and the door frame. "For God's sake, I already told Jason Bale . . ." *Everything?* I can't say it. It's a blatant lie. Instead, I breathe out slowly. "Honestly, this is ridiculous."

"Is it? Is it really, Mrs. Walsh?" The sergeant cocks her head, smiling crisply. "Well firstly, PC Jason Bale is part of our local policing effort, and this case has now been passed *up* to my team, the Protecting Vulnerable People Unit." Her emphasis on the word *up* translates to *lady, this is serious*. "Secondly, new intelligence suggests that there was a lot you *didn't* tell PC Bale." Pressure sweeps my body, like I'm losing oxygen underwater. "And while you're not under arrest at this time, it really is in your best interests to cooperate." She holds up a piece of paper. "Would you like to read this warrant that permits us to search your house and your car?"

44

Ellen

A scratched table. Three chairs. A wall-mounted camera. And, at last, company.

"For the tape, the date is Friday the twenty-ninth of October, and the time is twenty oh two . . ."

Eight o'clock. That surprises me. I wouldn't have guessed that I've been waiting in this oppressively beige room for the best part—or worst part—of three cuticle-picking hours. The long delay in getting started was due to Knowles insisting an HCP (a health-care practitioner) check me over—something she eventually gave up on when it became clear that the nearest available doctor (I'm not bowing to their acronyms) was going to be stuck for the next decade in a tie-up on the A413. In truth, I suspect the delay was more to do with waiting for updates on various searches, but as anxious as that makes me, at least I know they'll find zilch. They can rip up every floorboard, rifle every cupboard. There's simply nothing for them to see.

"Present are DS Roberta Knowles, DC Damien Flint, and Ellen Walsh. Mrs. Walsh has stated that she does not require legal representation at this time . . ."

Correct. I did state that. Partly out of petulance and a desire not to delay things any further, but also because of a possibly naïve belief that only guilty people request a lawyer.

"In accordance with the Home Office Circular 50/1995, I

am obliged to inform you that this interview is being remotely monitored . . ."

The preamble ambles on. The wholly familiar spiel that anyone with a passing interest in TV crime dramas could recite backwards.

The reminder that I'm under caution.

That what I say may be used against me.

That I don't have to say anything, but it might harm my defence if I don't mention when questioned something I later rely on in court . . .

And there's my cue.

With my hands anchored around a polystyrene cup of cold coffee, I say, "OK, there's something I didn't tell you. Well, I didn't tell Jas— PC Bale."

Knowles sits perfectly still. Flint jitters a foot against the floor, unable to hide his anticipation.

"And I *swear* I was going to report it today—voluntarily, I mean . . ."

"You are here voluntarily, Ellen," Knowles reminds me. "You're free to leave at any time."

"Yeah, yeah, I know, but . . ." I clutch the cup more tightly; the coffee rises a few inches. *Breathe.* "See, the thing is, Zane had a cut on his face when I picked him up last Sunday. Fresh. Bleeding a bit. Around here." I trace a moon around my ear. "And I didn't tell PC Bale because . . . well, Zane told me that Paulo had done it, that he'd hit him during this stupid row about the boiler, and I *knew* that wherever Zane was, he wouldn't want me landing Paulo in the shi— in trouble. So I didn't say anything. I'm sorry. I'm really sorry."

Knowles mulls this over, slipping off her suit jacket. Underneath, she's wearing a simple black T-shirt, and halfway up her forearm there's a small tattooed *J*.

"OK, fine," she says. "Poor decision, but I get the logic. But last night, PC Bale told you there'd been no such row with Paulo. Why didn't you mention this cut then?"

This cut, not *the* cut. An almost imperceptible difference, but *this* screams scepticism.

I draw a deep breath. I know this is going to sound bad.

"Because I had a Social Services visit to prepare for. Someone made a malicious complaint, so they had to do an assessment. And I just didn't want to get any more mixed up in all this Zane business until that was done and dusted." Did I *actually* say "Zane business"? Two unimpressed faces stare back at me. "And I know that makes me sound awful, and I'm certainly not proud of myself. But I *swear* I was going to drive to the station straight after and tell PC Bale or whoever about the cut. But I never got the chance, because Zane's mum turned up on my doorstep with this mental idea that he was in my house."

"I spoke with Julie Jackson just before, and it wasn't such a 'mental idea,' actually." It's the most I've heard Flint speak. I hadn't even registered he was Scottish. "There'd been some Facebook rumours about Zane's involvement with an older woman." He lets that sit. "Then around three p.m. today, someone texted his mum from an unknown number saying they'd just seen him entering your house. They gave her your full address. Naturally she jumped."

It's as though a camera flash has exploded in my face. I feel dazzled, exposed. I think I mumble, "What?"

Knowles confirms, *for the tape*, that the phone connected to the unknown number has since been switched off, and that the number can't be traced.

"Oh my God," I say slowly, still blinking away the shock. "So that's what your lot are searching for? You think you're going to find Zane hiding under my bed or curled up in the loft?"

Knowles gives a frosty laugh. "Not quite. If you remember, Ellen, we arrived at your house before we heard about Julie Jackson. We were looking for you, not Zane." She opens a grey folder, leaving the top page in plain sight—a printout of my internet search history. "Now, you don't follow Zane on Instagram, do you?" I shake my head. She tilts hers. "But you're a regular visitor to his page," she says, tapping the printout. "My daughter—she's slightly older than yours, but you know what they're like about social media etiquette—she'd call that 'a bit stalkery.'"

My skin feels hot even though I'm only wearing my tea dress. I'd ignored their advice to bring something warm. A childish attempt to assert control.

"I don't have an Instagram account, no." I shrug. "But in Zane's case, I like to keep tabs on what he posts."

"Oh yeah, why's that?"

"Because he's a complex young man. Vulnerable. And his Instagram page often offers a clue to how he's feeling. The quotes he posts, I mean. It's part of my job to be aware of that."

Which is true, if he'd ever been anything resembling a standard student.

"OK, sure." Knowles nods, sweeping a hand over her buzz cut. "And of course other clues come from his friends, and it's *our* job to talk to them." She dives back into the folder, has a quick read of something, then holds up four fingers. "*Four*, Ellen—that's how many of Zane's friends have made statements in the past twenty-four hours confirming that he told them, in some detail, that you and he were having a sexual relationship."

The camera flash again, even brighter this time, almost blinding.

"Well, that's a lie," I say, but it doesn't sound anywhere near forceful enough. Total disorientation has left my voice cracked and weak.

"Zane also said—and this is a friend directly quoting him, by the way—that you went 'proper schizo' when he attempted to cool things recently."

I burn with embarrassment even though what I'm hearing is pure fantasy.

Knowles powers on. "He *also* told his friends that you'd given him money and expensive gifts, that you'd basically been trying to buy back his waning affection. Apparently he found the whole thing a bit 'cringe' but said, 'the more desperate she gets, the dirtier she is in bed.'" She shakes her head. "Not nice, that, Ellen. Not nice at all."

The mix of pity and contempt kicks me out of my reduced state. "Definitely not nice," I agree. "But *definitely* not true."

She's disappointed in me. "Ellen, these are four separate friends. Only two of them know each other, but they *all* gave similar accounts."

"I'm not saying *they're* lying. I'm saying Zane lied to them." I strike a note of contemptuous pity myself. "Seriously, this is your 'new intelligence'? A teenage boy's fantasy and four other teenagers lapping it up?"

"But *these* aren't fantasy, Ellen." Knowles pulls several photos from the folder, slides them across one by one. "Custom-made Nikes—a hundred and sixty pounds. An Apple Watch. Brand-new AirPods. We found them in Zane's bedroom. Gifts he told his friends *you* bought him."

I study each photo, although I don't know why I'm bothering. Apart from overpriced groceries, I never bought Zane a thing.

Flint chips in. "Also, we don't have a photo, but he wore a Ralph Lauren T-shirt—limited edition—to a party on Friday night. That was from you too, apparently."

Shit.

My head swims. Should I admit that *was* from me—not a purchase, but a regift? My gut says no. If I gave him one gift, I gave him twenty. That's how they'll see it.

"I've never seen those things before. I didn't buy them."

"So why would he say you did?" Knowles asks.

"Because he stole them, maybe?" I suggest.

Any qualms I might have had about trashing his reputation went right out the window the minute he annihilated mine.

"Yeah, we thought that when we found them," says Flint, kind of chummy—*great minds think alike*. "And according to his pals, he wasn't exactly averse to a bit of the old ten-finger discount. But they reckon he'd have been bragging non-stop if he'd managed to lift items like these, so if he said someone bought them for him, then someone did. And that someone, according to the man himself, was you."

"The *boy*," Knowles says, looking straight at me. "You know, my youngest lad is seventeen. He barely needs to shave. Can't even work a tin-opener."

"Check my bank account," I say, not giving an inch.

"Oh, we will, you can be sure of that. But then you're a private tutor—you must be paid in cash quite often."

"Sometimes." And then before I can stop myself, I add, "Not enough to keep my teenage lovers in fancy Nikes, though."

A trace of a wry smile, then a complete change in direction.

"Have you lost a necklace, Ellen?" she asks, enjoying my confusion. "Because we found this in Zane's bedroom—down the side of his bed, actually. For the tape, the witness is being shown item TGR-8721." Flint produces a polythene evidence bag—inside it, my Tiffany circle pendant. The confusion swirling in my belly quickly turns to rot. "And, see, it *exactly* matches a pair of earrings the search team found in your bedroom. Your daughter kindly confirmed that you *do* have a matching necklace; your husband didn't know." She gives me a look—*Men, eh?* "But we couldn't seem to find it among your jewellery." She pushes the photo closer. "Could this be it?"

I block out thoughts of my *kind* daughter, of the devastation that awaits me.

"Could be," I say.

"And how would it have ended up in Zane's room?"

There's no way I'm admitting we occasionally worked in

Zane's bedroom. And in any case, it wouldn't explain anything. I've only ever worn that necklace on special occasions. As sure as I'm sitting here, I've never worn it in Zane's flat.

"I was wearing it last Friday," I lie. I have to until I can wrap my head around what's going on here. "It must have fallen off in the living room and he held on to it for safe keeping."

Knowles pulls a face. "Down the side of his bed?"

"Away from Paulo," I say, my brain firing on every cylinder. "He once pawned Zane's Nintendo to pay off a bar tab."

Or so Zane told me. But it looks like we've been matching each other pound for pound when it comes to telling lies.

"Zane saw you on the Sunday," says Flint. "Why didn't he give it back to you then?"

I make a cool gesture—*Who knows?* "Bigger things on his mind?"

Surprisingly, Knowles nods. "OK, that's fine. Shall we move on?"

To what? Christ knows. The blows keep on coming.

"Do you have a mole at the top of your inner thigh, Ellen?"

And there we have it, the next swerve.

"I do," I say clearly, keen to show I'm not rattled.

"And how would Zane know about this mole?"

I give a half-shrug, as though the question isn't worth a whole one. "I must have mentioned it, I guess." But I know I definitely didn't. I learned very early on not to give Zane open goals when it came to flirting. So a reference to my inner thigh? No way. Didn't happen. "It's changed shape over the last year, changed colour. I've been debating whether to have it removed."

Debating with Adam and Nush and Gwen and Kristy, and the woman in the dry-cleaner's, and more than one taxi driver, and *everyone* at Hot Pilates, and most of my students' parents, and frankly just about every living creature unfortunate enough to cross my hypochondriac path.

Except Zane.

Knowles is quiet as she stares, chewing over the plausibility. I try to read her expression, actually willing her to say something, but it's obvious she's holding back. The stretched silence forms a canyon, and eventually it's too much. I fall in.

"Look, this whole thing is pure madness. I have never had sex with Zane Jackson, or any other seventeen-year-old boy for that matter. And I've taught enough of them over the years. I can give you names right now. How many do you want?"

"Problem is, Ellen. We have a witness."

Knowles's stare is charged, but her voice is soft. As extra-time penalties go, it's not a smack into the back of the net, more a cool lobbed finish.

"A witness to what?"

"A witness who saw you and Zane standing at the rear of your car on Trensale Row, where you tried to kiss him and he rejected you."

She waits a beat, allowing me one "No!"

"And this isn't a horny teen lapping up idle gossip, Ellen. It's an independent, credible adult witness."

There was not a soul on that street. Was someone looking out of their window at us?

"No, no, look—*he* tried to kiss *me*. I know I should have mentioned it before, but it was nothing, a matter of seconds. I turned him down, *obviously*."

"Witness was very clear—*you* kissed *him*."

"Well, your witness needs new glasses then."

"They had an excellent view, Ellen. Spot-on recall of your car, of what you both were wearing, your faces. And if you'll give me a minute . . ." She pulls a page from the folder, gives it a speed-read. "Yep, thought so. Interestingly, given the level of detail they were able to provide, they don't mention anything about a cut on Zane's face. Obviously we'll check again, but . . ."

"Why would I make that up?" I say, my voice shrill with exasperation. I can't get a grasp on this, on anything. "What possible reason would I have?"

Flint takes over. "Because we're searching your car, Ellen. And you know that if we find a speck of Zane's blood, it gives you a plausible explanation." A seam of dread in my stomach says we're close to a point of no return. "See, the witness says you were arguing . . ."

"We weren't *arguing*. I was bit pissed off that he could have asked someone else for a lift."

". . . and that you hit him."

"*What?*"

"Witness said you hit him."

My eyes dart between Knowles and Flint. "Then your witness is lying."

"And why would they do that?" Knowles sounds as if she's had enough of me for one day. "A total stranger—what possible reason would they have?"

"I don't know. But I didn't hit anyone."

Flint launches the next ambush.

"Tell us, why did you change your clothes as soon as you got home that evening?"

"I'm sorry?"

"We took a statement from a Shay Hardwick a couple of hours ago. He says that when you got home on Sunday, you seemed 'on edge, kind of flustered.'"

The unutterable bastard.

A deep sadness descends. Kristy and I may never recover from this.

"Yeah, I was on edge with *him*, because I barely know him and he'd taken over my bloody kitchen!"

"He says that not long after you got home, you went for a bath, changed your clothes. He didn't think it odd at the time, but in light of our questioning . . ."

"I was damp!" I shout. I don't mention needing to be alone after reading the message that came with the flowers. "I'd gone straight from a rainy park to pick up Zane, and . . ." I stop dead, almost laugh. "Oh my God, what do you think I was doing? Washing off blood?"

Flint glances at Knowles, who, given the path we're headed down, looks fairly relaxed, almost flippant.

"Do you know what?" she says, leaning back, crossing her ankles under the table. "Let's not worry about blood today. Blood—*if* there is any—will take a day or two. Let's focus on right now." A pause. "On what we found in your car."

Fear makes me snippy. "Is it Zane? Did I forget I had him tied up in the back or strapped to the roof rack?"

She stretches forward, calmly sliding another photo across the table. "No. A condom wrapper, Ellen. Tucked away in the glove compartment between a child's drawing of a carrot, as far as I could make out, and an order of funeral service for a Dennis Kaye. Nice." Realisation hammers home. Reality takes a dreadful shape. "Durex Performax Intense. The *exact* same brand of condoms we found in Zane's bedside drawer. Only six left out of a pack of twenty-four. You've been busy." She sits forward; the scrape of the chair sends my rising pulse sky-high. "So what happened that day? Did you have sex in your car? Maybe a goodbye jump, as far as Zane was concerned . . ."

I zone out from the rest. I'm back in Danesfield, and Zane's asking if we can stop for paracetamol. He only offers to go in and get it when I'm already out of the car. Then I'm getting back in the car and he's closing the glove compartment. He says he was looking for tissues. His headache appears to have disappeared.

He told his friends lies about me.

He quite possibly broke into my house and stole my Tiffany necklace.

He planted that condom wrapper in my car.

He set me up.

But if I tell Knowles and Flint, they'll want to know why.

I have to get out of here.

I take a quick, steadying breath. "Look, can I still leave when I want, because it's clear you're not listening to me. I haven't been having a sexual relationship with Zane Jackson, and even if we sit here for another week, I'm not going to say any different."

It seems inconceivable that they'll let me walk, so I'm shocked to see Knowles nodding. I stand up straight away.

"Yes, you can," she says, looking up at me. "Repugnant as I find it, there's no law against having sex with a seventeen-year-old. But let me be clear—you are released under investigation, which means you are still *very* much of interest, and I suspect we'll be speaking again." Her face hardens. "See, we know you're lying about *something*, Ellen. And our guv'nor has a saying, doesn't he, Damien?"

Damien delivers the punchline. "A provable lie is the next best thing to a confession."

My hand is on the door handle when Knowles jolts suddenly in her chair.

"Oh, actually, speaking of sayings—before you go, could you help us with something?" It's a smooth shift in tone. She feigns surprise at my hostile look. "What? You do want to help find him, don't you?" I nod because I have to, but I'm honestly not sure now. "Could you take a look at this, then?" she says, handing me a photo of a sheet of lined paper. "You said earlier that the quotes Zane posts are often a clue to his feelings. Well, we found this written on the front page of a notebook under his mattress. There was nothing else, just this quote. Any ideas?"

SOONER OR LATER EVERYONE SITS DOWN TO A BANQUET OF CONSEQUENCES

"It's Robert Louis Stevenson." The world fractures and splinters as I realise just how much Zane hates me. "I've no idea what it means to him, though. Sorry."

But the truth is, I do.

It means I pulled the strings of his life.

Now he's pulling the strings of mine.

After I've circled the outside of the station three times, Adam finally flashes the headlights. It's hard to believe he didn't spot me before, which suggests he must have sat there watching as I wandered around freezing my tits off in my tea dress. I don't have the mental or physical energy to think about what that means.

"Oh God, take me home," I sigh as I slump into the passenger seat. "Seriously, I need a hot shower and a glass of wine, then I'll give you the lowdown."

"Sure you will, Ellen. Your version of it, you mean."

His anger is a dense weight, as real as another passenger. I stare at him, weighing up what to say, but then something catches my eye on the back seat.

"Hey, what's the bag for?" I ask.

"I've booked us into a hotel. The Falcon—just a cheap one."

"Hold on, why are we going to a hotel?" He starts the ignition, but I reach across, grab his forearm. "And the bloody *Falcon*?"

He turns to look at me for the first time and I instantly wish he hadn't. It's clear from his expression that he doesn't think much of what he sees.

"Oh, sorry, should I have booked the Ritz? Too good for the Falcon, are you? I thought as patron saint of the poor folk, it'd be right up your street."

My stomach flips, my grip loosens. Adam may be many things but he's not snide.

"What's going on, Ads?" I ask, my breath shaky. "Where's Orla? Where are the boys?"

He speaks slowly, his voice thrumming with controlled rage. "*Our* address, *your* name, has been *all* over Facebook, so let's just say we've had an audience. Trust me, you've had the easier ride." *Jesus Christ.* "So the boys are still at Gwen's, and I dropped Orla there half an hour ago. I'll work out the next few days in the morning. You don't get a say."

"No." I shake my head. "No way. I'm not being hounded out of my own home." Adam is silent. I raise my voice. "Ads, seriously, this isn't fair. I've done nothing wrong."

He explodes. "Fuck you, Ellen. Can you *actually* hear yourself? '*I've* done nothing wrong,' '*I* need wine,' '*I'm* not being hounded.' Do you *ever* stop to consider anyone but yourself? Because I can sure as hell tell you that *I* haven't done anything wrong here, but it's *me* who's had to fend off a million nosy phone calls. *Me* who's had to stop Orla from pretty much trashing the house. *Me* who's had to answer humiliating questions like 'Does your wife have access to any isolated property?' But do you know what's been worst of all? I've had to lie to the police—*the police*—about this boy, pretend I don't know—"

"What do you mean?" I say, cutting in. "You're not lying. You don't know him."

"Yes, but I know what this is about now." He gives me a look of unreserved disgust. "Orla just told me everything, Ellen. I know *exactly* who he is."

Third Bad Deed

The Knife

Orla

Esme shagged Zane. He blackmailed her. I took a stand against it.

And there concludes my testimony.

I wish I could say I don't regret a thing.

I definitely regret telling Mum; she caught me at a weak point, told me she'd fix things. I should have told Dad too, but Mum said, "Not a chance. Don't even think about it." Sometimes I wonder why they got married, although apparently their wedding was pretty epic.

"He's a skank, but so hot." That was my introduction to Zane Jackson. Not an *actual* introduction, of course; I'm never let within ten feet of Esme's conquests. But they were the first words she said about him. Kind of cruel, but precise and neat.

So, *obviously*, I checked him out on Instagram (lots of weird quotes, no photos of Esme), and unsurprisingly, he *was* hot, but surprisingly, I recognised him. It took a minute to remember, but then I realised it was from the Nook, this kind of sketchy café in Minton (I go for the hash browns; others buy their weed there), where, because of its location next to the main bus station, you get a real mix of teens dropping in.

And, you know, I didn't think he was a skank. There's *far* skankier at Foxton Grammar. Scotti Lund might throw great parties, but seriously, his fingernails—supergross. OK, so maybe this Zane didn't speak like Prince William, but that's the problem with Esme: she's only ever known privilege. And, like, I'm not being a dick, trying to claim *I* was raised in the ghetto, but I lived in a not-particularly-glam part of south London until I was eleven, and I don't piss my pants just because someone doesn't pronounce their T's.

But still, *Esme*. Esme, Esme, Esme. I craved her attention from my very first week at the grammar, and when she said, "Wanna come to mine? I reckon the squad could do with a token red-head!" I felt like I was standing on a stage on Broadway with bouquets raining down on me. I mean, don't get me wrong, she's a total bitch, but everyone agrees there's *something* about her. Maybe it's just the feeling that school life will be easier if you're a paid-up member of Team Esme.

It's a tricky team to stay on, though. So many jostlers, plenty of applicants. You can go from untouchable BFF to scapegoat without a clue what you did to displease. Sometimes it's because you wore something similar to her. Another time because you actually did your homework. But with me, the root of every problem is that I'm better-looking (and if that sounds arrogant, well sorry).

"But you're soooooooo basic, though, La-la," she always says (the ultimate put-down). "Do something interesting for a change. Don't you ever get bored of just being pretty?"

So, yeah, *bitch*. But whatever.

Anyway, for most of the month she was shagging Zane, me and Es weren't really speaking. I'd been banished once again from the kingdom for crimes against the queen. Actually, at least I knew what my offence was that time. It was "disrespecting Amber Keller." Apparently I shouldn't have called her out for laughing at a Year 8's crappy trainers. Not when her dad is "high up" at a record label (in HR and training; he's hardly Jay-Z).

And, see, I *soooo* badly wanted not to care, but *all* my friends were hitched to Esme. And it gets pretty lonely pretty quick when you've got no friends and no social life, just cello practice and homework and all four seasons of *The O.C.*

But then it happened. The thing with Zane. The video. And she told *me* about it first, of course, because when the shit hits the fan, and she wants support and endless sympathy, she doesn't turn to Amber Keller or Abi Devlin or Sophie Chu or Sinead Gallagher or Jodie Parks or Priya Prasad or Georgia Huckle. She turns to me.

"I told you he was a skank," she sobbed. "He's actually worse than a skank. He's a fucking criminal." She'd been ranting for nearly an hour. I'd thought Mum's vodka might calm her down, but it was sending her the other way. "He wants three hundred pounds by Friday or he's going to send everyone a video he took of me bent over my bed, playing with myself. And, I mean, I only did it because he said he needed something to get him off while I'm in Verbier over Easter, and all the girls on Pornhub are nowhere near as hot as me." She stifled a sob. "I thought he was being sweet."

Well, then you're an idiot, I thought, while I stroked her hair and called him a wanker. But even then, an idea was stirring. A plan to cement my position on Team Esme.

To "do something interesting."

"How will you pay him?" I asked, before offering her the £70 I'd been saving for new Converse.

"I don't need your money," she scoffed. I don't know why I was surprised by the lack of "thank you." "You know what my mum's like. She won't even ask what's it for as long it gets rid of me."

She was right. She got the money. Friday came, and she paid him. And he swore solemnly on his life that he'd delete the video and wouldn't ask for more money. But while Esme happily moved on—no sign of any video, no more requests for money—*I* couldn't help but come back to one question.

How dare he?

I mean, *really*. How fucking dare *any* of them?

How dare Declan O'Dell tell Scotti Lund that I let him come on my tits at Esme's party? He came in my hand after twenty seconds. I hadn't even taken off my fucking cardi!

How dare Callum Rudd leave a massive dildo on my desk, then call me uptight? *"It's only a joke, Orla."*

How dare Roan Howells think kissing on his bed is an invite to slip two fingers inside me?

And I did *nothing* when any of this happened. *Nothing.* Just scowled and sighed and had a bitch-fest with the girls afterwards. And they'd all had similar experiences. In Sinead Gallagher's case, far, far worse.

So the more I thought about it, the less it was to do with impressing Esme (although, sure, that was an attractive by-product). It was actually more to do with justice. Taking a stand. Settling a score. See, there was nothing I could do about Declan's lies now, or Callum's "joke," or Roan's fingers (except daydream about snapping them), and to be honest, if I sought revenge on any of them, they'd declare open season on me.

But this Zane, this stranger. He didn't know me. He'd never suspect me. I could get *him* back for blackmailing Esme.

I didn't mean for everything to go quite so mental.

Ellen

"Sweetie, *breathe*," I urged her. "I can't make out a word you're saying. But whatever it is, I'm going to fix it, OK? Whatever's happened, it's going to be fine."

I'd found her curled on her bedroom floor, hyperventilating into Princess Furryball. Sucking the edge of her stuffed cat's ear was how she used to soothe herself in her crib.

Her retreat into a childlike state had flooded my head with ink-black thoughts.

She was pregnant.

She was pregnant, and worse, she'd left it too late to have any choices.

She'd been raped or sexually assaulted.

She'd been raped and she was pregnant, and I was going to have to burn the entire world down.

My heart cracked in two. My baby girl was only fifteen.

Looking back, I often wonder if my cold, pragmatic response to Orla's unexpected revelation was a result of being braced for Armageddon. The fact I'd been expecting much, much worse. Because, as soon as I knew she wasn't hurt, that the situation was undeniably *bad* but not fatal, it was as though relief corrupted me. I became someone I'd never thought I'd be.

"So let me get this straight," I said slowly, needing to hear it in my own voice. Orla's delivery had been semi-manic, peppered with convulsive hiccups and snot and tears. "You walked into the Nook and you planted a knife in a stranger's school bag. And you did this on the say-so of Esme Eavis, who wouldn't piss on you if you were on fire."

When I'd said *you*, I'd meant *anyone*, but I was in no mood to spare her feelings. She wasn't pregnant or hurt in any way. She wasn't a victim. She was the aggressor.

That realisation, the recalibration from *my baby girl* to *you utter imbecile*, had rendered me speechless for a few seconds. But now I wanted detail, and if she wanted sympathy, she was out of luck.

"*Noooooo*," she howled, and I swear they'd have heard her across the green, if not in Bolivia. It was a small mercy—and God knows we needed one—that Adam had taken the boys to Splash n' Swim. "Es didn't tell me do it. She doesn't even know it was me. Nobody does. I mean, I *was* going to tell her. I thought she'd be pleased. That was the whole point. Well, no, it was part of it..." She made a stab at defiance, steadying her wobbling chin. "The other part was about making at least *one* boy pay for all the shit they get away with."

However, *this* boy wasn't an "entitled Foxton prick," and this was the crux of Orla's agony. She'd made the least privileged of them pay and she was crippled by retrospective guilt. *This* boy lived a tough existence on the Lomax and yet he'd aced ten GSCEs (she'd learned from Instagram). He'd also just written a post about feeling proud of himself "for the first time ever," because he'd finally been able to buy his elderly neighbour—who kept getting burgled—a security grille.

Orla insisted I look at the post—at the photo of the cutest old lady laughing as she cut a ribbon tied around her front door. I wasn't sure that putting her face on Instagram was the best way to guarantee her security, but it was hard to deny it was sweet.

"Don't you see?" she wailed, inconsolable. "*That's* what he wanted the money for."

"Oh, and that excuses what he did?"

"No. But it makes him 'stupid and desperate, not an out-and-out wanker.' *Your* exact words about Uncle Cahill, Mum. About all his fuck-ups, his burglaries. And now to make things worse, Esme's heard he was bluffing about the video anyway. But it's too late now. Everything's got so big . . ."

Big. The boy's permanent exclusion from school, nearly a year into his A levels. A possible criminal charge. At the very least, a referral to a youth offending team.

"Honestly, Mum, I thought he'd only get suspended. Vinnie Aldridge brought a *sword* to school last year, this ceremonial thing that his dad had, and *he* only got thrown off the football team. But, see, this Zane, he'd been suspended a few times already. Just truancy, Es thinks. Oh, and telling a PE teacher to get fucked once." She looked at me, pleading. "But how was I to know that?"

I was sick of her bleating, staggered by her stupidity.

"But a *knife*!" I roared. "A goddam effing *knife*, Orla! And don't talk to me about Vinnie Aldridge. He hasn't the got brainpower of a suet pudding. But you do. Or I thought you did."

"So what should I have done, yeah?" Belligerent Orla took the mic, a persona that didn't exist before Esme. "Drawn a cock and balls on his bag? Written 'Zane Jackson has a tiny pee-pee'?"

"If Esme believed he'd taken a video, she could have gone to the police. You could have gone with her to support her. Blackmail is a crime, Orla, not a tit-for-tat game."

"If she'd gone to the police, someone would've had to watch the supposed video. She was mortified."

Esme's dignity—although, bless her—was around #512 on my list of worries.

"Christ, where did you even get a knife?" I blurted suddenly. "I haven't noticed any missing."

The furtive shift of her eyes told me I wasn't going to like the answer.

"I stole one."

"From who?"

"Benny's Bargains on Minton High Street. I'd have paid for it . . ." She said this with a certain pride, as though it somehow restored her fine character, "but I'd been in there in my uniform. He'd have known I wasn't over eighteen."

"Oh, brilliant, Orla. Just brilliant." We'd moved to Thames Lawley for her education. We should have just shipped her up to Mum and Cahill. "So you're a shoplifter now, too? As well as a . . ." I couldn't think of the term. I could hardly think what year it was. "A *weapon-planter*?"

For the first time, I stood. I had to put some distance between us. Then I walked over to the bedroom window and stared out towards the village green. A young couple were trying to get a kite going, and in normal circumstances, I'd have thought: a kite, how bloody tedious. But right then, the innocence of their endeavour, the simplicity of it, almost broke me.

This is all my fault, I realised.

In her early adolescence, when Orla had needed a more intuitive style of parenting, the twins had been challenging babies, stealing my time and my sanity. Orla had got her first period the same day the boys were due their 6-in-1 vaccines, and as Kian had been grouchy afterwards, and Max biblically wrathful, I'd barely had time to acknowledge her milestone.

I'd failed her then and many times after. Suddenly it was overwhelmingly plain to see.

I turned back to her, quickly trying to chase my guilt away with more questions.

"So how did you even know he'd get caught with it?" I asked. "He could have easily looked in his bag and found it."

"I didn't *know*," she whimpered. "I just knew St Tommy More's were trialling these metal scanner things. I'd heard some kids talking about them. That's what gave me the idea." She paused, her face folding in on itself. "And I suppose I just got lucky that he didn't find it. Except I don't feel lucky, Mum. I feel like shit."

What she said next made my heart leap to my throat, then plummet through the floorboards.

"I think I should own up to what I did."

I stared at her, aghast. I knew that on some fundamental level I should feel proud that she wanted to take responsibility. But I worked in education. I knew what this would mean.

"No," I said unequivocally. It was as though the word had taken on fresh meaning. It wasn't an answer, it was a decree, and one that I'd enforce by any means necessary. "Absolutely not, Orla. No, no, no, no, *no*."

She pushed herself up to standing, genuinely shocked. "*Seriously*, you're telling me to say nothing?"

I took a step towards her. "I'm telling you to put it behind you. You did a terrible thing. Learn from it, move on."

"Except *he* can't, can he?" Silence passed between us. Orla waited, but I didn't buckle. "Seriously, Mum. Like, *wow*." She gave me a look of disgusted awe. "So even though I've pretty much screwed up his life—"

"Listen to me, Orla," I interrupted, desperate. "I went to school with boys like him. Always playing truant, always getting suspended. Trust me, ten GSCEs or no GCSEs, that kind usually screw their own lives up before too long."

"*That kind?*" The awe slipped away, leaving just contempt, plain revulsion. "My God," she said, staring at me as if seeing me for the first time. "So all that stuff about fairness and privilege that you've drummed into me since nursery, that's all bullshit, is it? It doesn't include *that kind?*"

Oh, to be young and principled.

How could I make her understand? To a fifteen-year-old, the future is something to be dealt with in the future. I was thinking about her *life*. Orla barely thought past the next weekend.

"Look, you're a really good kid who did a really bad thing,"

I said, trying flattery. "But regardless of what *you* did, this boy sounds like trouble, and I bet it'd only be a matter of time before he was expelled for something else." I *loathed* myself. This wasn't who I was, what I believed. But it wasn't a time for personal values. I needed to be a realist. I needed to be a *mother*. "*Blackmail*, Orla. That's what we're talking about here, and it's inexcusable. And you're not sacrificing yourself for a boy like that. No way. Not happening."

Her puffy eyes flared with challenge. "So you think I should get away with it?"

It was a yes-or-no question that made me want to poke my own eyes out, so I shouted, "What I *think*, Orla, is that you should bloody well *think* about what will happen if you admit to this. You'll be screwing up your own life. Is that what you want?"

She blinked. "They wouldn't expel me. I've never even had detention."

"For Christ's sake, wise up!" I'd never sounded more like my mother. "It's a criminal offence. Carrying a weapon in a public place, or whatever they call it. And then planting it on someone else probably carries some sort of other charge. And remember, you're not that idiot Vinnie Aldridge bringing his dad's fancy sword to show-and-tell. What you did wasn't just reckless, it was malicious and premeditated. Forget expelled; it wouldn't surprise me if you were charged. I'd say *definitely* a youth caution." She opened her mouth, but I was at full steam. "And you say you want to go to Oxbridge? Become a lawyer? Yeah, well, good luck with those applications. I presume you've heard of background checks?"

She nodded reluctantly, then threw herself on her bed, facing away from me and my double standards.

Finally, *thank God*, I'd made her see sense, unpalatable as it was.

*

So, your child or my child. Who do you save from a burning building? Because that's what it came down to. My daughter pitted against some random boy whose face I couldn't picture. My heart versus my conscience. Reality or an abstract thing.

See, I hadn't simply been trying to scare her when I'd outlined the potentially life-changing consequences. Orla could have been in deep, *deep* shit if she'd come clean. I believe that to this day. And while everyone knows that white middle-class girls don't exactly get the roughest ride in life, occasionally one gets made an example of.

Well, not this one.

Not *my* child.

Was that the "right" way to think? Obviously not, and Orla certainly didn't think so. If she was older, you'd call her a hypocrite, but she was fifteen, so you called her *fifteen*. Adam wouldn't approve either. Adam's always believed that as long as you do "the right thing"—which is always a set thing, never debatable—everything will eventually turn out fine and dandy. He's worse than a *Sesame Street* puppet with his one-size-fits-all morality.

Which is why I didn't tell him.

Orla followed my lead on that too, albeit with an air of martyred powerlessness. Fact is, she could have told him at any point; there was nothing I could have done to stop her. But it simply served her not to. *And she claims we're nothing alike.*

The secret created a gulf between us. You'd have thought it'd have brought us closer. But whereas I saw myself as her protector, Orla now saw me as her accomplice. And that's a tricky dynamic for a mum and daughter to navigate. It creates unhealthy, dysfunctional boundaries.

In plain English, she lost all respect for me.

I thought about the boy a lot over the week that followed. Occasionally I'd think of him as a blackmailer, but increasingly as a victim. And although I'd meant it at the time when I told Orla not to make comparisons, I thought about Vinnie Aldridge, too—the sweet but dopey son of one of the richest families in Thames Lawley, who'd brought a *sword* into school and barely gotten a slap on the wrist. Now, of course, everyone knew Vinnie wouldn't hurt a fly—he wouldn't have the wherewithal, even if he wanted to. But that wasn't the point. I'd read the school policy. Rules are rules. Or at least they should be.

They certainly are if you're from the Lomax, or the Highfield, or in fact any of the so-called "sink estates" where not too many have a dad whose hobby is collecting ceremonial swords and Bentleys. Funny how society's most disadvantaged kids are often talked about as though they're savages, but when they do wrong, they seem to be held to a far higher standard of accountability.

I mean, if this Zane had wielded a sword, would it have been passed off as "foolish high jinks"? And as for being suspended for swearing at a teacher? While I didn't condone disrespect, Nush's ex, Tom, once locked a teacher in a storage cupboard overnight. This resulted in his father having a single malt with the head and the school getting a refurbished gym.

Basically, life sprinkles glitter on some kids and sprays diarrhoea on others, and in protecting my daughter, I'd become part of the foul elite.

I began to feel sick—sometimes physically—about what I'd done. What I'd sanctioned.

And then the cute old lady, the security grille. What I'd said to Orla was true: it *absolutely* didn't excuse him. But the idea that he wasn't bad-to-the-bone made my stomach even queasier and sleep significantly harder. It turned my guilt into a living thing.

One day, after much restraint, I snatched a look at him on Instagram. I told myself I was being prudent, just making sure that Orla wasn't following him. To sum him up, he was handsome, he *loved* Hemingway, and he'd just made a one-pot chicken chasseur from scratch. The comments underneath were predictably glib:

> Chicken what-now, bruh??
> U gone gay, Z?
> Bet Gordon Ramsay's shitting himself 😬
> S'pose you gotta fill the days somehow.

It was his response to the last comment that mobilised me, offered me redemption.

> Too right. LEA still haven't sorted a tutor. Been
> 3 weeks now. Brain's going to shit bruh.

Three weeks, I thought. He's eager (that's unusual). And I knew he was in for a shock, too; he could easily be waiting three months. So here was an obviously bright lad who wanted to learn, and who I owed *something*. And I knew his name and the estate he lived on. It probably wouldn't take too much asking-around to track him down.

My guilt propelled me forward. My imagination crafted the story.

"God, it's the *maddest* thing, actually," I said two days later as I stood on his doorstep, looking at the blue-eyed teen dream with the slightly displaced air of a recently retired pensioner. "I was looking for chicken chasseur recipes on Instagram, and I came across your photo and your comment. And, well, would you believe it, I'm local and I'm a private tutor—mainly English lit—and I do the odd bit of work free of charge. I could maybe do Friday afternoons if you're interested. Any good?"

He asked me how I'd found him, though it was said with admiration, not suspicion. I said I recognised the Lomax from a photo, and I obviously knew his name from his IG profile, and that a little kid said he'd tell me what number Zane Jackson lived at if I gave him 50p.

Lies, so many lies, but all along I thought *I* was the only one lying. Now I'm left with endless questions.

Did he know who I was the whole time?

How long has he been planning this?

Where's he now?

What's his endgame?

45

Ellen

There was a wedding in full swing as we checked into the Falcon. Whitney Houston booming from a function room. The groom smoking with his mates outside. After a few minutes, the bride rustled past, headed for the loo and trailed by bridesmaids. I offered congratulations. Adam offered an ominous "best of luck."

In sickness and in health. I've always thought that to be an odd saying. It's a promise we give so much weight to, when really, loving someone when they're sick, or worse, dying, is an instinctive, easy thing. Loving someone when they're unlovable, when they're *unfathomable*, when they've fucked-up—*that's* what makes a marriage. That, and the freedom to point out that they're talking complete nonsense.

"*Seriously*, are you being deliberately thick?" I ask Adam as we sit side by side on the bed in gloomy Room 213. On the opposite wall there's a picture of a Spanish bullfighter, and over the past hour we've taken to treating him as a mediator, avoiding each other's faces and addressing all concerns to him. "You realise that if I come clean about Zane, I'll be hanging Orla out to dry."

He considers this for a long time. I feel his shoulders rise and fall as he tries to fashion an argument for that being OK.

Eventually he says, "I'd take a bullet for the kids, but you know what? I'm not sure I'd take one for you." I say, "Thanks."

Adam keeps going. "I mean, I'm not saying I *definitely*

wouldn't, but I can't be sure. Because it's different, isn't it? It's not unconditional. Marital love. Christ, it's not even constant."

"Shame the speeches have finished up downstairs. You could have offered your services."

He stares straight ahead. "The point I'm making is that I'd die for the kids, yet in *this* situation, this absolute clusterfuck, I'd choose *you* over Orla. I mean, the stigma of school exclusion versus the stigma of being accused of having sex with a teenage boy, of somehow being involved in his disappearance. There's no contest for me, Els. Orla's young, she's bright, she'll get back on the right path eventually. *You'll* never shake this off, though. The reputational damage. It'll be the end of so much."

Time to school Adam in the workings of the real world.

"Reputational damage? Sorry to break it to you, Ads, but that ship has well and truly sailed. I mean, you saw Facebook." We both did, for all of ten seconds. The general consensus is that I'm a slag. On the plus side, I'm "kind of hot." "People *want* to believe I was shagging him. It's a juicy story, so they'll cling to it. Even if Zane turned up tomorrow—which he won't—and denounced every single word, people are always going to think there must have been some truth in it."

"What makes you so sure he won't turn up? Because you realise that if he does, and he comes clean before you do, then *he* controls the narrative . . ."

"He's not going to come clean. It's much more fun to lie low somewhere and let the havoc unfold." Adam lets out a small breath, a doubting little huff. "Look, I *know* Zane is behind this now—that 'banquet of consequences' in his notebook proves it. But without the letter, I don't have proof. So, sure, we can go to DS Knowles and tell her the fucked-up tale that implicates our daughter in God knows how many offences, but how does that *actually* help anyone? Zane's still missing. I'm still the last person to supposedly have seen him. They still have a witness who says we were arguing, that I *hit* him. If anything, the Orla thing gives me a reason to want to hurt him. Maybe they'll think he was about to expose what she did, and I decided to stop him."

"So do you think he broke into the house? Stole your necklace, took the letter?" It's the first thing he's actually asked that hasn't been wrapped in an accusation or a dig.

"He must have done. He'd certainly know how to."

"And Social Services? Did you tell him about Max's hand?"

I didn't, I'm sure of it. But now I need to recast every conversation, to work out if there was a point where he seemed to change. Was he different before that day he saw Orla's photo on my iPhone? But Orla swore they didn't know each other. And even if he *had* vaguely recognised her, how on God's green earth would he have known what she'd done?

"Maybe Social Services is unconnected," I say, although at my core I don't believe it. "It *could* have been nursery. If not Mrs. O'Leary, then one of the mums. I don't know." I finally turn towards him. "What I *do* know is that Social Services doesn't remove your kids because you might have been shagging a seventeen-year-old. They do because of knives, though. And if I come clean about Orla and Zane, that's the *second* knife incident associated with us. And that's bad, Adam. Like, *bad* bad."

He nods. It's taken an hour, some shouting, and a level of vulnerability that has left me shredded, but I think I'm finally getting through to him.

"You know, we might have to consider moving," he says. "I'm not sure we can stay in Thames Lawley after this. I mean, I can handle a bit of gossip, but this is scandal, this is *dirt*."

I'm not ready for this battle yet. Neither the internal battle where I weigh up whether I can ride out the storm or not, nor the *actual* battle with Adam when I decide, yes, I probably can.

"Look, the only decision we need to make right now is to agree to protect Orla, correct?" I wait for his agreement, which comes in the form of a micro-nod. "Because if this gets into the media—and I've a horrible feeling it might—then 'Posh girl plants knife in disadvantaged boy's bag and disadvantaged boy seeks revenge on posh mum who covered it up' is a *much* better story than 'Woman rumoured to be shagging over-the-age-of-consent missing student.' And she's sixteen, Ads. A child. She'd die under that level of scrutiny. I'm old, I'm hardy. If it comes to it, I can tough it out."

"So that's the plan of action, is it? Cross our fingers. Tough it out. Hope the police go away."

"Pretty much, yeah."

And in the meantime, I find this witness.

Because Zane and I aren't the only ones who lied.

46

Jason

Jason circles his cracking neck, stretches his back, swallows two ibuprofen. He hit an all-time low last night, sleeping in his soon-to-be-repossessed car. He could have gone to a hotel, but he doesn't get paid until Monday and if he'd put it on the joint credit card, what would Emma think? She'd probably assume he was jumping someone's bones in a grotty local Travelodge. Although he doubts she'd be jealous. Most likely she wouldn't care.

Actually, a joint credit card expenditure would have reminded her that they need to separate their finances, get the divorce rolling. So he's glad he didn't flag that for her. He wants to cling to the belief that there might just be a way back.

Who is he kidding?

There's only one path for him now, and it doesn't involve happiness.

But he always knew he'd end up here. Now he just needs to see it through.

He's not sure what to do today. He can't go back to the house, not while it's swarming with Walsh kids. He can't look them in the eye, although "conflict of interest" was the reason he gave Gwen.

"Jesus, I can't be under the same roof as the children of a suspect in an active investigation! What were you thinking?"

She didn't answer. He didn't need her to. He knew exactly what she was thinking.

Be a good friend. Help Ellen. And to hell with what he wants.

He looks at his phone: 6:25 a.m.

He can put it off for another hour, then he'll have to call the station, say he won't be in again. It's crazy how anxious the idea of falsely calling in sick makes him, when if they knew a tenth of what he'd done, an unauthorised absence disciplinary would be the least of his problems. He wishes he hadn't said a migraine, though, because his boss said, "I get them all the time, they pass quickly." Reading between the lines, Jason knows he meant *Toughen up and get your arse back in.* But he's done his Google research, and he knows there's this thing they call the "postdrome." A kind of migraine hangover that lasts for days, leaving you mentally exhausted and slightly depressed.

Jason's whole life has been a postdrome. Mental exhaustion as rote as breathing. Emma eased it for a while, but then Ellen Walsh did what she fucking did.

And now *he* won't answer his phone and going to see him would be a huge gamble.

He'll give him another day to get in contact, then he might have to take that risk.

47

Ellen

When I wake the next morning—if you can call mainly tossing and turning sleeping—everything about the world feels the opposite of how it should be. The mattress is soft, not hard, and the windows don't rattle, they actually keep the wind out. But worst, my children are elsewhere. To think I've sometimes longed for this rarity.

And Adam hates me, that's a given. He doesn't say as much because he's a product of Sylvia and "we don't say *hate* here, dear," but it's there in every gesture, in his complete stripping of my agency. Within minutes, he tells me, quite matter-of-factly, that he's spoken to the builder and halted the renovation. Probably sensible, given everything, but the shard of triumph in his voice suggests it's less about sense and more about punishing me.

He doesn't even let me wash. We're leaving now, and he means *now*. I can shower when we get to his parents' empty rental cottage in Coombe, I'm told. That's where we're heading, apparently. It's all been arranged while I was sleeping (the implication being that *he* wasn't able to). It isn't a perfect hidey-hole, he admits, given that it's only a few miles from Thames Lawley, but at least it's away from the twitching curtains, and the brewing media interest I predicted.

There was a reporter on the lane this morning, according to

Muriel. She messaged Adam: *Don't worry, I told them to sling their hook.*

"Come on, move it," he snaps. "Gwen's bringing the kids to Coombe in an hour."

I shift to the edge of the bed, still wearing the tea dress that was supposed to charm Cathy Grantham. "I take it she's bringing other stuff, too? Clothes, toiletries?"

"No, I thought we'd go primitive." I smart at his tone, which he softens slightly. "Yes, look, stop flapping. It's all in hand."

Is it? How did I sleep through my life being so thoroughly taken over?

"Well, what about bed linen?" I say, needing to feel useful in some small way. "Is the Coombe place fully stocked? And towels. Do we need to bring towels?"

"Erm . . ." He doesn't have a clue. He sighs, annoyed; his "all in hand" exposed as cursory. "Look, if you drive, I'll try Mum. It's the middle of the night there, but I doubt she'll have been able to sleep." *So she knows then.*

"And did you tell Gwen to bring the Cetaphil?"

Another sigh. "The *what?*"

"Kian's cream—you know, for the eczema on his knees? Missing one night isn't a drama, but he'll scratch himself raw if I don't slather him this evening."

And with that, I dial Gwen's number, shooting Adam a defiant look. *See, I am good for something.*

Adam's parents bought the Coombe place in 1973 for £9,000. "About the price of a family holiday these days," so says Sylvia, who's clearly never taken a bus trip to Blackpool or caravanned in Rhyl. There was talk of us moving into it before we settled on Thames Lawley. Adam was keen ("minimal rent, Els, and two bathrooms"), but while the pale lemon cottage was cute, it was too rurally situated for my liking. No shop, no pub, no people would make Ellen a very dull girl indeed.

Perfect for now, though.

Gwen arrives with the kids while I'm in the kitchen, trying to fire up the Aga. It's Max I hear first. "Daddy, are we on holiday? Can we go the beach?"

His innocence, the sweet idiocy (he's in the car longer when we go to the supermarket) makes me crave being a child again. No sense of time or distance. Zero responsibility.

"This is nice," says Gwen as she takes in the *very* floral living room.

"Typical holiday rental," I say as we exchange solemn air-kisses. "Escape the stress of the rat race for a week by stepping back to the 1950s." Clutching a blackcurrant Fruit Shoot, Kian hurls himself at the sofa. "Careful, baby," I shout, although a stain on the chesterfield is going to be the least of Sylvia's gripes with me.

Adam comes in with the bags.

"Where's Orla?" I ask, glancing out the window.

"Yeah, about that . . ." Gwen kneads the back of her neck. "She, um . . . she didn't want to come."

I look at Adam. "Brilliant. So that means one of us will have to go and get her later."

"No. I mean she doesn't want to come at all." Her eyebrows crease. "I'm so sorry, Els. I didn't know what to do. I tried, but I couldn't *make* her."

I snatch Adam's car keys off the windowsill. "No, but I bloody can."

"You . . . you can't, apparently."

I stare at her, then break into a flummoxed smile. "Excuse me?"

Gwen looks wretched. "She's been researching it all morning. She said she spoke to someone at the NSPCC."

"We'll have to go home," I say to Adam, not leaving myself the space to feel heartbroken.

"Yeah, but hold on," Gwen says dismally. "She said if you come home, she's walking out. The NSPCC woman told her that as she's sixteen, she can leave the family home if she wants."

For one second, I feel an anger towards Gwen that's profoundly unfair. She's only the messenger here.

I drop to the arm of the sofa. "So what does she think is going to happen? That I'm just going to let her stay at the house on her own?"

Gwen throws her hands up, and I get the sense she's already had this battle with Orla. "She could stay with me, Els, but what with Jase being involved in the investigation . . . I mean, he walked out last night. Said it was a conflict of interest."

"Well, she's not going to Esme's," I say fiercely, as though someone suggested it.

"Mum and Dad have booked an earlier flight home," Adam says. "But it's not until midweek."

She's not staying there either; I'm not having Sylvia chip-chip-chipping away, delicately poisoning her against me.

"Kristy," I decide, prising my phone out of Max's hand. "I haven't seen hide nor hair of her for days, which isn't surprising given what that cretin Shay said to the police. But hey, beggars can't be choosers . . ."

"Um, yeah, that's another thing." Gwen really might cry. I might not be far behind her. "When I was packing your stuff earlier, I couldn't find Brown Bear anywhere, so I popped out to see if Kristy was in, check if she'd seen him, and . . . well, the cabin looked pretty empty. I think she might have gone. Like, *gone* gone."

Gone. I feel confused, then wounded, on about ten different levels. Because God knows, I don't deserve sympathy, nor its nobler cousin, compassion. But I'm not sure I deserve to be *deserted*.

While I sit on the pity pot, Adam finds the solution.

"Look, is there any way you could stay with her at our place, Gwen? You and Bella, obviously. We just need to get our heads straight, away from Thames Lawley. We'll come back in a few days—Orla should have calmed down by then."

Gwen looks doubtful about that, but she says, "Of course I can."

Later that night, Adam and I slouch quietly on the chesterfield. Him on his iPad, trying to numb himself with football scores. Me setting up a premium 192 account so I can get access to details about residents of Trensale Row. It's a long shot, for sure. I can't even be certain that the lying witness *is* a resident. But I know no one walked past, and Knowles said they had an "excellent view."

And I have to try something. *Do* something.

Around ten, Adam says he's going to bed. When he stops in the living room doorway, I assume it's to issue instructions. He had a *very* thorough chat with Sylvia earlier about various switches and plugs.

Instead, he says, "Orla knew something was up these past few months, you know? She thought you might be having an affair—that that's why you'd put the boys into full daycare every Friday. So you could spend the afternoon getting your rocks off with some . . . someone."

So that's what she thinks of me. I've had more charitable character assessments. But I guess that's the kind of person my actions suggested I might be.

"I wish you had been having an affair," he says, perhaps the most despondent statement he's ever uttered. "Some sordid weekly bunk-up with one of your students' dads, maybe. It'd have been preferable to this. This train wreck." He goes quiet for a moment, leaning his head against the door frame. "What I really want to know, Ellen, is why."

"Why? Why what?" There's a mountain of whys for him to pick from.

"Why did you feel the need to seek him out? Then to stick around for months, befriend him?"

My response is automatic. There's no nuance. It's clear and visceral and true.

"Because Orla had everything and he had nothing. And because despite the terrible things I've done, Adam, deep down I'm essentially good."

48

Nush

Nush was leaving the house when he arrived, the skyscraper detective, DC Damien Flint. When he stepped out of his Ford Focus (a strange choice of car for a man that height), she actually did a double-take, then immediately regretted it. Although she knows that standing out is the kind of thing you get used to. She certainly had to, growing up in semi-rural Oxfordshire. At primary and for most of secondary school, she was the lone brown face.

"D'you think I could have a word?" Flint asked, and his faint Scottish lilt made Nush wonder if he was one of *the* Flints, the renowned Cotswold hoteliers. She and Tom had sat next to the mother and father at a wedding a few years ago, and while they were most definitely Scottish—from Aberdeen, she seemed to remember—she didn't recall either of them being notably tall.

"Oh, I was just off to Pilates, actually," she lied, because there was no way she could tell him, or anyone else, where she was really off to. "I didn't go last Sunday, so I'm loath to miss this week. Will it take long?"

"I'll be quick as I can," he said politely. But his thoughts were as clear as the five-day stubble on his face.

Ladies and gentlemen, I give you another pampered housewife, filling her days with self-improvement and the spending of hubby's cash.

Nush felt like telling him that she'd been up since dawn,

actually, putting the final touches to an investor pitch that if it came off would make hubby's cash seem like pocket change. Then, after that, she'd washed the wheelie bins, changed the car's air filter and topped up the brake fluid. Later, as a personal challenge, she planned to have a go at resealing the bath.

People have always underestimated Nush. Not her general efficiency or capability, but her willingness to roll up her sleeves and do the necessary rough stuff.

"I assume this is about Ellen," she said to Flint, and then with a tinkly laugh added, "At least, I don't think I've committed any crimes this week."

Flint confirmed, "Aye, Ellen," then they headed indoors, where he said no to tea but yes to mango juice while perched awkwardly on a kitchen stool.

"So you're a friend of Ellen's," he said, presenting it as fact.

"I suppose so, yes."

This gave him pause. "I'm sensing a bit of tension in that statement." Nush nodded but didn't elaborate, so he prompted, "Has there been a falling-out?"

"I'm not sure I'd call it a falling-out. We haven't spoken for days, though. Things are . . ." She took a delaying sip of juice before saying, "A little raw."

"And why is that?"

Because she bulldozed me into teaching my flawed-but-adored husband a lesson, and now he's having a baby with someone who was born the year before I started uni.

"Oh, it was a misunderstanding, that was all. Someone reported Ellen to Social Services, and she suspected it was me because of a passing remark I'd made."

"So it *wasn't* you?"

"No."

He gave a tiny shrug, accepting this as either true or not relevant.

"And prior to this misunderstanding, would you say you were close?"

"We see quite a lot of each other, speak every few days. Is that how you'd define 'close'?"

"As good a definition as any." He smiled, although it was a forced smile—rusty, like it didn't get much use. "So has she ever mentioned Zane Jackson? I assume that even though you aren't speaking, you're aware of the events of the past few days."

Oh yes, very aware. Quite apart from all the gossip in the pub, and in the shops, and on social media, Adam had been keeping her in the loop, leaning on her quite hard.

"No, she never mentioned him to me, but then she doesn't talk about her work much. Ellen finds private tutoring elitist, you see, and she's always been slightly embarrassed to have joined the ranks, so to speak."

He nodded, reflecting on this, as though wondering if reverse snobbery was an indicator of criminality.

After a moment, he said, "Have you ever had the sense she might be having an affair?"

"No." She laughed. "But then I doubt I'd be her confidante." Flint had clearly noted the edge. His face demanded an explanation. "My husband had an affair." Six, actually, to the best of her knowledge. "And Ellen was *very* judgemental about it. So if she confided in me, she'd look like a first-class hypocrite."

"I see." He offered an apologetic frown. "Now, you might find this an uncomfortable question, Mrs. Delaney, but I have to ask. Would you say Ellen has ever shown an interest in teenage boys? An unhealthy one?"

Nush had a flash of the twins' Soccertots coach, Nathaniel. Ellen laughing with Susi Sands—"Shame they didn't build them like that when we were twenty years younger."

Or was it Susi Sands who'd said it and Ellen who'd simply laughed?

Actually, maybe Nush had laughed, too.

She must have looked stressed at that point, because Flint said, "We're going to be speaking to several of Ellen's friends, Mrs. Delaney, so please don't feel like the weight of the world is in your answer. I just need the truth as each person sees it."

And so that's what she did.

As those twenty years younger are prone to saying, she spoke her truth.

A little later, Nush receives a message from Gwen through Facebook. To see her name is enough of a surprise; they rarely have much to do with each other outside Ellen. But it's the anger in her tone, the lack of deference (if Nush is being completely honest) that really shocks.

Ffs Nush!! The police interviewed me earlier about Ellen. Told me what you'd said. What the hell do you think you're playing at???? Why did you say all that stuff???

49

Ellen

You'd think I'd be getting used to it by now, riding out one body blow after another, but even within the context of our shitshow, it's been an absolute brute of a day. News arrived via Gwen earlier that Orla—who's incidentally blocked my number—wants to move to Rog and Sylvia's once they're back. And they've agreed. *Of course they have.* On top of that, Adam declared an hour ago that he can't face going to work tomorrow, and he'll be calling his boss later to discuss taking a period of unpaid leave. Oh, and Gwen included a bottle of Malbec in the "essentials" she brought over yesterday, but I've turned the place upside down and there isn't a corkscrew in this sodding house.

So it's very much against the run of play, a stroke of luck I'm not expecting, that while Adam is out with the boys (taking carrots to a rumoured horse in a nearby field), a PC Lizzy Allen calls to say that DS Knowles has authorised the release of my property. In short, I can collect my car. That's the extent of the message, though, along with a reminder to bring my driving licence, and it's hard to gauge from her humdrum tone what exactly this could mean.

But *surely* it's good news?

And as an idea stirs, it's good news in more ways than one.

"Oh wow. Thank you. That's brilliant," I say, sounding stupidly chirpy, as though I've just been told I've won a raffle.

"I'll be straight over, then. Twenty minutes, maybe thirty? Does that work?"

"This is a police station, Mrs. Walsh, not a beauty salon. We're not squeezing you in for a facial. Come whenever, although you might have a short wait."

"Oh yeah, of course, of course," I say. "Totally understood. Seriously, thank you."

Jesus, Ellen. While it's good to appear grateful, dial down the Uriah Heep.

When I hang up the call, I automatically want to phone Adam—good news has been in short supply, and I'm *so* over being the prophet of doom. But if I call him now, he'll abandon "hunt the horse" and he'll want to drive me over.

And the idea that occurred to me a few minutes ago requires me to go alone.

I grab my bag and my coat, find my boots, then call a taxi. Then, scrolling past Adam's name, I make a more important call.

Once my car keys are collected and signed for, I'm asked if I can hang on for a minute. DS Knowles is just around the corner and she's keen to have a quick word. I'm tempted to ask if *she's keen* is the same as *she insists on*, but instead I plonk myself on a plastic chair and watch, with rising irritation, as half past three ticks closer to four.

I'm going through my third wave of *sod this* when she finally appears in reception, offering a sliver of a smile but no apology for my long wait.

"Come through," she says, opening the door to a small room I assumed was used for storage.

"So is this the 'quick word' room?" I ask, taking in the infinitely more pleasant surroundings than I found myself in on Friday evening. Two brightly coloured bucket chairs face each other next to a machine serving coffee and tea.

Her laugh is laced with dislike as she gestures for me to sit.

"I just wanted to very quickly update you on a few things."
I assume nothing seismic, or I wouldn't be getting the bucket
chair experience. "Firstly, we didn't find any blood in your car,
hence our releasing it back to you." She waits for a reaction, but
I'm not sure what's appropriate. Am I supposed to look pleased?
Smug? Nobly exonerated? Frankly, I'm surprised they *didn't* find
any, what with the boys constantly brawling on the back seat.
"And secondly, we do now have dashcam footage from a van
that pulled up close to Zane outside the Grapes. Zane's hood
was only down for a few seconds, but zooming in, we could see
that his face *was* cut, as you said."

Smugness is the *only* option here. It's been a while since I had
the right.

"So your witness does need new glasses, then."

Knowles gives me an arch look that warns me not to get too
cocky. "The right side of his face was angled slightly away from
the witness. This certainly doesn't alter the veracity of their
statement."

But it does. I know they're lying. I didn't kiss him. I
didn't hit him.

I stand up. "OK, well, thanks for letting me know. But if that's
all, I've got things to do."

Knowles escorts me to the entrance, which can't be ten steps
from the "quick word" room. As she pushes the door open, she
says, "Oh, by the way, it would have been nice to know that
you'd moved to another address, Ellen. We only realised when
an officer spoke with your friend Gwen Bale and she mentioned
she was staying at your house."

At the risk of sounding like one of *those* people, I know my
rights (I *googled* them, goddammit), and having been released
under investigation, I'm under no formal obligation to let them
know where I am. I don't actually say this to DS Knowles, but
I'm damned if I'm apologising. Instead, I offer a brittle smile and
say, "Don't worry, I won't go far."

Of course, what Officer Google *also* told me about being released under investigation is that "inappropriate contact with anyone linked to your case may be viewed as intimidation."

Oh well, I've done worse, I think, as I slip the car into first gear.

50

Orla

ESME: U coming to school tmrw

ORLA: Nope

ESME: R u ok?? Sinead and Priya said they've been messaging but u haven't replied.

ORLA: Why don't u just ask what u really want to ask?

ESME: La-la, obvs I have SOOOO many questions but really just want to kno ur OK

U were there for me when it kicked off with Zane. I'm being here for u now that it's kicked off with Zane too (wtaf??)

Call it symmetry

ORLA: I call it a bit late.

It kicked off on Friday. It's Sunday.

ESME: Er, my cousin's wedding remember????

ORLA: Strange, it slipped my mind.

Anyway yes I'm ok. Obvs I've been better.

Any good? Can you run with that headline? Cos that's all ur getting.

ESME: Don't be like that 😖

Can I come over? Sinead's mum heard from someone that ur mum's moved out!?

ORLA: Incorrect.

They're all staying somewhere else for a few days.

ESME: Because of reporters and shit??

ORLA: Rumours of "reporters and shit" greatly exaggerated.

ESME: Hold on THEY'RE staying somewhere else. So ur still there??

ORLA: Yup.

ESME: On ur own??? Have my mum and ur mum swapped bodies ☺ ☺

ORLA: Not on my own. Gwen staying for a few days

ESME: Oh right. Sweet.

Hey speaking of my mum did she drop u in the doo-doo on Friday?

ORLA: Huh?

ESME: Ur dad called looking for u after school. Mum said she hadn't seen u for months.

Ur dad was like "what?"

And like it's totally fine if u've been shagging someone and telling ur folks ur at mine . . .

But I've kind of got a situation here.

ORLA: Situation?

ESME: Abi-D freaking out BIG-TIME that the reason u being so low-key is cos it's Callum

ORLA: Just been sick in my mouth.

ESME: Who then?

Come on!! Ur mum's love life might be off limits ha ha ☺ but not urs???

Sorry. Too soon?

ORLA: I'm not shagging anyone.

51

Ellen

It's pure chance that I have Paulo's number. Zane's phone was out of credit a few months back, and so it was Paulo who messaged to ask if I could bring another copy of *King Lear* because Zane had spilled Red Bull on his. Oh, and if I was passing any shops, he'd added, could I grab him a pack of Camels.

I've brought cigarettes to this meeting. A hundred, though, this time. In fairness to Paulo, he didn't ask for anything as a condition of speaking to me. But as he was dithering when I called, saying could we make it tomorrow or the next day, then moaning that the Fox & Angel is "fucking miles away," I felt I had to produce some sort of incentive to get him here quickly other than offering to pay for a cab.

And he's right about the Fox & Angel. It *is* miles away; that's why I chose it. A safe ten miles from Thames Lawley, from twitchy reporters and prying eyes. Adam and I came here once for a gin evening and joked that it'd be the perfect pub to conduct an affair in. It's almost as if they've designed it that way, with its dimly lit booths and shaded little alcoves. Its monosyllabic staff who barely meet your eye.

Although Paulo draws attention, there's no getting away from it. And it's not because of his red tracksuit, which sets him sartorially apart from the standard Fox & Angel customer, but because he looks like he went ten rounds with Mike Tyson before a wardrobe dropped on his head.

"Oh Christ, look at you," I say, as he slowly limps towards me. One of his eyes is completely shut and half his face is purplish-blue.

"Yeah, I can kiss goodbye to that modelling contract," he says, cracking the glummest of smiles as he sits down with some difficulty. "Could be worse. Lucky I wasn't killed, apparently. I can't remember too much about it, to be honest. One minute I'm crossing Uxbridge Road, next I'm waking up in Ealing Hospital and they're talking about a pulmonary something."

"Haemorrhage?"

"That's the one."

"A bleed on your lung? Shit, Paulo."

I watch as he gulps a third of the pint I ordered for him when I got here then downs the double whisky chaser that he called me from the cab to request.

"Are you sure you should you be drinking?" I ask, quite sure that no, he really shouldn't be.

"My boy's missing. Getting out of my skull is about the only way I can deal with it." He knocks a knuckle against the table, jittery and impatient. "So what's this about then? What's so fucking urgent? 'Cos the only thing urgent to me, Ellen, is finding my son, and according to that sergeant woman—when she actually bothers to speak to me—*you* don't know where he is."

There's a bite to that *you*. Or maybe I'm imagining it. Either way, I need to address the elephant in the room.

"You know, whatever people are saying, Paulo, whatever you're reading, it isn't true. There was nothing going on between Zane and me. Nothing."

He lets out a bark of laughter, then winces, clutching his ribs. "Like I'd care if there was. Good luck to him. Every boy's fantasy, ain't it—shagging an older woman." I start to protest, but honestly, what's the point? Like I said to Adam, people will believe what they believe, and Paulo clearly isn't bothered. "Look, I don't give a shit about none of that, Ellen. I just want to know where he is, and I can't get anything out of that Knowles woman."

"Really?"

His lip curls. "Well, it was Jules who reported him missing, weren't it? She's like Mum of the Fucking Century to them. They can't see her for the proper slut she is." My hackles rise at the term, but I don't have time for *An Intro to Misogyny*, and anyway, I'm not sure I want to defend someone who called me "dirty paedo scum." "So that means *she* gets all the updates, and I get the odd scrap of information that she feeds me." He stares at the table, his face swollen and pitiful. "That first copper they sent—PC Bale. He was all right. Had a bit of time for me at least." He looks up. "Hey, did you bring those smokes?"

I fish them out of my bag, now slightly uneasy about handing them over. In my desperation to get him here, I forgot that what could be as interpreted as a thanks could also be interpreted as a bribe.

"You know, I keep thinking it's my fault," he says miserably, stacking the cigarette packs on top of each other. "What if someone I owe money to hurt him? There's this nasty bastard on the estate, Billy Comer—Billy Comb-over, if you've got a death wish. He's pulled stunts like this before. Threatened people's kids to make sure he gets paid."

I wish I could put him out of his misery, tell him I'm almost certain Zane's fine, that this is about *me*, not a minor drug debt. But I can't make any decisions until I know what I'm up against.

Which brings me to my whole point for being here. To "what's so fucking urgent."

"Paulo, can I run something by you? Some names."

The surprise of the question shakes him out of his wallow. "Names. Who?"

"But you *can't* tell Knowles, I mean it. Not that we've met up, or that we're even speaking. And *certainly* not that I ran names past you."

I'm playing a dicey game here, but I grew up around men like Paulo. And one thing they never, ever do, unless it's a matter of life or death, and sometimes not even then, is go squealing to the police. Answer questions, sure, but never volunteer.

"Listen, Ellen, I wouldn't tell that cow the time of day. And I certainly wouldn't get you in trouble." He fixes his one good eye on me. "I mean, I know what people are saying, but whatever did or didn't go on, you helped Zane. You made him feel good about himself."

Shame burns like an ulcer.

I take my phone out of my bag. Adam's called twice already.

"OK then," I say, quickly finding my saved search. "Tell me if you recognise *any* of these names. If Zane ever mentioned any of them." He nods impatiently. "Patricia Glassby, Geoffrey Glassby. Christopher Dillon. Susan Watkins, Donald Watkins, Eva Watkins. Hardeep Kaur . . ."

It takes a minute to go through everyone—the twenty-two Trensale Row residents whose details I managed to access on the 192 website. And as I roll through the list, I search Paulo's face for recognition. That's the reason I had to do this in person.

Sadly, there's none.

"Who are these people anyway?" he asks, frustrated, then suddenly hopeful. "Hey, do you think one of them knows where Zane is?"

"No. Well, I don't know." The hope in his voice means I have to tell him something. I take a deep breath. "Look, the police have a witness, Paulo, and they said they saw me hit Zane, but I absolutely didn't, I *promise*, so I need to—"

"Hold up—he said you *hit* Zane? The dude from Trensale Row said that?"

I nod.

He—that's a start.

Paulo shakes his head. "See, that's what I mean—that's the first I've heard of this. No one tells me anything." He laughs.

"S'a good one, though. You hitting anyone, never mind a bloody kid."

"But you'd believe I'd sleep with a 'bloody kid'?"

"Didn't say I believe it, just that I don't care much either way. I'd care a big fucking deal, though, if you harmed a hair on his head."

"I didn't."

He sizes me up, reaching a verdict within seconds. "I know that. I might not have any letters after my name, Ellen, but I've got street smarts, y'know? I know a wrong'un when I see one. And you ain't got it in you to harm anyone." He lets out a sharp, pensive sigh. "So, what's he said that for, then? The Trensale Row dude. The 'witness.'"

"I don't know. Mistaken, I guess."

"I went to see him yesterday."

My whole body goes weak. I swallow hard, trying desperately to keep my face neutral.

"Knowles wasn't best pleased. Oh yeah, she was on the phone pretty fucking quick then, I tell ya." He juts out his chin, a warning for me not to scold him too. "But I just wanted to hear for myself how Zane seemed, and he was the last person to see him, you know? Well, apart from you, and I didn't know how to contact you. Forgot I had your number, didn't I? What a pillock, eh."

"But you knew how to contact *him*?"

"Well, not exactly. Jules said the cops took a statement from some dude across the street from that cul-de-sac—I told you, she does throw me the odd scrap when she feels like it. So I headed down there, knocked a few doors. Could only be one of two or three houses, right?" He sighs. "Anyway, Knowles needn't have got her knickers in a knot, 'cos the guy wasn't there. It was his wife I spoke to, and she didn't know much. She couldn't get rid of me fast enough, to be honest." He points at his face. "I mean, would you want the Elephant Man on your doorstep?"

So, by the way, what was her name?
Did she mention her husband's name?
And what was the house number?
But I can't be that obvious, and frankly, I don't need to be.
"Across the street from that cul-de-sac" will more than do me.

52

Kristy

As daylight drains, Kristy realises she's been loafing around the park for two hours. She's not really a park kind of girl; never been in any way outdoorsy (so why she's moving to Cornwall, if she *is* moving to Cornwall, is a mystery). But as she hasn't got the money to do anything else, and she couldn't face another minute cooped up in Shay's bedroom-cum-holding-pen, Pointless Park it had to be. And it's been OK. She's fed some ducks.

Her phone buzzes. It's Shay. Well, who else would it be? she thinks pitifully. Since shipping out of Ellen's place on Thursday—partly to defend Shay's honour, partly to stop herself from saying something awful—her world seems to have shrunk to him and only him.

Where r u babe? Got someone here u need to meet x
Oh yeah who? she replies.
A surprise!
OK. Back in ten

A surprise. Oh goodie. As if there haven't been enough of those lately. Honestly, while he's a maestro between the sheets, Kristy's starting to wonder if Shay's a bit thick.

Like that thing he said to the police. "Yeah, Ellen seemed a bit on edge, kind of flustered . . ."

Seriously, is he *really* that stupid? He must have known he was handing them gold.

"That's what she's always bloody like," she raged after that copper had left the pub, practically can-canning with excitement. "That's her thing, Shay, her identity—'Ellen Walsh, the busy, flustered mum.' You made it sound like she was guilty of something."

"She is guilty of something," he said blankly. "Greed. Selfishness. She was happy enough to take your money when you were rolling in it in London, but now that you need a leg-up, she won't even give you four thousand lousy quid."

But, see, this is where it all starts to get a bit knotty for Kristy. Because she's realised that while *she's* allowed to think this, to give the impression that Ellen's a demon, she feels kind of scathing and increasingly suspicious of Shay's willingness to follow her script. It's as though he wants to stoke her hate, somehow use it, when surely if he genuinely cared for her, he should be encouraging her to build a bridge.

Everyone has an agenda, though. She understands that. She accepts it.

The problem is, she can't quite put her finger on what exactly Shay's is.

But anyway, this *surprise*.

The first thing she notices when she walks back into the Cricketers is that someone's put up a Christmas tree and there's an inflatable Santa on the bar. Bit early, she thinks, it's only November, but that's the pub industry. Then she thinks: he got me back here to meet Santa. She can't work out if this is annoying or ridiculously sweet.

"Oi, Kris. In here."

She settles on *sweet*, then reality bursts her bubble. Shay is waving from the back room, where as far as her blurred vision can make out, he's sitting with a blandly attractive blonde. OK, *now* she thinks she gets it. It's probably a Tinder thing, this surprise, then. She suddenly feels tired and deflated. She wanted an intro to Santa, not a threesome. Maybe Cornwall might be different. With a pub to run, he'd have more to occupy him.

"Hey you," she says listlessly as she hovers over the table. She's hoping he might read her mood, although they're years off reaching the telepathic stage.

He stands and gives her a kiss. The bland blonde looks on, well, blandly.

"So, er, Kris, this is Adele Ryder," Shay says, oddly formal and slightly pleased with himself.

Adele Ryder offers her hand to Kristy and says, "Thanks *so* much for agreeing to meet."

Kristy doesn't take her hand. Instead she throws Shay a *who the fuck?* face.

His response is a gloating grin.

"Adele's a journalist from the *Mail*. She's going to make us rich."

53

Ellen

DS Knowles shows up at Coombe the next day while I'm in the shower. Adam announces her arrival, almost regally, through a fog of steam as I'm shaving my legs. My monthly wax is booked for Wednesday, but I think I can safely say I won't be going. I can't even bring myself to call and cancel. Another job I'll outsource to Gwen.

Adam's right. We'll have to leave Thames Lawley. If I can't brazen out a twenty-minute leg wax, there's no way I can raise my kids here. Maybe moving back to London might be the best thing. Anonymity over community.

"Get a bloody move on," he says, holding out a towel to speed my progress. "I don't know what I'm supposed to say to her. You forget I'm not quite the accomplished liar you are."

I turn off the shower. "Did you ask what it's about?" *Surely, Paulo, you wouldn't have?*

"Well, *actually* no, Ellen, I didn't. But I think it's a fair bet it's not going to be about me."

He's been like this, off and on, since I got back yesterday evening. Distancing himself, sectioning himself off from me. Making it abundantly clear that from now on there's *my* problems and there's *his* problems, and the only time there's *our* problems is if we need a show of strength in front of the kids or someone in authority. Incidentally, Adam's problems, from what I can gather from the few words he's grunted at me, amount to a severely pissed-off boss who managed to make him feel like both a liability *and* indispensable, and a wife who assumes he's gullible enough to think it took two hours to collect her car.

Thankfully, though, he's all smiles and light refreshments by the time I come downstairs.

And he isn't the only one.

Knowles is smiling warmly as I walk into the living room, where Kian is presenting her with an array of plastic food that she then gamely pretends to eat. A fried egg. A doughnut. A chicken leg. An aubergine. She accepts them all and declares them delicious. The doughnut, in particular, gets a rapturous "Yum!"

Is this a tactic? I wonder. If you can't crack a suspect, get creative and confuse them. Let your laughter fill their living room, entertain their kids, drink their tea.

If it is a tactic, it's working. Sterling job, Knowles. I'm rattled.

I clear my throat. "Hi there. Sorry about that." *Why am I apologising for having a shower?*

"Not a problem." Her eyes flick towards Adam. "I was just saying to your husband, it's a nasty day out there. Cosy in here, though. I won't want to leave."

I glance outside. It's pelting. I hadn't even registered it was raining; I've been in a haze since seeing Paulo. Since "some dude across the street."

"Tea, Els?" Adam asks with overdone cheeriness.

"Glass of water, please." I shoot him dial-it-down eyes—we're supposed to be aiming for "solemnly united"—then sit opposite our visitor. "So, I take it you haven't come to talk about the weather?"

Max walks in, giving Knowles a confused scowl, then he burrows into my lap and says, "I love you, Mummy." *Attaboy.*

"No, I wanted to pick up on something you said to PC Bale, actually." My heart hammers against Max's ear. "He's been signed off sick, unfortunately, so I'm having to go from his notes here. But I believe you mentioned Zane having another tutor, someone appointed by the Local Education Authority."

"Yeah, Frances something. I don't know her surname. And it was only recently, maybe a month or two ago. It took them ages to sort it. Usual story—too many referrals, not enough resources."

I can't quite read her expression, but I sense there's something bad brewing. God knows what Zane told this Frances about me.

"Yes, well, obviously we've been keen to speak to her—it's good to get as many insights into Zane's state of mind as possible." Her head tilts. "But the thing is, Oxfordshire LEA confirmed this morning that they don't have any record of Zane being allocated a tutor. It's true he requested one, but nobody had been appointed and it's unlikely they would have been. Zane should have been attending a pupil referral unit. One-to-one tutoring is for special cases only—less able-bodied students, for example."

I shake my head at the floor, look up again, baffled. "But Frances—"

"Who Fw-ances, Mummy?" asks Max.

I kiss his head, say, "Just a lady."

Knowles shrugs. "We gave the LEA the name, Ellen. They don't have one single Frances either working for them or affiliated. Female *or* male."

Adam comes in with my water. I have the overwhelming urge to throw it in my own face.

"Have you spoken to Paulo?" I ask.

"Not yet. There was no answer at his flat this morning."

"Well, you need to," I say. "Because he's met her, this Frances. He must have done anyway, because he told me she's a stuck-up cow. Which doesn't mean she is—that's just Paulo. But what I'm saying is, there *was* someone."

Knowles sighs. "We've spoken to Zane's mum, and she knows nothing about any Frances. As far as Julie Jackson was aware, the only tutoring Zane was getting was 'a freebie off some posh sort,' which we assume means you."

Posh. That's a joke. Always has been, but never more so. Because sitting here in my hundred-pound leggings, in the almost million-pound cottage that my husband, then my kids, then possibly their kids will be heirs to, I've never felt more cheap. Less proud of who I've become.

In asking "Who Fw-ances, Mummy?" Max displayed more interest than his father. Adam barely speaks to me after Knowles leaves, except to confirm that yes, he's fine, and no, he hasn't seen a corkscrew. When the rain eases, I suggest a bonding game of family football to lift the mood a bit, "Although we'll have to wear our wellies," I insist. Max and Kian are delighted, finding the concept of wellied football hilarious, but Adam spoils the party, saying he isn't in the mood, he's going to read.

He's still reading later, or pretending to, when I start to lay the groundwork for what I plan to do tomorrow. What I need to do.

"Listen, I spoke to Cahill earlier," I say, not so much to Adam as to the cover of Andre Agassi's memoir.

"Could the day get any better?" he grouses.

"And he's been talking to Mum, and, well, she's got wind of what's happened somehow—Kristy, maybe—and apparently she's making noises about heading down here."

Adam lowers the book, giving me a look of abject horror. "Then stop her. Or tell Cahill to. Seriously, if he has to chain her to the bloody radiator, he is *not* to let her leave Leicester." He runs a hand over his head. "Please, Ellen, on top of *everything*, not your mother."

"I think I should drive up tomorrow. Explain the situation. Settle her nerves a bit." I give him a coy look. "Maybe throw her a few quid."

He rolls his eyes. "Fine, whatever. Although don't even *think* I'm coming with you."

Too right he isn't. I've no intention of driving to Leicester. The cover story carries the slight risk, of course, that one day Adam might mention the trip to Cahill (not to Mum—they haven't spoken since she called me a "heartless pig" at Dad's wake for closing the open bar at 6 p.m.), but on the balance of probability, the chance of them chatting is minimal. It's not that they dislike each other exactly, but they live on different planes, barely acknowledging the other exists.

I summon a deep breath, mentally crossing my fingers. "So, the boys . . . I mean, I can take them if you want some peace, but you know how she gets around children—"

"Absolutely not," he interrupts. "You do what you have to do, but my kids are staying here with me."

My kids. Not *the* kids. Not *ours*.

Even though my plan couldn't have worked better, I'm still stung by the undertone.

Leave my precious boys here and fuck off back to your good-for-nothing family.

54

Nush

"You're making yourself at home, I see."

It's strange enough being welcomed into the Meadowhouse by Gwen (well, not welcomed, *admitted*), but then to see Bella's socks drying on the radiator, to hear Radio 1 blaring around the kitchen (Ellen's a *strictly* Radio 2 girl) and to smell . . . well, Nush isn't quite sure what the cloying smell is, but it's certainly not Ellen's preferred basil and mandarin.

And the whole house feels *off* in a way Nush can't quite put her finger on. Not profoundly altered in any sense, but marinated in a slightly different way.

She moves a small crate of Bella's toys off the nearest kitchen chair. "Good Lord, Gwen, you only live across the green. Although Jasmine's the same—she packs everything but the kitchen sink, even if she's only going away for a few days."

Is that patronising, comparing a thirty-year-old woman to a nineteen-year-old student? Nush gets confused by the dates—is Gwen a Millennial or Gen Z?

"Yeah, well, it's bad enough having Orla out of sorts without Bella whining too."

Gwen sits on the window seat, pulling her feet into full lotus. Nush wants to ask her to turn the radio down, but she has the sense it'll make her sound old.

"So?" Gwen says, "I assume you're here about my Facebook

message? I saw you read it on Sunday, by the way. Bit rude not to reply."

"Civilised people iron out their differences face-to-face, Gwen. I've been busy these past few days."

Also, civilised people don't holler at each other across kitchens, battling to make themselves heard over Sean Paul.

"Oh, well, that's fine then, if you've been *busy*. Shame you weren't busy when the police came, hey?" Gwen shakes her head, exasperated. "I mean, why did you say all that stuff? You made Ellen sound . . . I dunno, *weird*. Like she's got some obsession with age-gap relationships."

Had she? Nush flashes back to her chat with the towering police chap. He asked her to tell the truth as she saw it, and that's all she did.

"I told him that when Ellen was *hounding* me to leave Tom, she seemed fixated on the idea of him turning his attentions to Orla or one of Jasmine's friends, and then how she *completely* overreacted when she saw Kristy's barman friend talking to Orla in the pub. I take it that's what you're referring to?"

"So you admit it?"

"Admit what? Suggesting she's always shown distaste for age-gap relationships. I would have thought that would help."

"Well, that's not how he picked it up—the big guy, Damian. He interviewed me right after you, and he mentioned what you'd said, asked me if I could add to it. Which, obviously, I didn't. But he seemed to think it was interesting, psychologically speaking, that Ellen sees potential relationships that just wouldn't occur to most people."

Damian. *Call me Damian.* Men get like that around Gwen. Nush despises herself for thinking it, but she's glad she never had to introduce her to Tom.

"Well, I can't help how he interpreted it."

It's no good. She simply has to turn off that radio. Gwen gives her a slightly withering look as she does it, but tough luck. This isn't her house.

As silence settles, the faint murmur of voices drifts from upstairs.

"Orla?" says Nush, surprised. "Doesn't she usually have after-school statistics on a Tuesday?"

"Does she? You're better informed than me. Anyway, she hasn't been to school this week."

Nush frowns. "Do Adam and Ellen know? She should really be at school. It's a crucial year."

Gwen laughs. "You want to try telling her that, Nush? Knock yourself out."

Nush mouths an *Oh*, although she can't imagine Gwen knocked too vigorously. Not that she should have to. She might be temporarily installed as Lady of the Meadowhouse, but Orla's education isn't her responsibility.

She sits back down, tilting her ear towards the kitchen door. "Who's she talking to?"

"Kristy."

"Adam said she'd cleared out."

Gwen raises an eyebrow. "She left something upstairs, apparently."

55

Kristy

"What are you doing?" Orla asks coolly, standing in the doorway of the spare bedroom.

Kristy jumps, surprised. Gwen didn't mention Orla was home. She straightens Ellen's fortieth birthday collage, now hanging crooked on the back wall.

"What am *I* doing?" She turns around. "What are *you* doing?"

"I live here."

"Yeah, but where'd you spring from?"

"I was hiding in Mum's en suite." Orla's eyes shift to the bag over Kristy's shoulder then the photo in her hand. "I was going to pretend I was in the shower if Nush came up to lecture me—wouldn't surprise me if Mum sent her." She rolls her eyes. "And you know what she's like. I don't need to be Nushed right now."

"Bad enough being Gwenned, right?" says Kristy, just for something to say.

"I'm cool being Gwenned. She listens to me, which is more than Mum ever does." Her gaze drops again. "Why are you taking that photo? You can't be missing Mum that much, surely?" She swoops forward, grabbing Kristy's wrist and angling the photo upwards. "And, God, you could have chosen a better one. That picture is next-level *gross*."

Not according to Adele Ryder, who thought that a miniskirted Ellen guzzling champagne on a bar with a sweaty teenage boy sounded the very opposite of gross, actually. Potential tabloid catnip. *"But he's definitely teenage, right?"* she'd asked. *"'Cos that's what gives us the juice. That's the 'public interest' angle."*

Orla laughs. "Hey, are you going to pin it to the dartboard at the Cricketers?"

She waits for Kristy to laugh, and to be fair, she would normally. She should have pinned Ellen's photo to a dartboard years ago; it'd have been a cheap form of therapy. But the odd thing is, since Sunday, when she sat watching Shay and Adele Ryder negotiate Ellen's public downfall—two people who've collectively known her for less than a fortnight—something seems to have shifted inside Kristy. It's not a tenderness towards Ellen. God, no. More a furious innate desire to protect her own, she supposes. And to snatch the power back from Shay, who, she sees now, has been riding the coat tails of her hate.

Her love/hate, actually. And a middle finger to anyone who says they can't exist in the same space.

"I'm taking it," she tells Orla, "because there's this woman, this journalist, who's willing to pay decent money for it. So I need to burn it, or shred it, or . . . fucking *eat it* before my parasite boyfriend—well, ex-boyfriend—gets his mitts on it."

See, Shay wasn't entirely honest that day—the day of the pizza lunch—when he said he only had a few cautions. Actually, he's got two spent convictions for burglary. He swears he's been straight for years, and maybe he has and maybe he hasn't, but with that journalist dangling £3,000—which would put a decent dent in Cornwall—Kristy wouldn't put it past him to break in to get the photo once she tells him she's out.

Seriously, though, £3,000. Not an amount to be sniffed it, but Shay pitched it as life-changing. Back in her modelling heyday, Kristy spent £3,000 on a velvet cape.

Which was moronic, but *still*.

"Wow. So you broke up with Shay to protect Mum." Orla shrugs. "Hey, your funeral, I guess."

"Well, I haven't *actually* broken up with him. But he'll get the hint when he sees my stuff is gone."

"Cold. *Very* cold. Auntie, I'm impressed."

"And anyway, it isn't just about your mum." Although it's felt good to bring the White Knight out of retirement. "It's because I've woken up to the fact that he's using me to fund Cornwall."

"Cornwall?" Orla looks at her blankly. "Say what now?"

Kristy shakes her head. "Doesn't matter. But basically, I think he came here, saw this house, heard how much the renovations were costing and thought, 'Excellent, I could use me a rich sister.' And then when your mum didn't come through, and all this craziness kicked off, he saw another way to get what he wants. And I'm sick of guys like that. I'd rather be on my own."

"Most guys are like that."

Kristy should probably say *that's not true* and they could have a lovely Hallmark moment. But she needs to get a move on. She's got a train to London to catch. An ex-boyfriend has offered her a two-week spot on his lumpy sofa (they'll probably end up shagging, but ultimately there are worse fates). Then when her head's straight, she'll come back. Patch things up with Ellen. No more drama. *Yeah, right.*

"So how much did this journalist offer, then?" Orla grins. "Just asking for a friend, obviously."

"Not enough to destroy your mum's life, let's put it that way."

And that's what it came down to for Kristy. A life. Her sister's life. Ellen, who before Courchevel wasn't her nemesis or her whipping girl. She was just an average sister. Occasionally adored, occasionally despised, predominately tolerated, always loved.

She does still love her.

She knows this because even though she thinks terrible thoughts about her, and ridicules her and steals from her, when handed the opportunity to *finish* her, to hang her out to dry in a tabloid newspaper, Kristy realised she couldn't do it. She couldn't irrevocably blow up Ellen's life.

And after what Ellen did to *her* life, that can only be because Kristy loves her, right? Not the patient and kind love that crops up in every wedding reading. No, the messy, inconvenient kind that you'd put a stop to if you had a choice.

Honestly, it genuinely amazes Kristy that Shay thought she'd choose him over Ellen. And it's now eating away at her—dangerously so—that he'd put her in that position in the first place.

One thing's for sure—once she's got her head straight and her sister back, she'll find a way to make Shay pay.

56

Nush

The front door slams. Nush calls out, "Nice to see you too, Kristy!" Then, turning to Gwen, she gets back to the matter in hand.

"Anyway, listen, why are the police so hung up on Ellen's supposed proclivities? Even if she was carrying on with that boy, it's not illegal. Is it actually relevant to his disappearance?"

Gwen shrugs. "I suppose because she's denying it, they want to catch her out in a lie." She throws Nush a strange look, somewhere between outrage and intrigue. "But wait a second, *if* she was carrying on with him? You don't seriously believe she was, do you?"

Nush knows she should say no, but if the past year has taught her anything, it's that life is full of lemons and curveballs and long-standing friends nearly becoming lovers, and finding out who your real friends are, and soon-to-be-ex-husbands purchasing prams.

So Ellen with a teenage boyfriend? Why not? Anything's possible.

"I don't think anyone truly knows anyone, Gwen, so I honestly couldn't say."

Gwen whistles. "Wow. That's *depressing*. Is it National Nihilism Day or something?" *Nihilism*. Not a word you'd expect from someone wearing a rainbow-striped sweatshirt. But it rather proves Nush's point: no one really knows anyone else.

"Or is it just your way of masking that you've got a really low opinion of Ellen?"

Nush bristles. "Excuse me? She thought I reported her to Social Services. I think if anyone's got a low opinion—"

"'Cos it's always been obvious to me," Gwen butts in. "And Ellen *does* notice, trust me. I've seen her face when you've said certain things. But she never bites back. Why is that? I've always wondered if . . ." She pulls her knees up close, as though pre-empting a blast. "Did something happen between Ellen and Tom? Is that it?"

A laugh bursts from Nush. "Ellen and Tom! My God, as if Tom would ever . . ." She stops herself before she says something monumentally bitchy. "Bless you, though, darling. That really made me chuckle, and it's been a while."

But Gwen isn't convinced. She mutters a flippant "OK," followed by a cynical "If you say so," and suddenly, almost physically, it's *essential* to Nush that this stupid girl with her stupid theories and her stupid rainbow-striped sweatshirt knows the truth about Ellen. About what she did.

"Ellen ruined my life, and she probably knows it. Maybe she even regrets it. *That's* why she doesn't bite back. Does that answer your question?"

"She *ruined your life*?"

It's Gwen's turn to laugh, although it's more shock than genuine humour. Nush is a little shocked too. It's the first time she's given voice to her feelings about Ellen, and she never in a million years imagined voicing them to *Gwen*. Although maybe she's the perfect audience, given that her opinion means virtually nothing to Nush. With her sparkly hair clips and lip gloss, it'd be like baring your soul to a disco ball.

"She shouldn't have told me about Tom and that woman. She knew I was perfectly happy in my marriage. Ignorance *can* be bliss, believe it or not. Adam even told her not to say anything, you know? He told her to let it run its course. That other people's marriages were their business. But oh no, she couldn't keep her big moralising mouth shut."

Gwen holds both hands up. "Hey, look, full disclosure here, Nush—I'm not your best bet if you're looking for someone to slam Ellen. It was a while ago now, but I once sent photos of this guy I knew was having an affair to his wife. And honestly, I'd do it again tomorrow. She had a right to know. *You* had a right to know."

"Fine, so tell me. And when I say, 'OK, thanks for telling me,' leave it at that. Don't bully me into taking action. Don't try to make me feel less."

"But . . ." Gwen frowns, "it was *your* decision, Nush. I never thought you'd play the victim. I mean, obviously I wasn't there, and I can totally imagine Ellen getting on her soapbox, but if you end your marriage on a friend's say-so, then I'm sorry, it wasn't much of a marriage."

"I wasn't ending my marriage! I only meant to teach him a bloody lesson!"

And there it is, the cathartic roar. Her anger detonating, then slowly settling. Gwen looks stunned, maybe a little embarrassed for her, but Nush doesn't care. She feels ten per cent lighter.

"I thought a few weeks at most," she carries on, almost to herself. "A few weeks of hotel living, then he'd realise what he was missing. And maybe it'd change him for the better. I had no idea he'd go straight to *her*."

Gwen hesitates, then says, "He might have anyway, given time. That would have been worse, surely? If *he'd* left *you*."

Nush shakes away the thought. She's trained herself not to even think it.

"No. No, she was just a fling until I kicked him out *on Ellen's instruction*. Kicking him out pushed them together, see? If Ellen had just kept her mouth shut, it'd have burned itself out like all the others, and then I'd still have a marriage, and he wouldn't be starting a new family, and I wouldn't be reduced to sitting outside a strange flat trying to get a glimpse of the only man I'm ever likely to love." She looks at Gwen's alarmed face and gives a tiny, exhausted laugh. "And I'm sure none of this sounds in any way rational to you, and maybe it isn't. But then is it rational to abandon your wife of twenty-one years for someone you've known five months?"

"Whoa, back up a bit." Gwen straightens up. "Sitting outside his house! That's *stalking*. That's a crime, Nush!"

Seeing herself through Gwen's eyes is sobering, but Nush wouldn't call it *stalking*. She's only ever done it once. The Sunday just past, in fact. She was leaving the house to drive past Jessie's apartment when the policeman turned up and waylaid her temporarily, although it was fortunate in the end, because going later meant she got her glimpse.

He was getting in *her* car, a Mini Cooper, which looked ridiculous. He looked even more ridiculous in that blue hoody. He always said hoodies were for chavs and thugs.

A bang on the door brings Nush back to herself and Gwen springing to her feet.

"Oh for God's sake. A reporter, I bet," Gwen says. "Those vultures don't know the meaning of *no*. Let me just get rid of them. I'll be back in a minute."

But Nush thinks now's a good time to leave. She's said too much. She feels off-kilter. So she follows Gwen into the hall, where's she opening the door and muttering, "Piss off."

But it isn't a reporter on the doorstep. It doesn't take the lack of a furry microphone to convince Nush of that fact.

The visitor stares at Gwen, then at Nush, then at Gwen, then back to Nush again. Then, before Gwen or Nush can get a word in, they say, "Er, what the fuck are you doing here?"

57

Ellen

It's kind of sad that the boys weren't grumpy about me "going to see Granny Rose" without them. They're usually desperate to go anywhere, even if it's just the post office or the dump. I always imagine they'd have liked Dad; he'd have bought them sweets, made funny faces. Mum thinks they're "up themselves." She calls Max "Little Lord Fauntleroy." Essentially, Granny Rose only likes Cahill and Mikey's kids, who are dyed-in-the-wool Hennesseys.

I reflect on all of this as I hunch down in my car, eighty miles from where I'm supposed to be. It's now late afternoon—the boys' dinner time, I note idly—and it's fair to say that today has been a total waste of time and mental energy. I've been parked on Trensale Row for almost three hours now, and the only thing of any note has been the marvel of the sunset—the autumn sky morphing from murky blue to a brilliant russet blaze. To think I actually worried about looking conspicuous, when in reality only a handful of people have passed me, and crucially, there hasn't been a flicker of movement from any of the houses across from where I dropped Zane.

So, maybe I should go.

No, I'll stay.

Not for too long, though. Another half an hour, maybe?

But then even if I stay, I'm still not sure what I intend to do here. I mean, while I was recklessly blasé about asking Paulo to meet up with me on Sunday, I knew that him snitching to Knowles was unlikely. It would go against every strand of his DNA. But *dude across the street* is an unknown entity, and hunching down in a car is textbook stalking. And it doesn't matter one jot that *I* know there's something iffy about this dude's statement; while I'm released under investigation, I can't tackle him on his doorstep. I could get five years for witness intimidation according to Google (possibly an exaggeration, but I'm not prepared to play the jail lottery).

So I should go.

I should definitely go.

Actually, what I'll do is to listen to Nush's voicemail. She called me five minutes ago, but I couldn't face speaking to her. To be honest, I can't face her voicemail either, but listening to it, then pondering it, then potentially getting quite pissed off about it temporarily postpones having to make the decision about whether I stay or whether I leave.

And who knows? Maybe she was calling to make peace. There's no question I could use a sympathetic ear.

I have my phone in my hand when it rings again. Not Nush, though. Adam.

I sit up straight, answer quickly.

"Hey," I say brightly. Perhaps a little *too* brightly for someone who's supposedly spent the afternoon being emotionally bludgeoned by Rose Hennessey.

"Hey. How's it going? Are you still up there?"

"Nope. I'm on my way back," I lie. "Over halfway. Just pulled off for a quick wee."

"So, how was it?" he asks. "On a scale of one to ten? One being Dante's ninth circle of hell, ten being broadly bearable."

I manage a laugh, buoyed by his seemingly improved mood. "Um, seven? It was fine. I mean, she was horrid, sweary, Mum-ish, the usual. But she's not coming to visit, that's the upshot." *So don't ask any more questions.* "The boys been OK?"

"Yeah. Well, kind of. There's loads of Disney DVDs here, so I thought I'd introduce them to *Dumbo*, but Max freaked out at the trippy elephants, and then when I tried *Pinocchio*, they both freaked out at the donkey scene."

"It's a fucked-up scene, to be fair," I say. "But weird, huh? They're not usually that jumpy."

"I know. But it's not really surprising, is it? They can sense something's up, Els." Silence hums down the line. "Look, I think we need to head home tomorrow. I know it'll be tough facing people, but the boys need some normality."

"Of course," I say, because what else can I say? "I'll call Gwen later, see where I'm sitting on Orla's hate-o-meter."

"You'll see Gwen later. You can ask her then."

"I will?"

In the rear-view mirror, headlights glow in the far distance. A car slowly turning into sleepy Trensale Row.

"Yeah, she's taking the boys to the fireworks at Whistlebrook. That's why I was calling—to check that's OK. It's aimed at little ones, apparently, and she's taking Bella, and it's over this way, so she thought it'd be nice to bring them too. It's six thirty till seven, so not a late one."

It's just past five now, which means it's possible they'll have left before I get back. I desperately want to say no. I am *aching* for a double hug.

But Adam's right, they need normality. Fireworks and toffee apples and hot chocolate sound just the job.

"Yep, fine. But tell Gwen to bring earmuffs, and not to take any shit from Max if he whines about wearing them. And wrap them up warm. Make sure they've got hats, OK?"

Then as Adam enquires, "Which hats?" because clearly head coverings are above his pay grade, the car that turned onto Trensale Row pulls up outside number 9, directly opposite where I dropped Zane.

I hunch down in my seat again, watching intently as the driver does nothing. Well, presumably they're doing *something*, but it's dark and I'm fifteen metres away, and this road could really use more street lights, and Adam's describing bloody bobble hats, and maddeningly, I can't quite see.

But then he gets out—definitely male—and heads not for number 9, but number 11. Halfway up the steps to the front door, he throws a hand back to lock his car. Even at a distance I can hear the faint beep.

Then he's on the doorstep, illuminated by the porch light, and nothing I'm seeing makes any sense to me. A hall light comes on, the door opens—another male—and then quickly, aggressively shuts in his face.

A hurricane swirls in my head.

"I have to go," I tell Adam.

I don't say why, or *bye*, or answer his panicked request for a hat ruling. And although I probably should, I don't tell him that I'm staring straight at Jason Bale.

Jason Bale, who, according to Knowles, has been signed off sick.

Who is, according to Knowles, to all intents and purposes no longer attached to Zane's case.

And who, by the look of the way he's now battering the front door, has serious and urgent business with the person inside this house.

And not police business.

58

Ellen

Jason leaves after a minute. Runs back down the steps and drives away again. I guess you can only take your anger out on a front door for so long before someone notices. And someone did notice. A plump middle-aged woman shouted from her porch while drying a colander. Through my slightly open window, I heard her threaten to call the police.

But Jason *is* the police. He was a senior officer in London. Something brought him to Thames Lawley. And what has any of this got to do with me?

I sit paralysed at the wheel, trying to get my thoughts in some kind of order.

So Zane lied about everything. And he knew about every-thing. *How?*

He lured me here, told me *exactly* where to drop him off, then disappeared. *Why?*

A "witness" pops up, but the witness lies.

Jason knows the lying witness, and there's clearly bad blood between them.

And then it hits me. Now that I know the number of the house, maybe I can get a name from the 192 website. And if I have the guy's name, I can ... *what?* What can I do?

I could sound out Gwen, see if she can tell me how Jason knows him.

Hands trembling, I bring up my search and find number 11.

The people listed at this address have an age guide of 50–54. Only two names are registered: Samantha and Marcus Tate.

I switch back to Google to enter their names, but before I have a chance, my phone rings.

Nush.

OK, so that's twice in twenty minutes. If she's that desperate to reconcile, maybe she'll be open to helping me out here. Nush was the one who first told me that Jason had "split up" from his former life.

"Ellen," she blurts. I don't even get a *hey* out. There's something slightly worrying about her tone, the breathless urgency. "Did you listen to my voicemail?"

"No, sorry, I've been—"

"Listen," she cuts in. There's a rustle of wind in the background. "Something really rather odd just happened . . ."

"Well, you've come to the right woman," I joke, trying to convey that there's no hard feelings. "After these past few weeks, I could do a PhD in rather odd."

"I was just at your house and—"

"My house? Why?"

"That's not important. But listen, as I was leaving, a man turned up at the door. I didn't know him, but from the small amount I gathered before I made my excuses and left—he was quite intimidating, frankly—it was the boy's father. You know, *the* boy."

"Zane?" I sit forward, hooking my spare hand tight around the steering wheel. A light comes on at number 11. "You mean Paulo Jackson was at my house?"

"If that's the father's name, then yes."

"Practically bald," I tell her. "Looks like he's been mauled by a bear?"

"That's him."

I sit back. "OK, well that's odd. I don't know how he got my address."

But of course, Julie Jackson. It says everything about my current life that I'd forgotten our doorstep contretemps.

"Forget knowing your address!" Nush takes an audible breath. "He seemed to know Gwen, *that's* the odd bit. He took one look at her and said, 'What the eff are you doing here?'"

An alarm sounds in my head, but for the moment it's kind of muted.

"Yeah, well, he's a bit rough and ready. He probably meant 'Who are you? Where's Ellen?'"

"No." I can picture her shaking her head in that way that brooks no argument. "No, it was obvious from her face that Gwen knew him too. She looked shocked—no, *caught out*. And I keep playing it over in my head, just in case I misread the situation, but I *definitely* know what I heard on the way out. And that was the oddest thing of all."

"What?"

"He called Gwen 'Frances.'"

59

Orla

ESME: Good news La-la!

ORLA: Forgotten what that is tbh.

Explain?

ESME: Everyone's over talking about ur mum at school.

ORLA: Oh right.

ESME: Well apart from Abi-D but who cares about that drama llama.

Want the bad news now?

ORLA: Sure.

ESME: Everyone's talking about u. Who ur shagging.

Declan O'Dell's started a sweepstake.

I told him to grow up.

ORLA: Course u did.

Anyway, u started it when u told everyone I'd lied to my folks about hanging out at urs.

ESME: I didn't tell everyone!!

ORLA: U tell Abi-D, u tell everyone.

ESME: Tbf ur creating the drama by being all CIA agent about it.

It's not a teacher is it? Mr. Fellowes?

Cos Jodie said he told her that green really suited her.

Weird-ass thing for a teacher to say, right?

ORLA: It's not anyone.

Look, I've been hanging out with Gwen. I didn't want my mum to kno because she's friends with her and she'd be weird about it.

But we've become really good mates. I can talk to her. She listens.

ESME: She's like thirty!!

ORLA: It doesn't feel like there's an age gap.

She says I'm really mature for my age.

ESME: So let me get this straight. Gwen's who u've been seeing??

Every time u've been telling ur folks that ur hanging out at mine, revising or whatever, u've actually been at Gwen's??

ORLA: Mostly yeah.

And sometimes I say I'm babysitting, and sometimes I am babysitting, but sometimes she doesn't actually bother going out and we just sit and chat shit for hours.

ESME: Okaaaaay.

Is it a lesbian thing?

Cos she never seems to have a boyfriend and u've gone SO anti-guy these past few months

ORLA: Not a lesbian thing.

A big sister thing I guess.

60

Gwen

Do you have any idea what £1,000 means to a boy like Zane Jackson? That insufferable cunt Orla would burn through it on ASOS in half an hour. Actually, it was £1,000, an Apple Watch, and some ugly Nikes. That's the going rate for hiring a seventeen-year-old to do your dirty work.

Although maybe I should have paid him more, because his execution was bargain-basement. He planted the condoms but messed up the blood. They didn't find any. Not one drop. He said he forgot, which beggars belief, as does his claim that it was my fault. My "non-stop stressing" over WhatsApp made him flustered, apparently.

I'll expect better for the final payment.

Ten thousand pounds means no cock-ups.

61

Ellen

"Marcus Tate, I *know* you're in there."

I pick up where Jason left off, ranting on the doorstep of number 11. A couple of knocks have gone unanswered, and I'm now down on my haunches and shouting through the letter box, watching as a typically haughty cat criss-crosses the mosaic hallway floor.

"Look, if I keep shouting, your neighbour will probably come out again. And I'll be honest with you, Marcus. I don't care if she calls the police. I think we need the police here." I absolutely don't. I'm bluffing. "We need to sort this out. My name is Ellen Walsh."

Silence.

"I took a video, you know. Of Jason." Except I didn't. *Why didn't I?* My former sensible self would have definitely done that. But she seems to have taken permanent leave. "And I know you're a senior partner at . . ." I look at my phone, at Marcus Tate's LinkedIn profile. "Sterling Kingsley Walters. Which means you're a solicitor of some sort, and we both know that giving a false statement could get you disbarred."

The cat stares intently into an open doorway, miaowing, as if asking its owner, *Who's the lunatic?*

"I don't even have to come in. You can talk to me on the doorstep. And if you answer my questions, I swear I'll be gone in five minutes. But if you don't open the door, I'll camp out here all night."

Nothing. I stand up. I give the door a frustrated, feeble kick, then turn to make my way down the steps again.

The door clicks open. I turn back to face Marcus Tate.

He's good-looking, a silver fox, although he can't be more than fifty. With his shoulders back and chest out, his posture screams senior-partner confidence. But his fevered stare screams panic. The eyes always give you away.

"Five minutes." His posh baritone voice rumbles with hostility. I don't think I've ever faced down such unapologetic hate. "My wife is on her way from Heathrow right now. She's around ten, fifteen miles away. And if you're still here when she gets back, I promise I *will* find a way to make you pay."

He turns and walks down the hallway, leading me into a small study off the kitchen, where a lavender-scented candle is fighting a battle with the smell of stale cigarettes.

"Five minutes," he repeats, perching against the windowsill.

"Fine. How do you know Jason Bale? And why did you lie to the police about me and Zane Jackson? And remember, I've got a video of you slamming the door on Jason—a police officer who worked on this case and who *clearly* has a personal issue with you. So the game's up, Marcus. I just need you to tell me what the game is, then I'm out of your hair."

He stares at me, blinking. That legal brain working overtime. He looks poised halfway between telling me everything and telling me to kindly fuck off.

With a deep, resigned sigh, he folds his arms and opts for everything.

"I only met Jason last week. He was the officer I gave my statement to. I had no idea he was Gwen's brother until he came to see me off the record and said he knew who I was."

"And who are you?"

"I had an affair with Gwen several years ago. The greatest regret of my life. Samantha, my wife, knows nothing about it, and I'd like to keep it that way for as long as possible, even if that's just another few days."

"Then keep talking."

He sighs again. "Jason said he'd been keeping tabs on me these past few years because he knew his sister had 'her hooks in'—his words, not mine—and he was scared that if I rejected her . . . well, he sort of implied that rejecting Gwen rarely ends well. As if I needed telling."

"Her hooks in how?" My head reels with this version of my sparkly, sweet friend.

"She fell pregnant during our affair. She wanted to keep it. Well, she did keep it."

Not *it*. Bella. A little girl. A lover of *PAW Patrol* and breadsticks.

My face says it all.

He's unrepentant. "Look, I told her as soon as I found out she was pregnant that I had no interest in playing Daddy. Samantha and I never wanted children. I certainly wasn't going to have one with Gwen."

"Maybe you should have been a bit more careful, then."

"Oh, I was careful. *We* were careful, as far as I understood. She said she was on the pill." A blush creeps over his collar. "*And* we used condoms. I insisted on it—to protect Samantha . . ."

"Noble guy."

"And yet still it happened." He shakes his head at the floor, then abruptly looks up. "I always wondered, you know. And then her brother all but confirmed it."

"Confirmed what?"

"That Gwen *always* gets what she wants. And she doesn't let the small matter of what other people want get in her way."

I snort. "You're saying she used you as a sperm donor?"

"Yes, but not out of any maternal longing. She wanted a

cash machine, not a baby." I look at him, confused, but I have a horrible sense of where we're going. "She agreed not to tell Samantha and that I would play no role in the child's life, but she wanted hush money. She framed it as child support. And child support would have been fine—I'm comfortably off, I'm not unreasonable. But what she's demanded over the years has gone *far* beyond new shoes and nappies." He glances at his watch, decides to keep talking. "Two weeks in Bali. Ten thousand pounds a couple of months ago—I asked what it was for and she said I didn't need to know any more than Samantha needed to know about Bella. And then there's her rent. She even demanded I help her *buy* a place a year or so ago—she wanted help with the deposit *and* for me to act as guarantor. I don't know what happened there, but thank God it fell through, because I'd have had to. She had me over a barrel."

After a few seconds of silence, I make the obvious, knife-twisting leap.

"So Gwen blackmailed you into saying you saw me with Zane Jackson. Kissing him, hitting him. She knew that as a solicitor you'd make a great witness."

"When she gets her hooks in, that's it." It's not an answer, but really it is. He looks defeated. "She wrecked some other poor chap's marriage, you know. She told me that herself—a warning, I suppose. Seriously, you have no idea what she's capable of. Ask her brother."

"Why did he turn up here tonight?"

If I keep asking questions, I can delay having to process this.

"He's got it into his head that I must know where Zane Jackson is, which I don't. And he won't ask Gwen anything about it, because he's scared he'll trigger her into doing something bad. Poor guy's lived his whole adult life in fear of what she'll do next. He left a good job in London, left his *wife*, because he felt he had to be near her, to keep an eye on her before she harms someone. He implied she's done it before."

I think about my conversation with Adam, which was, what, fifteen minutes ago? A conversation that ended on Gwen bringing earmuffs. My ever-helpful friend.

Oh Christ.

The earmuffs. The fireworks. I shoot a look at my phone. Almost 5:30.

I'm flying back down the front steps when Adam answers his phone. "What now?"

"Ads, it's Gwen. Gwen's behind all this, behind everything. I don't know why, and I don't have time to explain right now. You're just going to have to trust me, OK?"

Adam intercepts with "What the fuck?" but I shout breathlessly over him.

"Listen, I reckon I've got around forty minutes before she sets off for Coombe, so I'm going to floor it back home to get Orla and hopefully I'll intercept her there. But if she's gone, and she arrives at Coombe—whatever you do, *do not* let her take the boys."

62

Gwen

Regrets? I've had a few, ha. I'm not *completely* without feeling, despite what Jase says. Although he's given up saying anything. He thinks I'm beyond redemption. A lost cause. I think he partly blames himself for how I am (Ellen isn't the only one with a saviour complex), but he gave up on saving me a long time ago. I know he came to Thames Lawley to save her.

And he probably thinks he has. I mean, I've been "friends" with Ellen for a year now, and I haven't pushed her down the stairs or poisoned her cereal. And that's a relief to Jase, obviously, even though he's clearly not her biggest fan. Like me, he thinks Ellen's fake and spoiled and she drives a car that's far too big for her. But I guess he believes she doesn't deserve carnage. She doesn't deserve despicable me.

So, regrets.

Max's hand. Really, it was just a graze—that child sure knows how to make a meal of things. But it wasn't supposed to happen. *I* was supposed to find the knife, not him. I was supposed to shame her in front of everyone, set the groundwork for Social Services. *God, Els, that was a close one.* And she was supposed to wonder what she ever did before little ol' me.

So I took no pleasure in Max's pain, but, unfortunately, there's always collateral damage.

I wonder if that ever occurred to Ellen?

Call me cynical, but I doubt it.

63

Ellen

The last time I drove home from Danesfield, I flirted with the speed limit, desperate to get back to my family, to familiarity. Tonight, I crash through it defiantly: eighty on the motorway, forty in a thirty zone. Every red light is met with a guttural, primal scream.

Red lights. Red flags. Should I have sensed that something was off with Gwen? The speed of our friendship, how quickly she became a part of our family. Did I encourage that, or did she? The fact that apart from being a mum, and the occasional evening out when Orla babysat, her entire life seemed to pivot around being a supportive friend to me.

Truth is, I didn't look too closely because she was *easy*. Low maintenance. Was that her plan all along? To be everything I wanted her to be?

The Meadowhouse appears dark as I screech up barely half an hour later, although it's hard to tell with the blinds closed and the oak door giving nothing away. Gwen's car isn't outside, but would she have moved it here anyway? She only lives across the green.

The perfect spot for surveilling me.

I let myself in and call out for Orla, my voice echoing in the silent hallway. The hall light is on, but the kitchen's dark. The heating is up high. The air feels thick. When Orla doesn't answer—which isn't conclusive; she seems to have taken a vow of silence against me—I shoot upstairs and throw open all the bedroom doors. But there's nothing and no one to see.

I fly back down the stairs and head for the kitchen. I need to catch my breath. Call Orla. Call Adam. In the doorway, I reach for the light switch.

"I wouldn't bother, it's on the blink again. You never did deserve this house."

Gwen. Sitting in the near-darkness, and where else but on the window seat. She's facing out onto the back garden, watching green and pink explosions scatter the evening sky.

"Where's Orla?"

I ask the question calmly, not wanting to provoke her. For now at least. Once I know my daughter's safe, I can ask her why she's such a crazy fucking bitch.

"Of course, fireworks are better in the dark," she says, as though I didn't speak or she didn't hear me. "I used to turn off all the lights when I was little. It made the whole thing more magical, the colours so much brighter." She turns to face me. "But then you grow up and you realise that fireworks are a bit shit, really. Repetitive, kinda boring. Like a lot of things in life." She pauses, narrowing her eyes, making some judgement I can only guess at. "Actually, you probably don't find that, do you? Life's always been one big picnic for Ellen Walsh. Oh, sure, the Tales from the Council Estate might sound grim to the likes of Nush or Adam—'I had to share a room with my sister!' 'We'd never heard of avocados!' Try being branded with a cigarette because you had the nerve to ask for cereal, or being made to face the wall all day because you spilled lemonade on your dad's spliff."

"Where's Orla?" I repeat, panic leaking into my tone this time.

"Orla?" She gives me a faux-baffled stare, like I'm totally overreacting. "She's gone to get hot chocolate. We were going to take Thermoses to Whistlebrook, see. Obviously Orla, the spoiled brat, said we could buy it there, because she's like you—

no appreciation of money. But I always think hot chocolate tastes nicest out of a Thermos, don't you? It tastes of nostalgia, safety." She lets out a harsh, detached laugh. "I don't suppose we're going to Whistlebrook now."

"Where's Zane, Gwen? Have you hurt him?"

I keep my voice level, taking a few short steps towards her. Something stops me from getting too close, though. Her aura is a barbed-wire fence.

"Oh, that's actually quite sweet, Ellen. I mean, you could be asking *why*, but instead you're worried about pretty boy. He got under your skin, didn't he? You might not have fucked him, but you felt something. Admit it."

"Sure," I agree. "I admit I was fond of him. It's quite a normal human emotion. Are you familiar with those? Your brother doesn't seem to think so."

I chalk a point in my column, expecting a flicker of hurt to cross her face.

Nothing.

"Zane would have fucked you, you know? Although don't flatter yourself—they're walking hard-ons at that age. But he liked you. I know that. Does that make you feel better or worse?"

If I spent the rest of my life in quiet reflection, I'm still not sure I could answer that.

"But yeah, honestly, I couldn't believe it. Even after we realised that the Ellen I was telling him about was the *same* Ellen who'd been tutoring him for months, lying about who she was, he *still* didn't hate you. He said maybe you and Orla had done him a favour in the long run, 'cos he hated school anyway, preferred the home-tutoring. I mean, don't get me wrong, he was stunned. *I* was stunned. I'd only planned to pay him to send you a letter—an 'I know what you did' type thing to put the wind up you. But when I realised you'd conned your way into his life, I thought, oh, I can really have some fun here."

"So instead you paid him to set me up, stage his own disappearance, crucify me."

She shrugs, neither proud nor ashamed. *It is what it is.* "If it softens the blow, he only agreed to properly fuck you over when I mentioned five figures. And even then, I had to spoon-feed him—getting him to brag to his mates about you, coaching him to push your buttons, tug on your heartstrings, prepping him for Danesfield. *And* I had to practically drag his mum's phone number out of him, so I could text her your address." She blows out an exhausted breath. "Trust me, 'Frances' had a tougher job tutoring him than you did. He's a greedy little shit, but he didn't enjoy crucifying you. It was hard work."

The last words he ever said to me. *I really am sorry, Ellen. You've no idea how sorry I am.*

"How did you find him?" I ask, before a more pressing question strikes. "How did you find out *about* him in the first place?"

"Find him? Same way you did, I suppose. Tenacity, determination." Her expression shifts from blank to playful. "And how do you think I found out about him? Orla. Poor guilt-stricken Orla. She'd been bottling it all up, needed someone to offload to . . ."

"And she chose *you*? Some single mum nobody whose kid she sometimes babysits?"

I don't care what I sound like. I want her diminished. Humiliated.

Instead, she's amused.

"She hardly ever babysat, you know? I reckon in nine, ten months, she watched Bella maybe six or seven times." A loud bang from outside shuts her up momentarily. I stare at her, bewildered, as the sky fills with sparks. "Oh yeah, we love a cosy night in, me and Orla. Nice bottle of wine to get the lips loosened, secrets pouring . . ."

"You gave my daughter alcohol."

This amuses her even more. "Ellen, she drank eight shots of vodka at a party once." She cocks her head. "Although I suppose that could be bullshit. She's so eager to impress, isn't she? To be *seen*. She's felt invisible to you since the boys, which is self-pitying bollocks, really. I even told her that in slightly kinder words." That playful smile again. "See, I wasn't always dripping poison. I actually stuck up for you a fair bit." A surge of hate sweeps my body, cold and clear and deep like water. "And then, yeah, a couple of months ago, she has a bit too much Sauvignon and tells me *all* about Zane."

"Where is he? Paulo deserves to know he's OK, at least."

"And his mum!" She puts her hand to her chest in mock outrage. "God, you really do have mummy issues. No wonder you felt so sorry for poor 'abandoned' Zane—who's completely fine, by the way."

She stands and walks to the fridge, grabbing a bottle of wine, then, to my disbelief, two glasses. From day one, she always seemed at home here, but tonight she's the anointed queen.

"Why, Gwen?" The answer to this question is the only thing stopping me from hitting her. I'm guessing she'd be less inclined to tell me if she was sprawled across the floor. "Why would you go to these lengths? Because you've had a harder life than me and that sucks?" I shake my head. "No way, I don't buy it. In a crazy, fucked-up world, that might just about explain the breathalyser, the Facebook photos, the malicious calls . . ."

She puts the wine on the table. "You know, most of that stuff was your own fault, really. I mean, you *could* have been over the limit that day. And those Facebook photos—*you* posted them originally. And if you hadn't basically steamrollered Adam into buying the house and renovating it, I wouldn't have been able to softly influence him into calling the whole thing off."

How didn't I see it? It was the night after they'd been for ice cream that Adam first broached the idea of postponing. And they'd talked again the day Cathy Grantham came, although Gwen presented it as Adam lobbying her.

"This is insane." My voice is low, barely a whisper. "So you're jealous of my life, but all *this*. Why so . . . *ruthless*?"

"*Me?*" she roars, the word a bellow of pure fury. It's the first time she's raised her voice or dropped the mask of serenity. "You're the most ruthless person I've ever met, and the worst thing is you don't even fucking realise it."

The kitchen hums with silence. She seems frustrated by her own outburst. Then, in an instant, her face goes blank again. The perfect way of recovering control.

"What are you talking about?" I say, although I accept that covering for Orla was textbook ruthless. "And why all this now? You've known me for a year—this only started up two weeks ago."

"I had to get you to trust me. I needed free rein of the house; that sort of thing takes time. And it'd have looked a bit suspicious, wouldn't it, if the minute I came on the scene, your life fell apart."

"And why would you want that to happen?"

She stares at me for a second. "Have you ever hated someone on sight, Ellen? 'Cos believe me, it's pretty powerful."

"People don't hate other people on sight any more than they love them, unless it's their kids."

"No? Well, I disagree. And nothing you did after that first sight ever came close to changing my opinion. I mean, you're fun when you want to be. And you're kind if it makes you look good. But you are So. Fucking. Discontent." The loathing in her voice suggests there's no worse thing to be accused of. "And it's sickening to watch—like, *physically* sickening—when you've got everything I've ever wanted—"

I cut across her, practically foaming. "For Christ's sake, Gwen, you're thirty! I didn't have all this when I was thirty. It takes time to get your ducks in a row. There has to be more to this. Tell me *why*."

Instead, she hands me a glass of wine. I push it away. She shrugs, then sits back down. When she looks up again, she's smiling. "Do you know what, Ellen? Ultimately, the ins and outs of *why* don't really matter. What happens now does. Because there's two options. Two ways this can end."

She brings her glass to her lips. I picture myself slamming it against her nostrils.

"First way—I take my story to the national press. I tell them *everything* Orla told me about what she did and how you ordered her to keep it quiet. And then, of course, there's the even spicier story of how you hunted down and then seduced the 'missing' teen." She takes a slow sip of her wine, giving me time to digest the full horror of that option. "And a word of advice—don't think for a second I wouldn't do it. There's already a journalist from one of the national rags with her snout in the story, so all it would take is one phone call for you and Orla to become tabloid meat. Trial by TikTok, the works."

I swallow hard, trying to keep my voice steady. "You know, you don't hold all the cards here. You're not the only one with leverage . . ."

She looks at me, bored. "If you're talking about Marc, he called me. I've heard all about your bullshit video." *He called her?* I assumed she'd figured the game was up when Nush heard Paulo call her "Frances." It didn't occur to me that Marcus Tate would warn her. Clearly her power over him runs deep. "And he agrees with me that you were bluffing—if you'd really taken a video, you'd have shown him. So let's just say, after a minor dispute, me and Marc are back on the same page. I won't be taking Bella to meet Samantha, and he won't be changing his story to the police."

Motherfucker. If I didn't despise her, I'd be applauding right now.

Her eyes flash. "Do you want to hear the second way?"

I don't give her the satisfaction of a *yes*. She's obviously going to tell me.

"How about this? Zane turns up tickety-boo, saying it's been a tough year, he just needed time away to get his head straight. Oh, and he's honestly really sorry, but he made up all that stuff about you to impress his mates."

"And why would he say that?"

"Because he's being paid handsomely to follow orders. A decent wage every week he stays disappeared, then a *very* decent lump sum once you're gone for good."

"*Gone?*"

"Well, yeah, this hasn't been about embarrassing you, Ellen." She looks at me, disappointed, as though I've missed the point, didn't read the email properly. "I mean, if it was just about embarrassment, I'd have stuck to name-calling on Facebook and anonymous phone calls. No, I want you gone. And surely you can see that even if Zane says he lied, you're still finished in Thames Lawley. Mud sticks. No smoke without fire. You know what people around here are like. But you could start again somewhere else. This doesn't have to blow up any more than it has."

"And what's the catch?"

No hesitation. "Simple. I want this house."

I say nothing, then I laugh. I actually stagger slightly backwards. The unexpectedness of the answer hits me like a physical charge.

"What do you mean, 'I want this house'?" Her face is calm and resolute, as though her suggestion is entirely reasonable. I stare at her, wide-eyed. "Oh my God, Gwen. Are you having some sort of psychotic episode? Of course I'm not going to give you my bloody house."

There's a crunch of footsteps outside. A jangle of keys on the doorstep.

Orla.

"Let me tell you something, Ellen—there was a time last year when I was tempted to burn it to the ground, possibly with you in it, so when you consider *that*, asking you to give it to me doesn't actually sound that psychotic, does it?" This is insane. She's insane. I have to keep Orla outside on that doorstep. Better still, get her away. "But, see, I'm not even asking for that. This doesn't have to be unpleasant. I want you to sell it to me. I want to buy it." She looks me straight in the eye, channelling waves of pure hatred. "Like I *tried* to do last time."

The front door opens. I bolt into the hall, where Orla's annoyance at my presence gives way to confusion when she registers my face.

"Orla, get in the car now. The keys are in my bag, there." I point to the foot of the stairs. I can't afford to move a muscle. I need to act as a barricade between my daughter and this *thing*.

"I'll expect a reasonable price, though." Gwen's in the kitchen doorway now, glass of wine still in hand. "Certainly less than what you paid. I mean, you've run it into the ground this past year—no point keeping on top of things when you're planning to rip it to shreds, rip the heart out of it, eh?" She cranes her neck, looking past me to Orla. "Fireworks are off, I'm afraid. So be a good little girl and fuck off, yeah? Me and your mum have got big-girl things to sort."

Orla jolts at her tone, then looks at me, eyes filling. "Mum, what's going on?"

"*Please* just get in the car."

"Yeah, run along, La-la. Do what Mummy says." Gwen grins broadly. "It's what you always do, isn't it? It's probably best, to be fair, because you haven't got an independent thought in your pretty head. I mean, *God*, you drone on about Esme, but at least she's got some backbone, a personality."

My heart breaks for my ambushed daughter, standing there innocently with the jar of hot chocolate. At least I've had a short amount of time to adjust to the new way of things. And Gwen's pressing exactly the right buttons. The worst buttons, if you're Orla. While she might come across as confident, there's no doubt her friendship with Esme has muddied her self-esteem.

Gwen's not letting up. "Esme can't stand you—you do realise that, right? Actually, you probably don't. You might be 'Oxbridge potential,' but when it comes to people, you're a bit thick." She turns her stare, her scorn on me. "Guess she gets that from you, Ellen. I mean, do you have *any* idea how much Nush resents you?" *Resents me?* "No, didn't think so. And did you honestly think I wanted to sit night after night listening to you moaning about Adam and dodgy bladders and suspicious moles?" She grins. "Mind you, that mole on your inner thigh was solid gold info for Zane."

Orla takes a step into the house, her eyes on Gwen's wine glass. "Are you *drunk*, Gwen? Is that it? Is that why you're being so vile?"

"Er, you've only been gone twenty minutes. Takes a bit longer to get me drunk. I'm not a sixteen-year-old lightweight who can't handle her Sauvignon."

Orla takes another step forward. "What's *happened* to you?" I raise a hand to hold her back.

"What's happened, Orla, is . . ." Gwen takes a deep slug of wine, wipes her mouth, then steps back into the kitchen. "Oh, do you know what? I can't even be bothered to explain. I'm *so* fucking bored of you." Her voice takes on a grating, whiny pitch. "'Oh Gwen, Esme's so mean to me . . . Mum never has time for me . . . Roan Howells fingered me.' Like, did you *actually* think I cared? That we were friends? All I wanted was info on your mum. You're just a stupid, spoiled kid, Orla. You're nothing."

It all happens so fast then. A tidal wave of motion. Orla charging me out of the way, running at Gwen, elbows flying. The look of feral anger hardening the soft lines of my baby's face. Then the wine glass smashing on the tiles. A shout of "Bitch!"

A grunt of fury. The hot, taut, stinging sound of Orla slapping Gwen's right cheek.

Then Gwen raising her palm high. Orla bracing herself for the coming impact.

Me instinctively lunging forward.

Then with one hard shove, there's so much blood.

So much blood.

It instantly pools under the breakfast table, drips off the sharp corner where her head split open. I crouch down, but I can't bring myself to touch her.

Oh my fucking God.

What have I done?

Behind me, Orla's screaming, "Is she breathing? Call an ambulance!"

And so, dazed and barely breathing myself, I do exactly as my daughter tells me. But as I stare at Gwen's small body while I relay the chaos to the call operator, it doesn't enter my head to think *sorry*.

The only thing I think is *why?*

Fourth Bad Deed

The Meadowhouse

Jason

THE MEADOWHOUSE, CALDI-COTT LANE, THAMES LAWLEY

SOLD SUBJECT TO CONTRACT

gazump (informal—British) *gazumping*: when someone makes a higher offer on the house you are in the process of buying and has that offer accepted, thus forcing you out of the process, sometimes at a very late stage.

Example sentences:

He was devastated to be gazumped at the closing stage of the purchase.

The return of gazumping isn't surprising given the recent property boom.

While gazumping may be seen as immoral, it is not re-motely illegal.

Gazump.
Ga-zump.
A funny word if you're a toddler. Bella heard it screamed so many times by her permanently ranting mother, it soon became

her catch-all word for everything. She even started saying it outside the house.

So when Gwen finally moved to Thames Lawley, directly opposite *her* house, the one she'd had "stolen," she put a stop to it by telling Bella that it was a secret word, a scary word. It was only to be whispered in Mummy's ear or, at a push, Uncle Jason's. And if she said it outside the house again, the gazumpy goblins would come to feast.

A mean thing to tell a child, but Gwen's always had that mean streak.

And there was only ever one gazump goblin.

That was Ellen Walsh.

I always knew Gwen was different. Calculating. Vindictive. From a very young age, she'd lie and hit people, but above everything, it was the grudges that stood out. The sheer length of time she could hold one. The huge lengths she'd go to avenge one. The crazily out-of-proportion punishment she obviously delighted in meting out. In Year 3, a "friend" had borrowed her *Wind in the Willows*, then returned it with a page torn. *Six* months later, Gwen "accidentally" spilled orange juice down the front of the girl's Holy Communion dress.

She happily boasted about it to me, thinking I'd be impressed by her patience.

"See, if I got her back too soon, Jase, she'd have known it wasn't an accident. And anyway, I wanted to wait until I could do something that was really, really mean."

Like Freud, I blame the parents, although that's an unfashionable thing to say these days. It's become a cliché, but then it's also a cliché to point out that most clichés are broadly true. Because everything that was ever wrong with Gwen was either caused by, or learned from, those two neglectful, abusive wasters. She learned to lie to keep herself safe. She learned to hit because that's what they did. She held long grudges because forgiveness just wasn't a thing that was taught in our house. If you were wronged, you took a swing. If you wronged someone, you took the punishment. And Gwen took plenty in her early years. Far more than I did, I admit that. But then I was always happy to blend into the background, while even when it was patently against her interests, even in the face of violence, Gwen wouldn't be cowed.

So yeah, our parents were shit, and I blame them for what Gwen became and where she is now. But in a way that probably isn't fair, I blame Gwen's foster parents, the Merricks, too.

Gwen and I moved in and out of short-term foster care for chunks of our miserable childhood. Sometimes we'd get placed together, but sadly, it wasn't the norm. It's not always easy to place siblings, especially siblings with a six-year age gap. The age gap also meant that by the time Gwen turned ten, and our parents were finally deemed no-hopers, I was sixteen, almost an adult. Basically, I was allowed to live alone.

Gwen begged the authorities to let her live with me, but I was too young to be her legal guardian. And so she ended up at Wisley kids' home for a year, a place well-known for brutality.

But then came the Merricks.

Beverley and Malcolm Merrick of the Meadowhouse, Thames Lawley.

"Thames Lawley!" I teased her. "Check out my baby sis living the high life."

"Honestly, wait till you see my house," she said. *My house.* Quick as a flash, she'd staked ownership. "I'm not joking, Jase. It's perfect. Like something off a Christmas card or a box of chocolates."

The first time I visited her was over a week after she arrived there. I'd have gone sooner—even then, I was hypervigilant, always mindful to keep an eye on her—but I'd been on my first ever summer holiday. A cheap boys' jolly to Blackpool.

She answered the door holding a rabbit.

"Whoa, you look tanned!" she said.

I said, "Whoa, you look happy!"

And she did. She'd always wanted a rabbit, and what's more, she looked really healthy. Well fed, well cared for, and, if I was honest, well off. On her feet were a pair of pink Nikes that even in 2003 must have cost fifty quid.

The Meadowhouse was how it is now—cluttered, old-fashioned, but cosy and kind of charming. And the same could be said for "Bev and Malc," the ruddy, rotund couple in their late fifties who treated me like a VIP. We ate homemade scones as they gushed over Gwen, then Malc bored me to tears showing me around the front garden (I was seventeen; I couldn't get excited about hollyhocks). When we came back in, Gwen was sitting cross-legged on the window seat, making friendship bracelets. She'd made a purple one for me.

"This is my favourite spot," she said, as though she was showing the house to a prospective buyer. "You can feel the sun on your back, but you get to be inside at the same time. And I love being inside, Jase. Doesn't this place remind you of Badger's house in *Wind in the Willows*? It's even got a pantry!" She insisted I take a look, showing me pots of jam and tins of cake, bundles of herbs and strings of onions. "And they've bought me a bike, and I've got a sink in my bedroom. *And* I've got my own tree house, Jase. A tree house!" She paused then, slipping the purple weave over my wrist. "I feel so safe here. I've never felt safe."

It was nice, good to see her settled, even though as the months rolled on, it was obvious that Gwen was the Merricks' "poor kid project." For her twelfth birthday, they hired a princess bouncy castle, which seemed a bit babyish to me, but who was I to piss on her chips when she was reliving her lost childhood. For her thirteenth, they took her to Disneyworld. Christmas 2004 was the Four Seasons, Hawaii.

It was all a bit *My Fair Lady*, to be honest, which never sat quite right with me.

And then in late 2005, Gwen called me, hysterical. The Merricks' daughter had broken up with her husband in Australia and was coming back with her three children, and they were moving into "my house!" The upshot was, the couple were ending her placement. I was furious to begin with. It didn't feel right that they could just discard her. However, when I spoke to Gwen's social worker, she told me that it wasn't purely due to the unexpected change in circumstance. There'd been behavioural issues for a while—Gwen throwing monumental, threatening fits on the rare occasion she didn't get what she wanted—and that had meant the Merricks had come to the decision more easily.

Gwen was beside herself. Catatonic with grief, then wild with rage. She tried everything—*everything*—to stay in that house (because by then I realised it was the house more than the Merricks—it was what it represented: indulgence and safety). She tried flattery, good behaviour, making herself useful, making herself invisible. At one point she said she'd sleep in the tree house. They wouldn't even know she was there. But when that didn't work, she called them names I doubt they'd heard before. She smeared dog turd on the carpets—they didn't have a dog; she'd gone out of her way to acquire it—then set fire to the bedroom curtains.

She was supposed to stay with the Merricks for twenty-eight days after they announced they were ending her placement. She lasted thirteen.

Then, around eighteen months later, while Gwen was in the care of a far less indulgent couple five miles away, a male teen broke into the Meadowhouse and carried out what police called "a vicious, sustained, and totally senseless attack" on Bev and Malc Merrick. Thankfully, they survived, but Bev didn't walk for three months. Malc's hearing was never right again.

Gwen made no attempt whatsoever to hide her involvement from me.

"Yeah, shocking what some boys will do for a blow-job and fifty quid."

A while later, she tried to backtrack, claimed she'd been joking. But I *knew*.

After that, we grew apart. I couldn't stomach her, much less spend time with her. We'd occasionally talk on the phone, and there'd be the odd stilted meet-up, but I hadn't seen her in nearly a year when I was accepted into the University of Greenwich to study criminology and psychology.

Was my sister a psychopath? I suppose that's the question that drew me to my field of study. I felt a need to make sense of her (did she simply lack the tools to process disappointment safely?), and I also needed to work out if there was anything I could have done to have prevented the naïve but well-intentioned Merricks living out the rest of their days in fear.

I can't answer that question any more now than I could then. I *think* I believe that Gwen's badness wasn't innate. It was situational, environmental. She was neglected and abused, then abandoned by our parents, then superficially worshipped and overindulged by the Merricks for two years before being discarded.

Neither of those scenarios is a remotely good thing.

She certainly scored highly on manipulation, pathological lying, early childhood behavioural problems, superficial charm, lack of remorse, and failure to accept personal responsibility. But then so did half the country, if that's not too cynical (I *am* too cynical). And anyway, I didn't really need a label.

I knew she was dangerous. That was all that mattered to me.

Many years passed. I joined the Met, and Gwen did very well for herself—acing her GCSEs, then her A levels, and working her way up to something apparently quite senior in financial PR.

Our meet-ups were still irregular. I lived in London, she lived in Reading. She came to my wedding and for Christmas a few times, but it didn't help that Emma couldn't stand her.

"I don't hate her per se," she said to me once. "It's more your obsession with her. How you can't bring yourself to even meet her for a coffee, but you're always checking up on what she's doing. Stalking her from afar."

Then four years ago, Gwen told me she was pregnant. She was having a girl, she said. Bella or Belle, like the Disney princess. I asked her if it was a shock. She said no, it was something she'd been planning. And so I asked about the father. She wouldn't tell me, simply saying, "Don't worry about him, Jase, he's my problem." But the idea of Gwen and "problems" always had the power to utterly chill me, and so after what must have been six months of periodic surveillance, I discovered the father was a married solicitor named Marcus Tate.

I *did* actually wonder if a child could be the making of her. And when Bella arrived, she seemed happier. Less combative, more stable. Slowly, *very* slowly, we started to see a bit more of each other.

Then the Meadowhouse went up for sale, and the old Gwen came out to play again.

I knew she hadn't changed by the way she sat there rewriting history. All she could talk about was the happy times. How she'd never felt so safe. I did believe that bit, though—just looking at her in her rainbow jumper and her then-pink hair twisted into ponytails, it wasn't hard to conclude that she was stuck in some kind of arrested development, desperate to feel how she'd felt between the ages of eleven and thirteen.

On and on she went. When she bought the house (not *if*), she was going to make jam with Bella and pick hollyhocks from the garden like Bev had.

No mention of dog turds or burning curtains. Or the price of revenge being a blow-job and fifty quid.

"There's a few photos on the internet," she said. "Hard to believe, but it's barely changed from when I lived there. This feels like fate, Jase. It feels like mine."

I asked how she could afford it. She said Bella's dad had lots of money (I knew he did; I'd been keeping an eye on him). She'd also saved the bulk of her work bonuses over the years, before Bella, because buying the Meadowhouse one day had always been her dream.

"And it's going for a reasonable price! They've just reduced it slightly because the current owners are getting a divorce and are after a quick sale. Apparently it's in need of a revamp, so the agent said I need to factor that in. But apart from maybe a lick of paint, I'm going to keep it exactly as it is."

She was set. I couldn't stop her.

I also feared what could happen if someone else tried.

The one thing I did insist on—and this was to help her, albeit reluctantly—was that she stay away from the open-house viewing. *I* would go alone. I feared that faced with other prospective buyers, Gwen would do something erratic and put the sellers off. And anyway, there was no need for her to be there. She already knew for certain that she wanted the place.

I saw Ellen for the first time at the open house. We exchanged the briefest of thin smiles, had an "after you" dance in the kitchen doorway.

Sometimes I can't believe she doesn't remember me.

Other times I wonder if anyone really sees me at all.

Property sales are rarely fun, but to summarise the horror show that followed: Gwen made an offer, it was accepted, then six weeks later—kaput.

Literally two weeks before exchanging contracts, when she'd spent money on surveys and searches, bought furniture and hired movers, one phone call informed her that the Meadowhouse was going to be someone else's dream.

A last-minute buyer had put in a higher offer, actually going slightly over the asking price. Gwen asked for a chance to match it, knowing her only option was to fast-talk Marcus, but the seller wasn't interested. Truth was, Gwen had—surprise, surprise—been a royal pain in the arse throughout the entire process, quibbling about every little thing while haranguing everyone else for not doing their bit. And as the new people were cash buyers, the timeline wouldn't be affected. Basically, the seller, sick of Gwen, was more than happy to sell to someone else.

So she'd lost the Meadowhouse for a second time, that's how a truly distraught Gwen saw it. And if she hadn't paid a thug to attack the Merricks, I might have felt sorry for her. Instead, I felt sick with dread.

"Only in this fucking country!" she raged. "This wouldn't happen in the US. Even in Scotland an offer is legally binding. Did you know that eighty-five per cent of the public think ga-zumping should be made a crime?"

And when she wasn't obsessing over facts, she was cursing the new buyers. The "robbing, cheating bastards" who could afford to cash-buy a £600K house.

Later, once she'd cosied up to Ellen, Gwen learned that it was actually Adam's parents who'd bought the house outright. The agreement was that Adam and Ellen would then buy it off them as soon as their old house sold.

"It's all been a bit complicated," Ellen confided to her. "And costly too, although it was worth it. I do feel a bit bad, though— you know, for the people who'd already offered. Adam said we shouldn't do it, said it's bad karma. But hey, all's fair in love and property . . ."

But all *wasn't* fair, Gwen insisted. She had scrimped and saved to buy the Meadowhouse (she conveniently forgot about Marcus's money every time she mounted her high horse), and it was in fact unbearably *unfair*—and really, she *was* struggling to bear it—that the bank of mum and dad had swooped in and helped the Walshes out.

A few weeks later, when Gwen told me she'd rented one of the new-builds across from the Meadowhouse, I knew it was bad. I knew straight away she'd be planning something. She tried to play it coy, acting confused when I asked why she'd done that. She said she'd simply fallen back in love with Thames Lawley, and the Meadowhouse made nice scenery.

I said no more at that point, although I did something I wasn't proud of. Something I'd thought about doing a lot over the years.

I looked her up on the PNC.

I knew that improper use of the Police National Computer was a sackable offence, but I had to risk it. I had to know if, in the years when we'd barely seen each other, she'd ever hurt anyone, got up to her old tricks. There were no hits whatsoever, not so much as a caution or a minor parking offense, but then she'd got away with what she did to the Merricks.

The worst things people do don't always come to the attention of the police.

But it was Gwen's first mention of Ellen and how she'd been welcomed into the Meadowhouse, how she'd been trusted with Ellen's keys, with her *kids*, that made me realise I *had* to move to Thames Lawley. I wasn't able to protect the Merricks, but maybe I could protect the Walshes. I'd keep my eye on Gwen this time, even if it was at great personal cost to me.

So I told Gwen that Emma had kicked me out, which was kind of true, because she'd said, "If you go, don't come back again." And I told my boss I was suffering from burnout, which was kind of true, but not for the reasons he thought.

Little did I know the burnout was only just beginning.

Watching Gwen. Watching Ellen. Trying to pretend to Gwen

that I wasn't on to her. Knowing it was only a matter of time before she did something. It was exhausting. A full-time career.

But it was all *just* about manageable until the week Ellen showed Gwen the renovation plans. That turned out to be the fuel on Gwen's fire, the catalyst for everything. Because as Gwen saw it, the Meadowhouse—or at least her idealised version of it—was being taken from her yet again. Only this time, irrevocably.

"I won't recognise the house when it's finished, apparently. They're ripping it up and starting again—going all space age and open plan. She says it's costing the earth, but it doesn't matter, because it's their 'forever house.' They're never going to leave."

And that was when Gwen realised that unless she took drastic action, she'd never live in the Meadowhouse again.

Turns out now she never will.

64

Ellen

Three months after

Gwen never regained consciousness. I got two years for unlawful act manslaughter—the unlawful act being my "disproportionately forceful shove." My sentence was lenient on account of the "high degree of provocation," my "absolute good character" (a technical term, not a personal compliment), and my decision, after much debate and soul-searching, to plead guilty. My solicitor (referred by Tom Delaney; angels come in strange disguises) had toyed with self-defence, as Gwen's arm was raised, about to hit Orla. But the fact that Orla had struck Gwen first, and Gwen was the only one with visible injuries, made a self-defence plea risky, so it was hello HMP Holbeach for me.

And in any case, someone lost their life and someone has to pay for that. I get that. I'm also acutely aware that there's another victim here: Bella. A little girl. But while I'd never say this out loud, I think she'll be better off without her toxic mother. Although social workers presumably thought the same about Gwen when they removed her from her parents' cruelty.

But Bella's three, Gwen was ten. That's an ocean, psychologically. She might not even remember her in a few years. Which, while wholly depressing, might be a relief.

Marcus Tate gave a full statement, losing his law licence and a twenty-two-year marriage. I'm not sure how I feel about that, really. The best way I can describe it is a kind of serves-you-right sympathy. Then Jason Bale—another strange angel—provided the court with a detailed character assassination of his sister. He's visited me a few times, and his anger towards Gwen surpasses even mine. I hope he realises it'll soon be complicated by waves of crushing grief.

Truthfully, I'm not sure how I feel about Jason either. I respect him for taking Bella on, and his ex, Emma, for providing support with that. As long as he can mask his anger towards her mother, the best place for Bella is with family. But do I feel sorry for him? Do I forgive him? That's a tricky one for me to answer. After all, he admitted to me early on that he'd suspected Gwen was up to her old tricks again. So should he have stopped her? Maybe he couldn't. But should he have warned us? Absolutely.

Same for Tim Sharp, one half of the now notoriously divorced Sharps, who we merrily bought the house from. Turns out someone sent him an anonymous letter too, told him to leave the Meadowhouse or they'd expose his infidelity. He refused to bow to the blackmail. Three months later, his wife received damning photos. Like Jason, he should have warned us. But that's *their* guilt. I've got enough of my own to occupy me.

I think about Gwen a lot. Our smiling fixture on the kitchen window seat. And then I think about her on the kitchen floor, the ultimate victim of her own cruelty. But mainly I think about what I would have done if it hadn't got to that. If I'd chosen my "option."

Would I have sold her the Meadowhouse?

Of course I'd have sold her The Meadowhouse.

The devastating truth is we'd have sold up soon anyway. Gwen was right—I was finished in Thames Lawley. People remember. Mud sticks. And while *I* might have toughed it out, and to hell with what people thought of me, there's no way I'd have saddled my kids with the stigma.

So it didn't have to end the way it did.

Did I mention today is Mother's Day? I've received books, scribbled drawings, a pair of flip-flops, and nothing from Adam. Flip-flops are known in here as "shower shoes," because the shower floors are beyond grim. The best gift by far, though, is Orla. It's the first time she's come to visit. And in an act of divine normality, she's rolling her eyes and scowling at me.

"God, stop looking at me, will you? That smiley starey thing. It's freaking me out, Mum."

But I can't, and I won't. Frankly, she's lucky I'm not allowed to sniff her. I've been fighting the urge to bury my face in her hair for the best part of half an hour.

"Where do you suggest I look, then? We're not exactly spoiled with nice scenery." Although someone has created a Mother's Day display—fake flowers, pink balloons, gingham bunting. Something nice for visiting kids to paw at—it's for their benefit, not for their feckless mums. "Anyway, ever heard the saying 'even a cat can look at a queen'? It means that even a person of low status has basic rights. I'm the cat and you're the queen in this scenario, just to be clear."

Orla snorts. "I see prison hasn't changed you. Your chat's as dire as ever. I thought that hanging out with all the crims might have made you sound a bit more, you know . . . *street*."

I laugh. "Sorry to disappoint. I only really talk to two people." I take a quick glance round, make sure neither of my "friends" is within earshot. "One's in for major tax fraud and she never shuts up about her budgerigar. The other for causing injury by dangerous driving, and she's a sixty-one-year-old florist who'd make even Muriel sound *street*."

That gets the slightest tug of a smile. I class it as my finest ever victory.

"God, Auntie Kris wasn't wrong," she says. "You were never one of the cool kids at school, were you?"

Auntie Kris. Previously Cool Aunt. Now de facto mum to the twins and Responsible Adult. And while I dread to think what the boys are eating, what she's letting them watch, and what she's teaching them, I know she's taking good care of them in the only way that matters. All I want is for them to feel safe and loved.

"*And* I thought you'd be in an orange jumpsuit," Orla says. Another letdown, from her expression.

"You watch too much US telly, La-la. Actually, *I* watch too much US telly these days. Not much else to do in here." I want her to ask me what I'm watching, for us to find some common ground beyond secrets. When she doesn't, I say without thinking, "Well, not much else to do except dream of having a smoke."

"I've got some. You're not allowed, though, right?"

"Excuse me?"

She juts her chin; pure Hennessey. "Well, I have been a bit *stressed*, in case you'd forgotten."

"Then camomile tea's good. So's yoga."

She crosses one long leg over the other. "Get off your high horse, Mum. You started at my age."

Try fourteen.

Eventually Mum caught me smoking. I thought I was well and truly up shit creek. Instead she said, "If that's the worst thing you ever do, Ellen, I won't be losing much fecking sleep."

I wonder how she's sleeping now. And if she got my Mother's Day card, will she display it? I was supposed to be the kid she could brag to her mates about. She'll be hating this.

So that's a silver lining at least.

"Yeah, well, that was the mid nineties, La-la, when smoking

made you Kate Moss. It was cool then. I thought you kids were supposed to be the clued-in generation."

Even within the context of our wider wreckage, this hits hard. *My baby smoking.* And the way she just casually threw it in feels like the death of yet another boundary.

"So does Dad know?" I ask.

"Caught me the other day, actually."

"And what did he have to say?"

"Just the usual. That it's your fault."

Happy Mother's Day to me.

I sigh, kneading my neck. "So, I mean, how many are we talking? When did you start?"

"Four, five months ago. Not long before . . . well, you know, everything." Her face sours. "*She* said I should try one and I said no, I'd tried them before, couldn't see what the fuss was. But then *she* said menthols were much nicer. And they are." She shrugs. "It depends on how I'm feeling really, but I suppose I have between five and ten a day."

Gwen is now *she*. Orla set that rule as soon she got here. Refusing to say her name makes her "even more dead," she explained, and that can only be a beautiful thing. Being the grown-up, being the mother, I told her that that level of hate wasn't healthy. But now that I know Gwen intentionally got Orla smoking, and who knows how long she'll battle that legacy, I no longer care what's grown-up or healthy.

I'd cheerfully dig the bitch up and kill her again.

Fifth Bad Deed

The Invitation

Ellen

Two hours later and I've slightly mellowed. Camomile tea and basic yoga. And when I'm finished, I thumb through my new book from Orla—*An Idiot's Guide to Inner Calm*. Then a call with the boys lifts my spirits, even though every piece of news feels like a form of punishment. Max treaded water for the first time at Turtle Tots and Kian has a new favourite word—*wheelbarrow*. Oh, and they *both* tried "co-lee-fo-wer" and didn't hate it. Auntie Kris *insists* Max tries everything once.

Good for her.

Adam and I speak briefly about the house sale, then debate the best way to tackle Orla's new habit. It's actually the most we've spoken in weeks, given that he's started making excuses not to visit and he hands the phone straight to the kids when I call him. He proposes buying her Allen Carr's *Little Book of Quitting*, which would be fine if she bothered to read it. Ever the realist, I suggest paying her thirty quid for every week she abstains, although we'll want proof of that, obviously.

Adam says, "So on top of everything else, I guess I'm saddled with sniffing her breath, then?"

I tell him, "You have *no* idea how much I'd love to do it."

He says, "If you're looking for sympathy, Ellen, save your phone credit."

Kristy shouts in the background, "And your money. There's no way that girl's gonna quit."

Gwen. *Fucking Gwen.* Even from beyond the grave, she's causing misery. Even in my *dreams*, she's managing to stalk me. On average, I'd say she has a cameo every other night.

So am I glad she's dead?

Glad would be a harsh take. *Relieved* would be the better word. The lapsed Catholic in me believes all life is sacred, but the hardy pragmatist knows we're lucky she's not here to tell the whole tale. Because as far as the world knows, Gwen tried to shame me out of the Meadowhouse and recruited one of my desperate "disadvantaged" students to help her. There's only me, Adam and Orla who know about the planted knife.

And Zane, obviously.

While I thought about Gwen a lot, I thought about Zane almost constantly. I'd call Paulo to see if he'd heard from him, but he always hadn't, and he was always drunk. Depending on the number of cans he'd had, responses would range from "Y'know what? Fuck 'im" to "The day that boy was born, I won the lottery." Occasionally he'd turn his frustration on me. "Give it a rest, Ellen, would ya? You're like a stuck record. He'll turn up."

But *where* is still the hot topic. Where can he be, this Lord Lucan of the Lomax Tower? Apparently Facebook rumours have him in London. A few say Manchester. Others Italy.

They aren't even close.

His letter arrived three weeks ago. A postcard from Koh Phangan in a large brown envelope. On the front, a full moon and a standard *Wish you were here!* declaration. On the back, a message for me.

> <u>Totally</u> *wish you here. I've got kind of a beard now. We could compare chin hairs* ☻
> *Think about you loads.*
> *Lots-a-love xx*
> *PS I am sorry. What a useless word.*

He hadn't signed his name, presumably aware that prisoner post is always monitored and probably not quite sure if he was in trouble legally. It was obviously him, though. And not because of the reference to chin hair, but the apology—a Hemingway quote. I didn't know this automatically, but I had an inkling; it sounded quote-y. A few days later, using my enhanced privilege status (for being a good girl), I asked to use the internet. It's occasionally allowed, although restricted, and obviously social media is a no-go.

It was only part of a quote, it turned out.

The first part being "I love you and I always will."

I logged off, then called Paulo. He needed to be put out of his misery. He said, "Fuck me! Fucking Thailand. What do you bet Jules has known the whole time?"

And then yesterday, another letter arrived. A little longer and scrawled on letterhead, which meant he was either staying at the Culture Club Backpackers or he'd visited there at least. Another permitted internet peek revealed that *it's the place for you to be if you want to party under the full moon like there's no tomorrow.*

It's also the place to bare your soul, seemingly.

Ellen,

Hemingway said you should always do sober what you said you'd do drunk, so here goes . . .

See, I was shit-faced last night and talking to this South African dude about you—said I'd LOVE to see you again, or at least hear from you, and he said I should I tell you that then. And I guess I just did.

I'm staying at the CCB for a few weeks, so will you write to me here, tell me how you're doing (and maybe that you don't hate me, even if that's a lie)?? I'm tempted to stay in Koh Phangan a lot longer, btw. The vibe is me, and I've got ways and means of making money.

*And you can get really cheap flights you
know?* 😊 😊 😊
*And by the time you're released I'll be twenty.
Just leaving that there.
xxxxx*

PS I forgive you. Can you forgive me?

I should have torn it up, tossed it in the bin, this heartfelt paper hand grenade. These one hundred and fifty-three words that could cause untold damage to what remains of my life. Instead, I've read them a hundred times. I don't even think that's an exaggeration. And in between reading them, and thinking about them, and acknowledging the forgotten thrill of feeling wanted, I lie on my bed and think about Adam's dwindling visits. About our minimal chance of survival, and what that says about us as a couple. I guess our foundations weren't as solid as I thought they were. Our "years served" haven't equated to *true* commitment. And I guess Adam, for all his *Sesame Street* moralising, doesn't have it in him to truly forgive.

Then I think about what he'd say, what he'd do, if he knew that Zane had written to me. It'd certainly be the final nail in our marital coffin if I even thought about writing back.

I *might* write back.

For now, it's just a sweet letter under my mattress. Hungover words on cheap paper. I'll think about what to do with it another day.

Not much else to do in here but think.

Acknowledgments

Writing and publishing a book is such a huge team effort, it can be hard to know where to start. Perhaps the best place is with the first person I discussed *Five Bad Deeds* with—Eugenie Furniss, my agent extraordinaire. I still remember the fire in my belly when I left our lunch that day. The relief that you loved it. The feeling I was onto something. Thank you so much for your endless support and advice, and for talking me down from the occasional creative edge! Eugenie is fantastically supported by Emily MacDonald and Marilia Savvides at 42, who both played key roles in bringing this book to the shelves. Thanks also to Eleanor Moran for your early enthusiasm (and for seeing a great idea in my not-so-great pitch!).

It's fair to say that I hit the editor jackpot when I signed with Katherine Armstrong (Simon & Schuster) and Emily Griffin (Harper US) at the start of my career, and it's been a delight and a privilege to have worked with you both ever since. Enormous thanks for all you do—pushing me, praising me, working your magic with my words. Your beady eyes and intuitive edits made this book better by far. I'd also like to thank the maestros behind the scenes at both S&S and Harper—the PR, marketing and sales teams, the designers, the copy editors and proofreaders, *everyone* (with a special mention to Judith Long for tackling my messily scrawled page proofs with exceptionally good grace!). The crime writing community is an infinitely supportive place, and naming names would be a long task—I could literally fill a page. But you know who you are (!), and I *hope* you know how much I value you. For all the laughs (plenty) and tears (occasional), the WhatsApps and the lunches, the early reads and the cheerleading—thank you. An unexpected perk of being an author has been the emergence of such wonderful friends.

Not to forget my nonwriting friends, of course! You've been on this journey with me for a VERY long time now and while, again, there really are too many amazing humans to mention, a special shout to Helen, Cat, Carla, and Fiona. I always said I'd do this, and you never doubted that I would.

Finally, and above all, thank you to my family: Mum, Dad, and the substantial Frear and Naughton clans (including the pooches Millie and Zuma, who lay at my feet and proved to be excellent Creative Support Dogs at various points over the past few years).

And to Neil. My forever guy. I probably wasn't the easiest to live with during the writing (and rewriting and rewriting) of this book. Actually, scrap the *probably*. I was a nightmare—fact. Thank you forever for your patience and humor, and for loving me no matter what (but obviously I love you more—fact ☺).